CONVERGENCE POINT

Also by Liana Brooks

CONVERGENCE POINT

A *Time & Shadows Mystery*

LIANA BROOKS

HARPER

VOYAGER
IMPULSE

An Imprint of HarperCollinsPublishers

CONVERGENCE POINT. Copyright © 2015 by Liana Brooks. All rights reserved under International and Pan-American Copyright Conventions. By payment of the required fees, you have been granted the nonexclusive, nontransferable right to access and read the text of this e-book on screen. No part of this text may be reproduced, transmitted, downloaded, decompiled, reverse-engineered, or stored in or introduced into any information storage and retrieval system, in any form or by any means, whether electronic or mechanical, now known or hereafter invented, without the express written permission of HarperCollins e-books.

EPub Edition NOVEMBER 2015 ISBN: 9780062407665

Print Edition ISBN: 9780062407689

10 9 8 7 6 5 4 3 2 1

A toast to the survivors.
It didn't kill you, and you are stronger.

A BRIEF TIMELINE OF MODERN HISTORY (ITERATION 2)

2029—First human clone born

2037—Mexico, Panama, Costa Rica, Nicaragua, Honduras, El Salvador, Belize, and Guatemala sign the Central American Charter to form the Central American Territories

2043—The World Plague begins in China; an estimated 3 million people die in the next six years

2044—First law requiring all clones to have a genetic marker passed in Canada

2045—First clone with genetic marker created in the United States of America under the direction of an international team

2050—Canada signs the United Charter with the Central American Territories to form the United Territories

2053—The United dollar becomes the standard currency in North America

2057—European Recession cripples the world economy

2064—The United States of America votes to sign the United Charter

2065—The Commonwealth of North America is formed, and the first national elections are held in preparation for the writing of the North American Constitution

2069—Dr. Abdul Emir creates the first working time machine, a completion of his Grand Theory of Movement Through Time.

CHAPTER 1

If all life is sacred, then Mr. Gant is a blasphemer of the highest order. He is everything humanity strives not to be.

~ **Detective Samantha Rose** at the
trial of Nialls Gant I3–2071

Monday September 26, 2072
Brevard County, Florida
Federated States of Mexico
Iteration 3

Gracie, a bearded Latino man with a shiny bald head, punched Nialls Gant's arm. "Wanna a tat, brah? I got more ink."

Nialls kept his focus on the guards in the prison tower as they rotated.

"You hear me, brah?" The fetid odor of onions and poor hygiene entrapped him.

Blinking once, Nialls turned to the other inmate. "No."

"Come on, Gant. We could do a couple of teardrops

on you. Maybe a gun on your back," Gracie went on, oblivious to Nialls's focus.

"Prison tattoos make it easier for people to identify you when you're out of prison," Nialls said. "It's hard to run a con when you have your criminal record embedded in your dermis."

"Brah?" Gracie sat next to him, ignoring the burning metal of the prison-yard table. "You're serving consecutive life sentences. At this point, you ain't got to worry about what marks think. You need to be thinking what we think of a white boy in our yard."

"Don't trouble yourself with my integration," Nialls said. "I won't be imposing on your hospitality much longer."

Seven. There, the guards turned in to talk to each other and took their eyes off their prisoners. Seven rotations around the turret, then they had a three-minute conference. Long enough to move something forbidden across the open space. Long enough for a person to vanish into the camera's blind spot that the warden failed to fix after the last in-house murder. Inefficiency was the hallmark of the city's prison system. The fact that anyone thought he was going to linger here for more than a few months was insulting. Surely, someone knew he had better taste than that.

A flash of red caught his eye beyond the acres of barbed-wire fences.

The car paused for a moment, only long enough for the window to roll down as the occupant scanned the yard. Then it pulled away, tires squealing. It was gratifying to know that Detective Rose hadn't abandoned him entirely. The red-lipped harridan who'd terrorized him throughout his trial had wanted the death penalty. He hoped she stayed up at night worrying about what he was planning in his ten-by-ten cell.

He hoped it gave her nightmares.

CHAPTER 2

Peace is an illusion.

~ **excerpt from** *The Heart of Fear* **by Liedjie Slaan**

Monday March 17, 2070
Florida District 8
Commonwealth of North America
Iteration 2

Sam watched the EMT roll away the final lab-blast
survivors. In her hand was the name tag of the last
person—Henry Troom wasn't walking out of this one.
The police had pulled his plastic ID card out of the
wall.

"Agent Rose?" The lab facilitator approached her
cautiously. "I'm so sorry, but why aren't they taking
Troom out yet?"

"Because it's a crime scene, Dr. Morr, and because I
can't allow anyone in there who doesn't have the proper
security clearance. Someone will be here shortly," she
lied. Someone would be here, but it probably wouldn't

be soon, and it would probably cost her another lunch with Feo Petrilli from District 6.

Drenmann Labs was a major source of contention between Sam and her director at HQ in Orlando. Drenmann was a secure facility attached to NASA and sometimes used by the naval post and Patrick Air Force Base. All of which fell under the heading of Too-Classified-To-Think-About-In-Public and within the boundaries of Florida District 6.

Senior Agent Feo Petrilli had a complete staff with ten full-time agents and two full-time medical examiners with class-four or higher security clearance.

Senior Agent Samantha Rose of District 8 had one junior agent, an agreement with the local PD and coroner's office, and a bunch of retirees stretched along the space coast like beached albino whales. The crime rate here didn't justify keeping a larger CBI force. Drenmann Lab was the exception.

She stepped into a small conference room and locked the door behind her before calling the main office.

"Junior Agent Dan Edwin speaking, how may I direct your call, sir or ma'am?"

"Hi, Edwin, it's Rose."

"Agent Rose!" Her junior agent's voice cracked. He was an excitable puppy of a person. Sometimes it seemed like a miracle that he didn't jump up and lick her face.

"Did you get in touch with Petrilli yet? I need that coroner."

"Petrilli has one out on vacation, and the other is elbow deep in something. I didn't get details."

"That's not what I want to hear, Edwin. What I need to hear you say is, 'Yes, ma'am. Your medical examiner will be there in twenty minutes.' Can you do that for me?"

"Yes, ma'am. I called around, and there was a conference in Orlando. One of the doctors has clearance, so I had him pulled off the plane. He should arrive shortly."

"Orlando is over an hour away," Sam said with a sigh. "Good try though—it's better than nothing." Hopefully, Dr. Morr would accept her excuses. Of course, that would leave her with nothing to do for an hour but kick cleaning bots away from the door and wonder if she could get a contact high from the smell of pine-scented cleaning fluids.

"Not to worry, ma'am. The air force had a set of fighters doing emergency landing drills with the tower director there, so I commissioned one of them to bring the coroner to the local airfield, and there's a car waiting. They should be touching down now, ma'am."

Saints and angels. She could not have heard that right. "You scrambled a fighter jet?"

"You said it was urgent, ma'am."

Sam rubbed the bridge of her nose. "Tell me, Edwin, have you ever heard the term overkill?"

"Yes, ma'am."

Outside, Sam heard the whine of police sirens coming closer. "What kind of car did you have waiting for our kidnapped coroner?" She had a sinking suspicion that she already knew.

"I called the PD, ma'am. You did say fast."

"Thank you, Edwin. Remind me to note your diligence and willingness to think outside the box in your next performance review." Sam hung up the phone and shook her head. *Excitable little puppy.* If he hadn't been a six-foot-ten Viking with curly red hair and an eager smile, she might have broken down and used his nickname out loud.

Sam walked back into the main lobby as the medical examiner walked in with police escort, the broken lighting throwing shadows across their faces. Mentally she prepared herself for an angry tirade for interrupting their travel plans.

But he—and it was most definitely a *he*—wasn't what she expected. Six something, dark hair, well built, wraparound sunglasses, and wearing a thick black trench coat over black slacks and a black shirt. Wherever he was flying to, it wasn't in the South, where early-spring temperatures were already making it shorts-and-skimpy-dress weather.

"Dr. Morr," Sam called, motioning for the facilitator to come over. "Our ME has arrived. Do you want me to go back with him, or would you like to be there?"

"Um." Dr. Morr twisted a handkerchief in his hands. "Is it likely to be, uh, organic?"

"Most deaths are. It would help us immensely if you could look over the scene and comment on the position of equipment, maybe tell us if anything is missing." The doctor paled. "If you'd like to wait until after the body is moved, however, that's fine."

Dr. Morr nodded.

"Agent Rose." The voice made her smile in the shadow of death. Low and husky, it spoke of devotion and safety. "You are the only woman I know who would scramble a fighter jet just to see me."

She'd missed his voice. "What can I say, Agent MacKenzie; I wanted to show you my corpse." She turned toward him, trying to keep her expression neutral. They hadn't kept in touch since August. An occasional message here and there. He'd sent her a birthday card. Other than that, they'd moved on.

No: He'd *moved on*.

For her there wasn't anything to move to, and she wasn't going to drag him further into the mire that was her life. Especially since there was nothing left of the faded, nearly suicidal man she'd met last May. He deserved to be happy.

He took off his sunglasses and smiled. "So, to what do I owe the pleasure of being abducted from Orlando and my flight back to Chicago?"

Just like that, she was back in a sultry summer evening on a creaking front porch of an elderly house in Alabama. One smile, and she was home. "Come on back and meet my headache."

"What's the need to know?" Mac asked as he followed her back to the disaster scene.

"Drenmann Labs is the local think tank. It's supported by government grants, funding from the county, and public sales of some of the inventions they come up with here. You know Intuitive Design 3? The photo software?"

"Yeah, it's like the autopsy software we use."

Sam nodded as she lifted yellow police tape and ducked under. "That was invented here. All the scientists here spend some time on the main project, and then they have what they call a Tinker Lab. The scientists can go in there and play. Anything they invent with lab materials or help can be sold if they agree to split the profit with the government, the lab, and the county."

"Seems like a nice gig. What's the main grant for?"

"Disease control. Drenmann tracks malaria outbreaks for mutations that could lead to another World Plague and has a contract with the CDC. That happens on the far side of the building. It's under lockdown until this gets sorted out." She hesitated outside the lab. The *this* in this case was messier than most crime scenes, and when they'd first met, Mac could barely handle autopsies without triggering his PTSD. He *looked* fine—he looked better than fine, she had to admit— but she was worried. "There was a fire and possibly an explosion. Several people were injured. One is dead. There is blood—a lot of it. Can you handle that?"

A flash of worry passed through Mac's eyes. For just a moment, he was the same unsure, broken man she'd first met. But it passed, and he took a deep breath. "Wading through fire-suppression foam isn't my favorite activity in the world. What's the alternative if I don't go in there?"

"I find someone on the police forensics team, swear them in, and bring them back tomorrow. Meanwhile, the body rots, I lose evidence, and whoever did this gets away with murder."

He raised an eyebrow. "There's no chance this was a lab accident?"

"There's an excellent chance this was just a lab accident. I'm *hoping* it was a lab accident. I'm just too paranoid to believe it was a lab accident."

"Any particular reason you're paranoid?"

"Two reasons. First, this is the Tinker Lab. According to Dr. Morr, this is the brain box of the think tank. Lots of computers and simulations, zero chemicals or experiments in the room. It's supposed to be a nice place to write up your paperwork, eat lunch, and play with the graphics suite on the computer."

Mac's forehead creased in contemplation. "I could see a few ways to make a room blow up with just food and computers, especially if they have windows."

"I'm sure you could," Sam said dryly. Mac was full of surprises.

"Does the room have windows?"

"Yes. Sterile work is done on the other side of the building."

"That's two more ways. What was your second reason for paranoia?"

"Do you remember Dr. Henry Troom?" Sam asked as she snapped on her gloves.

Mac frowned. "It sounds familiar."

"Last time we saw him, he was working at Nova

Labs as Dr. Emir's intern. He graduated with his doctorate in physics in December and was lucky enough to win a spot here at Drenmann. This is a place that makes careers. Not many young doctors get a chance like this."

"Fascinating. And . . ."

"He's the only fatality."

"Do you think someone killed him out of jealousy?" Mac took off his trench coat and tossed it into a heap next to the door.

"I'm not ruling anything out. The lab's never had threats or protestors. The locals are pretty proud of this place, but I won't even guess at hypotheticals until I see some data." She stopped outside the lab and knelt by her crime scene kit. "Gloves. Mask. Shoe covers. Let me know if this is too much."

Six years ago, Mac had been a US Army Ranger, before the United States signed the United Charter to form the Commonwealth of North America with Canada, Mexico, and most of Central America. During the last, tumultuous days of the USA, Mac had gone on an extraction mission to the Middle East and been the only survivor of an ambush. When Sam had met Mac, he'd been a shadow of his former self—a shell of a man stitched together by antidepressants, sleeping pills, and a withered self-esteem. Post-traumatic stress was the diagnosis. Sam always felt there'd been more than a little survivor's guilt, too.

The events of last May couldn't have helped that.

"I'll let you know if I need to leave," Mac said.

Sam pulled a black, metal tube from the bag and twisted the cap off. A recorder bot skittered out onto her hand.

Mac eyed her mechanical assistant dubiously. "Shouldn't the lab be providing the scene readouts?"

"Yes. Do I trust them? No. This little gizmo will give me air samples, scans of the room, video of the initial investigation, and photos. By the way"—she grinned—"you're on the record."

"I'm excited." The sarcasm was thick enough to float a boat.

Sam pushed the door open and let the bot run forward. Smoke and the smell of charred flesh competed with the smell of fire-retardant foam to choke her. Lifting her mask across her nose, she walked across the lab and—waiting a few moments for the bot to test the air—opened the windows.

After a few minutes with the fans on and the slight breeze, the lab air was clean enough to breathe. The Tinker Lab was a maze of tectum-and-grass-cloth partial dividers. Desks nearest the door were untouched except for the mounds of cakey white substance covering them.

Mac poked a crusty white mound on one desk. "The foam dries faster than I thought it would."

"It's better for the tech than sprinklers with water."

"Yeah . . . but only if it doesn't soak the tech." Water splashed under his foot. "What's this from?"

Sam held up a partially melted water bottle, then

put it back as she'd found it. Looking straight back from the water bottle, she could see a clear line to a blackened workspace. "That's our target."

Mac stepped over the water carefully. "That bottle is melted, but the one on this desk is fine?" He poked at the bottle. It rocked under his touch. "What's the variable here?"

"Direct line of sight?" Sam guessed.

"Fire isn't usually that focused."

She looked at the melted bottle again. "A laser accident?"

"Laser falls over, melts the plastic, ignites paper or something similar, and starts the fire?"

"Possibly." That wouldn't explain Henry Troom's ID badge buried two inches into the wall outside, but it was a start. Setting aside her own emotions, she moved inward. Explosions hadn't always bothered her, but ever since seeing her body bruised and broken by one, she'd become leery.

Dried foam covered charred work material. A burned chair was stuck halfway through a divider. Desks and wastebaskets were overturned. A keyboard hung over the side of a desk, while a melted speaker still tried to play a cheerful tune from the radio.

She looked back at MacKenzie. "Tell me if you need to step out," she said once more.

His mouth was set in a grim line, but he shook his head. "I'm good. Let's see Troom."

Sam stepped into the workspace, cataloging the

placement of everything in her mind. "Whatever he was working on, it's ashes now." The desire to kick the offending ash was strong.

Very professional, she thought.

"Where's Henry?" Mac asked.

"Over there." She pointed to part of an arm stuck under a slagged chair. White bone showed easily through the charred flesh. "And over there." She pointed to a shoe with part of the leg still attached. "And . . . everywhere."

Mac was pale.

"I'm sorry. You can step out. I can get someone else," she rushed to say. "Do you need something? Breath mints?" she asked, only half joking. Orange Sun breath mints had been Mac's go-to placebo when he weaned himself off the sleeping pills.

He winced and turned away. "Can't take pills. Not since Harley tried to poison me. They all make me nauseous." Their former coworker had been a gem like that. Always ready to cut you down with an insult or poison your medication. Alabama District 3 had been a barrel of laughs.

"What do you need from me?"

Eyes clenched tight, he shook his head. "Computer records. What was Troom working on? Where was everyone when the explosion started? Where was everything originally?" he said, reciting the list in monotone. Mac took a deep breath. She looked at him with concern. "I'm good—honest. Can you get the surveillance tapes?"

"I'll get them."

He squatted and touched the body. "No RPC."

"RPC?" She raised an eyebrow. "Rapid postmortem cooling?"

Mac shrugged. "Does that put your paranoia to rest?"

"You made an acronym for that?" Their first case together had involved the mysterious death of Jane Doe, a woman tortured and ripped apart by an explosion that had also nearly frozen her despite the summer heat. Much to Sam's everlasting regret, the cold body on a sunny day was not the weirdest part of the case.

"I didn't know if I'd need it again." He stood up. "I guess I don't."

Muscles in her neck unknotted. "You have no idea how good it is to hear that."

"Yeah, I do," Mac said with a snort. "I was there."

The nightmares of the summer case they'd shared in Alabama District 3 still haunted her. Homegrown terrorists had tried to use a time-travel device to rewrite history. And even *that* wasn't the strangest part of the case. She'd been kidnapped by her senior agent, crossed into another timeline, come back, and almost died twice. Mac had saved her, he'd told her he loved her, and she'd walked away.

They'd never talked about it again. After the required fourteen hours of therapy, there was nothing more Sam wanted to do than forget that the summer of 2069 ever happened.

And yet here it was, back in her face. In the flesh. The tall, handsome flesh . . .

Choking back the despair, she forced a smile. "I'll talk with Dr. Morr and get the tag and cleanup team in here. Can you handle the autopsy for me?"

"No problem." He sighed and scowled back at the body. "And here I thought this trip was going to be uneventful."

Green light encased the shattered earthly remains of Henry Troom.

Mac tried not to gag at the smell of burned flesh or the sight of bare bone. There had been worse. Far worse when he was in the military, and even a few bad cases in recent months. In Chicago, he had the advantage of the being the senior medical examiner and passing the cases like this off to a junior as "on the job training."

He'd made the mistake of telling someone he missed real fieldwork last week before he left for the conference in Orlando, though. Fate was laughing at him now. It didn't get much more real than this.

A knock at the door made him nearly jump out of his skin. The little autopsy lab was a windowless room in a maze of government offices where Sam worked. He was pretty sure they'd wheeled the corpse past a WIC office. Some kid was probably going to need therapy because of that.

"Agent MacKenzie?" Sam's voice was soft, distant.

Mac had wondered what would happen if they ever saw each other again. He'd said "I love you" and she'd told him he had the kinder, gentler version of Stockholm syndrome. Now she was standing well out of reach with an invisible Leave Me Alone field in place. "Hey."

"Hi." Sam moved to the edge of the exam table. "Find anything interesting?"

"No." He finished the scan and saved the data to the case file. "The cleanup crew is still bringing me body pieces. I'm missing an arm, the head, his left foot. How do you lose body parts in a thousand square feet of flat room? It's statistically impossible."

"Maybe they disintegrated? But then why were his legs there and his foot not?" she asked, dismissing her premise immediately. Sam crossed her arms, clearly angry at the Gordian knot of a case and not at him. That was reassuring. "I know the explosion killed him," she said, "but do you know what exploded yet."

"Don't know, and I'm not guessing." Mac tried hard to focus on the corpse, but he wanted to look at her. He missed Alabama, the smiles, the laughter. The one night she'd come to his room and wound up in his arms all but naked. That memory alone fed his dreams for a day when she returned to him to do more than make sure he wasn't being stabbed to death.

She tapped the desk in front of him. "Earth to Planet Mac, it's past nine. Pack this up, and let's get you to a hotel. We'll have a rental car ready for you tomorrow."

His stomach rumbled. "Past nine? I didn't . . ."

"You never do." There was a hint of smug familiarity in her voice. She knew all his weaknesses.

She *was* all his weaknesses.

"It's easy to lose track of time when there's a dead body in front of you," he muttered. He didn't need her to break his heart again.

"Yeah? Well, you can get blissfully lost in corpse parts tomorrow. I'm starving, and Hoss needs to get walked."

He grabbed on to the safe conversation topic like a drowning man. "How is the slobbering beast doing?" Hoss was the South African mastiff Sam had adopted in Alabama. He was double her weight, and a slobbery pile of fur that looked like he might chew your leg off for fun. Luckily, the worst he'd ever done to Mac is take him for a run.

"Hoss is fine. He hates the heat, but he loves the beach. There's a pet-friendly one south of here, and we going running together most mornings."

Warning bells went off in his head.

Sam smiled like a shark. "You can come with us tomorrow if you want."

"Um . . ."

"Getting lazy up there in Chicago, MacKenzie?"

He covered the remains of Henry Troom and wheeled them to the cold storage. "Not at all, Rose. If you can find me some running shorts, I'd be happy to go running with you. Until then, you'll have to wait. My suitcase is lost in travel limbo."

"I'm sure I have something at my place."

Memories of black lace undies erased all other thought. "I don't think I'd fit."

"Let's go, Mac." She shoved him gently toward the door.

A sultry Florida night enveloped them in the scent of freshly mown grass as they stepped out of the air-conditioned building. Sam's silver Alexia Virgo was parked under a streetlamp in the otherwise-deserted parking lot. "People clear out early around here, don't they?"

"The streets pretty much roll up at nine," she said, hitting the auto-unlock. The cable connecting the car to the recharge station recoiled, and the headlights turned on.

The car was just like he remembered, everything neatly put away out of sight. Tidy and prim as the owner, except a huge muddy paw print on the floor of the passenger's side. "Hoss found something to play in."

She grimaced. "Sorry, it was muddy Saturday, and I didn't have a chance to clean it up yet. I have some napkins if you want to cover it up."

"Sam, it's dirt under my foot." He laughed. "I'm fine."

"Okay." She didn't sound convinced. "Let's find you somewhere to sleep."

"Food first. Please?" He didn't try puppy-dog eyes—to the best of his knowledge, Agent Rose was immune to every feminine instinct to fall in love with cuddly creatures. That's why she kept a man-eater for a pet. And was probably the only reason she gave him the time of day, seeing how he was even less cuddly than her dog. They headed east, turning just before the intercoastal bridge, then pulling into a very pink apartment complex. Mac gave her a questioning look. The only bright colors in Sam's life were her neon-yellow running shirts. Everything else was white, black, or bureau-regulation navy.

Maybe she's changing?

"No comments on the color. Three miles down, there's a set of apartments painted blue and purple."

Nope. "Seriously?"

"They like tropical colors here," she said in a flat tone that didn't invite further conversation. "Come on."

He followed her up to a second-floor apartment.

Hoss barked a welcome as she opened the door. "Hey, puppy. How's my good boy?" Sam petted the dog with obvious affection. "You remember Mac? He's the one who likes to go running with you." She shot him a puckish smile.

"Hey, Hoss." He took the slobber on his pant leg—and almost being bowled over—as a show of affection.

Sam turned on the lights, and it felt like he'd been punched in the gut. His old couch was here, the one they'd rescued before Hurricane Jessica drove him to find a new apartment and ultimately rent a room from Sam's landlady. The ancient wooden table sat in the breakfast nook. There was a scratch where he'd thrown a knife when they fought over the case one night.

"Mac?"

"I feel like a divorcee coming to see the ex. All that's missing are the kids."

"You left the couch in Alabama. Miss Azalea called and asked me to pick it up so she could get the new renters moved in. Do you want it back?" Her expression was guarded, unusually wary for a woman who always seemed to always tackle things head-on.

Mac shook his head. "No. It's . . . I have a new one. It's just strange. I know the furniture but not the house. Not quite déjà vu, but very surreal." The furniture was wrong in the apartment. In the old plantation house in Alabama, Sam's lacy curtains and the old brass bed— even the ancient wooden armoire—had all fitted together.

Here, the apartment walls were a glaring white even in the dim lamplight, the carpet was stiff and cheap. There was a sense of despair and desperation. It felt like a refugee camp. He watched Sam tuck her shoes away, close the curtains on the balcony window, and move around the house. "You aren't happy here."

"What?" she asked with a little jump.

"You don't look happy."

"I'm exhausted, Mac. I've been up since four, and the last thing I ate was a granola bar at six. Let me grab you some clothes, and we'll find some fast food before I drop you at the hotel."

"Sure. Sorry." She was lying, but he wasn't going to push. Last time he'd gotten too close, Sam had shut him out of her life.

She waved his apology away and vanished into the gloom of the back room.

He followed Hoss into the tiny kitchen. There were

steaks marinating on the counter in a bag. Two steaks. There would be potatoes in the cupboard, maybe some spring asparagus in the fridge. His stomach growled. "Sam?"

"Yes?" She walked out of her room, still dressed in her standard navy skirt with white blouse, holding a box with a pair of running shorts and a familiar shirt hanging out.

"What part of my soul do I need to sell to get one of those steaks for dinner?"

"Oh." Sam slumped with fatigue. "I forgot about those. I really need to cook them, too. I got them out Sunday and fell asleep before I got around to dinner."

"We could stay up for a little bit," Mac cajoled. "Grill them. Eat dinner. Pretend we don't have to be up at four."

"I need to run before work," Sam said, but he could tell she was on the edge of caving.

"The office doesn't open until nine, we could run at seven and grab a shower after." He picked up the bag and wiggled it temptingly. "Steak. Real food. You know you want this."

"We need to find you a hotel."

"I can sleep on the couch."

She bit her lip.

"I'll sleep better here than in a hotel room."

"Fine." Sam rolled her eyes. "You are so bad for me, MacKenzie!"

"I'm just making sure you eat properly," he said, radiating innocence.

"And it will be showers, plural, tomorrow morning. You are not hopping in the shower with me." She tossed the box at him. "Get the coals started. I'm going to change."

Mac raised an eyebrow. *Grab a shower* had turned into the suggestion they shower together in her mind?

Maybe there was hope for his dream relationship after all.

CHAPTER 3

*It takes a certain hubris to believe man can control
time. Hubris or genius. One often wonders what the
difference is.*

~ editorial published in *Aristegui Noticias* I3–2070

Sunday February 12, 2073
Brevard County, Florida
Federated States of Mexico
Iteration 3

There was something viciously beautiful about spring.
The way people cheered the end of a nice, clean winter
always made Nialls smile. Rabid plants brutishly destroying the earth around them to make space for
roots and branches, velvety-pink petals laced with se-
duction and death, it was a metaphor for life, really. A
brief, violent struggle, and in the end, the fastest would
win the day.

Or course, spring brought the occasional rare fog
to the sunny shores of Florida. Thick as soup and filled

with adulterated sounds like the cries of the damned. A local penitentiary was prepared for fires, floods, and hurricanes, but a thick fog made it impossible to see more than a meter or two in each direction. The watchtowers and cameras outside were useless. Only the locks inside stopped the prisoners from running loose. For now.

Nialls leaned back in his bunk and watched the open-circuit TV replay the news headlines. A triple homicide two towns south of here. A whole family murdered. No suspects. He smiled as Detective Rose, with her perfect black curls and trademark red jacket stepped in front of the cameras. No doubt, the newscasters were plotting murder in their minds as the detective upstaged them with the poise of a pageant queen.

It would do him no end of good if someone finally snapped and killed the woman. He'd personally pay to have it done on live television if the killer would guarantee that Detective Rose would die. The last unsung idiot who went after her found, much to his terminal regret, that Detective Rose kept a small ceramic knife concealed on her person.

A death sentence for the unfortunate man. A boon for Nialls, who learned from the deceased's mistake and made plans to take the detective out with a sniper rifle should the opportunity ever arise.

He toyed with the idea frequently. It'd be much easier to do everything he wanted if the only competent police officer in the area was in a shallow grave. But there was a chance, tiny and thin, that she might not die the first time he shot at her. That was enough to make him keep his distance—Detective Rose was not the kind of person who gave a man a second chance to kill her.

That, and—of course—the walls of this prison.

As if to remind him, knuckles rattled the bars of his cage. "Nialls Gant, up and at 'em. You know what time it is."

"Officer Breck, a pleasure as always. Am I in the kitchen detail today?"

"Laundry," Breck said. "Get your hands up here."

With a sigh, Gant walked forward and placed his hands through the slot to be cuffed. "Is this show really necessary?"

"How many people did you kill, Gant?"

"I was convicted of money laundering, not murder."

"Three was it?" Breck asked without bothering to listen. "Four? Five? Everyone knows you did it."

"If I did something, there would be evidence."

"Not if you're smart about it."

"Whatever happened to innocent until proven guilty, Officer?"

"The United States became a protectorate of Mexico in 2025," Breck said. "But it would be the same either way. You're a killer."

Gant rolled his eyes and waited for Breck to open the cell door. Shuffling with handcuffed legs and hands, he followed the now-familiar route to the laundry. Steam coiled up from the aging washing machines. "No company today?"

"Don't complain. You're out of solitary, aren't you? Working the shift alone means no one's going to shank you."

"Indeed." He watched the steam curl in front of the security camera.

"Hands." Breck held out his key, impatience written across his broad features.

Gant held his hands out.

Breck looked down, leaned forward . . .

Gant reached up and grabbed his head, twisting the officer's face until his fat neck popped. "Who needs a shank?" Bending down, Gant picked up the discarded keys. "Thank you ever so much, Officer." He unlocked his cuffs. There were two minutes left before Breck was due to check in again, long enough to wipe down Breck's body to keep the medical examiner from pulling a fingerprint. There was only a slim chance that anyone would find Gant if his plan came to fruition, but old habits died hard. Anyway, it was senseless to leave Detective Rose with any clues.

To further ensure no evidence, he deposited Breck's corpse in one of the industrial dryers.

He set it on "permanent press."

Days like this, he wished he had flunkies. There were so many things to do when planning a prison break: guards to watch, alarms to reset, bodies to hide. It was really quite distracting. Nevertheless, needs must, as they said.

He picked up Breck's truncheon.

Time to go muddy the trail.

Gant didn't saunter down the hall; that would have drawn attention. He kept his pace measured, quick, light . . . just like the pathetic errand boys who were trying to shave time off their sentence with good behavior. As if fetching and carrying for the guards was going to get them home faster than busting a few heads open.

The other inmates looked up when Gant walked into the cellblock without his guard or chains.

He smiled. "Good evening, gentlemen. May I recommend putting your shoes on?" He held up the master key. "I'm about the pull the fire alarm. All of you will be exiting the building in a disorderly fashion. Run. Jump. Cluck like a chicken. I don't care. As long as you leave the building in under two minutes, you'll only have to deal with the police."

Still smiling, he stuck the master key in the lockbox, twisted, and pulled the fire alarm. It was there only for life-threatening emergencies. Only meant to be used if the guards outnumbered the prisoners. It shouldn't have been built at all. Too tempting.

I'll never get over the stupidity of those in law enforcement.

"Come along, gentlemen. I haven't got all evening. Time and tide wait for no man. Stand up, stand up. Carmichael, why aren't you wearing . . . you know, never mind. Just go. You." Gant stopped in front of a cell where a younger man lay in his bunk. "Who are you?"

"Camden." The boy looked at him.

"It's time to leave, Camden."

"Ain't happening, man. I seen those guns in the turrets. I was here last time some jack fool tried to make a break for it. They took his hands off with bullets." Camden held his arms up like he was holding an assault rifle. "Rat-a-tat-tat. You know, man? That's a tune I ain't dancing to. You have fun. I'm staying here."

Gant sighed. "You're wasting my time, Camden." In one smooth motion, he raised the truncheon and brought it down hard on Camden's neck. "Stay here if you want," he told the corpse with the broken neck.

An alarm sounded lockdown on the far side of the prison. Someone had tried to bust a buddy out with them. He'd made plans for that. Or, rather, he'd made plans in case someone tried to use the prison break to take a detour and make some extra cash by offing a rival. But just because he planned for such an eventuality didn't mean the idiots had to go do it.

Out in the prison yard, gunfire rattled the windows. Rat-a-tat-tat indeed.

Best to use the parking-lot exit then.

Gant hummed as he strolled down the empty path, sirens wailing in the distance. Cell Block B was a great tomb—no, not a tomb—a cathedral to human ingenuity. Inmates were given one hour of computer time each month, but it had been more than he needed. One tiny computer virus and—on his signal—the sirens lost their voices. The lights were darkened, killed with a single keystroke. And outside the barred, bulletproof glass, the prison-yard lights illuminated the fog like the dawn of war. So poetic. Genius, even, if he would allow himself a brief moment of immodesty. He wished he could have recorded the moment for posterity.

One day, he'd have to blackmail someone to make a film of his life. If they didn't spring for the fog machine, he'd break their femur a quarter inch above the patella. A difficult infliction to master, but it always got his point across.

He pushed the prison doors open and took a deep breath of the vapor-choked air. Brilliant. Now, where was the coward?

Gant sauntered as he moved into the parking lot. The car-park lights far overhead were dimmed by the fog. The turret guards were distracted. At the far end of the lot, he could hear someone trying to start a car, but he couldn't see them. Which meant no one saw him as he approached the bright blue four-wheel-drive monstrosity with a temporary tag still in the window.

Officer Wilhite's aunt had passed unexpectedly a month ago, and she'd left her only surviving relative a tidy sum of money, a fact the bullying guard couldn't stop bragging about as he watched the inmates eat lunch. It couldn't have happened to a less worthy person. Wilhite was the kind of man roaches looked down on for not having enough class. He was a thing that fed off whatever the bottom-feeders left over. If he'd gone into crime—and Gant wasn't entirely sure the officer wasn't supplementing his income with some illegal activity within the prison—this was the guy the gang would leave for the cops to drag in.

No one wanted him.

Even the understaffed prison system hadn't objected when Wilhite gave his notice.

Gant hadn't planned on leaving tonight. He'd been waiting for Detective Rose to be distracted or for the weather to be perfect. A tornado or a hurricane that drove the guards out of the turret would have been ideal. But fog on a night when Detective Rose was chasing someone a hundred miles away and Wilhite was leaving early? It was as if God Himself had stepped down from his cherub-encircled throne and given Gant the key. It was divine intervention.

Or diabolical.

Someone swore in the depth of the fog.

Gant smiled, fading back into the darkness, giving Wilhite a path to his car.

"Crazy, sonofa—" Wilhite stopped in the ring of sickly-yellow light falling from the lamp overhead. He was watching the tower, head leaning this way and that as he decided whether to go back or not. The former prison guard shook his head. Turning back to his car, he fumbled with his new keys.

Gant moved in for the kill.

CHAPTER 4

Every wave loses energy in time. Collapses into a truer iteration of time.

~ **excerpt from Lectures on the Movement of Time by Dr. Abdul Emir I1–20740413**

Tuesday March 18, 2070
Florida District 8
Commonwealth of North America
Iteration 2

"Good morning, Agent Rose!" Edwin said. "You look cheerful this morning."

Sam froze in the doorway to her office. "I do?" She didn't feel cheerful.

"Very chipper and alert, if I do say so, Agent Rose." The junior agent beamed at her with all the enthusiasm of a floodlight. "I take it the case is going well?"

"It's going." *And so am I . . .*

She flashed a smile at Agent Edwin and retreated to the safety of her desk. Waking up to the familiar smell of Mac's soap, going for a run with a friend, letting Mac talk her into eating donuts . . . those were nice things. But she wasn't happy about it. Mac was dangerous . . . no, that was unfair, she realized with a sigh. She was the dangerous one. It was her life in a tailspin. It was her future that was filled with torture and death.

The danger was that Mac would insinuate himself into her life, again, and wind up getting hurt. She couldn't allow that to happen.

She spent a moment doodling stars on a piece of scrap paper, trying not to overthink the case. With a grumble, she finally shrugged off the dark premonitions and focused on the work in front of her. There was nothing major on the agenda today. A paperwork review, time scheduled to handle complaints, and a tentative meeting scheduled with Director Loren, the regional director for CBI in eastern Florida. Nine times out of ten, he told her to skip the meetings. No one needed input from District 8. Today, though, there'd be questions.

The main office phone buzzed. A moment later, Agent Edwin called her on the intercom. "Agent Rose? I have Agent Petrilli on the line. Are you available?"

Ugh. "Put him through."

Her phone rang, and, with another reluctant sigh, she picked it up. "This is Agent Rose."

"Agent Rose," Petrilli's voice dripped amusement, insincere goodwill, and condescension. "I wanted to talk to you before the meeting this afternoon."

"Uh-huh." She pulled up the files for paperwork

Edwin was approving, double-checking his work. If she caught the mistakes, she didn't have to deal with the complaints later on.

"I'm clearing Lawrence Dom to come over for the week."

She flagged a questionable tax rebate. "Dom? The medical examiner?"

"That's right," Petrilli said. "He was doing an assist up here on a car accident, but he'll be free by noon. That's soon enough, I hope." He made it sound like twenty-four hours after she needed an ME was a major favor.

"I don't need him at all. Thank you, though," she said, keeping her frustration out of her voice. "Agent Edwin was able to locate another ME for me yesterday. I have him working the case."

"Really?" Petrilli didn't sound convinced.

"I think I know an ME with a badge when I meet one, Petrilli." She flagged another file, circling the space Edwin had missed when checking the taxes.

He chuckled. It was a classic Feo, trying to make a social gaffe a weak joke, so everyone forgot he'd put his foot in his mouth again. "I meant, I thought that everyone was busy this week. There was a conference, and of course that hailstorm down south. District 6 is the only district with multiple examiners. Who'd you get?"

"Agent MacKenzie from Chicago. He had the clearance, and he was available." There was a baffled silence from the other end of the line. Sam smirked.

"You flew an agent in from Chicago to handle this?"

"Actually, we requisitioned him from the conference in Orlando. Considering the weather at home is calling for a late-season cold front, he was more than happy to extend his vacation." She finished approving the last tax file and opened the complaints box. "Did you need anything else? I have work to get done."

"No, no, of course not. I just wanted to let you know that District 6 is here to assist anytime you need. Ah, will this ME be coming to the meeting this afternoon?"

Sam raised an eyebrow at the phone. *Oh, right*: She'd mentioned that another competent male was in the district. Petrilli wanted to meet his new rival. "It's a meeting for senior district agents, unless I missed a memo. I know Chicago has a good reputation, but I don't think we're going to have the case wrapped by lunchtime. Give me at least twenty-four hours."

Petrilli laughed again. "Sorry. It's just my thing. I like to know who's working in the region."

"Mmm-hmmm." Petrilli's "thing" was his ongoing campaign to win her over. To his credit, it wasn't about sex. It was just that his ego couldn't understand the possibility that someone might not like him.

"Do you want to get together around eleven thirty for lunch? We can chat before the meeting, catch up, that sort of thing."

Sam silently shook her head. "Let me take a rain check on that. I'd like to have all my ducks in a row before I talk to Director Loren. Maybe another time. When I have less on my plate?"

"Sure thing. See you this afternoon."

"Good-bye." She hung up, dropping the phone like a venomous snake.

Feo Petrilli wasn't a bad man. He was a good agent—her highest form of praise—but he was too much like her ex-boyfriend from Toronto. The same charismatic charm, the same dark good looks, the same arrogant unthinking nature that had made her fall in love with Joseph. He was even a good Catholic boy, something that would have pleased her mother to no end if she and her mother were still on speaking terms.

That ever-strained relationship had been terminated after her mother suggested her memories of the kidnapping were clouded by stress and the Alabama heat. If she'd simply leave the bureau and get married, there'd be none of this kidnapping nonsense. As if a wedding band could miraculously change the world.

Certainly, there'd be fewer people shooting at her if she gave up her Commonwealth citizenship and moved to Madrid.

She could deal with people shooting at her, though. She'd rather deal with homicidal maniacs than become a trophy wife for her mother's cronies.

Frustrated, she sent the standard "I'll look into the matter" e-mail to all the complaints and shut off her computer. Grabbing her purse and the case file, she headed for the door.

Agent Edwin looked up from his desk as she walked out. "Do you need something, Senior Agent?"

"Nope, not unless you can schedule Petrilli for a

little trip to the vet. That boy needs to be snipped." Her junior agent whimpered in sympathy. "I'm kidding. Mostly."

"I . . . I can, um . . ." Panic suffused his face as he tried to find a way to obey the order.

"Don't worry about it." Sam smiled. "I'm going to talk with the ME. If it runs long, I'll leave from the morgue for my meeting with Director Loren. Do you think you can handle everything while I'm out?"

"Certainly, Agent Rose. Um . . ." His bushy red eyebrows furrowed. "Agent Rose? Do you know where Agent MacKenzie is staying? I don't have his hotel address, so I can't arrange for his rental car."

"Oh." She fervently hoped she wasn't blushing. Technically, there was nothing unprofessional about Mac's staying at her house. They weren't breaking any rules, and they weren't in a relationship, but it still felt wrong. Or right. Whichever, it wasn't the bureau's business. "I believe he's staying with a friend. Why don't you have the car dropped off here before lunch?"

Her junior agent beamed happily. "Excellent advice, ma'am. I'll have it ready within the hour. I'm glad Agent MacKenzie knows someone in the area. I was worried that pulling him into the case was going to cause problems."

"He hasn't registered any complaints with me." Not unless barely breathing between mouthfuls and telling Sam that he missed her cooking counted as a complaint.

"I know he doesn't have a wife or family," Agent

Edwin said. "I checked before I pulled him onto the case, but I thought he might have a girlfriend."

"Not that he's mentioned to me." To her own ears, her tone was noticeably cooler, but Edwin missed the change. It wasn't that she was opposed to the idea of Mac's dating, of course, she just figured he'd have mentioned if there was anyone significant in his life. That's the sort of things friends talked about over dinner.

Because that's what we are . . . friends.

"I'm sure he wouldn't, ma'am. You have a professional relationship, after all," he said with another ingratiating smile.

Whether he meant she was married to her work or that being an agent would keep her from stripping Mac naked, she wasn't sure. And she didn't bother to ask . . . mostly because she wasn't sure she wanted to know the answer. "I've got to run, Edwin. Call if you run into trouble."

"Yes, ma'am."

Some agents insisted on staying single because the future was too uncertain, and they didn't want to leave someone they loved burying them young. Her situation was quite the opposite. She knew exactly how and when she would die, right down to the six-hour window when she choked on her last breath. It was like living with a terminal disease.

Mac had buried enough friends. Of course, he'd already been to her funeral once, so maybe it wouldn't be so bad a second time around. But seeing her die wasn't a stress he needed in his life.

The heels of her navy pumps clicked on the tile floor outside the CBI office door.

Budget cuts meant she shared office space with everyone from the free clinic downstairs to the local drunk tank for the city police department. It was a situation that made her neck itch with paranoia. Any minute now, some madman was going to come charging through the tastefully decorated arboretum foyer and start shooting people because they had a grudge against the Commonwealth Bureau of Investigation. Or the police. Or the free clinic that offered referrals to adoption centers and abortion clinics.

The number of crazies in the world was sickening. Infuriating. A rational human being would take one look at all the head cases and lock themselves in a bunker. Instead, she kept a gun—which she hated—on her at all times and arrested anyone who looked at her funny.

Taking the steps two at a time, she headed upstairs to the lowest-budget morgue in the bureau. Mac was there, not bent over the charred remains of Henry Troom but seated at a computer terminal, leaning back in his chair with one foot on the long desk.

"That looks uncomfortable," she said from the doorway.

Mac pivoted fast enough that he almost fell. He caught himself at the last minute, grinning sheepishly. "My knees kept hitting the desk."

"What are you looking at?"

He motioned for her to look. "The lab layout. I'm

overlaying the original blueprints with the information from the data bots and the fire department."

"Looking for what?" She walked past the empty examination table to peer at the screen over Mac's shoulder.

"Here, sit." He moved out the chair so she could sit down as he pulled up a three-dimensional diagram of the lab. "This is the Tinker Lab. I figured they'd have everything set up for running a variety of experiments: gas, water, electricity, everything you'd see in a normal college lab setup. But they don't." Green lines seared across the screen. "See? Basic electric outlets but nothing else."

"Okay, but I thought we knew that. What's the problem?"

"According to the original blueprints, this room was meant to be a conference room. They added the electric outlets for the individual workstations later." Mac leaned over her, pulling up more schematics. He was close enough that she caught the scent of the soap on his heated skin.

Sam focused on the display. "Are you thinking faulty wiring caused an explosion?"

"I played with the idea, but everything was up to code. The readouts from all our scans look clean. A few of the scientists had models in their cubicles, but nothing that should have done this."

"We know at least one person had a laser near their desk. Maybe they were plugging them in? Or using battery-powered somethings?" Sam asked, turning to look at Mac. He had arms on either side of the chair and was hovering just above her. From the twinkle in his eyes, he was well aware of the fact, and it made her blush.

"Maybe. Has the lab director given you any a list of what everyone was doing yet?"

"No, he hasn't sent me anything. What are you thinking?"

Mac sat down on the desk next to the keyboard. "Possibly—and this is going to be hard to prove— there was a mixture of gases in the lab that caused the explosion. Remember how the air smelled when we walked in?"

"Anything gaseous or dangerous would need to be kept under a fume hood. No one would be playing with that in the Tinker Lab."

"Absentminded scientist walks in holding a vial of something, looks for his notes, the gas he's holding interacts with something else in the room, and things go boom."

Sam pursed her lips together as she thought. "My chemistry classes weren't focused on things that went boom. What's the likelihood of this actually having happened?"

"Low," he admitted. "We don't have the air samples all tested yet. Hopefully, that will give us something. My other running theory is that Henry was working with some form of explosive device, the laser that melted the water bottle set fire to the room, and whatever Henry was holding is what dismembered him."

She leaned back in the chair. "What's the autopsy say? Do we have a cause of death yet?"

"Not yet. His lungs are fine, he didn't die of smoke inhalation or superheated air. The tox screen came back clean."

"Have you looked at his bones yet?" Sam asked.

"For a radial pattern? No. I already told you there was no rapid postmortem cooling."

"Do it anyway," Sam said. "I want to rule that out completely." Henry's predecessor had killed at least two people with his machine. The radial fracture pattern on the victims' bones was the first clue they'd had that the cases were linked.

Mac nodded. "Any chance I can get over to see the lab director? The more I know what was in the lab, the better I can work my end of the case."

She checked the time on the computer. "I can drop you off there, but I have a district meeting. Agent Edwin is ordering you a rental car, so you could wait for that and go by yourself, and I'll meet you after if you're still there."

"I'll go with you now. There are enough questions here to keep me busy for the afternoon. The cleanup crew is still in there, and I'd like to see what they find." He stepped back and offered her a hand up.

"You really think you want to be there?"

Mac smiled, cool and confident, a completely different man than the one she'd met the previous year . . . or even last night. "I can handle it, Sam. If I have a problem, you'll be the first to know." He stripped out of his lab coat and opened the door for her.

They walked to the parking lot in silence, letting the sounds of the busy building fill in for conversation. An ocean breeze brought the smell of salt and stirred the humid air as they stepped outside.

Mac breathed deep. "I like this better than Chicago. All we get there is muggy smog." He caught her eye and winked. "Fewer bikinis, too."

"I don't have a bikini," she informed him primly as she hit the auto-unlock on her car keys.

"Does that mean no—" Mac cut himself off. It took her a minute longer to walk around the car and see what made him pause.

Her car was smashed.

The windows were broken, the front end was crumpled.

"Sam?" Mac moved closer, hand hovering over the car reverently. "Did you go to run errands after you dropped me at the morgue?"

"Nope." Her hands tightened around the strap of her purse. "Parking lot hit-and-run, maybe?"

"A hit-and-run that went through the shrubs and the electric hookup without leaving a mark? I don't think so." He bent down. "There's a note on the windshield."

"Don't touch it."

"I wasn't going to." He stood up. "Call the police."

"I *am* the police."

"You know what I mean."

"On it." The phone was already ringing. "Hi, this Agent Sam Rose from the CBI. I need a patrol car at the corner of Canal and Riverside at the city clerk's office. One of the cars in the parking lot was vandalized. Yes. Understood." She pressed her lips together as dispatch contacted a car. "Thank you, I'll wait."

Mac watched her expectantly.

"It'll be at least ten minutes, but probably more like forty. The county only has two cars, and they're on the wrong end of town."

"And vandalism isn't a high priority." Nor was it bureau jurisdiction.

"Facts of life," Sam said with a shrug, her hands itching to work. "There are a few dozen cars out here and no way of proving I was targeted. It's not like I get a special parking spot or have a 'Commonwealth's Best Bureau Agent' bumper sticker."

"At least I know what to get you for your birthday," Mac teased.

The note stuck under her windshield wiper waved in the ocean breeze. "Is it bad that I want to process this scene myself?"

"No, it just means you're you." Mac smiled. "Then again, I want to read the note."

"So do I. Then I want to dust it for prints, run the words by analysis, then do a microscan for DNA."

"I'd start with the microscan."

By the time the patrol car pulled up, Mac had the letter in the microscan and Sam was dusting the car for prints.

"Um, are you Agent Rose?" the officer asked as he stepped out of his car, his partner following.

"Yes."

Their name badges declared them to be Officers Ranct and Hadley. And while Hadley was abundantly female, it seemed she patronized the same barber as Ranct, one that specialized in a short, shaggy cut.

"Ma'am, what are you doing?" Ranct asked.

"Processing the scene before we lose evidence," Sam said. "What are *you* going to do?"

"Well, we can take your statement and maybe take some pictures," Ranct said with a note of uncertainty in his voice. He shared a pained look with Hadley.

"Do you want us to help with the car?"

"Sure." Sam brushed a sweat-dampened curl of black hair from her face. The building had security cameras, most of the shops across the lane had them, too. There were trees between the cameras and the parking lot, but she might catch something. "I need to call the insurance company about the rental they ordered for me."

"Late for a big date?" Hadley joked.

"Late for a meeting with my boss." She grimaced, but the police didn't echo her expression. *So much for fraternal sympathy.* Stripping her gloves off, she handed her data pad to Ranct. "Here are my notes. Have fun. Let me know if you find anything."

"Of course, you're a citizen of the Commonwealth and the county. We're here to protect you." Ranct beamed like he expected a camera flash to go off.

"And threatening a federal agent is a very serious crime. It's going to be hard to solve a murder if the only person trained for that in this district gets killed." Sam retreated to the welcoming cool of the office as her stomach growled for lunch.

"Yes, ma'am . . ."

A few people in the downstairs office watched through tinted windows as Ranct and Hadley walked around the car, taking pictures. But for the most part, the halls and offices were empty, victims of budget cuts and consolidation. There was some sort of logic behind the consolidation, streamlining all government functions so that welfare and health care weren't separate offices made sense. Firing 70 percent of the government workers in every district and relying on "aptitude awareness testing" made less sense.

Hopefully, they won't think to replace me with those two out there.

"Sam?" Mac was waiting outside her office.

"Any good news?"

"Whoever left the note was smart enough not to touch the paper. I found cow DNA from leather gloves, but it was vat-grown and mass-produced."

"So our vandal shops on a budget? Not super useful." She pushed the door to the CBI office open, and Agent Edwin bounced to his feet.

"Agent Rose!" If Edwin had a tail, it would have wagged.

Down, boy!

"Agent Edwin, this is Agent Linsey MacKenzie, the doctor you requisitioned from the conference."

"You can call me Eric," Mac said. "Everyone but my grandma does."

Sam rolled her eyes. He was never going to let her live down the fact that she told him he had a girly name when they first met.

"It's Linsey Eric MacKenzie on my birth certificate." He smirked, knowing he'd won the skirmish.

"Whatever. Mac, this is my junior agent, Dan Edwin. Don't scare him."

"Do I look scary?" It was a redundant question.

Mac didn't look scary until he switched from fluff-minded coworker to Death Squad, archenemy of Captain United in all the comic books. She'd seen Mac handle a gun, and not just the splat gun like she carried, with liquid bullets that delivered tranquilizers that were absorbed through the skin. No, Mac knew how to handle the kind of guns that came with lead bullets and killed people. His skills had saved her life, but *she* still found them intimidating. But she wasn't worried about Edwin.

That's because he looked scary *all* the time. He was a towering paragon of mixed Irish-Viking heritage who could crush a man's skull with his bare hands. But he was still more puppy than wolfhound. And, to Sam's amusement, he was deathly terrified of bugs. Anything with more than four legs wigged him out.

"Did you call Director Loren to let him know I wasn't going to make the meeting?" Sam asked, glossing past Mac's question.

"Yes, ma'am," Edwin said. "He asked you to send a report and call in this afternoon if you could."

"Shouldn't be hard, my schedule's pretty free." Especially if the rental agency didn't get her a car soon. "Edwin, what are your plans this afternoon?"

"Monthly inspections down at the boatyard of Braddock Creek and, at some point this week, I need to drive down to check on our pirates."

"You have pirates?" Mac looked at her with interest.

What was it with boys and pirates? "They're not real pirates, they're smugglers," Sam said dryly. "They smell bad and have the common sense of a concussed swamp mouse."

"We confirmed it was a salt marsh vole they had," Edwin said. "Not a swamp mouse."

Mac's eyes crinkled with amusement. "You're telling me this story."

"It's not a story." Sam sighed in exasperation. "District 8 covers part of the National Seashore: several inlets, a lot of rivers, and more back roads than anyone wants to count. So we have seed smugglers. Anti-GMO protestors meet ships off the coast before they head to a major port, then try to bring them through the national parks. Most the time the seeds they bring are nonnative, and contaminated."

"They're crazy," Edwin added with a happy smile. "They'll show you buckets of moldy corn and tell you about how the revolution is going to take everyone by surprise."

"Drug addicts?" Mac asked.

Sam nodded. "For the most part. They're considered nonhostile, but since they're squatting on national land, it's still the bureau's job to keep an eye on them. It's easy enough work."

"They'll do anything for marshmallows," Edwin said. "I bring a bag with me and check in to see what they're up to every few weeks. It's never led to any arrests or anything, but you never know."

Sam's phone rang, and she stepped into her office to answer it—leaving Mac and Edwin talking animatedly about pirates.

Boys.

"Agent Rose, how can I help you?" she asked, as the door clicked shut behind her.

"Ma'am, this is Rachel with the car-rental service. We have your vehicle ready to deliver to your address."

"Great—thanks."

Just as she hung up, Mac leaned into her office as he knocked on the door—he hadn't waited for her to tell him to come in. "Hey, what's the play here?"

"First off, you learn that you have to wait to be invited in after you knock." Mac grinned, and Sam just rolled her eyes. "Second, the car's on its way over." She stepped back into the main office. "Edwin, if you're not going to be back to the office by four, you can go home, but check in by phone or e-mail."

"Will do, ma'am."

"Drive safe," Sam said as she shooed Mac out of the office.

"Cute kid."

"He makes me feel old."

"He's, what, three years younger than you?"

"Two. And it feels like decades. I'm a bitter old woman."

"You'll survive." He held out a folded piece of paper. "The note from your car."

Sam unfolded it and frowned at the two words printed in all capitals:

NEEDS MUST

"This mean anything to you?"

"Not yet, but it will in time I'm sure. Still want to go to the lab?"

"Yes."

Days like this she missed Detective Altin from Alabama. The burly old man had been a reliable source and helper even in her rookie days when she was trying to bounce back from a series of bad life choices.

To be fair, they hadn't been my bad life choices, but I was the one who handled the fallout all the same. Someone like Altin had been such a rock to lean on.

District 8 was underfunded—at least in her mind—and understaffed. The way things were, she had exactly enough resources to handle a minor problem, singular. If she ever needed to handle a major murder investigation, she'd either need to beg them off the neighboring districts or rely on the police. Maybe she should bake Ranct and Hadley some cookies, see if she couldn't buy some favors with chocolate chips. She had a feeling she was going to need backup sooner rather than later.

CHAPTER 5

Time is no longer the enemy. Time is our plaything. A toy we can wind, and spin, and tangle to our heart's delight. Nothing is beyond us now. Everything, every time, is in reach.

~ Manuel Helu speaking at a tech conference I3–2069

Monday February 27, 2073
Brevard County, Florida
Federated States of Mexico
Iteration 3

Samantha Lynn leaned closer to the mirror to inspect her lipstick. The shade of her red lips perfectly matched the red in the Mexican flag pinned to her lapel. Another year or two of this, and she'd head for the senate. Every step was one closer to the presidential palace in the Plaza de la Constitución.

Her wall screen fizzed, artistic bubbles dancing up into the electric ether until they revealed the face of her second-in-command. "¿Sí?"

"We found evidence of the convict you were hunting," the man said in broken Spanish. His flat northern accent was an assault on her ears. She forgave him. He was an intelligent man despite being born on the wrong side of the border and growing up speaking a bastard language, the child of too many father tongues.

"Where is Gant?"

"The Plaza Carso, ma'am."

She frowned. "In Mexico City?" That was over three thousand kilometers away by bus, and unreachable by air, at least for Gant. If he'd gone through airport security, she'd fire every single guard at the place.

"No, ma'am, there's a cheap apartment complex forty kilometers from the prison with the same name. We've tracked Gant to the area and believe he's renting a house under an assumed name."

"Get the team in gear. I want everyone ready to leave in ten minutes." Gant was going back to prison, and this time she'd pay to see him executed. He would not escape a second time.

Detective Rose was on the news again. This time she was wearing a deep purple jacket the color of an old bruise that matched the dark circles under her eyes. Her lips were stained blood red as she assured the reporters that everything was being done to return the escaped convicts to their prison cells.

Gant wondered if Rose knew she was about to die.

He leaned back, and the once-overstuffed orange

armchair he was sitting in squeaked in protest. The thing was an antique, the stuffing matted, lumpy, and smelled of cat urine. He'd probably kill the old man who rented him the prefurnished apartment with the promise of cash on Friday, but for now it worked.

The doorknob jiggled as the coke addict from next door tried to get in.

"Wrong apartment!" Gant shouted at him.

The heavy wooden door buckled and splintered under duress. Wooden shards flew across the room. Gant stood up, ready to fight.

A tall, heavily muscled man with a military buzz cut walked in with a cocky grin. "Right door."

Gant offered him a grim smile. That was not going to be an easy neck to snap. "And you are?"

"Donovan."

"Should that mean something to me?"

"Right now, it won't mean a damn thing. A year from now, I'll be the difference between your life of ease and your life behind bars."

Gant raised an eyebrow. "I'm listening, and when I say that, I mean I'm listening for exactly three minutes because the police will be here in five."

"Did you call them?"

"No, but my landlord is picky."

"He's dead." Donovan's grin widened. "We're the only two people still breathing in this complex."

"You don't do subtle very well."

"You don't do smart very well." Donovan chuckled. "How long did you think you'd be able to keep the Wilhite thing going? Another week? Two at the most?"

"No one even knows Wilhite's the body they found in the parking lot. I made sure of that."

"They did an autopsy."

"Let them. The dental records were switched months before I left."

"But you forgot his bum knee," Donovan said. "He had it replaced three years ago after he ran into a particularly nasty bank crew. My crew. There's a serial number in him, and his friends reported him missing."

"Wilhite didn't have friends."

"He had more than you, but I'm about to change that."

"Are you now?"

"What if I told you I could take you to a place where the cops would never find you? All your crimes vanish."

"You have the shallow grave already dug?" Gant smirked. This was going to be a fun fight.

"Better than that," Donovan said. "Ever heard of the Timeyst Machine?"

"I've seen the ads. *'Visit history! See your own birth!'*" Gant shrugged. "It's a toy for the rich and stupid."

"It's also an escape route. A one-way ticket to the day before you committed the crimes."

"Are you saying I should stop myself?"

"I'm saying you should go back and skip town before the cops ever have you on their radar. You can leave the country before anything happens. Have a new identity before the cops find your fingerprint. It's foolproof."

"And you need me because?"

"It's a two-man job. My crew's in the clink. I could break them out, but then I realized you were loose. You know security. You're not afraid to get dirty. You can think faster than most cops. You can say no, but you'll regret it."

"Will I now?"

Donovan looked at the TV, where Detective Rose's muted mouth was still flapping open as she lied to reporters. "You think she'll let you go?"

"She doesn't know I'm out."

"She knows. She's hunting you. She's going to find you."

"Unless I go with you?"

"That's about the shape of it." Donovan's smile returned. "One little heist. One little trip back in time. You go your way. I go mine. No one ever finds us again.

"You'll be the first criminal to ever escape Detective Rose."

CHAPTER 6

*We do not know what effect traveling through time has
on the human body, let alone the human soul.*

~ activist Dr. Annie Lowell speaking at the
Conference for Time Theories I3- 2071

*Wednesday March 19, 2070
Florida District 8
Commonwealth of North America
Iteration 2*

Some people kept statues of the Madonna in their
house. Little altars to the saints who cared for the
small people. Ivy didn't pray to any god. Her altar was
built to a living hero, living, but no less distant than
the gods.

She stopped in her morning routine to look at the
poster of her hero. It was the eyes that always got her.
The dark eyes filled with fear, sorrow, and a new-
born, burning rage, like the look of a child who finally
reaches for their abuser's hand to stop the next blow.

Ivy'd seen the look a few times in the Shadow House before the city took her. The look of flowering hatred as the children there realized what their names meant. That the name Shadow was a death sentence for all but the lucky few.

Until the day the real Jenna Mills died, that had been her future. One day, the workers in white coats would come take her away from her group to a small room where her last sight would be a cold needle plunging into her arm. Her organs, genetically identical to those of Jenna Mills, would be harvested to repair the real Jenna Mills. If she was lucky, she'd only wake up with a limb missing. Most shadows never woke up at all.

Then the real Jenna Mills died.

The coroner said it was instantaneous. The driver of the car—the reports never said who had been driving—fell asleep at the wheel, and the whole family was killed. Police came to the Shadow House. She was sold to the city as a drone under the only name she'd ever known: Jenna's Shadow.

Now she was legally Ivy Clemens, police officer. She stopped to check her uniform in the mirror, brushing her fingers along the rough embroidery of her chosen name. And then, like the ritual it was, she looked back at the woman on the poster.

Agent Samantha L. Rose, the first clone to ever hold a bureau rank. Her brief speech on humanity had won the hearts of the clone population, maybe even swayed the hearts of the uterus-born idiots who still thought slavery was a good idea.

"I am not a thing. I am not your possession. I am a human being," Agent Rose had said when accosted by reporters at the Atlanta airport last summer.

Ivy had watched the speech live. When the poster with Agent Rose's stern visage and the words I AM NOT YOUR POSSESSION emblazoned went on sale, she bought it. The very first piece of art for her tiny apartment that was now, finally, legally hers.

Her phone buzzed. "Officer Clemens."

"This is Dispatch Operator Bogumil. We have a report of a dead body floating in the water south of Twenty-seventh Avenue Park."

"Great, why aren't you calling a patrol car?"

"I did, they told me to have a drone take care of it. A drunk swimming into a riptide is a waste of an officer's time. That's a direct quote."

Taking a deep breath, she looked at the angry-eyed poster. What would Agent Rose do? Silly question. Agent Rose would handle it. Agent Rose could handle anything.

Sam sat at her desk glaring at the dates on Henry's request forms that Dr. Morr had sent over from the lab. Something about them was troubling her, and she couldn't quite put her finger on it. They seemed . . . out of order almost.

Raw metal requested in late January, was that for the machine or for another project? The radio parts the second week of February . . . And then the answer formed like the shape of a rabbit coalescing in the clouds overhead. Tuesday, February 18, Dr. Troom went from ordering everything through the standard channels to applying for rush deliveries. Six extra forms to change the delivery date of the laser diode by a week. March 3, he'd paid triple the standard rates to have special silver and gold wires shipped from San Martin de Bolaños overnight.

Why was the original delivery date of March 26 not enough? A few weeks was nothing.

No, that wasn't quite right. A few weeks *should have* meant nothing. Unless Dr. Henry Troom needed his machine working before a certain date because something significant was going to happen. She stared at the large calendar hanging where a window would have been in a building with a more open design.

She shook from the memory of a purple light. The memory of a room that smelled both sterile and cruelly alien assaulted her.

The other iteration. He comes to my lab. He is stealing my work. Changing my formulas.

Agent Rose! Yes. Yes, of course, the paladin rushing to the rescue. It makes perfect sense.

The doctor, the soldier, the paladin, all the local einselected nodes near the machine have been deactivated.

I feel confident that we have reduced this iteration to yet another bad dream.

A gnarled brown hand gripped her shoulder, pulling her into the purple light. Cold air bit at her cheeks as her mirror image pulled a gun.

Sam tore herself away from the memory. From the hallucination. It was a stress-induced dream caused by an overdose of the drug Senior Agent Marrins had administered when he kidnapped her. Dr. Emir was dead, shot through the throat behind his laboratory by Agent Marrins. He hadn't come to rescue her from the small storage room.

The bureau therapist had reviewed it very carefully with her.

Sam escaped by herself. Picking the locks on the manacles chaining her to the wall, she'd kicked the door down and run for safety, only stopping because Henry Troom, then an intern at the lab, was captured.

She'd done the right thing, going back to save Henry, but the episode with Dr. Emir was a dream. Something conjured up by her subconscious to protect her from reality.

It didn't matter how many times she repeated the mantra, nothing made it real.

The memory of that other iteration was burned into her mind like a brand. Haunting her. Torturing her with a possibility she couldn't confirm.

Unless Henry had rebuilt the machine.

Grimacing, she checked the address of the shipments again and dialed a number from memory.

"Sammie!" Bri answered on the third ring. "Long time no contact, chica! What's up?"

"Not much, whatcha doing this week?"

"Aerial yoga instructor training and a half marathon on Saturday. You?"

"The usual: beach runs, weight lifting, and tracking down sociopaths. Want to do me a favor?"

"Always," Bri said cheerfully.

Sam smiled. "You remember that little self-storage place on the edge of town?"

"The one with the green roofs? Yeah, what about it?"

"My junior agent has been trying to reach someone at their office all morning, but no joy. Could you stop by there sometime this week and see if one of their boxes is still being paid for? I'll send you the number."

"Am I being recruited as a minion?" Bri asked suspiciously.

"Yes."

She laughed. "Sure; I can't make it today, but I can get there later this week. No rush, right?"

"No rush. It's a loose end. Probably nothing." Sam sighed and poked her pen at the pile of papers.

"You okay?" Bri asked.

Sam shook herself back to reality. "Yup. Never better."

"You are such a liar."

"Nah, I'm fine. Really. I'll call you this weekend and fill you in."

"I worry about you, Sammie. You need to be calling me more for sanity checks."

Sam smiled. "You're the best thing for me. Down-to-earth and always there."

"Hmmm." Bri didn't sound convinced. "But what are you going to do if I'm not here?"

"It's never going to happen," Sam said. "You'd give up oxygen before you gave up your phone."

Bri laughed again, a happy, carefree sound that was as alien to Sam as peaceful slumber or loving parents. As much as she'd hated Alabama, she missed having a friend like Bri nearby.

There was a knock at her office door. "Agent Rose?"

"I've got to get back to work," Sam said with a sigh. "Tell everybody I say hi, and I'll send them some more seashells after our next big storm."

"Love ya, Sam," Bri said. "Take care of yourself."

"Will do." Sam hung up and dropped the phone on its charger. "Come in, Edwin."

He had to duck to get through the door. "Sorry to disturb you, ma'am, but there's an Officer Clemens here about a dead body."

"Is she the one who notified Dr. Troom's next of kin?" Henry hadn't updated his contact information when his parents moved, and the police were having trouble tracking them down.

"No, ma'am—she's here about a different body."

Sam raised her eyebrows. "Another body? Our quiet little district is getting all kinds of wild and crazy. I'll be there in a moment."

Agent Edwin nodded and returned to the waiting area. Sam took a deep breath to compose herself, pushing the memories of the last summer away. Here and now was what mattered. Emir was dead and buried. Nothing she did would change that. She couldn't be *allowed* to change that. Even if the temptation and means were there, tampering with history was a crime, at least in her mind. Now all she had to do was convince the rest of the world she was right.

She slipped her shoes back on under the desk and went out to the lobby.

Edwin sat behind his oversized desk that almost met the proportions of his larger frame. In the metal-and-faded-fabric chair across from him, a thin woman with razor-thin nose and strawberry blonde hair tightly braided like a whip sat waiting.

"Officer Clemens?" Sam smiled.

"Senior Agent Rose, it's a pleasure to finally meet you," Clemens said as she stood up.

"Is it? I didn't realize I had any fans at the police department." She'd yet to make any real allies over there.

"Yes, ma'am."

Red flags went up. The little officer was buttering her up for something. "There aren't many people who could honestly say that."

"Most people don't have my background, ma'am."

A strange statement, but not one Sam felt like chasing to the ground just yet. She tucked it away for later examination. "Agent Edwin says you have a corpse for us?"

"Yes, ma'am, a man washed up on the shore with the tide this morning. He's late teens or early twenties and doesn't match any missing persons we're aware of. I had the EMT drop him at the morgue and came to report to you myself."

"Great." Of all the miles of shoreline in all the world, this drunk washed up on hers. "Good thing we have an ME on staff this week. Can you fill me in on the details as we walk to the morgue, or is the chief expecting you back before lunch?"

"I'm free, ma'am."

"Then let's walk." Sam led the way down to the morgue, Officer Clemens nipping at her heels and practically vibrating with suppressed enthusiasm. "First DOA case, Officer?"

"Yes, ma'am. My first real case ever, actually."

Sam glanced at the freckled woman out of the corner of her eye. "And they sent you alone?"

"I've served in the New Smyrna Police Department for ten years, but they were never my cases." Clemens lifted her chin. "I'm a clone."

She jerked her gaze toward the doors ahead. *Bloody, bloody clones.* It wasn't clones that were the issue, really. She supported the Caye Law—which said clones were not to be enslaved—and accepted that clones were human beings. But after being accused of being a clone last summer, and facing the possibility of execution for impersonating an officer of the law, she'd been skittish around them. The Caye Law hadn't granted clones equal rights to natural-born humans. They still couldn't hold elected offices or obtain a gun permit of any kind, and there was a strong anticlone coalition running the government right now. Her career wasn't stable enough to be seen sympathizing with clones.

"That's why I wanted to meet you," Clemens continued in a tone of hero worship, unaware of Sam's thoughts. "You're the only clone in the bureau."

What the heck? Did Clemens hate her? "I'm not a clone." Sam was amazed she managed to keep her voice calm. What this young woman was claiming—even as hearsay—could be the end of her. The bureau probably wouldn't hang her, not after they'd made her the sorta hero of last summer's debacle, but the rumor alone could kill her—literally. She'd find the other districts slow to respond for calls to help. Never know if the person backing her up would let her take a hit before they actually moved to help. Not unless she kept Mac as her backup permanently.

Clemens's jaw went slack with confusion. "B-but, what about all the reports from this summer? Every one said the bureau was covering up the fact that a clone was working as an agent."

"There was a cover-up, but it didn't involve clones." The icy-cold fear wrapped around her again. Jane Doe wasn't a clone. And Sam wasn't a clone of Jane Doe. They were the same woman separated by five years and one machine that broke the limits of time.

"Not even the Chimes girl?"

The memory of a young college student with tightly curled black hair and skin darker than Sam's rose in her memory. "Melody had a shadow, but that clone was never involved with the case." And she hadn't had the courage to follow up with Melody's family to see what had happened to her shadow. She hoped that they'd let the girl go in deference to the Caye Law, but she doubted that Melody's shadow had survived past the funeral.

Clemens deflated. "I'm sorry to have brought it up, ma'am."

"Don't be. It doesn't bother me," Sam lied. "I supported the Caye Law, and I support the integration of clones and shadows into society. Your humanity isn't based on how you were born."

"I hope so," Clemens said as she rolled her shoulders back.

Sam hid a smile. The little officer was a scrapper. "Stop hoping and start proving," Sam said as she keyed in the password for the morgue. "Now, tell me about our John Doe."

Clemens's pale face regained a little color as her confidence returned. "At 7:03 this morning, we received a call from a jogger who thought there was a dolphin or sea turtle wrapped in the kelp. They didn't want to get too close."

"A dolphin or a sea turtle?" Sam asked not sure how the two could be confused.

"The caller spotted the lump from the boardwalk. We're lucky they saw anything at all from that angle."

Mac peeked his head around the corner. "Hello?"

"You have a new body for me?" Sam asked.

"No, your body is lovely. However, the morgue does have a new client." Mac waved a gloved hand at Clemens. "Who's our friend?"

"Agent MacKenzie, this is Officer Clemens. Officer Clemens, this is our borrowed ME, MacKenzie. How'd the guy die? Drowning? Alcohol poisoning? Blow dart?"

"All three, actually," Mac said with a smile.

Sam's eyes went wide in surprise.

Mac laughed. "No, he was garroted—strangled from behind by something, I'm guessing a plastic rope or knotted bag. Something that was probably readily available. It certainly wasn't a professional hit."

"What?" Clemens eyes went wide with terror. "We . . . we thought this was a boating accident!"

Mac stared at her for a moment longer than it took Sam's eyes to start watering. "Adorable. Who thought that?"

"At the office, we have a sort of unofficial betting pool. People die every week: heart attack, car accidents, diabetes. The weather is finally warming up again, and people are getting their boats up."

"Meaning there's an increase in boating accidents," Sam finished for her. "No one checked the body before bringing it in?"

"The EMT at the scene took a pulse, declared John Doe dead at the scene, and headed here while I took the witness's statement." Clemens frowned at the memory. "It wasn't much of a statement. That stretch of beach is restricted for restoration. Our witness saw the lump and called it in thinking a dolphin had gotten tangled in a drift net. Animal control was first on scene. They phoned it in to us."

Sam looked at Mac. "Okay, tell me about John."

"John Doe is in his early twenties, has no ID on him, no fingerprints on file, and doesn't match any known missing-person report in the district. He died midday, between eleven and two I'd say, of asphyxiation when someone wrapped something around his throat and pulled back, choking him. There's subcutaneous bruising on his back where someone propped a knee to hold him steady."

"You said plastic," Officer Clemens said. "What makes you think the killer used that?"

"No fibers." Mac shrugged. "A metal garrote would have cut into the skin, a fabric like a scarf would have left trace fibers. They may be there when we do a microscan, but as smooth and as wide as the markings are, it looks like plastic to me. Just a hunch."

Sam nodded. "How long was he in the water?"

"Two hours, tops. And, you'll like this." Mac pulled up an image on the screen showing the John Doe's wrists. "See the red marks? Like his wrists were bound, but someone cut whatever was holding him off before the body was dumped."

"Trying to make it look accidental?" Clemens asked.

"This would only look like an accidental death if you'd never worked a homicide before," Mac said.

"Mac, how many people in this district do you think have ever seen a murder before?" Aside from Henry, the only cases that even merited a bureau phone call had been a drunken hit-and-run around New Year's and a domestic-abuse case before Thanksgiving. Neither of those had required an investigation.

He frowned. "Oh. Right." Another shrug. "It's still pretty hard to make strangulation look like an accident."

"A guy goes out for a swim, gets tangled in the

swimming line, manages to keep his head above water as he tries to untangle himself but it cuts off his air supply and he dies," Clemens said. "It's happened before. Last time was in 2067 during a minitriathlon at the beach. Run a mile, bike a mile, swim a mile. Cory Andrews was a seventeen-year-old high-school junior and in the lead until he swam into a fishing line. The crew on the rescue boat got to him in minutes, but he was already unconscious.

"After that, the mayor ran on a campaign to clean up the beaches. It was all over the news during fishing season or whenever the vote to up the cost of fishing licenses comes up."

Sam could feel a stress headache coming on. "So, there's a chance someone could have tried to copycat the accident? Wonderful." Serial killers were such a pain in the paperwork. Give her a nice clean shooting to report any day.

"I wouldn't look at local suspects first," Mac said. "Whoever did this didn't check the tide tables to make sure the body was washed out to sea."

She met his eyes and nodded. "Unprofessional." *Opportunistic.* "Maybe accidental? A kidnapping gone wrong."

There was a knock at the morgue door before Mac could answer. Agent Edwin smiled nervously at her, and Sam waved him in.

"What's up, Edwin?"

"This John Doe that just came in?" Edwin held a printout of John Doe's face. "I think I know who he is."

Sam's eyebrows went up in question. "Who?"

"Nealie. Nealie Rho. He's one of my pirates."

Mac kicked back in his chair, grinning. "Pirates? Murdered pirates are good. I love Florida."

"Shut up, Mac." Chicago has certainly taught him how to enjoy the job. Sam turned to Edwin. "How sure are you that this is your guy?"

"I recognize his face," Edwin said, looking a little flustered. "He's an easygoing guy, not one of my real troublemakers. The worse thing he's ever done is call me because a shipping container had one more box than usual. He liked to count stuff for fun. How many trips the tourist boat made. How many containers came into the shipping port. Little things. If the numbers were off, he'd call 911 to report suspicious activity. They always bounced it to me, so I finally gave him my home number. No big deal. Right?" His forehead creased in a worried frown.

"It's not breaking any laws," Sam said. "Can you run point on this, or are you too close to the victim?"

Edwin took a deep breath. "I can do it. Probably. I've never known a homicide victim before. Is it homicide or not? I really prefer not."

"Possible homicide," Clemens said.

"Definite homicide," Mac said. "It was someone he knew, and it was probably a crime of passion." He looked at Sam and shook his head. "This wasn't accidental."

"Passion?" Sam asked flatly. "Really? Running someone over is a crime of passion. Beating someone bloody is a crime of passion. Who strangles someone with a plastic bag in a fit of anger? No one stops and looks around and thinks, 'Gosh! That plastic bag looks like a great murder weapon! I'm so enraged! Let me choke you!' "

Mac shrugged and stood up. "Nealie and his buddy were talking, they start arguing over something. One of 'em's pacing, one's sitting. Nealie sits down with his back to the guy. Maybe he's pouting, who knows. The other guy flips, the argument's gone too far, and he grabs something he had on hand, wraps it around Nealie's neck, pulls back, and chokes Nealie to death."

"Then drags him to a boat he just happens to have lying around?" Sam asked. "And where do the cut arms come in?"

"Bondage play?" Edwin suggested.

All the air left Sam's lungs as she gasped in shock. "What?"

"Erotic asphyxiation is a thing!" Edwin turned to Clemens for support.

Clemens shook her head. "Not my kink."

Sam shook her head to clear that disturbing image. "Mac says passion, I say premeditated murder, Edwin has accidental, erotic-related death. Clemens, you want to get in on this? Mac's buying lunch for the winner."

"Me?" Mac laughed. "What if I win?"

"You're not. I'm right."

Clemens shook her head. "I'm going to go with accidental, nonerotic death." She blushed. "I like taking the long shots."

Sam walked Clemens out to the parking lot as Mac and Edwin got ready to leave for the swamps.

Clemens stopped beside the rental. "Nice car. I guess bureau pay isn't as bad as everyone says."

"It's a rental," Sam said. "I usually drive the Alexia Virgo, standard-issue car of lower-middle-class workers everywhere."

"What happened to it?"

"Somebody bashed it up in the parking lot. It's in the shop until they can get all the parts in to fix it."

"Wow, I hope the other guy had insurance."

"Don't know. Whoever rammed my car into something didn't stop to leave a number after their joyride. Just a nice, cryptic note and a two-hundred-dollar copay."

"Did you report it?" Clemens asked, sounding angrier than Sam felt.

She shrugged. "Two officers came in and took my report. They said they'd look at the security video from the street cams, but they haven't gotten back to me."

"Do you remember which officers you talked to?"

"Hadley and Ranct."

"They're good people," Clemens said. "Good officers. I'll talk to them and see if I can't get them to give your car some priority attention."

"You don't have to," Sam said. "I don't need special consideration, and I don't want favors I can't repay."

Clemens rolled her eyes. "Your drive-by vandalism is the second biggest crime in this town in weeks. If the patrol officers haven't gotten back to you, it's because someone in the tech department is too busy playing video games to check their in-box. I'm not doing you favors by reminding someone to do their job."

"Good for you, throwing weight around like that."

Clemens smiled. "I've got to start somewhere now that I have weight to throw around. Now that I'm a real person . . ." She shrugged. "I want to be a real person, you know? I want people to know I'm more than a vacation trinket created in the lab."

Sam knew exactly how she felt.

Henry's address, according to the lab employment records, was 12B Basilwood Loop, part of an apartment complex that catered to singles and young couples.

Sam knew where it was only because she'd run across it during her apartment hunt and remembered how out of place the Basilwood Apartments felt. Most apartments in Florida were cement blocks with stucco texturing and tropical colors. In fact, cement blocks were the preferred design aesthetic anywhere hurricanes were a common occurrence. Basilwood was synthetic wood with cuckoo-clock embellishments. She half expected to see a little woman in wooden shoes carrying tulips popping out of the arched windows of the main building as the clock struck the hour.

She drove around the loop until she found building twelve and parked in a vacant, unmarked spot. Two spots were marked 12B. Presumably one for Henry and one for his roommate. Lucky her, the roommate's car was sitting where it belonged.

Taking the stairs two at a time, she went up to Apartment B and rapped her knuckles on the door. From inside she heard the unmistakable sound of the soundtrack for War of Wars, a first-person shooter that was being advertised on every radio station and Internet site in the Commonwealth. Fake gunfire rattled inside. She knocked again, louder. Someone swore, and the music stopped.

"What do you want?" a lanky man with brown hair demanded as the door swung open. He glared at Sam, looked her up and down once, then changed his frown to a sleazy smile. "I mean, hey, babe. How's tricks?"

"Ha-ha," Sam said without inflection. "Funny. Are you Devon Bradet?"

"Um, yeah."

"I'm Agent Rose, I left you a message about meeting today?" Sam said, holding up her badge for inspection. "Do you mind if I come in?"

"Oh, right! The clone. Yeah, yeah, come in. I've been dying to meet you!"

She tilted her head to the side in confusion. "Officer Clemens is the clone. She isn't working this case. I'm here to ask you a few questions about your roommate, Henry Troom."

Bradet held the door open and gestured to a set of mismatched chairs. His high-end holoset was paused in the middle of a shoot-out between blue-fatigued soldiers and aliens in red shirts. "Do you play?" Bradet asked.

"No, I'm not a big fan of guns." And video games hadn't been at the top of the nuns' list of acceptable entertainment at school unless you wanted to play Deidre Duck's ABCs.

"Ah, man, you ought to try this! It's benjo! The top gamers' mags all say it's the next big batty-fang."

"I'm going to nod and pretend I keep up with youth culture," Sam said. The way slang changed these days, she felt she needed a dictionary.

"How old are you, grandma?" Bradet laughed, then suddenly sobered. "Oh, wait. Clones don't live that long do they? That must have sucked goat balls living in a lab and never getting out. How are you supposed to have a conversation like a normal person if you never see what human culture is like?"

Sam's eyebrows went up. "Once again, you have me confused with someone else. I'm not a clone. I'm a CBI agent, and I need to talk to you about your roommate. When's the last time you saw Henry?"

"But you are the clone!" Bradet protested. "My boss at the radio station was the one who started the petition to get you removed from our district last September. Remember? I know all about you. Go ahead, ask me anything. I had the whole file memorized, and let me tell you, whoever made your fake backstory did a lousy job. There are holes in it a mile wide. Kills me."

Now she wished she'd brought Mac along. He'd have either glared Bradet into submission or made a not-so-subtle threat that would shut the idiot up. "Mr.

Bradet, I really don't have time to indulge in your conspiracy theories. Can we talk about Mr. Troom now?"

"Okay." Bradet leaned forward in his chair, elbows balanced on his knees. "How about tit-for-tat. I tell you everything I know about Henry, and you give me the exclusive interview with the only known clone in the bureau? How's that sound? Pretty stellar, right? Am I right? You know I'm right."

What she knew was Bradet had had one too many cups of java this morning. "First, let me make this perfectly clear: I am not a clone. There is no conspiracy. There is nothing unusual about my birth or upbringing. Two, if you don't want to talk here, I can and will take you down to the holding cell and interrogate you there. That requires extra paperwork . . ." *and the sheriff's permission to borrow a holding cell* " . . . and I hate paperwork. If you make me do extra paperwork, I will make it worth my while by not only asking about your roommate, but also putting you at the top of my suspect pool. How do you feel about a complete and thorough examination of your finances? Did you pay taxes for these lovely games donated to you?" Sam nodded and smiled. She tried to make it a sweet, nonthreatening sort of smile that she'd always used to make people want to agree with her.

She was pretty sure it looked more like a grimace.

Somehow, she'd lost the knack for smiling like that over the past year. Edwin once said it was something about the look in her eyes—the one that threatened excessive amounts of imminent pain.

"Um, no. I mean, it's legal. The games and stuff I get to review because I'm paid to talk about them on air. The more people who listen to my station, the more ads we sell, the more freebies I get. That's it. Swear on my dad's grave."

"Good. Then the bureau doesn't need to recommend you be arrested for tax fraud." She flicked her tablet open. "But maybe it will need to look into obstruction of justice. Let's talk about your roommate, shall we?"

Bradet rubbed sweaty hands on his khaki shorts. "Oh, right. Um, Henry's a nice guy. Real quiet, pays his share of the bills on time, doesn't leave dishes in the sink. That's crucial to being a good roommate. He was the real deal, you know?"

"When did you last see Henry?"

He shook his head and squinted. "Sunday afternoon I guess? There was a beach volleyball game and barbecue I went to. Judged the bikini contest . . . and let me tell you we *all* won that day, if you know what I mean." She remained impassive. "Uh, guess not. Then I went to work. I clock in around midnight, go over my script, record any ads or whatnot, check the news. My show comes on at six and I'm off air at eight. I usually leave by nine, and Henry left for work early."

"Do you always work nights?"

"Yeah, I started with a midnight show. Liked to play some cool Indie stuff, music the college kids could relate to. I got popular enough, and they bumped me up to the morning show for weekends. I work Saturday,

Sunday, Monday at the morning slot, then Tuesday and Thursday I do the midnight show. Go in to work and go on air first, do everything else after. Friday nights it's all about the clubs, you feel me?"

"Not really." Spending her free time surrounded by sweaty, inebriated college students never appealed to her, not even when she was younger. "When you saw Henry on Sunday, did he seem upset at all? Worried? Distracted?"

"Nah. He did his thing like usual. Probably did breakfast before I woke up, I saw him when I had lunch, and I saw him making some noodles when I left for the beach. I asked if he wanted to come, but I knew he'd say no. Parties aren't his wiggle, you know?"

"Wiggle?" Sam tried not to say anything unprofessional, settling for, "I'm going to pretend that didn't come with a dance move. How long have you known Henry?"

"Three months or so? He got here just before the holidays. Knew an old buddy of mine who told him to look me up. I needed a roommate who could pay rent, he needed a place to crash, it seemed ideal."

"Did he have any friends? Girlfriend? Boyfriend? Family? Anyone ever come over?" The questions were textbook, but they made her squirm. Someday an agent would ask *her* neighbors the same thing, and what would they say?

"Henry? Nah, man, no." Bradet shook his head. "Henry never deviated from his schedule. He went to work, he came home, he went to his room, he came out for dinner at eight on the dot every day. Every day. Grocery shopping was Thursdays. I think he did laundry on the weekends. A man's shorts are none of my business, you know?"

"So, he didn't have any friends?"

"Maybe online?" Bradet guessed. "Once he was in his room, he'd turn on the computer, and that was it. No more communication from the Henry."

"Can I see his room?"

"Can you pick locks?" Bradet asked. He stood up and led Sam down the left hall. "Henry's bathroom, and his fortress of solitude." He batted at the combination padlock handing on Henry's door. "He was a very private man. But he paid his rent on time."

"Your roommate padlocked his bedroom when he left, and you weren't the least bit concerned?" She'd lived with a pill addict and hadn't ever felt the need to padlock her room. Either Henry was scared of someone, or he was scared of someone's finding what he kept in his room. Neither thought gave her much comfort.

Bradet raised his hands in surrender to the cruel fates of roommatedom. "What do you want me to say? He paid his bills. He washed his dishes. He could have been drinking blood and sacrificing gerbils to the elder gods for all I cared. As long as the house didn't stink, and the air-conditioning stayed on, I wasn't going to complain."

"You have very low standards."

He winked at her. "The lower the better, am I right, babe?"

"Don't," Sam said, stepping away as he encroached on her personal space. "Just don't."

He moved closer. "I'm just being friendly."

"And I'm clearly stating I want my personal space without you in it. Are we clear?"

"Yeah," Bradet said with a frown that said he clearly didn't understand why she wasn't thirsting after him.

She let it go. Bradet's insecurities weren't her problem. Besides—she had no doubt she could handle this slacker if it came to that. "Do I have your permission to enter the house when I find a bolt cutter for Henry's lock?"

He scratched the back of his head. "I don't know. Some of the stuff here is kinda, you know, important."

"Like what?"

"The games? My holoset? They're early models I get for working at the station, perks. I get them a couple months in advance. I'm really not allowed to have people around them unless I'm here. It's in my contract. I take most of my dates to hotels. And, you know, to respect my roommate's privacy." He nodded, like taking girls to pay-by-the-hour motels was an improvement. Then again, if the living room was any indication of the general state of Bradet's housekeeping, maybe it was a step up from his bedroom.

"When would be a good time for me to come back? Tonight? Tomorrow?" Next time she'd bring Edwin or Mac, some big, burly bureau shield who would make sure Bradet didn't try to climb into her pocket again.

"Friday afternoon would be best. I mean, you're

cutting into my sleep time." Bradet was giving her a beaten-dog look as if he were the victim.

Sam raised an eyebrow. "You do realize your roommate is dead, and I'm trying to find out what happened to him, don't you?"

"Yeah, but it was an accident at the lab. I know. I read the police report at work. It's tragic—he didn't pay money for April's rent yet—but it's not a murder or anything. If you thought there was something important here, you'd have come by on Monday."

"Henry's death was, we believe, accidental. I want to prevent future accidents. If Henry had notes about what he was working on or what he was planning to work on the day of the incident, it's important."

"Friday," Bradet said. "I'm usually up by four."

"Fine," Sam said. "I'll be here at four with some bolt cutters. In the meantime, if you think of anything, please don't hesitate to contact my office."

Bradet leered at her.

"And if you think of anything along those lines, I'll use the bolt cutters on *you* when I return."

Mac sat back and enjoyed the scenery as Agent Edwin drove out of what the locals optimistically called a city, south to the Mosquito Lagoon. Edwin's beat-up red Karoshi Legend rattled down a gravel road and stopped by a tree in an area not visibly different than the past ten miles of trackless gravel road they'd passed. "And this is?"

"The quickest way to the camp," Edwin said. "They used to live up by Webster's Creek, but a developer bought the area a few years back. Don't ask about the creek at camp. They protested it, and if they think you'll listen, you'll get a blow-by-blow story of it from Connor Nu."

"Connor Nu and Nealie Rho? Are those surnames real names?" Mac asked, as they climbed out of the truck.

Edwin grabbed two pairs of long plastic waders from the back of the truck and tossed a set to Mac. "One hundred percent invented. Nealie told me there's a society record, but I never got all the details out of him."

"You sound like you spend a lot of time down here with them."

Edwin shrugged. "Someone has to. The police don't care what they do. They're outside the city jurisdiction. Neither Volusia nor Brevard County wants to take responsibility for them if they get sick."

"Do they get sick a lot?"

"Not too much. Although one time I told them there was dihydrogen monoxide in the water around here, and three of them went to the hospital for dehydration." The younger agent flushed red with embarrassment. "Connor was on an anti-chemical kick. Kept saying that we shouldn't eat anything with chemicals in it. Lectured me on how I was poisoning myself eating grocery store food and refusing their all-natural fish and cattail biscuits. I got mad."

"Hey—it's not your fault they don't know basic chemistry."

"Yeah, but I should have known better."

"Better you play a trick on them than punch them in the face."

"I'm too big to hit people," Edwin said. "I played football my freshman year of high school. Knocked a guy out, and he quit playing because of the head trauma. I quit, too. I don't want to hurt people."

Mac nodded. "I guess hitting with your words is the mature thing to do, then." He pulled his waders on and looked at the dusty road. The humidity was near a hundred percent. Every breath was a gulp of hot steam. "How wet are we going to get?"

"In a mangal swamp? Don't bring anything that isn't waterproof."

"Is my wallet okay in the car?"

"Oh, yeah. Nobody comes out here but me and sometimes the park ranger."

Flattened grass and a faint tire imprint caught Mac's eye. "Any of your pirates have a car?"

"Not parked out here. I think a few of them have bikes at the marina. Mostly they get around on boats. All the waterways around here connect to Indian River Lagoon. You can take that all the way south to Sebastian Inlet. Or you go south of Mosquito Lagoon and hike everything across the A1A to the Atlantic. That's how they get most of their smuggled stuff in."

"So, this was the park ranger?" Mac pointed to the flattened grass.

Edwin shook his head. "Sheila Bingara is the ranger on duty up here. She doesn't come out here unless she calls me first."

"Are you two dating?"

Another blush. "I wish. Nah, she doesn't like being the only girl out here with a lot of what she calls bogans. I think it means hoodlums."

"And you haven't been out here in over a week?"

"Right."

"So let's get a picture of this tire mark and some measurements. This was probably Nealie's last ride."

Equipped with the bureau's standard crime scene kit, they took pictures, measured everything, and started hiking into the jungle interior. Long grass and gravel quickly gave way to thick trees, vines, and mud.

"Mind the orb weavers," Edwin said, pointing up. "They're usually not a problem, but you don't want to stretch in here."

Mac glanced overhead and saw spiderwebs stretched from tree to tree. Something scuttled past.

"Here." Edwin stopped. "This is what you're watching for." On the tree trunk next to Edwin's head there was a fist-sized yellow-and-black spider with strange horns on its carapace.

"Mutated?"

"Nah, orb weavers are spiky. Just watch for the little red-and-black ones. They like to make webs across the pathways. They're not poisonous, just pesky."

"And people are willing to live out here?" Idaho had spiders, too, but they were the normal little brown ones or the occasional black widow. Spiky spiders were something out of a kid's cartoon.

"People willingly live everywhere," Edwin said. "Ready to head into the swamp?"

"We aren't there yet?" *How could it possibly get wetter?*

"Oh, no, this is just the bike trail. We're in the swamp when you have water up to your knees."

"Oh. Yipee," Mac muttered. "There's so much to look forward to here."

"Not quite Chicago, is it, sir?" Edwin asked with a laugh.

Mac looked at the trees, ancient, gnarled creatures that looked like primordial ooze that had just found a solid form rather than the more prim maples lining the lanes of Chicago. "This isn't quite a walk past the linden blossoms, but it's not bad." Florida was less sterile. He took a deep breath, and the air soaked his lungs. "I could live with a little less humidity."

Edwin laughed. "This isn't humid, not yet. Come summertime, we'll have over a hundred percent humidity and triple-digit temperatures."

"A hundred percent humidity is called rain. We have plenty of that in Chicago," Mac said as he followed the junior agent down the suggestion of a game trail that might—if he squinted and used his imagination—be a path to a campsite.

"Down here, it gets so hot the rain evaporates before it hits the ground. It's like walking through a sauna."

"Oh, I remember days like that." He'd hated them

in Alabama until he realized those were the days Sam wore her thinnest shirts. On the weekends, she liked to wear lacy camisoles that the wet air plastered to her body like a second skin. "It wasn't so bad, actually."

Edwin looked over his shoulder at Mac. "You've been here before?"

"I was in Alabama. The humidity isn't quite so bad, but there were days."

"Right." Edwin snapped a branch and took a breath. "Ever eaten alligator?"

"Um . . . no. Am I about to get the opportunity?" Mac stepped behind Edwin and, much to his chagrin, had to go on tiptoe to see over the other agent's shoulder. "We found our swamp."

Edwin smiled. "It should be too early in the season for the gators to be this far north. They like to stay down in the Everglades until the weather really warms up, but there's always a risk of early migration and water snakes."

"Fun place, Florida. Why do these pirates live here again?"

"Cheapest rent in the district."

"Right."

Edwin waded into the murky water, and, with a reluctant grimace, Mac followed. "It's chillier than I thought it would be."

Agent Edwin pointed up. "Canopy cover. I'm not sure if this actually qualifies as a rain forest, but the upper-level foliage gets most of the light. Down here, it's dark and shady . . ."

"And humid, and buggy, and damp," Mac finished for him. "I think I see why Agent Rose lets you handle the pirates."

"Oh, she's come out here. Once at least."

Mac raised an eyebrow. It was hard to picture Sam wading through the mud for fun. "She didn't recognize Nealie."

Edwin shrugged and forged deeper into mangal swamp, walking around the mangrove roots and leaving slow eddies in the water. "All I know is they've mentioned her. I think she first came out here in late January. Nealie mentioned seeing her once, didn't remember her name, but I knew her from the description. Maybe she only talked with Connor Nu. All I know is Nealie thought she had a funny accent."

"Not that I've noticed." He replayed Sam's voice in his head.

"She doesn't have a noticeable accent, unless you count Commonwealth Newscaster as an accent. Agent Rose always sounds very polished. Maybe that's what he meant." Edwin stopped and looked around. He pointed in a southwesterly direction. "This way. I think."

"You think? That's not what I want to hear. Land-nav is not an exercise in guesses."

Edwin sighed. There might have been an eye roll. "I think this is the right island for the main camp. During high tide, it's easy to lose count and go down one too many. But I didn't hear anything, so it's probably this one."

"Fair enough," Mac said. He scrambled up the muddy bank after Edwin. "Sorry for, uh, you know."

"Questioning my every move?" Edwin said.

"Yup. That. Sorry."

"Don't worry about it. The only person who treats me like a real agent is Agent Rose. I don't think it's crossed her mind I might fail."

"Have you?" Mac asked.

Edwin looked confused. "Have I thought I might fail?"

"No, have you ever actually failed?"

"No."

"Then why would she think you'd fail? Sam expects the best out of people. She always has." Mac climbed the small bank and pushed aside a tangle of vines along with his thoughts on how Sam had first viewed him. She hadn't been a fan, but then he hadn't been someone worth rooting for when they met. But, if her flirtatious smiles last night over dinner were anything to go by, he was growing on her. "This is the camp?"

Edwin nodded. "One of them. They travel between the islands for fishing and whatnot, but this is the main base of operations."

There was a suggestion of habitation. A circle of cleared space on the muddy island. Fewer Brazilian pepper vines wrapping around the mangrove trees, and compacted earth suggested someone had been here recently.

Edwin walked in confidently and started scuffing the ground with his wet boots. "They were here."

"Yeah?" Mac walked farther into the circle and looked around. The dusty, dry ground looked rippled.

"Their bags are still here." Edwin pointed up, and Mac saw nets and plastic boxes hanging from a rope a good eight feet off the ground. "It keeps the bears away," Edwin said.

Mac nodded. "I'm sure it keeps it dry, too."

"Exactly," the junior agent said. "Here!" Edwin ran across the encampment, kicking up dust, and gestured for Mac to follow. "Tents and everything. Although . . . I wonder why they're over here."

Mac followed, eyeing the pile of broken tents and scattered shoes with distrust. He reached for Edwin's arm. "We should go."

"Why?"

"I need to talk to Sam."

Edwin frowned. "I thought you wanted to interview the pirates."

"I need to talk to Sam first, and there's no phone signal here." Mac took out his phone and snapped pictures of the camp. "Let's go."

He hoped Sam would tell him he was crazy. There were dozens of reasons the site looked like this. Maybe the pirates had decided to draw some geometric designs to fancy up the swamp, but the last time something had shattered in neatly concentric rings, people had died.

CHAPTER 7

Every expansion event is followed by a collapse. Every collapse is preceded by a series of decoherence events. One iteration of time collapses into the other like tumbling dominoes creating chaos and noise, but nothing more.

~ excerpt from Lectures on the Movement
of Time by Dr. Abdul Emir I1–20740413

Friday March 3, 2073
Broward County, Florida
Federated States of Mexico
Iteration 3

Gant regarded Bahia Corsario—or Privateer's Bay—with a dispassionate look as Donovan steered their stolen car down the well-lit boulevard as the car's AC breathed out tinny, recycled air. "It looks like a church."

"It is, almost." Donovan turned the car away from the buildings and down a side street lined with boutiques and pastry shops.

"What's the security like?"

"Tight. Zoetimax Industrial owns the complex. Twelve acres of paradise for the wealthy. A modern San Carlos, full of treasure."

"San Carlos held an army, not a treasure."

"It was a treasury before Mexico took their independence from Spain," Donovan said. He took another turn, and the difference between Bahia Corsario and the rest of the sheltered city of Pembroke Pines became visible.

Entire houses were missing. Empty lots choked by vines filled the places where humanity had been vanquished. "What happened?"

"Hurricane, three years ago. The whole area was destroyed. Pembroke Pines was far enough inland that some of the buildings stood. The government paid to relocate people to safer towns with low populations. Zoetimax bought up as much land as they could."

"Good for them."

"Everyone here works for Zoetimax in one way or another," Donovan said as he pulled up to a house and into the car park behind it. The metal awning wasn't much protection from sun, rain, or satellite, but most people weren't worried about the government sky cameras. "All those little businesses you saw? The mom-and-pop shops down the main jag? Zoetimax fronts. Zoetimax owns the bank. People get loans, open preapproved businesses, charge a set amount."

"Manuel Helu still owns Zoetimax, doesn't he?"

"Zoetimax and the senate and the palace if he can

get it. This is his *ciudad de la perfección*. His blueprint for the modern Federated States of Mexico." Donovan got out and looked across the withering grass of the house's backyard. "Makes me sick."

Gant rolled his eyes. Smooth-talking politicians weren't his business. Money meant security, and security wasn't what he wanted in a mark. "Whose house is this?"

"No one's. The owner ran into trouble with some buddies of mine. Took a fishing trip." Donovan met his eyes. "Fell off the boat."

"Tragic," Gant said. "Won't his boss be looking for him?"

"Not for a few more days, and by then we'll be long gone." He tossed a roll of lock picks to Gant. "Open the door while I get my gear."

Amateur hour. Gant hadn't had much time to research Donovan and his crew, but what he'd found was enough to keep him from slitting Donovan's throat while he slept. He walked the back of the house once, kicked over a rock, and picked the key and security code up. Honestly, sometimes he despaired at the intelligence of his fellow humans. A shiny plastic rock from the Peso General garden center wasn't how you hid a spare key. He grabbed the doorknob, and the door swung open.

"Depressing, isn't it?" Donovan said from behind him. "Company villages like this make people sloppy. They don't stop to think."

Donovan was wrong. People never even started thinking. "I'm beginning to be insulted you asked for my help," Gant said. "At this point, I could be replaced by a toddler with a toothache."

Donovan's mouth twitched up in a one-sided grin. "We haven't started yet." He pulled two sets of binoculars out of the bag and handed one to Gant. "Come upstairs."

The house was everything Gant hated about southern Florida: mold, mildew, alarming shades of green on the walls mixed with unnatural orange tiles on the floor. All the furniture was a knockoff from the set of *La Usurpadora*. All that was missing was for a beautiful woman in a tiny bikini to come screaming about how her husband had betrayed her.

That's pretty much all everything is missing, Gant thought.

The stairs creaked under his weight as they climbed to the second floor.

Donovan opened a door bringing in a gust of jasmine-scented night air. "The roof was never properly fixed. We can get a good view of the target."

Gant followed him into the tiled balcony that had once been a bedroom, perhaps, and onto the roof. Donovan looked north to the glow of Bahi Corsario. Gant took out his binoculars and did the same. "What am I looking for?"

"Security guards."

"I don't see any."

"Now you know why I need you." Donovan jumped down to the floor. "A building made of glass, and we can't do a smash and grab. Shame really."

Gant didn't say anything to that. From what he'd learned, Donovan's crew specialized in brute-force maneuvers. All of them were former Fuerzas Especiales, FES. Men trained by the military to do the impossible. Their war record was impressive, and most of it was available for public perusal. The socially acceptable rescue missions, at least. What puzzled Gant was that the record of Donovan's last year in service, and his reason for leaving the military, were classified to the point even Gant couldn't break the encryption. He had yet to find out how a decorated war hero had become the leader of one of the better heist crews in the northern territories.

Donovan hadn't been in a sharing mood.

"Coming down?" Donovan watched him. With good reason. His last job had ended when his second-in-command betrayed them. Two of his men had died, the rest went to jail. Donovan had escaped, his former friend hadn't.

Gant climbed back down. "When do we go in?"

"Two hours. The guards are behind bulletproof glass while they're on shift. Everything locks down if anything moves. Not a gnat gets through the building. Except during shift change. There's an eleven-minute window where the motion sensors are off. Six minutes of debrief when the sensors are on, and a ten-minute window where we can move again."

"More than enough time for you to get to the Timeyst Machine. Alone." Gant raised an eyebrow. "I'm your diversion, Donovan."

Donovan chuckled. "If I needed a salsa dancer, I'd have bought one off the streets in Miami. There are two things needed to make the machine work. Do you know what they are?"

Gant shook his head.

Donovan motioned for him to follow as he walked back downstairs to the kitchen, where their gear was waiting. "You know how all their ads end?"

"Yeah: 'Book now!'"

"Exactly. Book *now* is the key," Donovan said. "The machine only works sometimes. Something about stars aligning or some nonsense. You can't just punch in the date you want to go visit, there's math involved."

Gant closed his eyes. "Math? You hired me to do your math homework?"

"I hired you to get the key. The machine is locked behind several doors and three layers of guard posts. It's in the inner sanctum of the church of gratuitous wealth. The key is kept on the far end of the building in the offices of the operators. Director's name is Juana Carlisle. You've seen her on TV."

Gant narrowed his eyes as he tried to put a name to the face. "Blond hair, low-cut v-neck lab coat, plastic tits?"

"That's the one."

"She can't be the brains behind this."

"Doesn't matter. She's the *face*. Her office is in the south campus near the Fountain of Aphrodite." Donovan smiled. "I cased the place a few weeks before I found you. At first I thought a long con might get me in. Get myself hired, work on security, butter up Dr. Carlisle." Donovan shook his head. "There was a hiring freeze. Couldn't get in."

And I don't see you having nearly enough butter. "Why didn't you go in as a buyer?"

"Not enough *dinero*. It's two million up front to plan the trip. Another eight on top of that to go. Putting the funds together would have put me back on the *federales'* radar. And Dr. Carlisle was too well protected for me to kidnap her. This way's quicker. I neutralize the problems on my side, you get the key, we both skip town and go to a place where no one's ever heard of us." Donovan held out a laminated square of paper no bigger than Gant's palm. "That's your route. My pace count is a little longer than yours, so watch for the landmarks."

Gant nodded as he looked over the tiny map. Donovan had him breaking through a sealed door and several computerized locks. That made sense. Electronics and locks were his strong suit.

He'd started as a second-story man lifting jewels and smart watches. The murder had come later, an expansion of his repertoire as he chased larger dreams and embraced a simpler life. Breaking a neck was so much more efficient than talking himself out of a sticky situation. "How far between the south campus and the machine room?"

"Three-quarters of a mile, at most. You can run, can't you?"

"Ha-ha," Gant said dryly. "How close to the entry point can we get before go time?"

"Less than a block. There's a wrought-iron fence. Pretty, decorative thing. Don't touch it if you don't want to be electrocuted."

Skulking was never a necessity. Running between bushes looking like a hunchback only drew attention. Walking sedately down the road was the best way to approach a mark, be it a house full of priceless art or a gentleman who had failed to pay a debt. A person walking down the street had many reasons to be out, even at half past three in the morning. Anyone seeing an early-morning walker would make an excuse.

Early-morning skulkers got the police called on them.

So Gant walked, calm and relaxed, along the well-maintained sidewalk next to the terrifying wrought iron. Inside the grounds of Bahia Corsario, floodlights illuminated multiple fountains. Donovan had been wrong: the fountain wasn't Aphrodite. The artist had re-created Botticelli's *Birth of Venus* with luminous marble. The divine Venus Anadyomene seemed to glow with inner light, hinting at serenity and hidden knowledge with a cheeky nod to lust and power, impossible to miss.

No doubt the gift shop had postcards of this very scene, the fountains at night.

Perhaps he'd take one for himself. A memento of the night he escaped Detective Rose for good.

He slipped a handheld acetylene blowtorch from

his pocket and poked it into a nearby bush. There was a thunk and sizzle of torch meeting iron bars. He moved along, stopping here and there, always tracking the distance to Venus's fountain. Every fence had a weakness. This time he had to turn a corner to find it.

In a narrow alley between a shop selling gourmet dog biscuits and the business park, there was a small gate and a hedge-lined walkway. *Of course.* It wouldn't do to have the wealthy elite see the maintenance crew removing the trash. And this close to the coast, the tunnels inland cities used to hide their workers were problematic, if not entirely out of the question. The answer was naturally the concealed walkway.

Gant checked his watch. Thirty seconds to go. He peered down the walkway. There were no cameras marked on Donovan's map, but he didn't trust the other man completely. He scanned the bushes and eaves of the building until he satisfied himself that Donovan's information was good. Zoetimax was trusting to their reputation to keep people out.

Idiots.

And then it was time to go.

Gant pulled his blowtorch out and pressed the little red button. Searing hot flames poured out, melting the gate's lock. Copper oxide, magnesium, and aluminum—such simple things, but in the right quantities, they made a metal vapor torch that was the devil's gift to thieves. He ran down the walkway, pressed the button again, and cut away the lock of the metal security door. There was no handle, but he was able to nudge the door open with his foot. He squirmed past the still-cooling metal and looked down the back hall of Zoetimax Industries' temple to filthy lucre.

His heart leapt with unadulterated joy. If he'd only known this place existed as a younger man. Forget a smash and grab, he'd have gotten a job and taken this place apart. Art restorer maybe. Lift the real masterpieces and replace them with elegant fakes.

Gant walked down the hall, admiring the paintings. Rare masterpieces. *The Storm on the Sea of Galilee* by Rembrandt. *View of the Sea at Scheveningen* by Vincent van Gogh. *Waterloo Bridge, London* by Claude Monet. There was a king's ransom hanging here by the janitor's door. Those three paintings alone would get him out of the country and to a life of ease in any place he cared to name. He stopped, eyeing the frames. No. Anywhere he went, Detective Rose would follow. Better to go with Donovan into the past and come back to lift these paintings off the walls then.

The sound of heavy footsteps along the adjacent corridor propelled him forward. He took two more halls in haste, only realizing he'd lost his bearings when he nearly walked into a domed room with a gilt fountain. There was a map of the facilities on the wall, and Gant quickly reoriented.

Curse Donovan and his rushed endeavors—he'd left out a hallway.

Gant was certain he was going to miss his turn until he found the life-size painting of Juana Carlisle hanging on one wall next to a tasteful Degas. The director was no *Dancer with a Bouquet of Flowers*, but she certainly had an ego meant for center stage and the spotlight. He knelt, unlocked the office door in record time, and walked into a rotunda with a panoramic photograph of a pastoral scene printed on the walls. The place was familiar, but the artist's name escaped him (if the photograph was indeed meant to be the work of a classical artist, that is).

Each door in the office was discreetly hidden within the painting, but only one door was locked. Gant checked his watch, unlocked the door, and scowled at the director's office. It was lined with white binders on white shelves.

"Needle in a haystack."

He was going to kill Donovan. Rushed jobs were botched jobs.

Growling, he took a steadying breath and used an asset Donovan couldn't match: his brain. The plethora of binders had to be for show, they were out of fashion in the computer age. Gant did a quick search of the ornate rococo desk. The thin legs and elegant scroll-work hid nothing. There wasn't even a computer in the room. If Director Carlisle had taken her tech home, their chances of success had dropped to nothing. *No, wrong way to think.* He tried to think like a business-man. A wealthy, paranoid businessman.

There had to be a safe.

He scanned the walls, looking for a break in the monotonous wall of binders. No one was perfect. No one kept secrets. Not from him.

In the left corner, a shelf down from eye level, Gant found what he was looking for. Knowing the director was left-handed would have helped, but it was too late for regrets and dithering. He grabbed the binder, flipped it open, and skimmed the contents.

Dates and times of regressive jumps. Dates and times of lateral iteration jumps. Dates and times of future jumps. Well, that was interesting. Worth considering in ten years' time when he'd stolen enough money to visit as a customer. He snapped the binder shut and walked out the door. Three minutes until he had to hide from motion detectors.

Donovan put a lot of faith in Gant's ability to run a six-minute mile.

The first guard who crossed his path was lucky enough to only get the cold blowtorch upside his head. Cracked skulls were uncomfortable, but the second guard got a faceful of flame, his own private hell for the last moment of his life. Gant smiled at the thought of the superheated air cooking the man from the inside out as he slid into place behind a statue.

Six silent minutes ticked past.

Gant stood still, staring out the window at a fountain with dancing satyrs and an excellent view of the parking lot. Angry voices at the end of the hall signaled a break from the motion sensors as police cars filled the parking lot.

"Donovan." Gant swore creatively under his breath. He ran headlong down the halls, through a very broken door, and into the inner sanctum, where Donovan stood waiting next to a row of prone bodies. "You tied them up?"

"I like to give them the illusion of hope. Being tied up means they might escape."

Gant looked at the executed guards. "Seems like a waste of time."

"I was bored."

"A waste of ammunition then." Sloppy.

"I can always find more bullets. Did you find the right binder?"

Gant tossed the book at him. "This is the one. Carlisle has today marked as an ILJ. Do you know what that means?"

"That the machine will get us out of here."

"It better do it with requisite alacrity. Detective Rose is outside." And he wasn't going back to prison. He'd make a deal with the devil and testify against Donovan first.

Donovan frowned. "Impossible."

"Then stay here." Gant took the binder back. "I'm leaving." He turned through the pages, looking for instructions. There was a timetable, but he could only hazard a guess at what it all meant. "We should have grabbed Carlisle."

Donovan grunted agreement but stopped to dig things from his bag.

Gant rolled his eyes. Double doors led to a wide theater that reminded him of a scene from *The Wizard of Oz*. All the showmanship to mask the simplicity of the truth: A single machine with the power to change time.

He looked from the machine to the instructions. There was math, and an ON button, and very little programming. "Donovan, this is not a well-thought-out plan."

"Doesn't matter. The machine works, 'aight?"

"Yes . . ." Gant hesitated. "But we can't set it for a specific day. The machine uses a mathematical formula for a predetermined place and time based on when you turn it on."

"So, where are we going?"

"The year 2070, and Florida, if this is correct." Gant frowned. "What is an 'iteration'?"

"Who knows," Donovan said. "Do you think it matters?"

A muffled explosion sounded outside the room. Gant looked at Donovan as he slapped the ON button.

"I left a few surprises for your fan club," he said with a shrug, as smoke poured through the door. "But that won't keep them off us forever." An ethereal blue light twisted out of the machine. "You ready?"

"More than ready."

"Nialls Gant, you are under arrest." Detective Rose's voice boomed across the atrium.

He turned to see another flash of light and smoke tear the detective from his view. Smiling, Gant ran toward his past.

CHAPTER 8

Everything seems inevitable in the moment. Momentum, the weight of consequence, pushes on you like a tidal wave. It's only looking back that you can see with the clarity of hindsight and understand you should have made a different choice.

**~ private conversation with Agent 5
of the Ministry of Defense**

*Thursday March 20, 2070
Florida District 8
Commonwealth of North America
Iteration 2*

Mac woke to the predawn Florida light and stared up at the popcorn ceiling of Sam's apartment. It was funny how the little things always got him. His loft in Chicago had vaulted, square ceilings that the Realtor showing him the listing insisted was a classic art deco design. He didn't know enough about architecture to quibble, but he knew it looked wrong.

Ceilings were meant to be plain. Beds were meant to be soft. Apartments were meant to smell of lavender candles and vanilla hand soap and Sam.

Taking a deep breath, he drank in the smell of home. The underlying unwashed-dog smell of Hoss, the aroma of roasted chilies from last night's dinner, and the scent of Sam.

He rolled out of bed, checked the small hallway to see if Sam's light was on yet, then headed to the kitchen for breakfast. Chicago had taught him two very valuable lessons, first, take the pedway during the winter, second, if Sam wasn't around, he was going to have to feed himself something other than frozen breakfast burritos.

There was little chance that he'd ever reach her level of gourmet wizardry in the kitchen, but by the time she woke up, he had a small stack of fluffy pancakes and a bowl of scrambled eggs waiting.

She rested herself against the entryway to the kitchen, wisps of black hair curling loose from her braid, a sleepy smile caressing her face . . . Mac wanted nothing more than the right to lean over and kiss her.

He settled for smiling at her. "Good morning."

"Good morning. When did you learn to cook?"

"When I realized I couldn't get you to transfer up to Chicago, and I had to fend for myself."

She laughed and rolled her eyes. "I'm sure it was terrible, eating at all those fancy pizza places and forcing down all those designer donuts."

"Awful," Mac said straight-faced as he poured the orange juice. "I had to choke down the risotto at La Belle Vue, and all I could think as the truffle butter melted in my mouth was, 'I miss Sam's cooking.'"

"I'm sure that was it." Sam laughed as she plated her pancakes. "You wouldn't betray me by liking the cooking of a Corden-Bleu-trained chef better!" Her smile made his world complete.

Mac handed her the glass of juice he'd poured and sat down beside her. "Eat up, Pumpkin, busy day ahead."

Looking over a forkful of pancake, Sam raised an eyebrow in amusement. "Pumpkin?"

"Would you like Pookie better?"

She laughed again. "We're not doing pet names."

"We've known each other long enough, don't you think."

Sam rolled her eyes. "What part of the male brain connects 'let's solve a murder!' with 'let's give each other pet names!'? Where's the logic in that?"

"Who said there needs to be logic?" Mac asked. "Why can't we just have a little fun sometimes? This is a thing friends do. I know you call Bri 'Sweetie' half the time." Usually in a fake Southern drawl that he found adorable.

She did her head-tilt thing that he'd come to learn was her sign of semiagreement. "I don't like either of those names, though."

"Well, I'll keep trying," Mac said. "Eventually, I'll find one that fits."

"**O**kay." Sam scanned the appropriated conference room and looked at her team. Mac was there, dressed professionally and smiling. Agent Edwin had been dragged in as the liaison for the CSI team borrowed from the police. She turned the display screen on to show the pictures Mac had taken in the swamps. They needed answers, and the pirates had them. "I guess it's safe to say your foray into the swamps didn't get us the information we wanted."

Mac grimaced. "That's an understatement."

"The pirates have bugged out," Edwin said. "We went to the main camp, and it's gone. They left almost nothing."

"It wasn't like they had much left to leave," Mac grumbled. "No latrines dug, no shelters built. Sam, these guys make a Cub Scout Jamboree look high-tech. They had nothing."

Sam raised an eyebrow. "Do you think that's relevant?"

Leaning his elbows on the table, Mac said, "Die-hard survivalists keep themselves alive because they plan. There is no way to live off the grid—long term—if you don't have a plan of some kind. A base of operations."

"The pirates forage and trade," Edwin said. "During the colder months, they live off fish and panhandling downtown."

"No." Mac shook his head. "Not buying it. The tents out there weren't the good ones, they were the expensive ones weekend *glampers* buy to impress their girlfriends. None of the gear out there was repaired. You say they've been out there for years, but there's not one sign of duct tape on the rafts? No patches on the tents?"

Sam shook her head in bewilderment. "I've never camped in my life. What are you trying to say?"

"I'm saying that these guys have another base of operation. The tents aren't in use full-time. Either they're couchsurfing with friends, or they have a building out in the swamps."

She looked at Edwin. "What are the chances?"

"It's possible," he said with a shrug. "I know of three other camps, and we checked those. They move because of bugs or for better fishing. There's no sign of them. Connor's boat is still at the marina. We put a lock on it, but their bikes are gone."

Mac pointed at Edwin. "Where does a guy with no income get a boat? Where's he get the marina fee?"

"Connor's the leader of the group. He could have come from money," Sam said.

"I know sometimes they worked barter jobs," Edwin offered. "Did yard work in exchange for bike repairs, or cleaned restrooms at the gas station so they could get some snacks. Day jobs where they got paid under the table."

"Or he could be selling more than anti-GMO seeds," Mac said. "Every swamp in the Commonwealth has a history of smuggling, from moonshine to weapons. The black market for guns right now is hot."

Edwin shook his head. "Ma'am, I know these people. They aren't . . . they're pacifists. Most of the time, it wasn't a reformist movement as much as an open-air soup kitchen. Connor and Nealie were the two who were always there. During the winter, the camp grows to twenty people. One time Connor told me there were over thirty. They welcome transients. But the only other people I knew were in the camp were Cogs, Spik, and Tracks."

"None of those are legal names," Sam guessed. Saints and angels, she hoped they weren't legal names.

Edwin snorted in amusement. "Obviously. Cogs is a local kid with a juvie record. He got busted for tagging crates in the freight yard. No violent crimes, but he ran with a group of wannabes. Kids who saw gangs on TV and think wearing chains and selling cigarettes to each other after school is what gangs in the inner cities do."

"Not a likely suspect for our case," Mac said. "Connor is probably the killer."

Edwin nodded. "Nealie followed him everywhere. If Connor said jump, Nealie leaped without asking how high. When I'd go talk to Connor, Nealie would hover."

"Does Connor have a record?" Sam asked.

"Not here. I asked at the station, and none of the local cops know him, but without his real name, I can't run a check in the database," Edwin said. He bit his lip and shook his head. "I hate saying this, but if it was a crime of passion, that's Connor. He's the passionate one. That's why he was in charge. He could get worked up over anything. Give a speech that would make people die to protect soap bubbles."

"Okay, let's put an APB out. Ask the police around here to keep an eye out for the group. Edwin, contact Petrilli in District 6 and Mada over in District 4. They're the nearest to us, and they need to know that trouble might be headed their way. Other than that . . ." She held her hands out in defeat. "Any genius ideas you two want to share?"

Mac shook his head. "I'll do the autopsy today, see if I can find a fingerprint from the killer, or at least something that will narrow down where he was killed. Other than that, I dunno, I want to say follow the money."

"With me, they stuck to the same story all the time. They were off the grid, barter only, no cash, no taxes," Edwin said with a sigh. "Connor was very careful not to mention business when I was around."

"Fine," Sam said. "We'll start by running Nealie through the system, see if we can find what his real name was. Then we'll go from there." She shuffled her notes. "Next order of business, Henry Troom . . . how's that going?"

"The major autopsy is done. The head hasn't appeared yet," Mac said with a frown, "but the last of the wreckage should be cleared out today. From the damage to his neck, I believe Henry was decapitated postmortem by falling debris. The cut isn't very clean, but at high enough velocity, even a piece of paper can feel like an ax."

"You sure it was postmortem?" Sam asked.

"I know it wasn't the cause of death," he hedged.

"The blast was fairly instantaneous, wasn't it?"

Mac shrugged. "The blood pattern and cut is wrong."

"Was the wound cauterized because of heat?"

Mac shook his head. "Nope. Henry's body shows only minimal signs of heat damage. I thought super-heated air in the lungs might be the cause of death, but it's not. His jacket's lightly singed, but it would have been the kind of burn you run under cold water and grumble about, nothing fatal."

"What about a toxin screen?"

"I should have those results this afternoon."

Sam sat in her chair and wished she could run her fingers through her hair. Or pull it all out in frustration. "Does anyone have *good* news?"

"My college basketball team has a shot of being in the playoffs this year," Edwin said.

"That's nice. Is it going to help me find a killer?"

"Probably not."

"Too bad."

Gant threw a tasteless burrito wrap stolen from the corner gas station on the table with a growl. "I hate this place."

"Noted," Donovan said, not looking up from the device he'd liberated from the college student they'd met on arrival.

Nice enough kid. Bit whiny. Screamed in the end, but now they had his car, his computer, and his wallet, which had enough cash to buy the worst Mexican food ever made. Donovan had even managed to get a little information about the local *federales* out of the kid before he'd lost his patience and squeezed a little too hard.

"The food is horrible. Their accents are abominations. The whole place makes me itch. This isn't the past, it's hell. You found us a gate to hell." He sneered at Donovan. Under any other circumstances, that man would be dead already, but Gant needed him, as a barrier between him and the strangeness of this place if nothing else. Donovan was his anchor, irrefutable proof that the real world existed and so did this strange alternate universe where English was still the dominant language of North America and the food wasn't fit for dogs to eat.

Donovan looked up. "I see beaches, pretty women in bikinis, and palm trees. This is Florida. What's wrong?"

"The food!" Gant slumped into the motel-room chair, beige this time, and an improvement over the one he'd had after the jailbreak. "I miss El Cardenal." The national restaurant of Federated States had an amazing breakfast. His abuela had taken him to one every year on the Monday after Easter as a boy. They'd go and celebrate with a big breakfast, fresh-baked bread, and the Dona Olivia hot chocolate. This Florida was a pit stain with the strangest food he'd ever seen outside of a reality TV show. "What is poutine anyway?"

"Unimportant," Donovan said. "I found him."

"Him who?"

"The Timeyst Machine was created by who?" Donovan asked in response.

Gant shook his head. "I don't know. Someone rich?"

"It was designed by Dr. Abdul Emir, and built by his protégé, Dr. Henry Troom," Donovan said. "Troom owns a controlling but silent share of the Timeyst Machine. Zoetimax Industries owns the other half. He built the machine, they market it, everyone wins."

Hope blossomed in his chest. "He can get us back?"

"He can at least tell us what went wrong," Donovan said.

Gant jumped to his feet. "Good. Let's go get him."

"We'll need a vehicle first."

"There are dozens lining the streets. Pick one."

"Such a socialist, Mr. Gant."

Gant smiled. "Opportunist." And, should the opportunity present itself, murderer once more. Once he had Troom, there'd be no need for anyone else.

Donovan's calm was grating on his nerves. Everything from the smell of the beach to the colors of the buildings screamed to him at an animal level that this was not his place. Never in his entire life had he felt so wrong.

All he could think is this wrongness was what ordinary people felt when confronted with the idea of murder or sacrilege. All those dear, rosary-clutching nuns who came to pray for the prisoners, this is what they would feel if they felt a stranger's neck snap under their hands. Like a part of them was being ripped away.

Like they were about to shatter into a thousand points of madness.

Donovan stood up, folding the clunky device in two. "Are you ready to go?"

"I'm always ready." Gant walked out of the motel room and sauntered to the parking lot away from the manager's office. Donovan kept insisting that leaving a trail of bodies would draw unwanted attention. Gant actually agreed with him on that. Couldn't have police from hell chasing them. He grabbed the car door and pulled it away from the frame. He then dropped a slim rod from his pocket, extended it, and pushed the unlock button. The door opened and within a few minutes it was running. "Where to?" Gant asked, as Donovan took the passenger's seat.

Donovan put a toolbox at his feet. "Go out to the main road and turn left. I'll give you the directions from there. And, this time, no swerving off the road to hit squirrels."

The directions Donovan gave led them to a hideous apartment complex that ought to have been condemned.

"Third building on the left," Donovan said.

"You want me to go up and knock?" Gant asked as he parked the car.

Donovan picked up his toolbox. "What would be the point of knocking?"

They walked up the stairs, and Gant touched the knob; it turned easily in his hand. Grinning, he pushed the door open. "Knock, knock."

A man sitting in front of a fancy television jumped to his feet. "What? Are you the maintenance guy? The sink's fixed."

Donovan pulled his gun out as he closed the door. "Are you Henry Troom?"

"Henry?" the man said, eyeing the gun like a rabbit seeing a wolf. "Yeah. Right this way. His room's this way." He hurried around the corner, and Gant shook his head.

"The idiot's running."

Donovan sighed, pushed his way past Gant, and fired down the hall twice. The sound of the gun was followed by the sound of glass shattering. "He fell out the window."

Gant followed him around the corner, but his eye was caught on the metallic lock on a bedroom door. "Go shove the body in the trunk."

"You go get the body," Donovan said. "I have a bolt cutter."

Weighing his options, Gant decided being near the getaway vehicle and away from any chance of booby-trapped doors was the safest option. If Donovan entered the room without injury, then he'd come back upstairs. If Donovan blew up, well, he had Troom's friend. That would be enough leverage to get a ride back home.

Downstairs, the jumper lay on the grass, still breathing but shaky. There was a crunching sound from the apartment above and a string of curses.

Donovan looked out the window. "Troom isn't here."

"Is anything there?"

"Bits and bobs, but not enough."

Gant hefted the shivering man to his feet. "This one's breathing. Let's go find a private place to talk to him." The man started shaking. Gant checked his shoulder. "Just grazed," he told the boy. "You'll live. Maybe. If you cooperate."

The man's eyes were black, pupils dilated with fear. It had been a long time since Gant had seen that look. Too long, really. It made him feel warm all over. This place was wrong, but that fear was right. He smiled. It was good to be back in control.

CHAPTER 9

We need no longer fear the future. We need no longer stagger blindly forward grasping after hope and lies. From this day forward, every action will be done with an awareness that the path is set, the future immutable.

~ Dr. Abdul Emir speaking at the inauguration the Future Command Force complex I1-2064

Friday March 21, 2070
Florida District 8
Commonwealth of North America
Iteration 2

There wasn't such a thing as a basement in Florida.

Half the potholes along A1A were below sea level, and anyone wanting to plant roses needed to accept the fact that a hole deep enough for the roots would fill with water on any day ending in Y. Still, it was weird looking out the morgue window at a parking lot below him. Mac was used to looking at trees and grass slightly above his head. As his junior agents in Chicago liked to joke, morgue people evolved from mole people. The bright Florida sunshine filtering through the tinted solar-panel windows was unnatural in every respect.

He sat down between the two preserved bodies of Henry Troom and Nealie Rho as the computers scanned them. The police forensic team had brought the last pieces of Troom's corpse—including his head— over the night before.

There was a beep outside the door before it swung open. "Hey," Sam said as she stepped in and locked the door behind her. She sat down in the spare chair. "How's your day going?"

"Pretty good. We finally found Henry's head. What's left of it, anyway. I'm doing the postmortem scans now. Should have the autopsies done by tonight." He tapped his computer stylus on the counter.

"Cause of death: being ripped apart by explosion," she said in a nasal TV-announcer voice. "Which I still don't understand, by the way. How does an explosion rip someone apart?"

"Physics," Mac said, as the computer scan beeped, marking an anomaly on the corpse. "Everything's waves: heat, light, sound—matter when it comes to it. A sound wave can kill you, but with an explosion like this, it was probably heat and a lack of oxygen that killed him. Probably."

Sam knew him well enough that she rolled her chair closer. "What are you seeing?"

"An anomaly on the preliminary scan." He frowned

and typed in the command to have the computer redo the test.

"Tell me." Sam's voice was cold with fear.

"Our theory is that the head was lost in the debris, right? Nice, logical, slightly improbable for a room that size, but not actually impossible. Right?"

"Right." Sam's lips flattened into a grimace. "Let me guess. The head is colder than room temperature, and much colder than it should be. With . . ." She held up a hand to her closed eyes like a television psychic, "with no evidence of decomposition." Her eyes opened, and they were flat with anger. "Almost like it magically appeared out of nowhere."

"Not magically," Mac hedged, "but you're onto something. We should at least rule it out."

Sam said something in French that he guessed wasn't considered polite. "What else would it have been? You think one of his coworkers smuggled his head past me and kept it in the fridge for a few days? No one would do that."

Mac turned the screen so he could see what the computer had found. "Maybe not. But . . ."

"What did you find?"

"A bullet hole at the back of the cranium. Henry was shot."

"No one is going to be at the lab," Mac protested, as Sam parked her rental car, a red Xian Congsun, with a squeal of tires. "Everyone's going to the memorial service."

"People don't matter. I want the security tapes."

Mac hopped out of the car and jogged to catch up. "I already looked at the tapes."

"Then you missed something. Henry was shot at the lab before the explosion, and no one saw that? No one heard anything? How is that even possible?"

"A bullet in someone's head doesn't mean there was a gun, not during an explosion. This could have been shrapnel."

"Because people keep random bullets in their desk?"

"Yes!"

Sam glared at him. "No."

"Yes."

"Normal people don't keep bullets in their desk."

"But Henry might have. His mentor was shot last summer. He almost died last summer. What if he went and bought a gun for protection?"

"That seems very unlikely."

"Not under the circumstances."

She pulled open the door.

The guard looked up at them in surprise. "Can I help you?"

"Yes, I'm Agent Rose, and this is Agent MacKenzie. We're with the CBI, and we need to review the security footage of the day of the accident." Sam flashed her badge like a shark showing its teeth.

"I can help you with that, ma'am. I'm Earl. Earl Mosely. I work graveyard shift most days and caught the weekend." He wiped a hand across his forehead. "You want the conference room, ma'am? I can set it up for you."

"That'd be fine," Sam said.

Mac tapped her arm as Mosley hurried around the corner. "He's nervous."

"I noticed."

Mosely came back and waved them through the foyer. "This way. Conference room two is quiet." He led them into a room with the security footage already on display on the projection screen. "I've been going over this myself."

"Oh?" Sam said, as the guard closed the door.

"Young Dr. Troom was a friend of mine. Always came in early and we'd talk. I used to work at NASA, back in the day. I had a stroke and took early retirement. Couldn't quite do the math anymore, but Henry was nice to me. I was worried about him. Real worried."

Sam sat down, datpad in front of her, and gave Mosely her full attention. "Why were you worried?"

Mosely pointed at the chair opposite her. "Can I sit?"

"Be my guest."

Mac kept his place by the door.

"Henry signed on in late December. Fresh young graduate, usually they come in with stars in their eyes, but he burned. Burned something awful. It's not a bad thing, wanting. That drive got man to the moon and back. To Mars and back! But it was burning him from the inside, and he didn't have any balance. He was coming in earlier and earlier. Sometimes only a few hours after he checked out. Said he was having trouble sleeping."

"Did Henry tell you anything about his dreams?" Sam asked.

"Lots. He told me about last summer, how some men tried to kill him. He told me about how his mentor died. And he told me he thought he was dying. Kept dreaming about it."

Sam nodded. "Did you tell anyone about Henry's behavior? Or ask him to see a therapist?"

Mosely shook his head. "He'd been seeing therapists, and I figured it was normal. You have a gun pointed at you, you start thinking about your soul. But Henry wasn't doing it right. He fixated." The guard took a little book and put it on the desk. "He gave this to me the morning of the incident. Asked me to lock it up in my locker. Said it was important."

"And you're just showing us now?" Mac asked, but Sam waved him off. She picked it up and flipped it open.

"Did Henry say what this was about?"

"His big project, I guess." The guard shrugged. "He didn't tell anyone about it. I've been trying to make sense of it. Reading through his notes during the quiet times at work, but the old brain box ain't what it used to be," he said, tapping the side of his head. "Not since the stroke."

"What is it?" Sam asked.

Mosley scratched the white stubble on his chin. "Quantum physics mostly. I've heard of a couple of the theories, but not all of them. Some of it sounds made up, like a bad science-fiction novel. The thing that got me was the checklist in the back. He had a calendar with numbers, and each number lines up with a dream he had about dying."

Sam quickly turned the pages. "Car crash. Car crash. Multicar pileup. Car hits him crossing the street. Car hits him in the parking lot. Gunshot. Gunshot. Multiple gunshots and bleeding out. Execution by firing squad. Explosion. Explosion." She turned the page. "The last week was nothing but dreams about explosions and guns."

Mosely nodded. "The boy was real worried. Didn't know it was this bad. It ain't good to focus on how you're going to die. Sucks the life right out of you doing that."

"What do you think it means?" Sam asked.

"I don't know," Mosely said. "I know there's no such thing as precognition. People don't see the future."

Not like this they didn't. Unless Henry had been bouncing around other iterations trying to catch a glimpse of his future, there was no way he could have predicted his own death. At least, there wasn't one she knew of, but a year ago she hadn't believed in time travel, either. Her fists clenched as she offered a silent prayer for protection from the fools of the world.

"There's a pattern, though," Mac said, drumming his fingers on the table. "His dreams came in sets. Maybe he was influenced by something he saw."

"Like what?" Sam looked up at him, eyes dark and focused.

"Television show? Movie? Internet video? When we get to the office, I can run a scan of available media and see what was available for viewing."

"Showtimes mean nothing. He could have watched something from six months ago, or ten years ago."

"Then we'll get a warrant for his house and check the television and his cloud network. If he was storing schedules and movie listings, we can find them."

Mosely turned to look at both of them. "How long have you two been together?"

Sam frowned at Mac in confusion. He shrugged, not sure why the guard was asking. "We've worked a case together before," he said

"One case?" Mosely asked.

"Yes, we just . . ." Sam floundered.

"Think alike," Mac finished for her with a wink. "Great minds and all that."

"Right." Mosely crossed his arms. "You two think you can find out what happened to Henry?"

"Yes," Sam said, as Mac said, "Probably." They both shrugged.

"We'll find Henry's killer," Sam said.

"Killer?" It was Mosely's turn to frown. "What killer? I thought there was an accidental gas leak in the lab. No one said anything about its being intentional."

"That could have gone better," Sam said as she strode to her car.

"It's nice that Dr. Morr is keeping everything low-key. A natural-gas explosion seems innocent. Accidental."

"A bullet to the head is murder." The car lock unclicked, and the plug retracted from the charging station. Water in the engine gurgled as the rental car turned on. "There wasn't anything on the security footage, though."

"I know."

Her heart sank. "I think I know what happened."

"Yeah?"

"It's a lousy guess, though."

"Does it involve a time dilation or time travel?" Mac asked.

"It does." Her worst nightmare come back to haunt her.

"That's a lousy guess."

"It's a lousy situation. No one's going to believe me. The regional director isn't even cleared to know what happened in Alabama." Ninety percent of her current bureau files were sealed. It didn't make her popular at district mixers.

"So we sort it out ourselves and don't tell anyone," Mac said. "You broke the stupid machine once, all we need to do is find it and break it again."

"And I know where to look. Let's go pay Henry's roommate another visit."

"**B**asilwood Apartments?" Mac peered out the rental-car window at the faux-wood buildings. "Mechatrees and biogen grass. I wonder if they included a mechanical alligator in the retention pond, too."

"It doesn't look that bad," Sam said, as they pulled to a stop in front of building twelve.

"It's so fake, it makes my teeth hurt."

"But it's hurricaneproof."

Of course it was. The trapezoidal brown buildings squatted under engineered southern pines like squashed mushrooms. Crabgrass had been replaced by a pollution-absorbing lab-created monstrosity with leaves like razor blades. Not that crabgrass was very soft, but at least it didn't throw shrapnel when it was time to trim the lawn.

"Apartment B on the second floor," Sam said.

Mac looked around at the mostly vacant parking lot. All the cars were over five years old, most of the apartments had the blinds closed, and there was a notable lack of kids' toys or barbecues. "This isn't a family apartment complex, is it?"

"It's unofficial student housing for the local colleges. One- or two-bedroom apartments only. No pool. No playground. No pets allowed. I looked into it when I moved down here 'cause the rent's right, but even if Hoss could have come, I didn't like it."

"There's a sort of Pacific Northwest vibe," Mac said, as they walked up concrete steps and a faux-wood shingle caught at his pant leg. "Pine trees and alpine shacks."

"I think it's meant to be European."

"Circa 1970?"

Sam shrugged and knocked on the door. It swung open.

Mac raised an eyebrow and reached for the gun at his hip. "That's not a good sign."

"Time to put gloves on and get the recorder out."

"You get the gloves, I'll have the gun." He frowned at the recorder. "When did you start using that?"

"Standard policy down here. All law enforcement officers or agents entering a crime scene must use a visual and audio recording device." She held up a Commonwealth flag pin he'd mistaken for decoration. "Yay for button cams?" With a click, the little device turned on, and Sam pinned it back on her blouse. "This is the home of Devon Bradet. We are here to speak to Mr. Bradet about his deceased roommate, Dr. Henry Troom, and have found the door open."

"The doorjamb is cracked," Mac said for the camera's benefit as much as Sam's. He knocked on the splintered doorframe. "Hello? Anyone home? This is CBI agents MacKenzie and Rose. We need a verbal declaration of your presence, or we will enter the premises." A soft breeze blew a napkin across the floor. "No answer."

"Then we have permission to enter." Sam stepped in first, panning the camera around the room.

Mac followed her and looked for evidence of some personality. "Interesting layout. Two chairs, but no couch." Most homes had pictures on the wall. Art or posters or photographs of the occupants. "Even student housing usually doesn't look this bad."

"It's a bachelor pad. A place a guy crashes without expectation of ever getting laid. You should feel right at home," she teased with a smile.

"I have pictures up!" Oversized black-and-white prints of the skyscrapers of Chicago he'd found cheap at the art walk during a date. He couldn't even remember the woman's name anymore, only that they'd had a bland conversation at a disappointing café, and he'd spent the entire time wishing he were there with Sam.

"At the new apartment, not your old one in Alabama."

That place had been a trash heap. His addiction to sleeping pills had left him too despondent to care about anything, much less cleaning or decorating the dump he lived in. "Yeah, well. I'm better now." He walked over to the chairs. "One new gaming throne with plugins."

"Is that relevant?" Sam asked.

"Gaming thrones cost over nine hundred dollars when they first came out, and that was on the cheap end."

"And it's still here . . ." she said, nodding. "So not a robbery."

"Probably not." Mac pulled his gloves on and opened the entertainment center. "TV is still here. There's a miniholo set, a prototype for the one Lingen Industries is releasing this fall."

"Bradet said he got it because of his radio job. He told me I couldn't come check Henry's room when he was away because of the confidentiality agreement. I thought he was just being difficult."

Mac shrugged. "Might have been, but some of those confidentiality clauses for new tech are evil. Either way, the door definitely wasn't broken by thieves. They wouldn't leave something like that behind."

"Okay," Sam said from the kitchen. "Come here real quick and tell me if you see what I see."

The kitchen was a narrow rectangle with an island that doubled as a breakfast bar. Two mismatched stools were placed at opposite ends. "No blood," Mac said, only half joking. "That's always good news."

Sam opened the fridge. A strip of black electrical tape ran down the middle. One side had reusable water bottles, tofu, and almond milk mixed with assorted vegetables and a whole-grain loaf with packaging that promised organic nutrition in large, friendly letters. The other half had discount beer, a half-eaten sub sandwich, and a pile of grab-'n'-go diet meals. Sam carefully turned the pile of diet lunches to show an expiration date of January–2070. "Someone wasn't into healthy eating."

"Or sharing with his roommate," Mac said. "I'm getting a very strong this-is-mine-this-is-yours vibe from this place."

"Let's check the bedrooms." Sam stepped into the tiny living area and frowned at the two halls that went in opposite directions. "Okay, the two-bed, two-bath floor plan has a shared kitchen, with suites on either side. Henry's room was to the left. Let's check Bradet's room, make sure he isn't just sleeping through our intrusion."

Sam took the right hall and knocked on Bradet's door. There was no answer.

"There's some light down here," Mac said, looking down the left hall. "What's down there?"

"There should be a laundry cupboard and a fire window with a rope ladder. It's part of the fire code out here."

He walked down the hall, and something rough crunched under his shoes with a familiar cracking sound. "Found some broken glass. It's the fire window." Someone had smashed the window open. Down on the ground, he could see the imprint of a fallen body in the neighbor's overgrown flower bed.

Sam stepped up beside him, recording the images. "The intruder breaks through the front door, Bradet runs for the fire window, breaks it with—what?—and then falls? That's not good. I'll have Edwin start calling the hospitals."

She dialed and waited for her junior agent to pick up. "Edwin? I need you to start calling the hospitals. We're looking for a man named Devon Bradet. Yes, the radio DJ. Call Officer Clemens and see if he's called the police to report a home invasion, then call his office to see if he's at work. Okay. Good. Call me back as soon as you hear anything."

Mac wandered back to Bradet's room. A radio station's banner hung over a twin-sized mattress that smelled like it had seen better days. T-shirts and cargo shorts littered the floor. Socks and boxers were bunched in pile in the corner, but the games were organized in neat columns around a dual-screen gaming computer.

Sam stepped up beside him and regarded the room with a wrinkled nose. "Ugh. I'm guessing it's untouched."

Mac looked at the chaos. "Unless they came to pillage the man's underwear, yeah. The computer and the games are the valuable things."

"I want to see the Henry's room," Sam said, marching down the hall. "Oh." She stopped.

Mac followed her gaze to the padlock, still locked and shining but no longer attached to the shattered door. "We find Troom's head with a bullet in it, and now his home's been invaded." Mac kicked the shards of door away. He looked on the inside of the door to see an automatic locking mechanism used in offices of the rich and influential. It was set on a timer, or it had been. "Looks like they used a fire ax."

"There's probably one missing from the stairwell emergency kit." She shook her head. "I should have made Bradet let me into Henry's room when I came over the first time. This is a stupid, rookie mistake."

He walked into the room. "A desk, but no computer," he reported for the sake of the audio pickup. "Mattress has been torn open, books are all on a heap on the floor."

"What's this?" Sam picked up a sculpted piece of glass from the wreckage. "The Misakat Award for Excellence in Research Science." Her voice quavered with an edge of fear. "Find me the plaque. There should be a stone base for this with the winner's name engraved on it."

He knelt and dug through the mattress fluff and books until he found the rock. "Here you go," he said, holding it up for her inspection.

"Abdul Emir." She sunk enough venom into the name to make it a profanity.

Mac caught the award before Sam could throw it through the wall. "Henry kept it?"

She walked over to the closet and pulled a windbreaker off the hanger. "DRENMANN LABS," she said, showing him the logo. "Troom probably took the award as a memento after Dr. Emir died."

"Do you think he took something else?"

"Like Emir's research notes?" Sam asked darkly. "I imagine he did."

"I really want to say, 'But Henry knew better!' " Mac said. "But I get the feeling he didn't."

Sam stomped her foot and screwed her mouth up as she choked down whatever it was she wanted to say.

"It's going to be okay, Sam."

"No it's not. I have one dead researcher and now a missing DJ. This district hasn't had a homicide in three years, and now I have possibly three in a week? And Nealie's just a random transient." She stomped again and pivoted to fume at the wall.

"These things happen. You didn't kill anyone. Stop beating yourself up and get back to work."

She shot him a glare that made him smile.

"Come on, Agent Perfect. You're the senior agent, stop pouting and get to work."

"I hate you some days." She sighed.

"Consider it payback for the many early morning runs you literally dragged me on."

Her smile was coy. "*I* didn't drag you anywhere."

"You made me hold Hoss's leash, and he ran."

"You could have let go. Letting go was always a choice." She looked around Henry's room and sighed again. "Okay. I'm officially declaring this a crime scene. I'm going to alert the apartment manager and have Edwin get over here to help us process the scene. And then I'm going to co-opt Clemens and have her run a manhunt for us. I want Devon Bradet found."

"**I** come bearing burgers!" Agent Petrilli from District 6 ducked under the police tape covering the door as he beamed at Sam. "I even brought chocolate milk shakes."

"Mac! Dinner is here." Sam took the bag from Petrilli. Drool pooled in her mouth at the scent of deep-fried goodness.

Mac stepped around the corner, stripping off his gloves. "Food? I could kiss you."

"I don't swing that way," Petrilli said with a laugh. "But if Agent Rose wanted to kiss me, I wouldn't deny her the pleasure."

"I just want food," Sam said. "Thank you, for this

and for loaning me your crime scene techs. I need to petition for our own in the budget this year."

"Not a problem. I'm all about interdistrict cooperation. I even told my ME to get out here tonight after he's done with the tox screens he's doing."

"Oh, you can tell him he isn't needed. I have Mac for that."

Mac waved, a half-finished burger in his mouth.

"He doesn't look familiar," Petrilli said. "Is he the one you were telling me about?"

Mac offered a ketchup-stained smile. "I'm from Chicago."

"I still can't believe you couldn't find someone closer," Petrilli said. "What about that nice gal working for Mada down in District 4? She seemed easy to work with."

"He was in town for a conference, he has clearance, and he didn't object to staying a few more weeks. It was supposed to be a simple two-day autopsy. Not this mess."

"No one misses me," Mac said. He took a gulp of his shake. "We're overstaffed with college interns right now. If I were in Chicago, I'd be playing Tetris and dying of boredom. This is a much better use of taxpayer dollars."

Petrilli shot Mac a trademark grin, the one that Sam was certain he practiced to dazzle cameras, and held out his hand. "Senior Agent Feo Petrilli, I'd hate to see a fellow bureau brother stranded here without a friend. You give me a call if Agent Rose works you too hard. I hear she likes to crack the whip."

"Eric MacKenzie," Mac said, taking Petrilli's hand. "And the only thing I've ever seen in Sam's bedroom are handcuffs."

Sam choked on her milkshake. Her eyes went wide. "You did not . . ."

Mac tried to hide a grin.

She punched him in the arm. "This is a crime scene." She glared at both of them.

Petrilli held his arms up. "I came bearing food. No comments. No . . ."

"Oh, don't even try that, Petrilli. You were both sizing each other up like a pair of—" She cut herself off.

Mac raised his eyebrows. "Of?"

"Don't you even start with me, MacKenzie."

He chuckled.

"I didn't realize you were in a relationship," Petrilli said.

"I'm married to my work," Sam said.

"She just keeps me around for my brains." Mac jumped back before she could hit him again. He was enjoying this, dammit all.

Leveling her best Senior Agent glare at him, she said, "You're drunk-on tired, that's what you are."

Mac's smile didn't dim under her scowl. "Considering it's past ten at night, and we've been up since five? It's a possibility."

"It isn't dereliction of duty to get some sleep,"

Petrilli said. "My techs are good at their job. Go home. Get a few hours of sleep. Let my people do what they're paid to do and tackle this again in the morning."

"Listen to the man," Mac said, as he put an arm around her shoulder. "We have Troom's room cleaned out and tagged. Unless Edwin calls saying he found the guy in a hospital, there's nothing more we can do until we're clearheaded enough to understand his notes."

Caught between the desire to finish the case and overwhelming need to see her pillow again, Sam relented. Edwin would find Bradet, and tomorrow's sunshine would make everything much clearer.

CHAPTER 10

*With this we step out of the darkness into a brighter
dawn. We will not simply await the future, we now will
change it.*

~ Dr. Abdul Emir speaking at the inauguration
the Future Command Force complex I1–2064

*Saturday March 22, 2070
Florida District 8
Commonwealth of North America
Iteration 2*

Ivy pulled her car to the side of the road and leaned
her head against the steering wheel. If scientists had
the common sense evolution gave a caterpillar, the ge-
neticists who'd made her would have thought to give
her a better-functioning body than the normal human
one. Goodness and the great beyond knew the department worked her like she was a robot. In before seven
in the morning, still chasing down leads at three the
next morning, with one meal in between and a shot of

an Extra Energy Lime drink that left her jittery for an hour and desperately in need of sleep now.

"Patroller?" the dispatcher's voice floated through the car like a ghost.

"This is Officer Clemens. I'm in the armpit of nowhere following lead 391. Sending GPS coordinates now."

"GPS coordinates received, Officer," the dispatcher said. "Check-in scheduled for twenty minutes from now."

"Check-in scheduled," Ivy agreed. "Exiting the car now." She slammed the door shut on the dispatcher's response. A waxing gibbous moon hung low over the eastern horizon, not quite above the palmettos shivering near the bay. There was worse weather for a manhunt than 60 percent humidity and low seventies with a sea breeze.

The tipster had called dispatch to say he'd seen a man matching Devon Bradet's description north of Ponce Inlet along A1A. And by matching they meant he looked about the right height and weight and might have been Caucasian, it was hard to say the in the dark, might have had a maroon shirt on, maybe purple.

All it meant to her was she was chasing a transient hitchhiker through Mosquito Central.

Grabbing a flashlight, Ivy started humming a billboard top-ten song to stay awake. Halfway through the chorus of *"A clone would never love you like me"* she was at the mile marker where the tip had been called in. She shined her flashlight on the ground, looking for any indication someone had been here an hour before. Gravel and dust looked like gravel and dust to her.

No candy-bar wrappers, abandoned shoes, or cooling corpses to indicate that the tipster had been anything other than drunk.

Ivy checked her watch, an old plastic one she'd bought with her first paycheck because it was green and waterproofish. Seventeen minutes until check-in.

The beam from her flashlight arced across the water and to the foot of the bridge. There was an old road there. With a sigh, she plodded forward. There was half a chance someone might be sleeping under the bridge. She stopped and redid the math. Okay, no one smart was going to sleep in the sand with the fire ants and mosquitoes this close to the inlet, where there might be gators. But no one said she was looking for someone smart, and it wasn't a bad place to stash a body. The ants would swarm it, then the crabs would come. A corpse might only last a day or two in a place like this.

She jumped over the guardrail and landed softly a few feet lower than the highway on the curve of the dirt road. A bat swooped low over the river and swept past her, clicking in a chiding tone. Ivy laughed. "Look at me, I'm a regular cartoon princess complete with animal sidekick." The bat flew away. "Or not."

The smell of rotten fish assaulted her as she walked under the bridge. Bycatch left to wash up onshore and rot under the sun, nothing more. She toed the muddy bank but saw neither signs of a freshly dug grave or a corpse. Leaving her with another dead end. Eleven minutes to check-in.

She shined her light across the road. It curved west behind a copse of fiddlewood shrubs to a broken wooden sign where the faded words SPRUCE CREEK were still legible. Her memory ticked over to, pulling up information from her early years on the force. Back in, what—Sixty-four? Sixty-five? Something like that— there'd been rumors of the Spruce Creek Cannibal. Ol' Crazy Ivan, a shadow who had gone mad, run off to the twisting fens to eat raw fish and unwary tourists. Ivy rubbed her nose and choked down a cough.

Crazy Ivan.

Crazy Ivy was more like it.

Nine minutes to check-in. She shined the flashlight back at her patrol car. It was five hundred yards away, a quick sprint up loose gravel. She might skin her knee, but she was confident she'd make it to the car before any homeless clone got her. She stretched a tension knot out of her neck and slowly walked away from the main highway, flashlight beam dancing madly in front of her.

There was an old wooden bait shack, roof missing and one wall shattered, an old airboat tilted and rusting on the silty shore, and a quiet chorus of tree frogs excited by the light. A snake slithered across the road and rattled the grass still yellow from winter's drought. The place looked forgotten but not threatening. She walked around the hut once, shined the light through the broken wall at the forgotten spiderwebs, and turned away. There was nothing here but the memories of bygone days paddling through the waterways taking pictures of blue heron.

Three minutes to check-in. She hurried up the gravel road, heartbeat rising as she exerted herself, and the caffeine wore off. There was a muffled thud. Ivy turned, frowning at the darkness. Nothing. Maybe a frog jumping onto the old boat, or her mind playing tricks on her. She ran to the car as the dispatch line lit up.

"Patroller?"

"This is Officer Clemens," Ivy said. "I've checked under the bridge."

"Nothing there?" dispatch asked.

"Nothing but bycatch." She hesitated. "There's an old shack around the bend. A bait shop. I'm going to walk down the road a bit to see if there are signs that anyone was here." Maybe she'd get lucky and find a lost wallet with the phantom's name in it.

"Check-in in twenty," dispatch said.

"Check-in in twenty," Ivy agreed. "But it shouldn't take that long." She glared at the darkness as she leaned against the car. There was a warm blanket in an air-conditioned apartment just waiting for her at home. She reached through the open window of her car and grabbed her water bottle. A quick swig, and she headed back for one last look at the shack.

Nothing stood out for her. Moonlight splintered on the quiet water. Mosquitoes swarmed overhead. Gnats chased her. Frogs croaked. Bats skimmed the water. A fish leapt out. It was a nature biopic only missing a sound track and a soothing voice to narrate the scene.

She closed her eyes.

Thud.

A faint echo of metal and boot meeting each other. She walked toward the broken bait shop. Nothing. She circled toward the boat.

Thud. Soft, faded . . .

Thud.

"I don't think it's frogs," she muttered.

"Help!" The muffled cry was almost drowned out by the chorus of frogs.

Ivy ran to the boat and stood on tiptoe to look at the deck. She shined her light on the peeling deck. "Hello?"

Another thud, from the stern of the boat.

Tucking her flashlight into her utility belt, Ivy let her eyes adjust to the dark, then climbed the side of the listing vessel. There were holes in the transom. Probably spiders lurking under the boards, too. She tested her weight on the floor and said a small prayer to anything that might be listening that she wouldn't fall through rotted boards as she let go of the side of the boat.

The boat rocked precariously in the wet sand.

"Hello?" Ivy said quietly. "Is someone there?"

Another muffled thud reverberated through the hull.

She sidled sideways, sliding her booted feet across the rotting boat, never quite trusting her weight to any one spot.

At the stern of the boat, there was a jerry-rigged lockbox that had either held catch or gear at one point. Now the lid was closed and latched over something.

Ivy lifted the latch, edged three fingers under the lid, and threw it up and jumped back all in one motion.

An unpleasant cocktail of smells of urine and sweat overpowered the stench of rotting fish. Ivy grabbed her flashlight, switched it back on, and shined the beam into the wide eyes of a bedraggled man wearing a torn T-shirt.

"Hi."

He held up duct-taped hands.

Ivy took his arms and pulled him out of the hole, then stripped the duct tape off his mouth. "Are you Devon Bradet?"

"Yeah. This is not funny."

"You're telling me," Ivy said, as she cut the duct tape with her pocketknife.

Bradet looked down at her hands. "Is that Hello Kitty?"

"Don't knock it. I'm not officially allowed to carry lethal weapons and no blades over two inches." Officially was the key word. Her extra-heavy flashlight was technically not a weapon, but it could break skulls as well as any truncheon. The Caye Law, making things almost-kinda-sorta equal if you squinted and thought the Constitution of the Commonwealth only applied to people born through "natural forms of conception and birth." Which technically made people conceived by in vitro unnatural, clone-like barbarians who couldn't be trusted with weapons, but no one seemed to mention that when the legislation went through.

"I'm going to die," Bradet groaned.

Ivy rolled her eyes. "Calm down. I'm a trained officer of the law. I don't need a weapon to pull people out of boats."

In the shadows away from her flashlight, someone chuckled. All the hairs on the back of her neck stood on end.

"We're going to die," Bradet whispered. "They told me. They want Henry, but I can't find Henry. Henry is dead."

Ivy patted his arm. Her hand came away sticky with blood. "Just . . . just be calm. I'm going to radio this in, we'll have you to the ER in no time."

The boat rocked. "Hello, little girl," said a voice from the shadows.

Ivy's jaw tightened. "Hello? You're the big bad wolf, I presume. Is that how this story goes?" She tightened her grip on her flashlight. Powder guns with beanbag rounds and powdered mustard gas were standard issue in the department. Her badge hadn't come with one. Instead, she had a five-pound flashlight, a one-inch Hello Kitty pocketknife, and a pair of steel-toed boots. She tucked the knife into Bradet's hand and pushed him flat on the boat deck. "My name is Officer Ivy Clemens," she said as she stood up. "Want to walk into the light and introduce yourself?"

A muscular man with buzz-cut hair and a wicked-looking fillet knife stepped up to the boat. "Name's Donovan, and I like killing cops."

"Wow. Great intro. You use that pickup line on all the girls?" Ivy smiled as her hand slipped to her radio.

She turned the volume down and hit the distress button. "Nice knife. Compensating for something, Donovan? You come out here to Spruce Creek to do a little late-night fishing? Using my buddy Bradet here as gator bait maybe?" Cold sweat beaded her forehead. *Come on, Dispatch. Get the hint. I'm not making check-in. Send backup.*

Donovan chuckled. "Why don't you come down here? Pretty girl like you, I'll make it quick. Slit your throat. Quick burn, and it's all over."

Ivy licked her lips, her heartbeat rising a tick. "Your people skills need work."

"Considering how much I dislike people, not so much." Donovan walked toward the boat, pushed it so she rocked.

Ivy took two steps and jumped, rolling across the ground and coming to her feet behind Donovan. She hesitated, not sure if she should run for the car or stay to protect Bradet.

Donovan turned. He kicked something in the grass. Her radio. He stepped on it. "You weren't hoping for backup, were you?"

"They're already on their way. Let me arrest you. I'll make it quick and easy."

His first kick knocked her flat on her back. He followed up with his knife hand.

Ivy kicked back, arching her back and slamming both booted feet into his chest. Donovan staggered backward. She lunged at his legs, knocking him to the ground. With one swift motion, she slammed her flashlight into his nose. Jumping away, she ran for the boat.

"Bradet? Bradet you there?"

He sat up.

"Hurry up. Get off the boat. My patrol car is waiting up there. We can run."

"Can't . . . can't run." He swayed as he spoke.

Ivy grabbed his arm and pulled him to the side of the derelict boat. "I'll carry you. We need to leave. Now. Before he gets up." Donovan wasn't unconscious, just stunned. In another minute, he'd have adrenaline enough to work through the broken nose and come after her.

Bradet fell down in front of her. Ivy picked him up by the armpits dragging him into a standing position. "Up the hill. It's not much. My car is right there on the highway." He was heavy, a good thirty pounds more than she weighed, and barely walking.

He turned to look at Donovan scrambling to get up. "He's going to kill us."

"If he tries, I'll hit him again." She brandished her flashlight like a sword, but her legs were trembling. As if to echo that sentiment, the beam of light quivered, blinked, and faded, leaving them alone in the moonlight.

"We're going to die," Bradet repeated in a quiet whisper.

"You're in shock," Ivy said. She glanced over her shoulder. Donovan was watching them, the shadows of night making his face a harsh mask, but he wasn't following.

They reached the crest of the small hill and found the road empty.

"Car?" Bradet asked weakly as he sagged against her.

Ivy looked up and down the road. "I don't . . . I don't understand. I left it here."

Headlights flared up ahead. For the briefest moment, she hoped it was backup; and then she saw the license plate. It was her car. Someone had stolen her car and was approaching at a reckless speed.

At the last second, she pulled Bradet to the relative safety of the guardrail. Nothing but a handspan of cement between them and the inky inlet below. Ivy looked down at the dark water and wondered if Bradet could swim in his condition. If they jumped, where exactly could they swim for safety but back to the bridge and Donovan?

The car's tires squealed on the asphalt as the driver turned sharply. It rushed toward them, then stopped with the screeching tires and the smell of burning rubber. The window rolled down, and a man leaned forward. "Hello."

Ivy's jaw clenched in anger. "That's. My. Car."

The driver looked casually at the lit dashboard and the torn-out dispatch radio. "It needs repairs."

"Get out. I'll make sure you get the mechanic's bill." She stepped in front of Bradet.

"That's not how I work."

"You are under arrest."

The driver shook his head.

Bradet screamed, and there was a sudden draft of chilly night air behind her where he had been. She turned in time to see Donovan's knife flashing toward her. For a precarious second, she balanced on the edge of the cement railing; and then she fell.

When she resurfaced, she could hear her car peeling away. She smashed her hand down on the water, but only gave herself that moment of frustration before finding Bradet—floating facedown—nearby. She flipped him over and, feeling for a pulse, found a faint one. Then, with one arm looped under his arm and across his chest, she dragged the young man to shore. He lost consciousness as they climbed the hill.

Sitting on the wet sand and shivering, she waited for backup to arrive as Bradet's body cooled beside her.

Sam walked into the morgue with a scowl for Mac. "You skipped breakfast and didn't wake me up. I take it that means you found Bradet?" That was the only reason she could imagine that Mac would sneak away like an embarrassed one-night stand. As reluctant as she was to admit it, she was growing accustomed to seeing him every morning, even if it was just the view of him snoring shirtless on the couch as she left for a morning jog.

"Clemens did." Mac nodded to the clone sitting in the corner. His face was tight with worry.

Ivy's face was paler than usual. Dark bruises marred her body. "I'm sorry, Agent Rose."

"What happened?" Sam asked, breakfast woes forgotten.

Clemens stared at the wall and shrugged. "I've had better days."

"I can see that." The officer looked like she'd had better years. Sam turned to Mac for an explanation.

"She had to get a pint of blood at the hospital because clones from her generation don't clot well," Mac said. "It's a minor miracle she survived until the ambulance arrived. Bradet wasn't so lucky."

"It's just scrapes and bruises," Ivy argued.

"Scrapes, bruises, and a run-in with a knife-wielding maniac out in the swamps." Mac gave Ivy a look of near-paternal disapproval.

"Start at the beginning," Sam said.

Mac cleared his throat. "Devon Bradet of Cowansville in what used to be the Quebec Territory of old Canada. He's twenty-seven with a mixed racial profile, brown eyes, recently shaved head—"

"It was for charity," Ivy said in a weak voice. "He shaved it Thursday on air for child-cancer awareness or something like that."

Mac nodded. " . . . and a master's in communication arts from Elon University in North Carolina. Moved here a couple years ago and took the job of radio intern. He's been working his way up since then."

"How'd he die?" Sam asked, watching Ivy. The clone shrank away from her gaze, but Sam couldn't tell if the other woman was scared or suffering from loss of confidence. Worse, she didn't know how to make Ivy better.

"Blood loss and internal hemorrhaging. There's a graze mark along Bradet's neck. Officer Clemens said he was bleeding when she found him. It looks like he was shot while running away from someone."

"Like a home intruder?" Sam guessed as she silently berated herself. She should have gone looking for Bradet first and had someone else process the scene.

Mac nodded.

"Clemens?" Sam turned to the injured officer.

Ivy shook her head. "We had a tip-off that a man Bradet's height was seen walking along A1A near Ponce Inlet. I went up there and found him duct taped and locked in a boat. I thought we were alone, but there were two men. One said his name was Donovan—he had the knife that killed Bradet and sliced me. The other didn't give his name, but he snuck up and stole my patrol car." She closed her eyes. "I'm an idiot."

At least she wasn't scared. "Could have happened to any of us," Sam said.

"If it's any consolation, I don't think the knife killed Bradet," Mac said. "He had the bullet wound already, and the knife wound was shallow. Neither were fatal, but there was severe internal bleeding. They worked him over thoroughly before locking him up."

Clemens looked up. "Bradet said they wanted Henry, but that Henry was dead. It didn't make any sense to me."

"Henry was his roommate. He died in a lab accident on Monday. There was no evidence of foul play." At least not in the details they'd released to the public. His killer was almost certainly not running loose in the current timeline. Probably. The thought gave her headaches. If Henry had survived, Sam felt certain she would have strangled him for this nonsense.

"And now we have Donovan," Mac said.

Sam nodded as the gears started turning. "I'd like to speak with Mr. Donovan, wouldn't you, Mac? Ask him why he wanted to talk to our boy Henry?"

Mac nodded; so did Ivy. It was good to see the team working together.

"There were security cameras on the complex entrance and at the gas station across the street," Sam said. "We have video of everyone going in or out of the complex. So we're going to take those videos and talk to every single person who went in or out of the complex on Thursday."

Clemens hunched her shoulders. "Sounds fun."

"Most police work isn't fun," Sam said. "It's chasing down every clue like a terrier, following leads, following hunches, and worrying about the safety of strangers every hour of the day."

Ivy's lips creased with a resigned smile. "The academy made it sound so much simpler."

"Well, you have to lie to cadets," Mac said. "No one would try to get through basic training if they knew about the paperwork that was waiting for them."

Sam nodded agreement. Paperwork was the bane

of her existence as a senior agent. A shadow of a thought begged for attention, and she frowned until the memory of Nealie Ro's face surfaced in her mind. "New topic, where are we with the pirate?"

"Oh!" Ivy held up a datastick. "I almost forgot, I found this in our files. Nealie had a history of calling the police nonemergency line. He was the only one who called for months. I pulled the records yesterday afternoon before I was sent out looking for Bradet. His last one says he'll meet with someone, said six in the morning, but didn't give a date or place."

"Wrong number?" guessed Sam.

"Maybe," Ivy said. "But I'd like to see his phone records." There was a pause, and her face turned bright red. "I mean, if it were my investigation. Which it's not. So I'll shut up now."

"He didn't have a phone," Mac said.

"Right," Sam said. "Edwin told us the pirates weren't on the grid at all. No bank accounts or credit cards, and that would mean no cell phones either. Where was Nealie calling from?"

"Are there pay phones?" Mac asked.

Sam blinked in confusion.

Mac raised his eyebrows.

"Sometimes I forget how old you are!" Sam said. "Pay phones died with the dinosaurs. Are you really that ancient?"

Laughing, Mac shook his head. "Pay phones are a real thing in some countries!"

"Not since the 1950s," Sam said.

"They were a little bit more recent than that," Mac argued. "I think."

"No," Ivy broke in, "the city doesn't have ancient technology or landlines. The last ones were phased out in 2048 as a health hazard. Telephone posts fall in high winds and can cause damage. Cell towers and wifi relays can be spaced away from property and fenced in so no one is near them if they do accidentally fall."

Sam snapped her fingers. "What about those tire tracks? Have we figured out what they belonged to yet? If one of his friends had a car, he might have borrowed a cell phone."

"The tire tracks belong to an older-model Alexian Essence," Mac said. "The bureau database couldn't narrow it down much more than that."

"Then we have two leads to chase down," Sam said. "Find out whose phone Nealie had so we can get the phone records and see who called him back. Can you chase it down, Clemens, or will the department get mad that the bureau stole you?"

Clemens smirked as she got up to leave. "They'll never notice me missing. I'll give you a call when I find out anything. And I'll see if anyone's reported an Essence lost or stolen."

"Check the impound, too," Mac suggested.

Sam sighed as Ivy walked out the door. "That means we're stuck with no minions to read through Henry's work folders."

Mac looked over at her, his eyes filled with an emotion that was half hunger, half something she couldn't quite define. It was a look that made her want to cross the room and lean in close. To touch him and reassure herself she wasn't alone.

"Sorry I left without telling you," Mac said quietly. "I won't do it again." He waited a beat. "Shoog."

"Shoog?"

"Like sugar?" Mac smiled unrepentantly.

"No." Sam shook her head. "And no more possessive-boyfriend routine with Petrilli. We aren't in that kind of relationship." She wasn't sure she could label what they had between them if pressed.

"What are we then?"

Sam shot him an annoyed glare. "I don't know. We're . . . something. But boyfriend sounds too immature. You're my Mac. I like eating breakfast with you in the morning and dragging you out for runs. It's easy to fall into the habit of having you around."

"That could be a dangerous habit." His words were playful, but his smile was pure masculine pride.

"Especially since Chicago wants you back," Sam said with a sigh. "I had a friendly inquiry in my in-box this morning asking if I was done with you yet. I think your district director is getting ready to send down an extraction team."

He chuckled. "Did you tell them you're done with me?"

"I told them I was petitioning my district director to have you transferred full-time."

Mac froze, and she couldn't tell if the expression on his face was one of shock or horror.

"Don't worry about being forced to give up your penthouse overlooking the park," she said quickly. "There's no way to fit you into the budget."

He rolled his eyes. "I live in a third-story walk-up apartment. It's not as fancy as you think."

"Whatever. You're not in danger of having to pack and move a second time." The moment stretched between them, full of unspoken possibilities. What-ifs and maybes crowded the silence. Until duty, ever sovereign, demanded Sam's attention once again. "I'm going to go talk with the apartment manager about their security footage."

Mac looked down at his desk. "I've . . ."

She cut him off before he could drag them back to dangerous territory. "You can stay. I don't need backup on this."

"Be careful?" His eyes were filled with emotions she didn't want to acknowledge: yearning, fear, desire, love . . . Powerful emotions reined in by an inner strength Mac rarely acknowledged.

She smiled. For him, she'd be careful. "Always."

Ivy sat cross-legged at the end of her bed, flipping through the dead-wood papers filled with phone numbers. The nonemergency police line kept a record of the time of the call, the phone number, a name if given, and the complaint. Some of the calls were marked with a small asterisk that indicated emergency assistance had been sent, usually an ambulance.

There was no pattern. Not at first. She tried marking all the same numbers in the same color, but there were few repeat calls, and those that existed were usually within a few minutes of each other, probably because a caller had another question. In one peculiar instance, the same man had called three times trying to order pizza.

She wiped dewing sweat from her face and leaned over to switch on the AC unit fitted into her window. Muggy, barely cool air came with a harsh buzzing sound and the scent of garbage from the alley on the other side of the fence. Another few months of saving up, and she'd be able to buy a new one during an end-of-season clearance sale.

She looked at the file. Patterns were the natural order of things. Waves, clouds, genes . . . all of them had set patterns. Even phone numbers had patterns eventually. *If only I could see this one . . .* Then, like watching a cloud take the shape of a pirate ship, she saw it. There *were* repeat numbers. The same number repeated a dozen times, but scrambled so the time, date, and phone number made the same repeating pattern. Twenty repeated digits, sixteen when she crossed out the four digits designating the year. She ordered a fresh printout from her computer and highlighted them.

Even with the times doctored, she saw the pattern. The person had called every day ending in a prime digit between the hours of eight in the evening and two in the morning. She got a drink of water from the tap and went to work untangling the phone number. Theoretically, there were scramblers on the market like this. High-end tech toys used by paranoid billionaires. It made sense that a pirate might have something like that . . . almost. Except Agent Edwin said the pirates weren't tech users. They were off-the-grid eco-terrorists.

She stabbed her pen into the paper and willed the numbers to give up their secrets.

Two long hours later, she had ten digits in her hand that were, most likely, Nealie Rho's private phone number. Logging into the limited-access police database she could use from home, Ivy ran the numbers.

Jamie Rex Nelson-Gardner.

Ivy rubbed her eyes. Gardner?

As in Sheriff Gardner?

She'd only met the man in passing, but he wasn't the fatherly type. He didn't have a spouse at any public events. Not that she was an expert on families. She'd been raised with thirteen other clones in a Shadow House, where the closest she had come to parents were men and women in lab coats monitoring their diets and making sure they had plenty of exercise and very little communication with the outside world. Speaking to non-shadows, aside from answering questions for the doctor, was discouraged although not actually punished. The keepers couldn't risk scarring the precious, expensive skin of a shadow. But minds? Well, everyone knew a clone's mind wound up in the trash. Eyes and tongues and teeth might be harvested for the

Real Person, but the rest was waste. A shadow's brain was its least valuable organ.

She smiled. Life after the Shadow House was proving her mind was her most valuable asset. *Eat that, White Coats. I am more than a body for you to sell.*

Ivy sighed and flopped back on her bright pink sheets. There weren't difficult answers, only complicated questions. Living a double life, doing one thing and saying another, that led to complicated questions.

If you said murder was wrong but allowed yourself to get enraged and think about killing every day, then your life was complicated. If you knew killing was wrong and treated everyone with respect and admiration no matter what they did, life was simple.

As a police officer, it surprised her how often people chose the complicated life. How they were willing to break the law even though they knew the odds were stacked against them. She shook her head. It was a nonsensical gamble.

No one ever won betting against the house.

She sat back up and pulled her clunky laptop off her desk. It wasn't a nice sleek datpad like Agent Rose had, but it was what she could afford on her salary. She typed in Jamie's name and pulled up a picture of a wide-eyed boy staring mournfully at the camera. The headline read, LOCAL BOY REMANDED TO FOSTER CARE AFTER CAR WRECK KILLS MOTHER.

She clicked the link and read on. "Local boy Jamie Gardner has been placed in foster care following the accident that killed his mother, Dolores Nelson (46).

The boy's father is also a local resident but waived parental rights. Miss Nelson and Mr. Gardner divorced three years ago, after their son's autism diagnosis." The article went on for several more paragraphs about how the rise in neurally atypical children in foster care was draining national resources and listed several clinics that would test for genetic abnormalities.

Right—this nonsense.

It was before she was aware of the outside world, but for a few years the public had believed that there was a way to determine if a fetus would be neurally atypical—unable to act like a "normal" person—with the goal of either preparing the family for the "horrors" of a high-needs child or to persuade the parents to terminate the pregnancy. It was a shot of snake oil, but for a few years the abortion rate had skyrocketed as media outlets proclaimed it was the end of crime. No more sociopaths, no more narcissistic personalities conning people out of money, no more unusual children who didn't quite fit into the standard models for schools. No more square pegs in round holes.

She tasted bile on her tongue and realized her blood pressure was rising.

Poor Jamie had been born into that mess. His mother was old enough that her pregnancy would have been considered high-risk even with gene therapy. Born less than ten years after the Yellow Plague had erased half of humanity, at the height of clone technology and the height of antihospital sentiment.

She'd bet a milkshake that Miss Nelson hadn't even

gone to the doctor for basic birth control. That was the old States back then, and very few birth-control measures were sold over the counter. Not when the whole world was rushing to repopulate. The poor woman had probably thought it was her patriotic duty to have a child, like some chilling remake of *1984*.

According to the date on the article, Jamie had gone into foster care thirteen years ago. It wasn't hard to imagine his never getting adopted. Being bounced between foster homes and crèches that weren't much better than Shadow Houses without the constant threat of death. And then? Where would a boy with a dead mother and a hateful father wind up?

With Peter Pan in Neverland. In the swamps of Florida with the other lost boys.

Her lips twitched into a smile. There was a whole group of barely educated man-children playing at being pirates. It was so laughably obvious she wondered why no one had thought of it before. Checking her hunch would mean a late-night run to the precinct, but if she was right, she'd just found a way to track down the pirates and find Jamie's killer.

CHAPTER 11

The difference between animals and man is the latter's willingness to change their circumstances. A dog may sense the coming storm, but it will never reach out to move the clouds.

~ excerpt from the *Oneness of Being*
by Oaza Moun I1—2072

Sunday March 23, 2070
Florida District 8
Commonwealth of North America
Iteration 2

Gant's hands shook as he finished wiping down the stolen car and slammed the door shut behind him. Everything was going wrong. The man they'd taken hadn't known anything about the Timeyst Machine and kept saying Troom was dead. And the cop Donovan had killed hadn't looked dead to him although Donovan swore he'd gotten her.

He should have snapped Donovan's thick neck the

minute that blundering fool stepped into his house. Everything was fine until then. And what did Donovan know anyway? Detective Rose couldn't have been close to finding him.

Shivering in the hot morning sunshine, he stripped off the gloves. Dumping them near the car he'd just wiped down wouldn't help. There were too many ways to pull a fingerprint. But he'd passed a friendly-looking apartment complex on his way downtown, and a pair of cleaning gloves in the Dumpster there wouldn't draw anyone's attention.

Walking the few miles back to the motel would cool his head. Settle him down. Maybe give him some good idea of how to deal with this mess. Donovan was keeping calm about the disaster, but it was clear he wasn't going to find a solution.

He scratched at the stubble on his chin. Zoetimax didn't exist here. Donovan had taken a shower last night, and Gant had taken the chance to use the stolen tech he'd been hoarding to look. English was his birth language, but he hadn't used it since he went to school, but it wasn't rusty enough for him not to know that the maps were wrong. None of the search engines brought up familiar names or places.

Donovan didn't have the drive to get back. Last night, Gant had caught him looking at a Want Ads site for jobs. As if they were going to settle in and stay here!

He'd never worked a nine-to-five job in his life. He'd lifted his first wallet at nine. At fifteen, he'd pulled his first second-story job. By the time he'd reached adulthood, he already had a reputation. People respected him. More to the point, they paid him what he was worth. That was what he was going back to: fame and luxury.

He hadn't broken out of prison to work at an office-supply store.

Gant shook his head and pretended to take an interest in the ants scurrying across the sidewalk as a man with a very large dog jogged past. The dog gave Gant a sympathetic look and loped off after its master.

Sighing, Gant walked past the shrubs toward the pink apartments. Cute, tropically themed balloons were tied by the community pool. There was a playground with a bright blue plastic slide that was probably hot enough to fry eggs on. He didn't care about any of it—what he wanted was the large green Dumpsters at the back of the property.

A woman doing laundry looked out the window and waved at him. Gant waved back. Like skulking, people remembered the emotions they felt rather than the faces they saw. An angry man stalking through the complex was going to get remembered; an average-looking guy who waved a friendly hello to the neighbors wasn't.

He chucked the gloves in the Dumpster. Turned. Froze. A very familiar face was approaching him.

Gant rubbed his eyes.

The gray car drove past and parked not thirty feet from where he stood. Gant stood motionless as Detective Rose stepped out of the car, wearing the most casual clothing he'd ever seen on her. Logically, he knew the woman had times when she wasn't wearing power suits or courting future voters, but he'd never imagined something as casual as jeans.

His eye twitched.

Detective Rose took a handful of bags from the trunk of her car and climbed the apartment steps two at a time. Not once did she notice that he was there.

His lips curled into a sneer. So, the detective had followed them through the portal. That was fine. If she knew how to get here, she knew how to get back. Getting the information from her would be easy as robbing a corpse.

Exactly as easy.

Sam's phone rang as she walked up the stairs to the apartment. "Agent Rose, how may I help you?"

"Rose?" asked a woman's voice on the other end. The single word was filled with confusion and sadness.

The wooden steps creaked under her feet. "Yes, ma'am. Who were you looking for?"

"Eric."

"Eric?"

"Eric MacKenzie?"

"Oh, Agent MacKenzie isn't with me right now." Sam balanced the grocery bag in one hand, clenched the phone between her ear and shoulder, and unlocked the front door. Hoss didn't run to greet her, which meant Mac had come back at some point to fetch the mutt and take him for a walk.

"I thought this was his phone," the woman said.

Sam kicked the door shut, dropped her groceries and purse on the couch, and took the phone away from her ear. "Oh, dang it. This is his phone."

"Oh?" There was a curiously accusatory harmonic to the simple sound.

"We, ah, were at a meeting, and these government phones all look the same. I must have grabbed Mac's by mistake. Who did you say you were again?"

"I'm Mrs. Mackenzie . . . Eric's mother."

Sam looked at the phone again, at the caller ID and 208 area code. "His mom?" Her voice squeaked only a little. "Well, I, um. I'm so sorry, Mrs. MacKenzie. I don't know where Mac is right now. I will have him call you back."

"He never does." The older woman's voice cracked on the edge of a sob. "I've called every other day for the past five and a half years, and I never get anything. He changed his phone number last year."

"With the move to Chicago," Sam said. "I know. How'd you get the number, then?"

"A friend from church knows someone who knows Mac and had his new number. She sent it to me."

Mac's mom went to church? Had Mac gone to church? How did someone from their church get access to a restricted government number? What kind of religion did they belong to?

"Is he doing well?" Mrs. MacKenzie asked. "Is he . . . is he all right?"

"He's great," Sam said. "Healthy, happy, wonderful. You raised an outstanding son, Mrs. MacKenzie. Everyone loves him."

"Is he dating?" she asked, as the front door opened, and Hoss bounded in.

"Hey, Sam," Mac said as he unclipped Hoss's leash. "Agent Edwin called. I grabbed your phone by mistake."

"Is that him?" Mrs. MacKenzie asked from the other end of the line.

"You have a phone call," Sam said, shoving the phone at MacKenzie.

"Hello, who is this?" Mac asked cheerfully.

"Your mother!" Sam said about the same time Mrs. MacKenzie must have announced herself.

Mac's face went white, and he started shaking his head. He held the phone away from his face. "No, Sam, I can't."

"You will say hello," Sam ordered.

Reluctantly, he lifted the phone to his ear. "Hi, Mom." His shoulders tightened into a defensive hunch. "I'd love to talk, but I'm really busy."

"You have some time now," Sam said loudly enough to be heard all the way in Idaho. She crossed her arms and raised an eyebrow at Mac.

His mouth twisted into a snarl, but he sat on the couch with the phone still on. "Yeah, Agent Rose is a friend from work. Yes. She's very intelligent." Mac nodded in agreement and shot Sam another angry look.

Hoss, seeing one of his humans available, strolled over to the couch and lay down for a belly rub.

Mac was sufficiently well trained to drop a hand and pet the dog. "I'm sorry I didn't call, Mom. No. No, I didn't go to church last week. Or the week before. I've been busy."

Sam hung behind the couch, listening to Mac's half of the conversation.

"How is everyone? That's good. Yeah. Tell them I love them." Mac's knuckles were going white. "Look, I know. I've got to go. I'm sorry. Yes. I'm sorry. Bye." He dropped the phone like it had burned him. "Sam. I don't talk to my mother," he said in a flat monotone.

"If you don't want to talk to her, block her number. Or put Do Not Answer on the caller ID. How was I supposed to know it was your mom? The phone rang, I answered. That's what I do when phones ring." She sat down in the armchair next to the couch. "She sounded upset. Is everything okay at home?"

Mac closed his eyes and sat up straight, leaving Hoss bereft of affection. "Yeah."

"Mac?"

He looked over at her, face tight and eyes red. "I haven't talked to her since before Afghanistan."

"What?"

"I . . . I couldn't. I couldn't call her up when all of my soldiers couldn't call their parents. I couldn't go home without them." He pressed his lips together.

Sam moved to the couch. "Everyone else lost their children, so your parents had to lose you, too? How could you do that to her, Mac? That's so selfish! No one would want that." She knew she was bullying him, but what was she supposed to say? *You're right, Mac! You should be dead with everyone else. Go hop in a grave.*

Rubbing his back, she rested her head on his shoulder and softened her voice. "If you asked the families who lost soldiers, they wouldn't tell you to punish your family because you survived."

He shook his head, tears running down his face. "I couldn't. *I couldn't.*"

"Why didn't you answer her phone calls? I mean, okay, yeah. I get your not wanting to talk to her when you were drugged and depressed, but why not now? Why not at Christmas?" She slammed herself back into the couch. "Do you know how much I would have loved someone to call on a holiday to say they loved me?"

"That's why I couldn't talk to her," Mac said. He'd pulled his emotions under control, but it left his voice cold, void of everything that made him *him*. "I couldn't face her, or any of them. I couldn't live if I saw how much I'd disappointed them."

"How did you disappoint them?"

"I went to Afghanistan with six men to rescue fourteen others. I came home alone."

They sat in near silence for a moment. Hoss rolled over, looking as concerned as was possible for a perpetually cheerful Boerboel.

Sam's mind raced, trying to catch up with the

enormity of the thought. "You hated yourself. So you thought everyone else would hate you, too?"

Mac shrugged his shoulders. "What else was I going to think?"

"Do you still hate yourself?" Sam asked, reaching for his hand.

"Some days." He wrapped his hand around hers, warm and strong. "Other days aren't so bad."

"Your mother loves you, Mac. I heard it in her voice."

"I know." He pressed his lips together again, and she could see he was fighting back more tears.

Sam squeezed his hand. "You're a good person."

"I try."

"You're worth loving. You have to believe that."

"I'm trying."

She leaned her head on his shoulder. After a few minutes she said, "Mac?"

"Yes?"

"I'm making you call her next Sunday."

Sam's phone rang again—her real phone this time. "This is Agent Rose speaking."

"Agent Rose, this is Ivy. I think I found a lead on the Nealie Rho case," Ivy said. "Can you meet me at your office?"

Sam's eyes widened. "I'll be there in twenty minutes."

Ivy paced the carpeted floor outside the bureau office as she waited for Agent Rose to arrive. She'd fallen asleep at her desk at home only to rush to the office at first light to double-check everything. There were certain things that weren't done, and digging into the history of state-raised juveniles was one of them. Her gut twisted in guilt.

Footfalls echoed in the stairwell. Light, even steps with the distinct click of high-heeled shoes. Ivy turned in anticipation as Agent Rose opened the door.

"Officer Clemens, sorry to keep you waiting." Rose passed her hand over the scanlock and opened the door. "Let's use my office."

"I am so sorry to drag you out on your weekend," Ivy said preemptively.

Rose's face was emotionless. "It's not a problem." The flat tone said otherwise, but Ivy couldn't guess what part of this mess made her angriest.

"Last night I was reading through the police nonemergency-line phone logs, trying to find a phone number for Nealie."

"And you had luck?" Rose asked as she unlocked her office door and sat down behind her desk. The office was spartan, decorated with simple pencil sketches of buildings around the district and a desk that was twin to the one in the front office. There was no hint of Agent Rose's personality here. Nothing personal. A reminder that even bureau agents were replaceable.

Like shadows . . .

Ivy hastily sat down. "I found some anomalies." She pulled the highlighted papers from her bag and put them on the desk, facing Rose. "At first I didn't think there was anything, but then I noticed a repeat of the numbers across all columns. Not the same times or the same phone number, but there's a pattern."

Rose shuffled the papers, scanning the columns with a small frown. "This looks like a scrambler pattern."

"I think it is." Ivy took a deep breath and held it.

"I've never seen these outside bureau training." Rose's eyebrows went up in surprise. "Good job."

"Thank you." Ivy blushed. "Once I realized there was a scrambler in use, I did a little more digging. Once I had a large enough sample set, I was able to find the scrambled phone number."

Rose looked at her. "That can't be easy math to do."

"I'm really good with numbers and patterns."

"So what did you find?"

She took a thin datpad out of her bag and passed it to Agent Rose. "This is the file for one Jamie Rex Nelson-Gardner. He was raised in the foster-care system after his mother's death."

"Gardner?" Agent Rose fixed on the name like a hound dog, just as she had. "Like Sheriff Gardner? Any relation?"

"Jamie was his son," Ivy said. "I had to log in at the police station this morning to double-check, but he is. The sheriff divorced his wife before she died and refused to take custody of Jamie."

"Was it an accidental death?"

"The mother's? Yes, there was a full investigation."

Agent Rose rocked back in her chair, eyes staring at the wall as her thoughts wandered. To Ivy, she looked like an all-seeing empress on her throne. Rose steepled her fingers. "Do we know why the sheriff refused to take custody of his son?" she asked in a slow, cautious voice as if she were sneaking up on an idea.

"There's no official reason given . . ."

"But you suspect something. Did Gardner deny paternity?"

"No"—Ivy smiled—"but you're right. There was an article about the accident, and that made me dig into the divorce files. Those are in the county record and not nearly as secure as Jamie's—or the sheriff's—personal files. There's a transcript of the divorce proceedings, and several times Sheriff Gardner argues with his wife that she should put Jamie into a home. He was diagnosed as neurologically atypical at age three."

Rose's eyes narrowed, and her nostrils flared. "Gardner wanted to abandon his child because he wasn't normal enough?"

"He was diagnosed with speech apraxia, obsessive tendencies, and a minor developmental delay. From what I can tell from reading between the lines, it looks like they wanted to put Jamie on the autism spectrum. There are little signs here and there, not enough for a real diagnosis, so I'm guessing. I did find a few other articles about him. He won a science fair in fifth grade and had one of his poems published in the city newspaper when he was in tenth grade. He played on the soccer team." She sighed.

Rose shook her head. "What a waste of a good life. What a wasted opportunity."

"I can't imagine a parent's leaving their child for anything," Ivy said.

Agent Rose winced. "I can." Her lips puckered like she'd bitten a lemon. "A lot of people are willing to put careers before children, even when the child doesn't have special needs."

Ivy bit her lip and looked away. The emotions on Rose's face were frightening in their bitterness.

The bureau agent washed it away with a sigh. "Okay, we have a name. How much legwork can you do on this case?"

"The chief is officially loaning me to the bureau until the homicides are all wrapped up. I'm supposed to be running support for the Bradet case, but I can work on this one, too. No one will stop me." She wouldn't let them. Jamie was one of hers. He was a forgotten child, an underdog, someone who knew what it was like to be unwanted. He was her people.

Rose nodded. "Good. Then, if you don't object, I'd like you to run down as much information on Jamie and his habits as you can. See if he had a home outside the swamp. See if he was dating anyone, look for a place he might have shopped a lot or was a regular. Cousins, friends from school, past coworkers. I want to build a timeline of his life the week before he died. Look for anomalies again, anything that didn't fit in, then see if we can find out who saw him last." She froze for a brief second, then laughed. "That's a request, by the way, not an order. If you don't want to do this, I can have Agent Edwin run this all down."

"Oh, no! I'd love to do that," Ivy said quickly. "It's no trouble at all."

Rose smiled like a proud parent. "Great. Agent Edwin knows Nealie's pirate group pretty well, so feel free to pick his brain. I have him working on some other things, too, but utilize him. And don't— under any circumstances—go chasing after a suspect by yourself. You call the bureau for backup. You wear your tac vest. And you do not, ever, go alone and run into a situation blind. Promise me that."

"I promise," Ivy said solemnly.

"You have a bright future ahead of you," Rose said. "I don't want to see you throw that away because you get caught up in the chase."

Somewhere around age four, Sam remembered a sleepless week where she wrestled with the fear that everything disappeared when she closed her eyes. From a clinical standpoint, and from an adult perspective, she could view it as the last stage of understanding object permanence, or the first step to studying theoretical physics. Either way, she recalled being terrified of closing her eyes at night in case the bed disappeared and she hit her head on the floor.

Of all the things she'd worried about the most, it had been her bed. Not her friends disappearing, or her already-absentee parents never returning. No. That would have made sense. Instead, her younger self had feared losing her bed.

The nuns had tried in vain to explain it away. They'd offered her prayers. They'd made her close her eyes and touch the bed to show her it wouldn't disappear. But it wasn't until Sister Gabriel volunteered to sit and watch Sam's bed as she slept that Sam was willing to finally fall asleep.

Looking at Mac in flannel pajama pants and a faded gray T-shirt making his bed on the couch, she felt that same rock-solid reassurance that nothing bad would happen. She leaned her cheek against the wall and watched him move through the shadows of the apartment. "Bathroom's free."

He looked up with a warm smile.

In another life, she might have crossed the distance to him and wrapped her arms around him. In another life, she might have risked loving him. She wasn't lying when she had told him that he deserved to be loved. And a part of her was willing to admit she did love him on some level that the English language couldn't ever convey. What she felt wasn't a physical lust although he was handsome in an unconventional way, and if there wasn't a headstone with her name on it, she would have been happy with a physical relationship. She felt more than that, though. Mac was her pillar of strength. Even though he had just returned to her life, she knew with a certainty that when everything else went wrong, he was the one thing she could count on.

"You're staring," Mac said. She was a flash of teeth as she smiled in the darkness. "What is going on in that busy brain of yours?"

"Nothing," Sam lied as she moved to rest her shoulders on the wall.

"Nothing? Really?"

She shook her head. "Just staring off into space, thinking of things."

"Not staring at me?" Mac teased.

"Nope." He lifted his shirt over his head. *Yum.* There was nothing soft about Mac. The doughy, swollen man he'd been while lost to drugs and depression was gone.

Mac chuckled. "Still not looking?"

"Of course not." She knew he could hear the lie in her voice. "Why would I be watching a sexy man strip in my living room?"

"I don't know," Mac said, as he sauntered toward her. "Maybe you like the guy. Maybe, you'd like to get closer to him." He stopped just out of reach.

"Maybe." Sam tilted her head to the side. "Maybe I've thought about it once or twice." About how wonderful it would feel to wake up with his arms around her. About how much she'd love to kiss him good-bye every time she walked out the door, and hello every time she found him again. She could imagine the taste of his lips on hers, though, and it was the taste of blood. The scent of death that hugged her like a jealous lover was always between them.

Mac took a step closer. "Want to do more than think?"

"I don't want to hurt you." The same refrain. The same argument. Again and again and again—it was starting to get old even to her. "There's never going to be a right time for us." Reaching out was a mistake. The feel of hot skin beneath her fingertips was too tempting, too promising. She closed her eyes and pulled away. Burned. "I'm sorry."

"Don't be." The air grew warm as he drew closer. Soft lips brushed her forehead. "I'm not going anywhere."

Sam ducked her head as she grinned. "Get in the shower, MacKenzie."

He kissed her head again. "Yes, ma'am."

I'm in trouble.

CHAPTER 12

A human being is more than a mere tangle of DNA. Humanity is the gift of sentience, art, civilization . . . To be human is to create and to destroy.

~ excerpt from *Among the Wildflowers*
by Andria Toskoshi

Monday March 24, 2070
Florida District 8
Commonwealth of North America
Iteration 2

For centuries, Florida thrived on tourism. The constant influx of capital from visitors did everything from pave the roads to pay for the new playgrounds at the schools. As with any large tourist area, there were hideaways, secret places that the natives kept hidden from outsiders so *they* could escape. Gator Trap was one of those places. It was a combination gas station, marina, bait shop, and restaurant on the edge of Shipyard Canal that had an unlisted number and no Web site. So far, that was enough to keep the tourists away.

It also made it an excellent hideout for the kind of people who didn't like clones or police. Knowing that, Ivy had opted for casual wear, or at least as casual as she dared let herself wear. Jenna Mills had been a very pretty girl in life. Ivy wasn't sure what her gene donor acted like, but there was something about strawberry blonde hair and freckles that made people assume she was going to have a cute Southern accent and wear shorts no longer than a bikini.

She went out of the way to defy those expectations. Her only concession to the springtime heat was a thin pink T-shirt with cap sleeves. The shirt and her jeans were both baggy in an attempt to hide her body from prying eyes.

Sitting on the front hood of her car, she watched the people watching her and hoped no one decided to pay any closer attention. She checked her watch, bit her lip in worry, and kept an eye on the empty stretch of road.

A few centuries seemed to pass before a familiar red truck pulled into the dusty lot. She'd told Agent Edwin to come in casual dress, which for him seemed to mean khaki shorts and a faded university T-shirt with a fraying hem. He waved.

Ivy waved back and hopped off the hood. "Hi. Thanks for meeting me out here."

"No problem," Edwin said. "It's this or read through physics notes for Agent Rose. This is definitely better."

"Not a fan of physics?"

Edwin shook his head. "I barely passed it in high school. Everything we're reading from the lab is so far over my head, I need the Hubble telescope to see it." He clapped his hands together. "What are we doing here, and does it include lunch?"

"Should it include lunch?" The aroma of deep-fried fat was overwhelming, and not in a good way. Fatty foods weren't a part of her shadowhood. Adulthood and freedom hadn't changed her views.

"They do a great fried-gator sandwich. It's life-changing."

"I'm sure it is for the gator."

Edwin sighed and rolled his eyes. "If we're not here for lunch, why are we here?"

She rocked to the balls of her feet and bounced with nervous energy. "I, um, might have reached out to someone and told them I was a friend of Jamie's and that I wanted to meet." She bit her lip anticipating a reprimand.

"Who's Jamie?" Edwin asked.

"Your pirate? Nealie? His real name was Jamie Nelson. I contacted Connor Houghton, who was Jamie's foster brother of sorts. They spent at least three years in the same foster home during high school. Connor was a year older . . ."

" . . . and you think he's Connor Nu?" Edwin nodded. "That makes sense. You want me to ID him?"

"And make sure no one feeds me to the gators," Ivy said. "Self-defense laws don't apply to people like me."

He squinched his face and looked at the ground. "It'll be fine."

"I'll feel safer having you as backup."

Edwin beamed. "Then lead on."

She crinkled her nose and laughed. It was kind of adorable how the big, tough CBI agent was willing to play backup for her. She walked into the Gator Trap and picked a corner booth overlooking the water in the screened patio. Edwin saw her seated, then wandered off—presumably hunting for his fried-gator sandwich.

Ivy took a deep breath, checked the water for gators, then started watching the parking lot. She'd heard about Connor from the rumor mill at work. A few years ago, there had been talk around the station that the pirates were clone sympathizers. The chief wanted them prosecuted for sedition. She'd accidentally shredded the orders, and no one ever followed up.

At the time, it hadn't occurred to her that she might one day have to meet one of the pirates and learn the truth. She shifted uncomfortably in her seat. No one could tell by looking at her what she was, but she'd sat silent while the people around her ranted about wanting all clones dead enough times in her life already. They were welcome to their opinions, but she was never going to go out of her way to help one of the bigots. If he was a clone hater, she was going to kick herself.

She dug in her purse and pulled out a laminated card that fit in her palm. It was a print copy of her emancipation letter with the details of the Caye Law printed on the reverse. For other people, there were prayers to gods and saints. For her, there was a law that declared her human.

"Connor!" Edwin's voice echoed off the wooden rafters.

"Danny Boy!" a tenor voice shouted back.

Ivy nodded to herself. Most voices were just voices, but this one was musical. The voice of Oberon welcoming Titania home to the moonlit forest. It was a good voice for a mysterious pirate. She turned, trying to catch a glimpse of him through the crowd.

A shadow fell over the table, and Ivy jerked back, startled.

Edwin grinned down at her. "I got you some gator nuggets and sauce."

If it were possible for a clone to turn green, she was doing that now. "Gator nuggets?"

"They're like chicken nuggets but saltier," he said as he sat down and pushed a basket of unidentifiable deep-fried lumps, a white sauce with green chunks, and french fries at her.

"I've never had chicken nuggets. Aren't they chocolate? For Easter time?"

Edwin stared at her, sandwich halfway to his mouth. "What?"

"What?"

"You've never had chicken nuggets?"

"I grew up on a vegetarian diet." Ivy squirmed in the wooden booth. "Is that wrong?" Other humans lived as vegetarians. She knew they did. There were cookbooks just for vegetarians. Clones couldn't be the only ones buying the books.

He shook his head too quickly. "No, it's just . . . you eat meat right?"

"Sustainably caught fish and occasionally grilled chicken." That's what normal healthy people ate. She'd read that in a book at the library. A healthy diet for an adult female consisted of a balanced diet full of nutrient-dense food such as vegetables, fruits, and wild fish sustainably caught. Her heart raced with fear. "What did I do wrong?"

Edwin shook his head. "Nothing, nothing. It's just a little weird, you know? Most people try junk food eventually."

Ivy frowned at the basket of food. "I . . . I didn't want to. Not when my body was finally mine. I didn't want to hurt my body. For the longest time, it wasn't even mine, but now it is, and sometimes I feel it's the only thing I own."

"I'm sorry." He frowned. "I wasn't trying to break you. I just thought you might like it. The gator's real tasty."

"Danny!" the tenor voice said, interrupting them. A man sauntered up to the table. He was striking in a very magazine sort of way, Ivy decided. Brilliant hazel eyes, sandy-brown hair, a five o'clock shadow even though it was one in the afternoon, and well-defined muscles that looked like they took six hours at the gym every day to maintain.

"You're frowning," Edwin said.

Ivy shrugged. "I thought the pirates would be more . . . scraggly. Malnourished. Ragged. Real pirates were riddled with sexually transmitted diseases, parasites, and lice. They weren't—"

"Handsome?" Connor hit her with a megawatt smile. His eyes met hers, then traveled leisurely down, resting longer than was polite on her breasts and legs before making a leisurely trip back up. He made sure he had eye contact . . . and then winked.

She burned with embarrassment.

"You are beautiful."

"Thanks," Ivy said weakly, "I was designed that way." Connor moved to sit down beside her, and she had to scoot to the end of the bench to avoid being sat on.

He took the seat opposite Edwin with another wink for her. "This isn't the bad old days, beautiful. We're not keelhauling anyone. Modern pirates are ecoterrorists. We want to preserve our natural heritage with heirloom seeds and eat foods that weren't lab-created."

"Rotten sunflower seeds and low-yield tomatoes," Edwin said between bites. "That's not how you build a revolution."

"I don't want my garden produce to be owned by a company," Connor argued.

Edwin rolled his eyes, and Ivy got the feeling the two had debated this at length many times.

With a nervous smile, Ivy risked touching Connor's arm to get his attention. He responded with another blazing smile . . . but there was ice in his eyes. "Actually, I wanted to talk to you about Jamie."

"Jamie?" Connor shook his head. "Don't know him."

"Jamie Nelson," Ivy said, setting her face in a practiced look of disapproval she'd modeled after Agent Rose. "He went by the name Nealie Rho after graduation. Before that, you two lived in foster care together. I have pictures," she added in case he tried to wriggle his way out of the conversation.

Connor stole one of Edwin's fries and chewed on it while stared at her. Finally, he shrugged. "So I knew him? So what? Is that a crime now?"

"N-no." Ivy stuttered. This would have been so much easier if she'd worn her uniform. Tiny women with freckles never got respect. Badges did.

"Anyway," Connor said, "I haven't seen Nealie in a while. He buggered off with the others."

She looked to Edwin for help. He was eating his french fries with no more interest in the conversation than she had in attending a college football game. Taking a deep breath, Ivy said, "Nealie's dead."

"What?" Connor turned to Edwin. "How?"

Edwin glanced at her. "He died of asphyxiation. Ivy"—he carefully avoided her title—"found the body. She's been helping the bureau in the investigation."

"Because, what, you're a good citizen?" Connor scoffed.

"I was the first officer on the scene." She lifted her chin a little, trying to act as if his opinion of her didn't matter. It would be so much easier to fake if the opinions of people like him couldn't sign her death warrant.

Connor frowned and shook his head. "Nealie was fine last time I saw him."

"Which was when?"

"I dunno." He took another fry from Edwin. "Last week maybe? We got into a bit of a fight. MacKenzie and Troom had Nealie's head all twisted up talking about changing the world."

Ivy's hand started to shake. "MacKenzie? *Agent* MacKenzie?"

"Yeah," Connor said. "Why?"

Edwin frowned. "Agent MacKenzie from the bureau? Tall guy with dark hair."

"Looks like he knows how to move in a fight?" Ivy added. "Possibly has anger management issues?"

Connor shook his head. "No, Agent Mackenzie's a girl. Short, black hair in a braid, Aussie accent. She and Troom came out to our camp and asked for help. I didn't like her, so she went to Nealie." He looked at the table as if eye contact was too hard. "She knew everything about him. His mom's name, his history with his dad, all of it. Wrapped him around her finger faster than you can gut a fish. I tried telling him . . ." He sucked in his cheeks as his face turned red. "I told him she was trouble."

"But he wouldn't listen?" Ivy asked.

"First time in his life Nealie doesn't listen to me, and he winds up dead." He shook his head again. "I've known him since we were kids. We weren't placed together on purpose, but we wound up in the same homes a lot. I was the only one who remembered his birthday. Even Nealie didn't. All he remembered was his mom's death date."

"Which was?" Ivy slipped her notebook out.

"March 19," Connor said. "Every year, he'd ask me to go out to his mom's grave with him. He didn't like going alone."

Ivy's hand hovered over her notebook. The date couldn't be a coincidence. "Was he depressed when he went to his mother's grave?"

"No, not really. He understood she was gone, and he'd done his crying a long time before I met him. He brought me in case his dad was there."

"This is Sheriff Gardner we're talking about, right?"

Connor nodded. "Yeah, though he wasn't sheriff when Dolores died. When we were younger, he'd get drunk and yell at Nealie if he saw him. He sobered up. Did rehab, I think. We never saw much of him after graduation, but we stayed out of his town, too. If we were there, I don't doubt Gardner would have made our lives difficult just because of Nealie. He hates him."

"Do you know if Nealie went to his mom's grave this year?"

"I guess he would have," Connor said. "He didn't ask me to come with him if he did, though." His eyes narrowed for a second, then he shrugged it off. "He's not a kid anymore."

Edwin finished his fries. "Tell me more about this Australian agent and her buddy Henry."

"Do they matter?" Connor asked.

"I'm curious," Edwin said.

"She showed up near the end of January. Seemed to be in a rush. They needed a place they could work on a project off the grid. At first it didn't bother me. He seemed nice, and she was . . . whatever. I don't like her. She's creepy."

"What kind of creepy?" Ivy asked.

Connor stole one of her fries since Edwin's were gone. "Just weird. She'd say things that made no sense. Talk about stuff that was going to happen like, 'Next month when you do this, make sure you don't leave trash all over the place again.'"

"You made a mess at that one protest," Edwin said. "I yelled at you, too."

"You yelled *after* we made a mess," Connor said. "She was reading me the riot act two weeks before we planned the event. I hadn't even decided we *were* doing it. Tell me that's normal."

"Do you have a history of littering?" Ivy asked.

Both Connor and Edwin shook their heads.

"My people don't litter," Connor said. "We're earth-conscious and ecofriendly. Everything we use is renewable, sustainable, and fair-trade. But we had some antigovernment types stop at the protest. They had plastic water bottles!" He sounded outraged at the idea. "Never mind the oceanic gyres or the needs of sea turtles. They had plastic they left on the ground. I even made sure we had recycling bins."

Edwin frowned. "You don't usually have recycling bins. I thought you upcycled everything."

Connor shrugged. "The lady creeped me out. Told me I'd get a fine if I left a mess again." He held up a finger. "Again? It's the again that gets me. Like she'd already lived through all of this. Between that and Troom talking about rewriting history, I dunno. I didn't like her."

"But Nealie did?"

"She was kind to Nealie," Connor said. "She left, then Troom left, so I figured Nealie had gone with them."

Ivy looked at Edwin again. He shook his head. She nodded. Connor really ought to know.

Connor caught the gesture. "What's up?"

"Edwin wants to eat my gator nuggets," Ivy lied. She pushed the basket of deep-fried reptile across the table.

Edwin pushed it back. "Try one first."

With a reluctant grimace, she snatched up a breaded piece of meat, dipped it in the white sauce, and took a bite.

Edwin and Connor laughed at her expression.

"I told you gator was good," Edwin said. He pushed the basket back to her. "Connor, go grab another basket. You owe me for all the fries you stole."

Connor laughed. "Fine. You want a drink."

"Water is fine," Ivy said.

Edwin pulled his wallet out and gave Connor some cash. "Bring some of the icy lemonades?"

"Sure."

Edwin raised his eyebrows as Connor walked away. "What do you think?"

"That this isn't a coincidence. Henry Troom *and* Jamie Nelson are both dead. Jamie died on the anniversary of his mother's death?"

"Do you think the killer picked the date?" Edwin asked.

She shrugged. "It's a working hypothesis."

"It's sickening."

"Well, serial killers are usually a bit messed up in the head, aren't they? Maybe this one was trying to 'right history' and kill people they were supposed to."

"Then Nealie would have died in a car accident."

"You don't know that. Kids die from asphyxiation in cars, too. A seat belt across the neck or an airbag to the face? That kills kids."

"That's tenuous."

"This whole thing is tenuous," she said.

Edwin stole one of her nuggets. "Agent Rose isn't going to like this."

"Look on the bright side, at least we don't have to tell her that her Agent MacKenzie is a suspect."

"Great, now all we need to do is find a short woman with black hair and an accent. That only describes, what, 40 percent of the country?"

Ivy smiled. "At least now we have a lead."

Sam sat at her desk listening to the sough and whine of the air-conditioning as she read over two lists. One was the visitor registry for Sea Pines Memorial Gardens, where Dolores Nelson was interred at a family plot. The other was a list of activities on the sheriff's schedule. The name Jamie appeared on the visitor record, no surname given, and the sheriff's schedule put him at the cemetery that day, too, but he hadn't signed the register.

She really didn't like the idea forming in her mind. It sounded . . . sick. Yes, sick was the only word she could think of. Sheriff Gardner had been the last person to see his wife alive. His statement to the investigating officer was in the files Ivy had found. Gardner had met his ex for a brief conference at a public library, where she'd given him a box of his things left at the house after the divorce. The next time he'd seen her was at her funeral.

It was stomach churning to think that the sheriff had suffered the same trauma twenty years later with his son. Her phone rang as she made a note to talk with Sheriff Gardner. With luck, he would have some insight for her. Maybe Jamie had brought a friend along that day.

The phone rang again. "Agent Rose speaking"

"Sammie!"

She smiled. "Hey, Bri, what's up?"

"Remember that little scavenger hunt you sent me on?"

"It wasn't a scavenger hunt. I asked you to go talk to someone because they wouldn't answer their phone. Were you able to go?"

"Done, and done," Bri said. "The storage place did have a locker rented out to the phone number you gave me, but it was cleared out over Christmas by some guy in Florida. Does that help at all?"

"It does, actually. Did the storage owner know what was being kept there?"

Bri blew a raspberry. "Sam, please. The place was a roach-infested money-laundering unit. There could have been bodies stored in there, and the owner wouldn't have known. I could barely get him to look at me, and I was wearing a low cut v-neck!"

"Professional interrogation shirt of PIs everywhere?" Sam laughed. "TV shows lie, Bri. They lie like dogs."

"Don't knock it 'til you try it. Cleavage gets you everywhere you want to be."

"And a few places where I'd rather not," Sam said. "You're setting feminism back a hundred years, you know that, right?"

"Nah. Feminism means I have the right to do whatever I want with my body. If I take advantage of the way men objectify me, that's evolution at work. Survival of the smartest."

"It's 'survival of the fittest.' "

"Which is still me," Bri said.

Sam could practically see her smug smile. "I know. How was the marathon last weekend?"

"Great! I took four minutes off my last run time."

"That's great," Sam echoed.

"And, this summer, Jake and I are taking the kids on a spelunking tour across North America."

"I thought you were going to New Zealand this summer."

"Oh, no no no. We're going to New Zealand for *their* summer. We're leaving in August or September. Jake hasn't worked out all the details yet, but it's a four-year contract. We'll have plenty of time to go exploring. You'll come visit us, right?"

"Of course!" Not that the bureau would approve an agent's going down to New Zealand, but she could pretend. "Any chance you'll get to Australia while you're there?"

"Ha!" Bri laughed. "Not happening. Ever. Their borders are closed tighter than a nun's knees. The only reason the Kiwis are letting anyone in is because their population is critically low. And even then, it's taking months to get them to approve our moving there temporarily."

Mac knocked on the door and poked his head in.

Sam held up a finger to tell him to wait for her and motioned for him to leave. "Bri, I got to get back to work. Thanks for running to the storage place for me," she said, as her door swung shut.

"Anytime, sweetie. Send me pictures from your date this weekend."

"I don't have a date this weekend."

"You always say that. I always ask. One day I will get a picture of you on the beach having fun."

"Right," Sam said, trying not to be sarcastic.

"For me?" Bri asked. "I worry about you."

"I'll put on something sexy this weekend and take a picture," Sam said, as Mac opened the door again.

He raised an eyebrow.

" 'Bye, Bri."

The other eyebrow went up. "You're sending sexy pics to Bri now?"

"You were supposed to wait outside!" She sighed. "Bri wants me to go on a date and be happy."

"I agree with her."

"Really?" Of course he did. Sam tucked her phone away. "What did you need that couldn't wait three more minutes."

"You should go out with me this weekend."

Sam rolled her eyes. "We've had dinner together every night since you got here."

"So it's tradition." He grinned.

"Focus, MacKenzie. Whatchya got for me?"

He held the door open. "The ballistic reports for the bullet that killed Henry Troom came back. Come on down to the morgue?"

"Tell me there's a match in the database," she asked as they walked down to his office.

"There is," Mac said, smiling with manic glee as he unlocked the morgue door, "and the suspect is already dead."

"What?"

"The bullet matched the ones fired from Marrins's gun when he shot Dr. Emir last summer."

Sam nodded, already seeing where this was headed. "Henry went to the field behind the lab . . ."

" . . . and picked up one of the stray bullets from the tree line," Mac finished. "He kept it as a souvenir, and during the explosion, it hit a velocity high enough to kill him. It's a nice theory."

She rubbed the back of her neck as a stress tightened her shoulders. "Okay, but is that how bullets work? A spent bullet shouldn't be able to achieve that kind of velocity."

Mac smiled in approval. "You've learned something about guns in the last year."

"You're working up to telling me it isn't a stray bullet from the tree line, aren't you? That's where this conversation is going."

"Ten points to Agent Perfect."

Sam slugged him in the arm.

"It's a freshly shot bullet," Mac said.

"From the gun of a man who is dead?" Sam stared at the wall. "Marrins is dead. His gun went to evidence. It was melted down. Right?"

"I've no idea," Mac admitted. "That's what *should* have happened."

"So let's check on that."

"On the to-do list." Mac looked at her. "Do you want to call Alabama, or do I have to do it?"

"You get to make phone calls. I'm going to check out a storage unit Henry rented in January. I've got a hunch it might be an interesting visit."

Henry Troom's storage unit was on the western edge of town. Conspicuously out of reach of the faulty street cameras down a cracked road the county hadn't gotten around to repairing yet. If one were inclined to be suspicious, one might almost say it was like Henry wanted to hide something.

Sam parked her rental by the main office, mouth tightening with annoyance at the lack of hookup. At least she'd have her car back by the end of the day. The repairs weren't done, but it was drivable. Tossing her hair, she walked into the office.

An older woman with lines etched into her deeply tanned face looked up with sullen eyes. "No vacancies," she croaked in a nasal Jersey accent mixed and softened by Florida's sunny tones. "Try Billie's down the street. He's got a couple sheds free."

"I'm Agent Rose with the Commonwealth Bureau of Investigation." Sam pushed her badge across the Formica counter for inspection. "I need to get into locker 324. The owner is Dr. Henry Troom, now deceased."

The woman sighed, heavy chest heaving under her faded floral shirt with a sigh. "Only the investigating officer or next of kin can enter the premises. If you want something, you gotta wait until the auction. If no one comes to claim the property six months after final payment, we sell it off. What's in there, honey? Nude photos? Sex tape? Trust me, I seen it all."

"I *am* the investigating officer, and I'm looking for motive." Since it wasn't bureau policy to show civilians paperwork or get warrants unless it was a domicile or involved a living person, she felt confident that would be enough. Henry wasn't getting any deader, as they said, and even the broadest definition of the word wouldn't qualify the rental units as domiciles. "How many inquiries have you had about this place?"

The woman frowned. "Oh, let's see. There was that smarmy boy. Talked like a lawyer and had oily hair. Jailbird if I ever saw one. I know someone who's done time. All three of my husbands did time. Sometimes together."

Sam's thought process lurched to a stop. "Don't you mean ex-husbands?"

"Nah, divorces are expensive. Nobody checks the paperwork anymore. They're all dead now, anyway. Wasn't even them killing each other like my mom said it would be. Twenty years of three husbands, and nobody said a word."

"That's illegal," Sam said, amused despite herself.

The woman shrugged. "So's speeding, honey. You ever gotten a ticket?"

"No . . ." She was a careful driver.

"See? Now, next was the lady with the purple suit. Very pretty I thought. A real bulldog, ya know? She was a reporter for the one of those Spanish-language channels. Told me she was a detective following a lead, but her badge was fake as my tits. Her accent was so heavy, I didn't even think she was speaking English at first."

"Which lady?" Sam asked.

"The one who wanted to see locker 324. She bunged up the car she was in trying to get out. Drove forward instead of back. Cracked some paint off the pylons."

"Oh, that's not good," Sam said, confused.

"Nah, it was only an Alexian Virgo. Girl like that ought to have a better car. You can't get rich husbands driving working-class cars."

Sam rested her arms on the chest-high counter, fascinated. "What did you say your husbands went to jail for?"

"Fraud, mostly." She sighed again, then slid open a desk drawer and pulled out a lollipop. "You want one, honey? They're cinnamon-flavored. My therapist says I should have one every time I think about going man-huntin' again. I'm too old and too rich to waste my time chasing money pots."

"No thanks. I'm good. Who else came by about the locker?"

The woman unwrapped her lollipop and tossed the wrapper in the recycler. "Let's see, lawyer, then the re-porter, then this guy with a shaved head. All muscled up with some really nice tats. I offered him a joyride in exchange for the keys to the locker, but he turned me down."

"That's technically prostitution. Also illegal."

The woman's eyes went wide. "Joyride! Joyride, honey! Ain't you never . . . ugh. Girls. Youth is so wasted on the young. I was going to take him out in one of those classic cars we have stored here. There's this businessman from beachside who parks his cars here when he goes to his vacation home in Tulum, down south. Gorgeous classics."

"So you use the cars without his knowledge. That's illegal, too."

"No—I just borrow the cars sometimes. Make sure the engines are running. It's practically charity work. Driving in a ragtop in the hot sun. I started charging him extra for the good sunscreen. Well, I had to. I couldn't be driving around like that in cheap SPF 10 could I? Skin cancer is no joke, honey."

"Do you do *anything* legal? At all? I'm just curious."

Flowers trembled as the woman sucked in her breath, it came out again in a wave of humid, cinnamon-scented despair. "I pay my taxes regular-like."

"Great. How's this. I'm going to pretend you aren't in my district because this is technically a gray area, and you could be someone else's problem, and while I'm on the premises checking out this storage unit, you are not going to do anything that reminds me I have a badge. How's that sound?"

"Sounds like I'm not going to get paid," the woman said. She gave her lollipop a thoughtful lick. "You gonna tell me about the stiff."

"No."

"Fine, you're the private type. I get that. My second husband was like that. Very quiet man. Liked horses. Liked shooting bookies more though, the poor soul. It was an affliction."

Sam stared at the woman noisily sucking her lollipop. "Have you ever done anything normal?"

"I almost graduated once."

That sounded about par for the course. "Key?"

"Sure, honey." The woman heaved herself off her stool and waddled to the back room. She came out with a key ring dangling on one finger. "Do I gotta walk you out there?"

"I can find the locker myself."

"Okay." The woman handed her the key. "The three hundreds are the big storage garages. You can use the side door, but not the front door without the fingerprint of the owner." She paused and her mouth drooped into a horrified frown. "You don't have his hands, do you?"

"They're both at the morgue, attached to the body."

"That's good. Dismembering people gets messy."

Sam nodded but didn't ask the woman how she knew. Maybe the old girl had a lively imagination. Or not. As the door swung closed behind her, she reached for her phone. Petrilli was going to love investigating this place. She sent him a quick text with the address and a note to check in one of these days.

The pedestrian gate swung open as the woman inside pushed a button. Sam crossed the parking lot, already baking in the Southern sun. The heat felt good on her skin.

Building three hundred was near the back of the lot. Licking her lips, she looked at the keys. If he had . . . if he'd rebuilt the machine, this was probably where it was. A far safer choice than in his apartment or the lab.

She reached for the camera pin in her pocket out of habit, then paused. Officially, in the reports everyone else in Florida had read, Emir's machine didn't exist. Time travel had never been discovered. She'd never crossed timelines into another place or seen another version of herself. If the machine was in there, and she caught it on camera, there wouldn't be any more secrets. Some four hundred pages of classified information that was locked under a mountain in Colorado would be exposed to public inquiry. Her life would be shoved under the microscope of public opinion.

Again.

Heart racing, she dropped the pin back into her blazer pocket. Some things were best left off the record. Her lips tightened into an involuntary frown as she unlocked the door, her movement turning on the motion-sensor lights.

And she held her breath.

Color filled the room. Huge canvases leaned against every wall. Skinny ones barely wider than her torso that scraped the eight-foot ceiling. Long ones that were still taller than she. Paintings of wild cities in colors that seared across her soul with burning emotion.

There was some order to the chaos. On the left of the main door, the first paintings were subdued, cityscapes all in shades of gray and all slightly alien. The proportions of the buildings were odd, the angles . . . not quite right. The gray paintings included one small portrait, a square no bigger than her hand. The face was hers painted in ash.

Next to the gray cities were paintings of Alabama. She recognized the café, and the courthouse in the town square across from her old bureau office, and N-V Nova Labs, where she and Henry Troom had first met while he worked for Dr. Emir. The painter had picked other vistas; the feral fields choked with weeds and dying cotton plants, the main highway out of town at sunset, maybe sunrise, and a field with high grass burned golden by the sun. A chill ran down her back.

Jane Doe had been found in that field.

Next to Alabama was another set of paintings. Some of them showed the same buildings, but this time the signs were written in Spanish, and a Mexican flag flew over the courthouse.

As she walked, the paintings became brighter. The painter had chosen more vivid colors, deeper contrasts. The strokes went from blueprint precision to wild, almost angry strokes, as if the painters had been trying to exorcise a demon through their art.

In one corner, a stack of smaller canvases lay scattered, paint side down. There was a hole there, large enough for a person to squeeze through. She pulled out her phone and turned on the camera light to look through the hole to the neighboring storage unit. Dust motes danced in the light, but there was nothing more.

Pulling out a pair of examination gloves from her pocket, Sam slipped them on and picked up one of the fallen canvases at random. It was another painting of her. She leaned it against the table and picked up another. Again, her. She turned them each over with morbid curiosity.

Her with her hair up.

Her in her work clothes.

Her with her hair down.

Her bruised and bleeding.

Always her face.

Always looking away.

Bile churned in her stomach.

She left her portraits and went to the first gray painting, the one that seemed to be on the far end of the painter's spectrum, either first or last. The painting was maybe six feet across and came to just below her chin. Gingerly, she rested her gloved fingertips on the side and eased the canvas away from the wall. There were more gray paintings behind it, smaller ones lying hidden, but that wasn't what she was after.

The artist hadn't signed a name to the paintings, not one she could see, but . . . she looked across the pale back of the painting until she found the scratch marks of faded pencil lines. Shuffling the painting she got close enough to read the words:

"Iteration 1"—Abdul Emir May 9th, 2067.

Sam put the painting back on the wall and picked up the gray portrait of herself.

The back read:

"Commander I1"—Abdul Emir August 3rd, 2067

Nearly two years before they met. She would have still been in the academy. So how had he seen her? A press release? Some information bulletin from her mother's political campaign? Or was the knowledge of her impending death making her paranoid?

She turned her phone on and dialed a number by memory. He picked up on the second ring. "Mac? I found Henry's old storage place. I need a crime scene unit down here."

"Did you find a body?" Mac sounded almost hopeful.

"No." She looked at the hole in the wall, the curiously empty space nearby, and the sea of portraits. "I'm not sure what I found."

CHAPTER 13

It doesn't matter that we survive. All that matters is that our world survives.

~ Private conversation with Agent 5 of the Ministry of Defense

Tuesday March 25, 2070
Florida District 8
Commonwealth of North America
Iteration 2

Gant crouched behind the bushes in the predawn light.

"Are you sure it was her?" Donovan asked again.

"Positive. You think I wouldn't know Detective Rose when I saw her?"

Donovan craned his neck to look at the apartment. "Should we rush the building?"

"No. She's always got weapons on her. Probably sleeps with her gun. We have to attack when she least expects it."

"The shower?" Donovan asked. "I don't mind that view."

Gant looked at him in horror. "You are a very sick man."

"You never thought about what she looks like naked?"

"No. I think about what she looks like dead. Alive, she thinks about what I look like dead. That's how we interact." He turned back to the apartment with a shudder. "There's nothing appealing about a woman who wants you in front of a firing squad."

"Sometimes the sexiest ones are the girls who want you dead." Donovan grinned. It took all of Gant's willpower not to slit his throat then and there.

The door to the apartment opened, and Detective Rose stepped out wearing jogging clothes and carrying her purse. Gant frowned. Who went jogging with a purse?

A car alarm beeped.

Nasty, twisty mind that detective had. Naturally, she wouldn't run near home. She was probably using her jogging time to try to triangulate his position, or the machine's. Either worked for him.

Gant patted Donovan's arm. "I've got an idea. Car wreck. We'll follow her to where she's going jogging and T-bone her car in an intersection. She'll never know what hit her."

Donovan frowned as Detective Rose drove away. "We need a certain kind of car to pull that off. Something with extra weight. Unless you want to snap your neck in the process."

"City maintenance vehicle?" Gant suggested.

"Good idea." Donovan nodded. "Let's tail her."

It wasn't hard to find the little gray car driving on the empty street. Detective Rose didn't check for a tail or try anything fancy. They watched her drive into the parking lot of an auto-body shop and jog off. "Easy enough," Gant said. "You want to stay here and watch the car, or do you want to go lift the other one?"

"Boosting cars isn't my strong suit," Donovan said with a grimace, as if Gant hadn't guessed from the scars on Donovan's knuckles what the other man's specialty was. Donovan was a wet-works man all the way.

Gant smiled. "I'll be back within an hour. If she tries to leave, stall. Give her a flat tire or something."

Forty minutes later, Gant pulled into a side street and parked the large truck used for breaking up trees that had fallen in storms. The wood chipper welded to the back gave the truck a nice heft. He climbed out of the cab and looped around the corner to where Donovan stood leaning against the chain-link fence. "Anything?"

Donovan shook his head. "She went for a jog and changed. Came back about ten minutes ago. She's inside now. That's her car there. Almost done."

The little gray car was having its tires filled. Gant could taste the anticipation of death on the air. He felt light as a feather—effervescent—and with a good kick off the ground, he could have flown. Removing Detective Rose from the equation would remove the lodestone from around his neck. Everything he'd ever wanted was here in this moment.

"You think she knows a way out of here?" Donovan asked.

"She wouldn't have crossed timelines if she didn't." Gant licked his lips in anticipation. "Can I drive the truck?"

Donovan raised an eyebrow. "If you want. Don't see what's so exciting about smashing a car."

Typical of the man, really. He was all hot and bothered with seeing Rose alive, but put her in the ground where she belonged, and Donovan was getting squeamish. "She dies, and everything is better. It's letting the tiger off the leash. Once she's gone, no one can stop us."

"No one's *trying* to stop us."

"Shut up," Gant ordered. Detective Rose walked out of the shop, waving to the man behind the counter. It was good that she looked a little less than perfect today. Her black hair wasn't as glossy in the humidity. Her signature purple jacket had a crease in it from sitting in the shop. The flaws made her look human, a little more mortal, a little bit less scary. She smiled as she climbed into her car, and so did Gant. Everything was perfect. "Into the truck." He shoved Donovan.

He ran toward the vehicle, hoping he'd planned it right. If she headed back to the apartment, there were two stop signs between her and the truck. Traffic wasn't heavy, but she wouldn't be zipping along, either. He didn't bother waiting for Donovan to close the door before he started the engine and pulled forward. The little side street had a stop sign.

Detective Rose didn't.

Gant held his breath, heart racing in anticipation.

The little gray car drove toward destiny.

There was a perfect moment. The synchrony of fluid movement as the car drove past and the truck surged forward. Metal met metal with a cacophonous crunch. Gant was thrown back in his seat, but he lifted his head grinning. *It had worked!* Everything he'd ever wanted.

Like a child racing to see the presents waiting for them on Three King's Day, he leapt out of the truck to survey the damage.

Detective Rose's head lay on the steering wheel of her car. The horn's blaring was the trumpet of God. The final proof that all was right in the world.

Donovan opened the side door. "Here, she's got some tech and papers. Let's take it and go."

Gant nodded, unable to take his eyes off the beautiful scene. Perhaps, in a perfect world, she would have seen his face as she died. The look of shock and fear would have heightened the experience. He knew it from other victims, but her look of terror would have been special. He sighed.

"Gant!"

"What?"

"We have to go before the *federales* arrive. Is there anything else we need?"

Gant reached through the broken glass and pulled Rose's head back. Lifeless black eyes stared back unseeing. "No. Let's go."

The jagged rhythms of Draxton's *Third Modern Symphony* pulled Mac from a dreamless sleep. "Sam?" He sat up and looked around the apartment, letting the phone ring. Hoss ran over to the couch, nubbin wagging. "Sam?"

No answer.

He punched the on button on his phone. "'lo. This is MacKenzie."

"Agent MacKenzie?" a quavering voice asked. It sounded vaguely familiar. For some reason, the color red popped into his mind.

"This is MacKenzie. Who's this?"

"Junior Agent Dan Edwin, sir. I . . . um . . . can you come over to the county hospital? I need some help."

Mac scratched his head and yawned. "Sure. Gimme a minute to get dressed. You're not bleeding to death or anything, are you?"

There was a sniffle from the other end of the line. "No. No, sir."

"Hostage situation?"

"No, sir." Edwin sounded like his puppy had just died. Poor kid. Probably got into trouble with some girl and didn't want the senior agent to know about.

Not too smart calling the senior agent's roommate. "Hold tight, Edwin. I'll be there in fifteen minutes." Mac hung up the phone. "Sam! Hey, Sam, you in the shower?" He waited a second before shrugging and heading to her room. Not his fault if she couldn't hear him from back there. If he accidentally walked in on her in a towel, it wasn't like he was going to cry. And Sam was never overly body shy.

He smiled and opened her bedroom door. "Sam?"

The room was empty, the shower off. Her gym bag and car keys were missing from her dresser.

Mac looked down at Hoss. "She left? Without me?"

Hoss wagged his stub of a tail with enthusiasm.

"You only say that because you want part of my breakfast." Heading back to the kitchen, he dialed Sam's number.

After three rings, the phone beeped. "This is Agent Samantha Rose of the Commonwealth Bureau of Investigation. I'm not able to answer my phone at the moment, but if you leave a detailed message and a contact number, I will call you as soon as I am able." The phone beeped again.

"Sam, it's Mac. Edwin just called me from the hospital." He balanced the phone between his ear and shoulder and pulled a loaf of bread from the fridge. "Poor kid sounds pretty tore up." He took the peanut butter from the cupboard and smeared it on the wheat bread to make a quick sandwich. "I'm not sure where you are, but I'm going to take my rental and go see if I can help. I'll give you a ring if it's serious. It's, uh"— he glanced at the clock—"just after eight. I guess you took off early to hit the gym or something. Call me around lunch if you're free. I'll swing by your office later and be home by seven at the latest." He swallowed an "I love you," before choking out, "See ya," and hanging up.

But he realized something: It was love. Not hero

worship or lust, but pure love. Sam was the first thing he thought of when he woke, his last thought before falling asleep. His internal compass swung due SAM. In the past decade, she was the only thing he was sure about. Even if she could never see that, he loved her. They might never be more than friends, and he'd accepted the fact that eventually she'd probably fall in love with some-one else, but between now and then, he was going to make the most of the time he had with her. Tonight, he planned on convincing her to teach him how to cook. Something basic and hands-on. Something that would mean she spent an hour or so standing next to him.

He held the butter knife out, so Hoss could lick it, and scarfed down his sandwich. A swig of milk, a minute to brush his teeth, then his shoes were on and he was out the door following the rental car's GPS to the county hospital on Beachside Road. It was a wide, squat building painted the same pale gold as the sand on the beaches, with crushed coquina shells decorating the arches. It had probably looked good forty years ago when it was new. Now it looked faded, half-forgotten. The large parking lot was three-quarters empty, and a monument to local plague victims, carved in obsidian, stood between visitors and the main door, looking like a promise of death.

Grimacing, Mac walked past, trying not to look too closely. It had been nearly thirty years since the last victim was interred but it still wasn't long enough to make the fear of the plague fade.

Agent Edwin was pacing the empty lobby when

Mac walked in. The younger man looked up with red-rimmed, tear-swollen eyes. "Thank you." He closed his eyes and rocked on his heels. "Thank you for coming, Agent MacKenzie."

"My pleasure." Mac tried to smile, but the plague statue outside had put fear and doubt in his mind. Please, God, if you're out there, don't let it be the plague. "What'd you need me for?"

Edwin took a deep breath. "There was a . . . an accident. Hit-and-run."

"You look okay," Mac said.

Edwin nodded. "Agent Rose . . ." The younger man looked up at him with his lips set in a flat line. "They brought her here."

"Sam?" His voice cracked and thundered, shaking the bulletproof glass of the lobby doors. His calm shattered. "Why the hell didn't you tell me it was about Sam? I'd have been here in minutes. Where is she? I can . . ." He took a deep breath. "Do they not have a surgeon? I can do that. I mean . . . yeah. Where is she? Get me some gloves. This'll be fine."

A woman in medical scrubs with bright pink and green flowers came through a heavy metal door. "Agent Edwin? Is everything all right?"

"Um . . ." Edwin looked panicked between the nurse and Mac. "This is the senior agent in the district right now. Agent MacKenzie. He's a medical examiner from Chicago."

"Where's Sam?" Mac demanded, doing everything he could to get his temper under control.

The nurse frowned with disapproval. "Maybe you should calm down a little before you come back."

"No," Mac shouted.

She stepped back.

He swallowed, then coughed. "I mean, I'm fine," he said in the calmest voice he could summon. "Sam's my best friend. I'd like to see her, please."

"I'm . . . I'm sorry." The nurse pulled a green curtain back as she turned. "Dead on impact."

His world tilted, spiraled away, colors fading as he realized what he was looking at. Sam lay lifeless on the hospital cot, neck twisted at an unnatural angle. Oxygen fled the room.

"It happened instantly," the nurse said in a consoling voice. "She didn't feel anything."

"Sam." His knees hit the tiled floor. "Sam?"

"I can get you a chair," the nurse offered in a calm, rational voice so at odds with what he felt. "We tried to contact her next of kin, but her mother was in a meeting, and her father didn't pick up."

"He's dead," Agent Edwin said. "And she doesn't talk to her mother."

"Oh."

"I called Agent MacKenzie because he's listed under her family contacts," Edwin said. "At least on her bureau file."

"How irregular."

Mac reached for her hand. She'd painted her nails lilac. It was . . . cute. He'd never seen her with her nails done before. "Her hand's cold."

"Yes, she's been dead for over an hour now," the nurse said. "We just needed you to come in and confirm her identity. Officer Hadley was first on scene, and she recognized Miss Rose, but there was no purse or wallet found."

"Probably stolen," Edwin muttered.

"This is Sam," Mac said with all the emotion of his dead partner. "Samantha Lynn Rose, CBI senior agent."

"Wonderful! You have the condolences on the loss of your coworker. Would you like her cremated? We can have her in an urn by dinnertime, just say the word."

The ghost of Sam Rose, Agent Perfect, rose over his shoulder with her arms crossed. Something clicked in his brain. The emotions drained away, locked behind steel walls of practicality. Mac stood up. "You said it was a hit-and-run?"

"Yes," the nurse confirmed.

"Is that common for this area?"

"We have one or two every year, but not really. It was enough to shake up the three witnesses, for sure—they're all being treated for shock. When we do get them, it's usually drunks driving around after holidays, but there's no evidence of that."

"No evidence the drivers were drunk?"

"I'm sorry, there was no one on scene. No witnesses." The nurse frowned. "Is that a no on the cremation? Only, anything else is a lot more paperwork. If it's all the same to you . . ."

"A CBI agent killed under suspicious circumstances is treated as a homicide investigation until the culprit is found and the situation explained." He looked down at her lifeless face, already starting to swell from decay. There was a pale mark on her neck, like a scar he'd never noticed before. "Have the hospital finish any work they need to do, then have the corpse transported to the CBI office. The medical examiner will need to do an autopsy."

Never refer to the deceased by their name—it was an old army trick. A corpse was an it. A dead friend on the ground was an inoperative combat unit, a fallen hero. But no one said Johnny was dead. Mac swallowed hard. The ghost of Sam raised a phantom eyebrow in challenge.

"Agent Edwin, you're with me. Nurse. Make this a priority. I want the body in my morgue in under an hour."

The bright Florida sunshine hit him like a gut punch as they exited the hospital. He was going to get Sam to go to the beach with him. There was a little seaside restaurant he'd spotted on their drive yesterday that looked like it could knock out a good po' boy. He was going to take her there. She wasn't supposed to leave him like this. Not here. Not now.

They had time.

He knew that, eventually, Sam would die. She'd done it once, five years in the future, then been caught in a madman's nightmare that sucked her back through time. Her face on the diagnostic screen kept him up at night, but they had time. To solve things. To stop her murder. To be together.

He slammed his fists down on the hood of his rental car, searing his hands with the heat.

"Sir?" Edwin looked at him with puffy eyes. "Sir, what do we do?"

"Do?" Mac raised an eyebrow, a perfect imitation of his Agent Perfect. "We do what we were trained to do and solve the murder. We'll start with this morning. Retrace her steps. Find out where she went and why and with whom. We find her killer, and we interrogate them until their gonads shrivel in fear. Then we lock them away for the rest of their miserable life. And then we get therapy."

"Therapy?"

"Lots of therapy. Trust me on this." He unlocked his car. "Get in, I'm driving."

Edwin didn't look happy with the offer, but he climbed in, tall frame bent over and beefy shoulders hunched. The junior agent buckled himself in and pulled out his phone.

"I don't need the GPS," Mac said.

"Oh, no, sir. I was just . . ." He waved the phone near Mac's ear as if that explained something. "She was really dressed up today, I thought."

It took Mac a moment to realize Edwin was talking about Sam. He nodded as they waited for a light to change. "She had her nails painted. I don't remember her ever doing that when we lived together in Alabama."

"It was the purple blouse that got me," Edwin said with a heavy sigh. "She looks good in gem tones, but

I've never seen her wear them to the office. Do you think her boyfriend gave them to her?"

Mac hit a curve a little too fast, and the brake too hard as they came to a stop sign. The tires squealed in protest. "Boyfriend?" He kept his voice flat, but he could feel the muscle under his high tic.

"You, ah, didn't know? She used to talk about some guy she lived with in Alabama. And then I think this week she was with someone. It sort of slipped out. I thought, maybe, he bought her some stuff."

Praying for patience worked for some people. He'd seen Sam do it when she was frustrated with him, but closing his eyes while weaving in and out of erratic south Florida traffic seemed like a bad idea. "Edwin, *I* lived with her in Alabama. *I'm* the one who just showed up in town."

"Oh!" Edwin swiveled in his seat. "You? You seem so normal."

"Why wouldn't I be normal?"

"Agent Rose talked about you like you were a genius. I pictured some heroic-looking guy who was, you know, taller."

"I'm six-two!"

Edwin shrugged, rubbing his shoulders against the fabric-lined car seat so it was audible. "Seems short to me is all."

Mac growled as he turned into the bureau parking lot. A bright turquoise Montero Sunlit sat in Sam's parking spot. It was an exquisite car that breathed sensuality and wealth like a French vintner inhaled the scent of grapes on a hot autumn afternoon. He'd never wanted to destroy a car so much. "How dare they?"

"What?"

He pressed his lips together, picturing the brazen gez who'd violated her space.

"Sir?"

"I'm fine." He refrained from punching the car only because he knew from firsthand experience that it would deploy the airbags, and those things hurt. "Let's get inside. I need you to pull up Agent Rose's schedule, then I need all the traffic data for the area. Find out which businesses have security cameras facing the street." He glared at the Montero Sunlit as he locked his rental car. Damn, Sam would have looked gorgeous in that. With a little black dress and those extra high heels he'd seen at the back of her closet one day. Just picturing her there made his knees weak with pain.

No more Sam.

He couldn't process the thought. One step at a time. Find a cause of death. Find a killer. Mourn later. Mourn after he'd done everything else he could do for her.

Following Edwin into the CBI building, he could almost smell Sam's perfume. If he closed his eyes, he could hear her heels tapping a delicate staccato across the marble floors upstairs. She was there, only in spirit, but she was there.

Agent Edwin opened the office door and collapsed behind his impeccably tidy desk, staring into the distance.

The thousand-yard stare. Mac knew it from too many mornings catching his own reflection in the dirty mirror in the dingy apartment he survived in before Sam came along. She'd pulled him out of the depression and given him a reason to live again.

A light at Edwin's desk flickered as he turned the phone back on. "She was so pretty in that shirt. Why'd she never wear purple to the office?"

"Regulation states a white blouse or button-down shirt with tan, navy, or black slacks or skirts are appropriate attire," Mac said offhand. "She said the black made her look like a stewardess."

The door behind him slammed open, and Mac jumped, hand dropping toward where his sidearm should be.

"Edwin, if you're going to be late, call me," Sam said.

Mac started shaking.

She was right there. Navy skirt three inches above her knee, two-inch navy kitten heels shined to a fine polish, regulation blouse that was still just tight enough to emphasize the swell of her breasts.

And she was looking at him. "Mac, did you walk Hoss before you left?"

"Agent . . . Agent Rose?" Edwin stood up unsteadily. "Um . . ."

"I hate the word 'um,'" Sam said with an oh-so-typical eye roll.

The junior agent turned pale, blood draining from his face. "I don't know how to tell you this, ma'am, but you're dead."

Mac's strangled sob turned into a choked laugh. He covered his mouth and dropped into the stiff secondhand couch that completed the government office set. There was a god, and that god was probably Loki, possibly Coyote. Definitely a trickster god bent on torturing Mac until the last of his sanity dribbled away.

The clock ticked as he giggled madly.

Edwin shuffled like fire ants were crawling up his trousers. "Ma'am, it's nothing personal, ma'am. It's just that you are dead, ma'am. I . . . ah . . . um . . . went to the hospital. You died. In a car accident."

Sam's shiver, such a strange movement, focused Mac's attention.

"Sam?" He tasted the salt of tears on his lips.

"I had a dream last night that I was hit in a collision. My neck ached like it'd been snapped. I couldn't get back to bed, so I dropped my car off at the auto-body shop to get the dents knocked out and went for a run. Wound up here, showered and changed in the locker room downstairs." She rubbed her neck. "I was surprised Agent Edwin wasn't here, but I must have left my phone in the car . . ." Sam's word slowed to a halt under the weight of his stare. "Mac? Can you please explain why you're crying?"

"Edwin called me this morning from the hospital. Forty-five minutes ago, I arrived and was told you'd been killed in a hit-and-run accident."

Horror suffused her face, and she ran to him. "Oh, no! Are you okay?" She hovered just out of reach.

"Am I okay?" Mac laughed. "Me? You're worried about me when you're the one I saw dead?"

Sam's eyes went wide, and she looked between him and Edwin. "I'm fine. You're the one who just saw his best friend in the morgue. All I had was a bad dream."

He took her outstretched hand and pulled her almost close enough. The scent of her perfume surrounded him like the blessing of a saint. Warmth radiated off her body. Her pulse beat a steady rhythm that calmed the wild despair.

Agent Edwin cleared his throat. Mac tightened his grip on Sam's hand and looked at the younger agent, professional behavior be damned. "Yes?"

"I . . . I hate to be the one to bring this up, ma'am, sir, but how do we know she's Agent Rose?"

"Who else would I be?" Sam demanded.

"A clone. A spy. A plant or actress of some kind. We positively identified the body at the hospital as Agent Samantha Rose," Edwin said. "Both Agent MacKenzie and I know her very well. What is the likelihood of someone with your physical description, in your car, not being you?"

Sam took a deep breath and let it out. "Statistically, I admit the numbers aren't in my favor. However, there are instances of this sort of thing's happening before."

"I've never heard of them," Edwin said belligerently.

"You don't have the right security clearance," Mac shot back, instinctively siding with Sam.

"Sir, I don't want to question your judgment, but doesn't this strike you as the least bit fishy?"

Mac looked up at Sam. Agent Perfect in her uniform and office smile. He let her hand go. "Fine. DNA test?"

Sam shrugged. "If this is what we think it is, the DNA test isn't going to be conclusive."

"What?" Edwin asked.

Mac waved his question away. "Twenty questions?"

Sam nodded. "Agent Edwin, there is classified information that only you and I would know, correct?"

He frowned in puzzlement. "I suppose."

"What about the contents of your primary evaluation when you first reported to this station? I described you as overexcitable and too trusting."

Edwin licked his lips clearly caught between a desire to believe Sam was the real Sam and his loyalty to the truth. "With all due respect, ma'am, anyone could know that. Especially since you arrived at the office before I did. Anyone walking in could have hacked into our system and checked Agent Rose's comments on my review."

"Especially since our password is 'ice-cream-for-all-6-7-8-9,' " Sam said. "All right. When Agent MacKenzie came I told you to find me an ME and you scrambled a fighter jet. I said it was overkill."

"Again, ma'am, dozens of people were in the building with you when we had that conversation. It doesn't prove anything."

"I have one," Mac said. He looked Sam in the eye.

"The first time we met, what bra were you wearing and why did I see it?"

Sam's cheeks flushed. "I can't believe you're asking me that in front of my junior agent."

"Just answer the question."

"Black, and you saw it because my white shirt was wet. The maintenance man turned the sprinklers on and said it was an accident. I reported him, and Marrins laughed and told me I should have come in right away if I wanted to file a complaint, not go home to change and whine about it later."

Mac nodded. "She's Sam."

"Then . . . who is the hospital delivering to the morgue?" Edwin asked.

"Probably also me," Sam said. "Sit down, Edwin, I think it's time we had a little talk about the facts of life."

"Like, the birds and the bees?"

"No," Sam said with a shake of her head. "More quantum physics and the transient nature of reality. Don't worry, I'll talk slow, and Mac will fill in any of the gaps in your education."

Edwin looked at Sam dubiously. "A time machine? I don't think that's how time works, ma'am."

"That's what we said." She punched in the code to the morgue and scanned her hand for verification. "Dr. Emir started with a theory."

"The idea of a multiverse has always been very popular," Mac said.

"In science fiction!" Edwin looked at her pleadingly. "The idea that someone bent time and space, though? I'm sorry, it sounds ridiculous."

"It *is* ridiculous," Sam said. "But so are birds that can't fly, giraffes, and someone named Zoe Frillmumper running for president of France—but they all exist."

Mac went to the morgue cooler and rolled out Jane Doe.

Sam picked up the name tag that read SAMANTHA ROSE and tossed it in the recycler angrily. "We can't call her Jane Doe. We already worked a Jane Doe case. Jane is Jane. This is . . ." She stared at Mac waiting for help.

"Jane the Second? Jana Doe? Jillian Doe?" Mac shrugged. "We both know it's you again."

"Again?" Edwin's voice cracked into a squeak. "How many times have you done this, ma'am?"

"This?" Sam pointed at her doppelganger on the autopsy cart. "Dying? This is the second time I've seen a corpse that looked exactly like me. It's not like I make it a hobby or anything."

"That's two more than most people see," Mac said.

She rolled her eyes and refrained from punching his shoulder. "Let's pretend we don't know this is me. What we have here is an unidentified woman in her midtwenties to midthirties who was the victim of a hit-and-run accident, possibly in a stolen vehicle. We need facts, boys, not guesses."

Mac and Edwin both nodded, one looking grim, the other looking terrified.

"Edwin, pop quiz: In a case like this, what is the first thing you do?"

"Check for identity carried on the victim such as a citizen ID card, driver's license, or passport. But none of those were found at the scene of the crash."

Sam raised an eyebrow. "Mac?"

"Check the car for prints, see if there is security footage covering the area, then check the missing-persons database to see if Jane matches anyone on the list." He looked at Edwin. "Solve the murder first and get the killer off the street. Identity cards can be forged or stolen. It takes five minutes and a pair of scissors to make something that will pass a cursory inspection."

"Exactly," Sam said. "Although I'd really love to know why this lady had my car. Edwin, get me the security tapes from the body shop. See if they think they have my car still or if she came in and impersonated me. If they gave the car to her, find out how she paid for the repairs. We might be able to backtrack and see where she's been."

Edwin made a note on his datpad and nodded. "I'll call you as soon as I have information, ma'am."

As the heavy door clicked shut behind him, she let the gut-churning sensation of fear creep over her. Bile crawled up her throat at the sight of the dead body, and she turned away. "How long do you think she's been wandering around our iteration?"

"I'm not sure there's a way of knowing," Mac said. "You could go around asking people if they've seen a lady who looks like you wearing a purple jacket."

Sam closed her eyes and swore under her breath. At this point, a few more Hail Marys for blasphemy were the least of her worries.

Mac raised an eyebrow. "What?"

"The lady who rented a storage unit to Henry Troom said a lady in a purple jacket came in asking questions. She thought the woman was a reporter."

"You think it was Jane?"

"Jillian," Sam said. "The first one was Jane Doe. This one is Jillian Doe. The lady said the 'reporter' was wearing purple, speaking with a heavy Spanish accent, and drove a gray Alexian Virgo which she drove into the pylons."

"Ah, well, that explains the vandalism at least," Mac said. He looked at the cold body on the table.

Her body, swelling from decomposition, bruised and bloody from the crash. She looked away.

Mac cleared his throat. "So . . . our Mystery Sam is more of a Juanita than a Jane?"

"Maybe." She rubbed her aching neck with a cold hand. "Put her in the machine. Let's get the autopsy going."

"Are you sure you want to stay for this?" Mac asked.

"We could be barking up the wrong tree, you know. I can think of at least one very plausible explanation for all of this that doesn't involve time travel at all."

He looked dubiously at her. "You know a Spaniard who wants you dead?"

"Maybe not dead, but my mother would love for me to forget about the bureau and time machines.

It wouldn't be hard to find a woman my height and skin color in Madrid. A little cosmetic surgery . . ." Sam shrugged. "My mother likes mind games. She wouldn't be above ruining my career by sending an imposter to start a scandal or destroy the evidence so she can gaslight me."

Mac was watching her intently.

"What?"

"You're getting more paranoid than I am. That's not good."

She rolled her eyes. "Just get me a DNA sample and her age."

"She's not a countdown clock," Mac said. "You can't estimate the time of your death based on her accident. I don't think that's how the timelines work."

"Really?" The autopsy scanner clicked shut and hummed softly. She turned around and looked at the metal coffin. "Does she have a healed fracture on her left ankle?"

"Sam . . ."

"Does she?"

Lips pressed into a flat line Mac checked the readout. "Yes, there's sign of a fracture."

"And her other scars and injuries? How many of those are going to line up?"

"I don't know. I can't even compare Alabama Jane to Florida Jane because of the damage Alabama Jane took in the accident!"

"I hate those names."

Mac gave her sideways look of frustration. "Noted."

"Gene scan?"

"Unofficially, you. Officially, I'm going to run the tests through the Birmingham lab."

"Orlando has a good gene lab."

"But I know the people at Birmingham, and I know they can run all the tests I need done the way I want them done." He frowned. "I'm half-tempted to take this whole case to Chicago and run the tests there myself."

"That's not a bad idea." He was brittle. This was a trigger in too many, she could see that. The PTSD that had driven him into depression and self-abuse was only a breath away.

Mac gave her a narrow-eyed look that managed to convey disgust, disbelief, and a general unwillingness to give an inch on his position.

"I'm serious. This is the end of the case. Juanita has been here long enough to steal my car, twice, so that's handled. She took my car when she saw an opportunity. She worked with Troom to build a new machine, so she could get back, and she died. No one is targeting me."

"But why does she come back at all? Henry dies from a gunshot nine months after the gun is fired. Nealie dies, what, fifteen years after the car accident that should have killed him. This extra agent dies in a car accident, so what? Who killed her? Who killed Bradet? You're going to tell me you don't think this isn't tied to his murder?" He was inches away and fuming.

"Don't be snarky with me!"

"I will be as snarky as I want! I saw you in a morgue today, Sam. Dead."

"Exactly." She stepped away taking a deep breath. "Let's face it, I'm very good at ending up dead."

"That's not funny."

"I'm not laughing. I'm saying you should go home."

Mac's eyes narrowed with outrage.

Sam held her ground. "You're ready to break, and I'm not letting you do that to yourself. You're still recovering. This isn't going to help. It would be irresponsible of me, as a senior agent, to let you stay. It would be selfish as your friend to ask you to stay."

He rolled his shoulders back, ready to fight.

"The threat's past," Sam said. "Now it's time for me to pick up the pieces. There's an APB out on Donovan. He can't hide forever.

"I don't like the report I'll have to write for Henry, but I will, and I'll send it to Director Loren with most of it blacked out. He'll use sarcasm and grind his teeth, but it won't kill my career. Nealie and Miss Doe here weren't killed by Marrins. If Miss Doe killed Nealie, then there is evidence in this mess somewhere. I'll find it."

"I'm not leaving, Sam."

She crossed her arms across her chest. "I'll be calling Chicago within the hour to tell them we're booking you a flight home. I'm a big girl. I can arrest reckless drivers all by myself. Your job isn't to protect me, Mac. You've got that Captain United look in your eye. Reel it in."

"I am not a fragile flower in need of protection, Agent Rose." He ground her name out like a curse.

Sam crossed her arms across her chest. "And I'm

not a monster who's willing to hurt you, Agent MacKenzie." Two could play the name game. Mac was hot stuff, but he couldn't out-Prim her even on his best day.

He took a deep breath, nostrils flaring, and shrugged. "Fine. Call Chicago."

She glared at him. This was definitely a trick.

"I already put in for leave. Told them I wanted to use up some of my vacation days."

"You cannot vacation in my morgue!"

His face lit up with a wicked grin. "Watch me."

Sam put her hands on her hips. The power pose didn't help. "You are such a stubborn cuss some days!" He smiled. "I swear, MacKenzie, why can't you listen to reason?"

"I'm being perfectly reasonable."

"I'm very tempted to handcuff you to a piece of furniture until this is over," Sam said. *Saints and angels, this man would tempt Mother Mary to swear.* "I just . . . I don't want you hurt."

"I won't be." He stepped forward and pulled her gently into a hug. "Listen, I'll be fine, Sam. If I can't handle it, I'll let you know. But we make a great team. Let me help you." Lips brushed across her forehead in a tender kiss.

She leaned against him for a moment longer than was appropriate for an office setting, then broke away.

"Fine—let's find out how I keep dying."

CHAPTER 14

*No matter what we want to believe, we cannot change
the past. We can change the world around us, but our
own personal histories never change. I can't undo
what I did ten years ago. Going back and stopping my
younger self doesn't change my history, it only splinters
the world's future.*

~ **excerpt from *Thoughts on Einselection***
by Saree Tong I1—2076

Wednesday March 26, 2070
Florida District 8
Commonwealth of North America
Iteration 2

Sam walked the perimeter of the conference room,
trying to see the individual details of the paintings
collected from Henry's storage unit instead of seeing
them as a whole. The problem was that they were a
cohesive whole. Ordered by the dates on the back, the
large paintings created a complete cityscape that bled

from futuristic metropolis to decaying wasteland in a faded rainbow of colors.

Mac propped his feet on the table and leaned his chair back on two legs. "This is a mess."

"We'll tag them as evidence and store them later."

"That's not what I'm talking about."

"They're paintings, Mac, not windows into another world or glimpses of the future."

"Wanna bet money on that?"

She looked over her shoulder and glared at him. "There's a connection here. Miss Doe did not wind up in this iteration—in my car—by accident. Henry had the answer to how she got here. If we have a How and When, we might find a Why. Once I have a Why, I'll have the killer."

"I'm glad to see you let the reckless-driver thing drop," Mac said.

They'd argued about the case over dinner, and again after their morning run. Life would be so much less complicated if the deaths weren't tied together, but neither she nor Mac was a believer in coincidences. Not anymore. "I'm not ruling out reckless driver yet. But I'm thinking more about timelines at the moment, trying to figure out who saw what when."

Mac tapped his pen on the table. "Did you get the sheriff to confirm he'd seen Edwin's pirate at the cemetery?"

"Not yet. I'm waiting for him to call me back."

There was a knock at the conference-room door,

and Agent Edwin shuffled in, sidling past the art blocking the main door. "Good morning?" He looked around the room in confusion.

"How'd your bedtime reading go?" Sam asked, nodding to Henry's notebook that Edwin had in his hand.

"Um." Edwin scratched his head. "There is nothing in here that you are going to want to hear."

"Really?" She raised an eyebrow.

Edwin shrugged. "It's nonsense. Just ramblings about dreams and calculations for things that don't exist. It's . . ."

"Nonsense?" Sam offered. Edwin nodded. "Henry wasn't insane," Mac said.

"You wouldn't get that from his journal." Edwin slid the book across the tabletop to Mac. "He wrote in pen on dead-tree paper, which gives you a hint of where his mental state was."

Mac frowned in confusion. "He liked vintage style?"

"He was paranoid," Edwin said. "People who don't use electronics are always paranoid that someone is after their secrets. But the thing is, there are no secrets in here. He was documenting his nightmares. All you can glean from this is that Dr. Troom needed to see a therapist."

"What did he dream about?" Sam asked.

"Dying." Edwin shrugged.

"We got that from skimming it," Mac said. "What else did you see?"

"Notes on convergence events and decoherence. Sounds physics-y, but it was just scribbled in the margins. I thought they were partial notes from a lab project."

Mac flipped the book over onto the surface of the smart table and did something. A moment later, a picture of sine waves weaving in and around each other appeared on the conference-room screen. "This drawing appears on multiple pages," Mac said. He touched his screen and enlarged the picture. "Look here, where multiple sine waves hit the same point on the graph? Troom called it a Convergence Event."

Sam sat down and pulled her own tablet out. "All right. So what's a Decoherence Event according to Henry? Is that when these iterations pull apart?"

Mac flipped through the pages. "Doesn't look like it. He has the timelines moving apart labeled as an Expansion Event."

Edwin sighed. "The first two pages have drawings and the word 'decoherence,' " he said as he took a seat at the table. "It made my head ache," he added with a guilty look at Sam.

She shrugged. "Physics wasn't my best class either."

"It doesn't make any sense!" Edwin said in frustration. "Time is linear. It moves forward. You don't just have multiple timelines."

"It's the Many Worlds Hypothesis," Mac said. "The theory that anything that can happen does happen in some variable universe. Dr. Emir called them iterations of time, and that's the school of thought Henry was working from."

"What I don't get is *why*," Sam said. "He knew this

theory killed Emir, so why go and try to re-create the past mistake?"

Edwin and Mac both stared at her as if she just grown a second head.

"What am I missing?"

"Why does anyone try to re-create a scenario?" Mac asked. "Why does your brain replay embarrassing scenes from high school at 3 A.M.? Why do you go to the place you went on your first date on the anniversary of the day you broke up?"

Sam shook her head. "I don't know."

"You do it because you want to change something. Emir created the machine to pass messages, to stop tragedies like terrorist attacks. Marrins wanted to use the machine to change the nationhood vote. Troom . . ." Mac shrugged. "What one event do you think he wanted to change the most?"

Sam bit her lip as the truth slowly took shape. "Emir's death. If Henry could have changed one thing, that would have been it, right? To go back and save his mentor?"

"He had everything he needed," Mac said.

Edwin cleared his throat. "So, the bullet? From the original crime scene in Alabama? Are you saying Dr. Troom was shot with his mentor?"

Mac raised an eyebrow and shrugged in a sort of what-else-is-there? way. "It fits the facts."

Sam pushed her tablet across the table in disgust. "The backlash of the machine's collapsing would have created enough force to cause the lab explosion."

"Lots of little electrical fires as the collapsing time wave short-circuited the tech in the room. Friction burns." Mac shook his head. "Cause of death? Arrogance and stupidity."

"Stupid idiot. What makes anyone think messing around with time travel is a good idea?" Sam frowned at Henry's notebook like it was about to bite her.

"Most people make mistakes," Mac said. "They have things they want to undo."

She reached for her tablet and made a mark next to Henry's name. Case closed. "Fine. Henry was an idiot. This will be super fun to explain at the next district meeting."

"It's all classified," Mac said. "What are the chances they won't ask too many questions?"

"Poor." That was not a day she was looking forward to. Director Loren hadn't gotten to his current position by not asking questions. Her fists clenched at the thought of the fight they were likely to have.

Edwin cleared his throat. "Um. I'm going to go see if the lobby has any donuts left. You want some?"

"Chocolate glazed," Sam said.

"Anything but cake donuts or strawberry frosting," Mac said, as Edwin hurried away. "Did we scare him?"

"Maybe a little." She sighed. "This doesn't feel right, you know?"

"Of course it doesn't—you didn't get to lock up the killer. A murder case where the shooter was dead before the shooting is not something they cover in the academy textbooks."

"It's more than that." Sam stood and started pacing past the paintings. "I feel like . . . I'm working the wrong case, maybe? That I'm looking at this and seeing the wrong thing. Like in Alabama. A break-in didn't quite make sense, but we ran with the idea because there was no other explanation."

Mac rested his elbows on the table. "You think we're missing a bigger crime?"

"Not a crime, a threat. This is a threat," Sam said, gesturing to the paintings. "There's something here. Bits and pieces, and I put the puzzle together wrong."

She stared at the paintings of Alabama. "There was this book when I was a kid with this fuzzy blue guy scared of the monster on the last page. You turned the pages, and at the end, the guy is standing alone."

"Is this a 'you have nothing to fear but fear itself' thing?" Mac asked

"More of an existential thing. Only you can destroy you. You are the real monster." Sam walked toward the gray landscape.

"And you bring this up because?"

"Because this was a story. Emir was trying to tell a story with his painting. We know how this story ends." She stopped in front of the first gray portrait of Iteration 1. "It's the story of Sam, and, spoiler alert! Sam dies."

"A Sam dies," Mac said. "One possible you."

"Jane died. I died. Then I died again. In, what? Three years? Two? A car crash is better than torture, but I'm still dead. Can you hear the clock going tick-tock? I'm going to die, sooner rather than later. I know how. I know where. I've got a good guess as to why, but I'm missing the *who*."

"Spoiler alert, Sam: everyone dies! That's what 'THE END' means. Life isn't Happily Ever After and riding off into the sunset. Life is death. You die. I die. We all die. Doesn't matter. All that matters is that you die knowing you did something."

"What I want to do is find my killer and put him in the ground. I feel like raging against the dying light."

"Well. Good. Juanita Doe is a homicide, let's solve it. It's one more death in the ten thousand."

"The what?"

"Every life is ten thousand deaths. You've never heard it before?" Mac asked. Sam shook her head. "You exist because of death. People who lived and died and in between had children who lived and died as your ancestors. All the plants and animals you consume. They die so you can live. Ten thousand deaths, and the goal is to make your death one of the ten thousand that brings a new and better life to the world. "

Sam frowned. "Ten thousand? That sounds low. If we're talking about every lettuce leaf or grain of rice, ten thousand barely covers a week."

"It's a poem. It's meant to be metaphorical."

"Terrible poem. That's going to bother me, you know. Instead of wondering about sodium content of my dinner, I'm going to wonder how many trees I've killed before they could grow because I'm eating almond slices. Thanks."

"Anytime."

"We have a problem," Edwin said as he slammed the door open.

"No donuts?" Mac asked.

"There's a guy who sent a thing to the news saying he killed you, ma'am," Edwin said as he gulped in air.

"A guy sent a thing?" Sam raised an eyebrow.

Edwin waved his hand. "A video thingy? It's playing on the channels downstairs, and the office phone keeps ringing. There's a news crews outside!"

Sam shut her eyes. "Of course there is."

"What are we supposed to do?" Edwin asked.

"I'm going to go down and hold a press conference. I'll tell everyone I'm not dead. And then I'm going to schedule a meeting with the regional director and explain this."

"Does the regional director have the security clearance for this?" Mac asked.

"He's going to have to get that expedited."

There was quite the crowd outside when Sam arrived. Traditional camera people and reporters were vying for spots with the automated media bots, all creating a ruckus that would put a rowdy preschool to shame. The head of the WIC office glared at Sam and told her the CBI was not invited to this year's Christmas party. Sam just adjusted her blazer and painted on a sardonic smile.

She stepped out into the sunshine, briefly wishing

she were home in Toronto, and raised her hand. "Quiet down please. Thank you. Thank you for responding so promptly. Our field office had just received the news of the death threat when the junior agent noticed you gathering." She didn't add that a flock of vultures had more decorum. Saints and angels knew she'd gotten an earful after snapping at a reporter during the trial last summer in Alabama. "Now, if we can do this in an orderly fashion, I'd like to answer your questions and get back to work. Let's not waste the taxpayer's time. First question?"

A woman in a red blouse raised her hand at a fraction of the speed of light. "Mandy Martin, Channel 9 news. Is it true that your car was in an accident this morning?"

"Yes," Sam said. "My vehicle was taken from the repair shop by an unidentified woman. She was subsequently in a fatal hit-and-run accident. The police are working with the CBI to identify the driver of the other vehicle."

A man crowding his way to the front jumped in as she took a breath. "Agent Rose, is it true that you are a clone?"

She raised both her eyebrows. "No. Are you from Channel 2?"

"Stach Christel, Channel two evening news, indepth reports on everything you need to know," the reporter rattled off in a single breath. "You were accused of being a clone a few months ago. Do you still deny it?"

"I do. My blood work was made public and tested by independent labs," Sam said, teeth grinding together as she smiled.

Another hand. "Richone Lawley. Agent Rose, was the woman killed in the hit-and-run this morning your shadow?"

"No," Sam said. "I don't own a shadow. I don't support cloning though I do continue to openly support clone rights and equality. The victim of this morning's accident has yet to be identified, but we will be doing genetic testing."

"What about the man who claims to have killed you?" another reporter shouted. "Do you know who he is?"

Sam took a deep breath and smiled beatifically. "I haven't had a chance to watch the video sent to the news stations, but this"—she held up a packet of manila folders—"is the current death-threat log for this bureau office for the year. Three months into the year, and this is our seventeenth death threat. All of them are fully investigated. We invite the public to help us. To that end, copies of the death threats will be sent to every media outlet in the district. Citizens are invited to review the files and report their findings to the bureau. Additionally, since this is a hit-and-run accident, the county has offered a five-thousand-dollar cash reward—nontaxable—to anyone with a tip that leads to the arrest and conviction of the other driver."

There was a buzz in the crowd, and the reporters called in to their station executives.

Mandy Martin's hand raised again. "Agent Rose,

does the bureau have a record of events like this happening before?"

"Hit-and-run accidents or car theft?" Sam asked. She shook her head. "The bureau is aware of similar incidents, but there's no known record of someone's targeting and killing bureau agents with vehicular trauma." At least not to her knowledge. People hunting bureau agents hadn't ever been something she felt the need to study.

"Agent Rose, why were *you* targeted?"

"You'd have to ask the man trying to kill me I'm afraid. His motives are a mystery to me. If he'd like to turn himself in so we can discuss his concerns, I am more than willing to sit down and speak with him." Sam held up her hand. "One last question, please. The rest of your concerns can be directed to the field office and will be responded to in a timely fashion." Poor Edwin. She probably owed him dinner for putting him on phone duty.

"Agent Rose—Fellis Marr of Channel 7 news. My station can find no record of a felon named Nialls Gant on the public record. Is there a reason his record is not public? Is it true what they're saying on social media, that Gant is a government agent? Is this the start of a political coup in Florida?"

Sam really wished she'd had the time to watch the blasted video before she'd come to the conference. But, that was politics. You lied and you smiled. She smiled. "To the best of our knowledge, Nialls Gant is an alias. The bureau has no information on him. The bureau welcomes citizens to send us information that they have. If the bureau finds information that the public needs to know, we will make it accessible through the usual media channels."

She tried not to think of the last time the bureau had updated the regional Web site. Probably not since the last round of budget cuts in '68. She'd have to pull out the handbook on bureau transparency to see what she was actually allowed to share. Usually, it was just enough information to keep the public asking questions and not enough to let them form vigilante mobs.

With a final smile, she retreated to the air-conditioned bliss of the office building. She didn't relax until she was in the elevator headed upstairs, but even then, she felt like she'd painted a bull's-eye on her back. Someone wanted her dead, and now she knew his name.

"That . . . that . . ." Gant struggled to find the proper term for Detective Rose.

"Starts with a B," Donovan said. "Ends with an ITCH."

"No, she's more than a common street cur." Gant's lip curled in a sneer. "She's a disease. A plague. A destroying angel from the pits of hell. How, in the name of rational thought and humanistic endeavor, did that woman survive? How did she get through the machine? I thought if she left at a different point in time, she'd go somewhere else."

"Maybe she followed straight after and landed somewhere in the city instead of the swamps," he said as he pulled out a knife and rag.

Gant rolled his eyes. "Impossible. Even if she had, how did she find us?"

Donovan finished wiping down the knife blade he was polishing. "Probably followed the same lead we had. There's one way back home. Detective Rose can't want to stay here any more than we do. The window's closing. We want out. She wants out. We're all after the same thing. We're bound to cross paths."

"We did cross paths," Gant reminded him. "Violently." He stalked back to the other end of the motel suite and flicked the TV on. The local news stations had been playing variations of Detective Rose's interview all morning. The navy blazer was a ghastly dull color on her, but it made her blend in. The reporters nattered on in English. Detective Rose responded in kind. It was a carjacking gone wrong. Someone had stolen her car. She was uninjured. No, they had no leads. They didn't know who Nialls Gant was.

They didn't know who he was! Nialls Gant, the man who was the focus of the nation's largest manhunt. His had been the trial of the century! For weeks, he had dominated the headlines. He'd commanded the attention of everyone from the northern territories to Tapachula. How dare the media act as if they'd never heard of him! As if he'd never been born.

Cold fingers of dread curled around his spine, raising gooseflesh on his arms. "Donovan?"

"Eh?"

"This place, this period of history, were we born here?"

Donovan shuffled, moving his gear around. "Who knows? Probably."

"Probably isn't an adequate answer. You said you knew how the machine worked."

"I do. I got it to turn on, didn't I?"

Gant closed his eyes and counted slowly to ten. In Greek. Then Swahili. "Understanding how to turn a machine on is not the same as understanding how it works. Turning a doorknob isn't the same thing as picking a lock!"

"You okay?" Donovan moved in front of the TV with a serious frown. "Why does it matter? We're leaving here."

"We left our own time and came here instead of going back to the day before I committed my crimes, which was—if you recall—the original intent of this expedition."

Donovan shrugged, his shoulder holster sliding as he did. "Who cares? It was a miscalculation. No one's chasing us."

"Detective Rose is chasing us."

"Nah, we're chasing her. The bimbo on the TV doesn't have a dime on us. She doesn't know us from God Himself." He kicked the TV so sparks flew as the glass cracked. "Enough of this. We're getting the machine, and we're leaving. You're still with me, aren't you, Gant?"

Gant looked coldly at his erstwhile partner. "Naturally."

"Then gear up. I'm tired of listening to people speak English all the time."

Sam tossed Henry Troom's day planner on her desk. There were still several notebooks retrieved from his apartment to read over, plus the reams of paper found in boxes at the storage unit. Edwin had given up on the notebook and passed it off to Mac.

Crossing her arms, she laid her head on the desk. Poor Henry. It must have seemed like such a clever idea. He already knew how the machine worked. Controlling it was a matter of math. With the right formula, he was able to calculate when and where he needed to turn on a machine to connect to the morning of July 4, 2069, behind the lab. Going back to save Dr. Emir probably made perfect sense. Troom controlled every variable.

Except the gun.

The real shame was that if Troom had used the stupid machine the way Emir intended, he wouldn't have been at risk at all. He would have sent a paper airplane through to his past self and warned him. Told him to call Dr. Emir or the police.

No, that wouldn't have worked . . . because she'd ignored those messages.

The guilt still ate at her.

Emir had called in the wee hours of the morning.

He'd been on the phone minutes before he died, and she'd done nothing. Fear had kept her locked in place. She liked to think it was a sensible fear.

Chances were good that if she had driven out to the lab before dawn that day, she would have been just as a dead as Emir. Marrins was a senior agent who was both racist and sexist. He wouldn't have let her walk away. But the choice still haunted her. Maybe it had haunted Henry, too. Only he'd had the guts to try.

Sam poked her computer. Theoretically, the calculations could be done backward. She knew when and where Henry had gone, so she should be able to calculate where he'd started the journey, but the math wasn't adding up.

The door to her office swung open as someone knocked.

"You're supposed to knock, *then* enter, Mac." She put her head down.

"Funny you knew it was me," he said. There was the sound of one of the cheap metal chairs from the front office being dragged across the floor.

"Everyone else knocks and waits for a response."

He snorted in amusement. "That's great for them. I have a question for you, purely bureau business. Have you ever taken advanced physics?"

"No." She lifted her head. "Why?"

Mac tossed the journal on her desk. "Agent Edwin gave up before he got to the good parts. Does that handwriting look familiar?"

Sam turned the journal around and read over the

notes made in purple pen. "That's . . . my handwriting? What in the name of the saints is going on?" She flipped the pages. "How much is there?"

"Quite a few pages."

"But . . . how? Why? Why would anyone mimic my handwriting?"

The look he gave her suggested sarcasm without saying anything.

Sam blinked. "You think this is *my* writing?"

"It probably belongs to the Jane Doe with the purple shirt," Mac said. "She's a variation of you. An iteration of you, I guess."

She read over the notes again. "What is a stabilizing core?"

"I've no idea."

"Iterations . . . half of this is gibberish."

Mac's smile was one of fatigue but not quite defeat. "Tell me you have good news."

"Come on up to the conference room. Edwin and Clemens have cooked up a plausible theory."

Her eyebrows went up. "Is it going to lead to the end of this madness?"

"It's sort of like a road map on how to get there."

"Yeah?"

"Yeah, where X marks the apocalypse."

"You need to work on your pep talks, MacKenzie."

Ivy looked up as laughter echoed through the hall. Agent Rose and Agent MacKenzie walked in, joking about something, their eyes never leaving each other. She sighed. One day someone's eyes would light up when they saw her. And not with greed as they realized what she was and mentally priced out her body parts at a chop shop.

"So," Agent Rose said, "I hear you two have solved the Grand Unification Theory? Ready to share?"

"It's not quite particle physics," Edwin said. "But Officer Clemens has linked almost everything together."

All eyes were on her. "I'm not sure how much of this will hold up in court," Ivy said hesitantly. Agent Rose didn't move to stop her, so she went on. "Dr. Troom's journal shows two set periods of time."

"Arguably three," Edwin said.

"You wouldn't win that argument," Ivy said. At least he wouldn't win it with her. "The journal starts with very basic notes about how the machine could work, what might be needed to contact other iterations, and a detailed list of his dreams. Dr. Troom seemed to believe that he wasn't dreaming so much as witnessing the end of an iteration." She nodded to Edwin, hoping he'd help.

He nodded. "Troom made notes of three major kinds of events: expansion, decoherence, and convergence. During expansion, the iterations break apart. During decoherence, they collapse into each other. During convergence, the iterations run parallel . . . struggling for dominance."

Agent Rose and Agent MacKenzie both looked perplexed.

Officer Clemens tried to think of an analogy that would work. "Think of a hundred particles of light racing in a sine wave, up and down, up and down. Each color of light travels at a different speed or wavelength. Some particles reach higher or dip lower along the wave pattern. But at some point, they overlap. That's what we think timelines are doing. Each iteration is traveling at its own pace, but sometimes they run parallel, and we have a convergence. The woman who died in the car wreck had to cross over during a convergence event," Ivy said.

Agent Rose nodded. "All right. That's a start, I guess. So are we still in a convergence event? Does that mean Mr. Gant from the TV crossed over with her? And, should we be expecting more intrusions from the other iteration?"

Ivy shook her head. "I can't say for certain. It's possible."

"How possible?" Agent MacKenzie asked.

Ivy shrugged and looked at Edwin. "Better than seventy percent? Maybe?"

"The convergence points are, according to the notebook, very narrow windows in time. Sometimes the overlap lasts a few hours, sometimes only for minutes."

"How long was the convergence that brought Juanita over?" Agent MacKenzie asked.

"Dr. Troom didn't leave the calculations in his notebook. His notes say that every convergence is followed by either further expansion or destructive decoherence. There a formula for calculating the events, and he was predicting a catastrophic decoherence. The loss of multiple iterations."

"That made him have bad dreams?" Agent Rose took a seat at the table.

"More like a redundant memory," Edwin said. "The dreams were real events of other iterations that had failed. Troom was tracking them."

Agent MacKenzie sat down across from Agent Rose. "Is there a patron saint of nightmares?"

"Saint Raphael," Agent Rose said without looking up, "but I don't think he's going to help us. If every dream for every person is a failed iteration . . ."

"No," Ivy said, shaking her head, "that's the thing: It's only for certain people. There are notes on einselected nodes: individuals or events that exist in every iteration. They're kind of like glue, or the bond between iterations. I don't know if Dr. Troom even understood the concept fully. But he considered himself to be einselected."

"Was that ego talking?" Agent Rose asked.

"Possibly," Ivy conceded, "but it doesn't really matter in the end. The theory Agent Edwin and I came up with is a lot simpler than that."

Edwin bounced in his seat a little. "You're going to like this."

She smiled, too. "All the equations require a location code to operate from. So I started breaking down all the numbers the way I did with the phone numbers, and I found a pattern."

Agent Rose didn't look like she appreciated any of this, but she motioned for Ivy to continue.

"The machine only operates predictably at a certain geographic location. You need starting longitude and latitude to calculate a destination. For Dr. Troom to calculate the precise arrival in another iteration during a convergence, he had to know his exact starting location."

Agent Rose's face lit up with a fierce smile. "Tell me you have those coordinates."

Ivy held up the strip of paper she scribbled her calculations on. "Longitude and latitude of where Dr. Troom operated his first machine. It's somewhere in the swamps." Not her favorite place in Florida, but it made sense in a way. People didn't go out to the swamps for fun anymore. Hunting wasn't allowed, and the touristy airboat tours were restricted to set stretches of waterway. If someone wanted to get up to less-than-legal shenanigans, the deep swamp was the place to go.

"Which is how Nealie and Connor got involved," Edwin said. "They must have bumped into Troom at some point."

Ivy held up a hand. "There was also a second set of coordinates that match the longitude and latitude of the lab. We think Juanita Doe crossed iterations, possibly with Mr. Gant, possibly following him. She wanted to go back," Ivy said. "She worked with Dr. Troom to rebuild the machine. There was one in the swamp, then a second he used at the lab."

Agent Rose frowned. "Why two machines?"

Ivy and Edwin both shook their heads.

"We don't know yet," Edwin admitted. "Although there are a couple of notes about a stabilizing mechanism. Something that could control the energy of the machine."

"Let me guess," Agent Rose said, rubbing her temples. "No control, and the machine explodes?"

"That's possible," Edwin said. "Though Troom hypothesized that a stabilizing mechanism wouldn't be needed under certain circumstances."

Agent Rose quirked her lips into a bitter smile. "I think it's safe to say he proved that hypothesis wrong. Mac, can you and Edwin check out the swamp location?"

"You don't want to come get dirty with us?" Agent MacKenzie teased.

"Not particularly, no. Officer Clemens, thank you for your help."

Ivy hesitated. "There is one more thing."

Agent Rose quirked an eyebrow up in question. "Yes?"

"I tracked down Sheriff Gardner since he wasn't returning your calls. He's staying at home. I drove by and knocked on his door, but he yelled at me. He's very, very drunk."

"I would be too if my kid had just died," Agent MacKenzie said.

Agent Rose wrinkled her nose. "I think it might be more than that. Ivy and I will go over and talk with him. Call me when you get back from the swamps."

Rose gave her a calculating look. "Do you have a tac vest?"

"A . . . a bulletproof one?" Ivy shook her head. "Why would I need one?"

"Standard-issue for bureau interactions like this. You never know when someone will get violent." Her lips pressed into a thin frown.

"And because I think we'll need it."

It had never occurred to Sam that she hated being the passenger in the car. As Ivy took another left-hand turn faster than Sam felt was safe, she had ample time to reflect on why she was always behind the wheel. Being the driver gave her control. And the clone's driving gave her more near-death experiences in fifteen minutes than she'd had in her entire life . . . and she'd already died twice.

Her knuckles turned white as she gripped the seat belt, and Ivy slammed on the brakes. "When did you learn to drive?"

"When I became a city drone," Ivy said calmly. "They gave us cars and a training video, and we worked it out on a dirt lot."

Sam quickly reviewed her saints, trying to remember who the patron saint of drivers was. St. Frances of Rome, wasn't it? Or was there another one for race-car drivers?

"Are you okay, Agent Rose?" the officer asked, maybe catching on that Sam was nervous.

"Have you ever considered professional race-car driving?"

"No, ma'am," she said as she took another turn at qualifying speeds.

Sam closed her eyes and whispered a prayer. "You missed your calling in life." She snapped her fingers.

"What?"

"St. Richard," Sam said. "He's the patron saint of NASCAR."

Ivy hit the brakes and slowed to something closer to the speed limit. "My driving isn't that bad."

Sam looked over at her.

"Not all of us drive like old ladies!"

With a guffaw of laughter, Sam turned to look out the window. "Some of us are able to see the speed-limit signs as we go past and actually follow the law."

"What is the point of flashing blue lights and sirens if I don't get to use them?"

"You aren't," Sam pointed out.

Ivy shrugged. "I don't need to. Everyone is at work or school." The car slowed some more. "Is that better?" There was a note of beaten uncertainty in her voice that Sam didn't like.

"Your driving is fine," Sam lied. "I was teasing." Ivy's insecurity was worse than taking a turn on two wheels.

"We're here," Ivy said. "The blue house on the left."

Sam looked at the overgrown, winter-browned grass with a frown. The gutter was sagging, and a weather-beaten flyer for a local pizza place fluttered in the door handle. "Are you sure?"

Ivy nodded. "He forgot his running shoes at work once, and my commanding officer made me run them over."

"I didn't picture him as a runner."

"He's not. He wears the same pair of running shoes in every morning, and it's been the same pair for at least three years. It's all for show."

That seemed an apt summary of Sheriff Gardner. More politician than policeman. More sycophant than politician.

Sam walked up to the door and knocked. There was a crash inside, followed by a man's cursing.

"Sheriff Gardner?" Sam called out. "Sheriff? Are you all right?"

Silence.

"Sheriff, it's Agent Rose from the bureau." She knocked again, louder this time. "Do I have permission to enter?"

Ivy closed the distance behind her. "Maybe we should wait."

"He might have hurt himself. Our first duty is to protect the citizens, no matter what part of the government we work for. We exist to keep people safe." She reached for the doorknob. As she touched it, the door was wrenched inward with violent force.

Sheriff Gardner stood in front of them, wearing a stained white tank top, wrinkled uniform pants, and reeking of alcohol.

Sam tried not to judge him.

She failed miserably.

"Sheriff? How are you doing?"

"Get off my property," Gardner said through clenched teeth.

"I will," Sam promised with a smile. "I just need to ask you a few questions. First, did you see your son, Jamie, at Dolores's grave on March nineteenth? That would have been last Wednesday."

The sheriff's eye twitched. "I know what day it was." Sam waited. The sheriff looked away. "You saw Jamie." His body language gave everything away. She'd seen the same hunched shoulders and guilty look on her father's face when he sobered up and realized what she'd given up to take care of him.

Gardner turned away.

"I need to know what happened," Sam said. "Did you fight? Did he argue with you?"

Gardner's shoulders hunched inward. "I gave him a car."

That . . . was not what she expected.

"I was trying to make things right. Get him a good life." He shook his head. He turned around, face contorted with anger and sorrow. "I got a bonus last year. Enough to send Jamie to college like Dolores wanted. She always said he was smart."

"He was very smart," Sam said. "Got good grades. Won a poetry contest, I think."

Gardner peered back into the gloom of the house, avoiding eye contact.

Sam scanned the room trying to guess what had Gardner's attention. The TV was off, the house covered in empty beer bottles and frozen-food containers. There was movement in the far corner, an old electric picture frame playing through a series of dated photos. Sam couldn't see the faces, but the clothes were a good twenty years out of style: Mango-orange and sunset-pink dresses were visible. She made an educated guess. "You loved your wife, didn't you, Sheriff Gardner?"

"Of course I did!" His nose scrunched as he tried not to tear up. "Tried to. We were fighting even before Jamie was born. She had moods. Liked to sulk for days. Wouldn't talk to me sometimes because she was mad. It was worse after he was born. Doctor said it was post-partum depression maybe."

"And when he was diagnosed, she was worse," Sam guessed.

Gardner shook his head and sighed. "There was a recession. I couldn't get a job that paid enough, and she wasn't ever happy. I thought it'd be better just the two of us. I could keep her happy, and she wouldn't have to worry about him. Jamie'd be safer. That's what I told myself."

Ivy walked up beside Sam, frowning. Sam shook her head.

"Sheriff, what did you and Jamie talk about when you saw him?"

Gardner shrugged. "Math. Physics. He said he thought it was really interesting. He was always like that, getting hyperfocused."

"And you were already planning to pay for his schooling, so that was good." Her suspicion that the sheriff had killed his estranged son was rapidly falling apart. "You bought him a car?"

"A cheap one, to get around town in. A 2060 Alexian Essence. Blue. Dolores's favorite color was blue, and it was the right price.

Cheap. "What did Jamie say he was going to do after that?"

"Go home, pick up some things, then he had class that afternoon. A fourth-quarter pickup class on intro to college life or something like that. He would have been on campus early. Except, I don't know if he made it. The cemetery opens at five in the morning. I was there first thing. We talked. We bought that car off the lot at eight. By noon, I was getting a call someone had found him washed up on the beach."

Sam looked over at Ivy. "Mac said they found tire tracks near the swamp. Did we ever find out what kind of car it was?"

Ivy shook her head.

"Go call it in and see if Mac has an answer." She watched Ivy walk back to the car before turning to the beleaguered sheriff. "Is there any other information you can give me? Names of friends? Someone else your son might have seen that day?"

"No." Gardner shook his head. "We weren't . . . He didn't talk about his life. We didn't talk much ever except when I was drunk and yelling. He had the boys out in the woods, but I don't know who he knew in town. High school friends, I suppose."

"All right," Sam said. "We'll see if we can trace the car."

His eyes went wide. "Wait. I have . . . I have a picture. The guy who sold us the car . . ." He stumbled into the house and attacked the disaster inside. Empty take-out boxes tumbled off the coffee table in an avalanche. Gardner grabbed a flimsy piece of shiny paper. "Here. The dealer took this." He shoved the photograph at Sam.

The picture showed Gardner in a dark brown suit two sizes too tight and old enough to be the one he wore to Dolores's funeral. Jamie stood next to him, hair pulled back in a ponytail, jeans ripped, T-shirt faded and stained. Around Jamie's neck was a knotted scarf of . . . "Is that plastic?"

"Trash he picked up," Gardner said. "Plastic bags and whatnot that wound up on the beach. He made scarves out of them. Sold them as 'upcycle couture' at the farmer's market during the summer. I used to patrol there just so I could check on him."

Mac had said Jamie was garroted, probably with a plastic bag found at the scene. Jamie had been wearing the murder weapon all along. "Can I take a picture of this?"

Gardner nodded. "Will it help?"

"If I can track down where your son's car was, I can find where he was killed. Once I find that, I'll have some evidence." She pulled out her phone and took a picture that she sent to Mac, Edwin, and Ivy. "I'm sorry for your loss, Sheriff. You'll be the first person I call when I find out who did this."

CHAPTER 15

> *Decoherence is the winter of time. All things die until*
> *spring returns. In the spring of time, we have Expan-*
> *sion, a million possibilities bloom in front of us, and we*
> *are blinded by the brilliance of our future.*
>
> **~ Dr. M. Vensula head of the National**
> **Center for Time-Fluctuation Studies**

Thursday March 27, 2070
Florida District 8
Commonwealth of North America
Iteration 2

Static filled the radio as the map led Donovan and Gant deeper into the fetid swamps. Gant turned it off with an angry slap. There wasn't good music here anyway. Something buzzed past his ear. A high-pitched annoying hum that made him want to break things.

Without warning, Donovan slapped his own arm.

Gant looked over at him.

Donovan lifted his hand to show him a splattered bug.

"This place is disgusting."

Donovan grunted agreement.

It wasn't enough. Gant could feel himself unraveling. Losing his focus. "Don't they drain swamps at home?"

"Yup." The car bucked as they drove over another muddy rut in the road.

"This is like driving through a sewer. I can feel things crawling all over me."

"Noseeums," Donovan said. "Read about them in the guidebook. They're little bugs that crawl on you."

"How informative," Gant said dryly, eye twitching. It struck him that Donovan was having fun in this nightmare. In a strange way, it made sense. Even hell had to seem attractive to someone. He pulled Detective Rose's briefcase onto his lap and snapped it open. With a frown, he checked the GPS clipped to the front dash of the car. "Is that readout entirely right? Another hour to drive ten miles?"

"The roads aren't good," Donovan said. "No sense breaking the car trying to get there fast."

"We could walk faster." He did the calculations in his head. "Perhaps not. But there must be a better way to navigate this . . . jungle." No word had ever crossed his lips with such loathing.

Donovan grunted again. "I see dirt bike tracks."

"Is that a problem?"

"Means the locals probably don't drive a POS car stolen from an old lady to get out here."

"She was on a respirator and had cataracts. We did

her a favor by recycling this old heap," Gant said virtuously. "Besides, an old woman who can't get out of bed won't report a missing car from her garage. The caretaker was on his phone playing video games. Not the conscientious type."

Under normal circumstances, Gant would have been just as happy to leave both of them dead. This, however, was not the time to get sloppy. Gant didn't consider himself a superstitious man. Nor did he spend much time reflecting on the truths of God or the possibility of judgment after this life. Those things were beneath an intelligent man such as himself. But, in the privacy of his own mind during the dark watches of the night, he'd begun hypothesizing his own little theories about Detective Rose. There were certain things about her survival that didn't quite add up.

And there was the word "clone" floating around now.

Sure, he had heard of cloning. A kidney here, a bone there, that sort of thing. But this hell of an alternate reality seemed to have taken cloning past the point of sense and started cloning full humans. If that were the case, he was facing the impalpable possibility that there were multiple Detective Roses to deal with. It made the idea of escaping all the more desirable.

Donovan tapped the window. "I can see a roof over there. Bit of green that doesn't fit. You see it?"

Gant leaned forward. There was something out there across a deceptively flat field. "Can we drive off-road in this?"

"I'm pretty sure that's swamp," Donovan said. "No

telling how deep the water gets. But the road should loop back around."

The GPS now estimated their arrival time in twenty minutes. He pitied the criminals of this world. Inefficient tech. Dirt roads. There wasn't a hint of refinement in the entire place.

Nothing good ever came of 3 A.M. phone calls. Sam rolled over, obstinately ignoring her ringing phone until Hoss put his cold nose to her leg. She growled at him and reached for the phone before the ringing woke up Mac in the living room. "Who is this?"

"Are you Rose?" The voice on the other end sounded faded, distant, and fevered and not at all familiar.

"No," Sam said. "Are you drunk?"

"You are Detective Rose."

"Agent." Sam yawned. "I don't go by Rose, and my friends don't call me Rose. So—QED—you aren't a friend. Which begs the question why in the name of Saint Mary you are calling me at 3 A.M. Are you dead? Probably not. If you're dying, try nine-one-one. Good night."

"I'm coming for you," the voice said, as she took the phone away from her ear.

She sighed. "Yeah?"

"Does that frighten you?"

"At three in the morning, nothing frightens me. You could tell me a giant spider is trying to break through my window, and I wouldn't care. I'm tired. If you want to threaten me, call me in the morning." She hung up.

The light flipped on.

Sam threw her pillow in the general direction of the door and flopped over on her stomach. "Go away."

"Did someone just call and threaten you?" Mac's voice was low and far too calm to actually be calm.

"Yes."

"And your reaction to someone's walking into your room is to throw a pillow?"

Sam pointed at the dog. "I have Hoss." She heard the dog wiggle across the room to get a belly rub from Mac.

"Fearsome."

"I'm not dead yet."

"Where's your gun?"

"In the safe in my closet, locked away from idiot mastiffs who think guns look like chew toys." She pushed the blankets back and propped herself up on an elbow. "Can I have my pillow back? I'm tired. This is bedtime. We can talk tomorrow."

Mac folded his arms over his chest. "Safety should be a priority when someone is hunting you. Not sleep."

"No one is hunting me."

"Someone just called you, Sam."

"So? If they meant to do something, they would have just done it. Calling means they're not ready, even if they are planning to do something."

He raised an eyebrow.

"I'm not an idiot, MacKenzie. I take threats seriously when I need to, but at this moment, I don't. Go to sleep. I will not die between now and when the alarm goes off. Swear on my father's grave. But if you don't let me sleep, I am going to tie you up in the kitchen and gag you."

"Really?" He handed her the pillow.

"Really?"

"I'd love to see you try."

"Don't make me get my handcuffs, MacKenzie."

He chuckled and turned out the light.

CHAPTER 16

Every life is created with ten thousand deaths. Every
breath I breathe steals a moment from another. Selfish
I. Selfish love. Selfish broken man.

~ excerpt from the poem "A Living
Death" by Jorge Sabio I2—2068

Friday March 28, 2070
Florida District 8
Commonwealth of North America
Iteration 2

Mac sat in the living room, back propped up against the outside wall of Sam's bedroom, and watched the sun rise. In the service, he'd known soldiers who could sleep anywhere. Guys who could drop onto any surface, close their eyes, and be snoring in minutes no matter what was going around them. Explosions and gunfire wouldn't rattle them. Until a few years ago, Mac would have put himself in that elite group of snoozers. The ambush and depression had changed all that. He'd lost sleep but never been alert. Now . . . he rubbed a hand across the stubble on his chin and tried not to think about Sam.

At least she'd been wearing clothes this time. The problem was she was as sexy in an oversized T-shirt and shorts as she was in a lacy bra and panties.

He bumped his head on the wall to clear the memory. Sam didn't know it. She never noticed how his heart skipped a beat when she stepped into the room. She never noticed him.

Cursing quietly, he looked at his phone. Leave days would only get him so far. Eventually, he'd have return to Chicago. Go back to the apartment in the city and not seeing Sam every day. He'd break a little. She'd probably not notice his absence.

A shadow fell over him, and he looked up where Hoss's face should be. He saw knees. He looked up higher at Sam, frowning down at him. "Did you not sleep at all?"

"I was sleeping fine until the phone rang."

She sat down next to him. "I'm sorry it woke you up."

"I wasn't that tired."

"You're a terrible liar."

"You're not much better if you think I couldn't fall back asleep just because the phone rang."

"Then what is it?"

Besides the fact that you smell like cinnamon and vanilla? "Maybe the contents of the call?"

"I told you not to worry about that." She leaned sideways, resting her head on his shoulder. "Should have known that wouldn't work. But I know what would make you feel better."

"I doubt it." Her scent taunted him, speaking of home and all the things he'd never have.

Sam held up her phone. "Last night, I had the bureau techs in District 6 run a trace on the creeper who called me. I thought we could have breakfast, then go arrest him." She smiled. "Yes? Fun times?" She moved away from him. "What's wrong?"

Mac shook his head. "Nothing. I was just in a weird place when you walked in."

"You're mad at me." It wasn't even a question.

"No."

"Your shoulders are tight. You won't make eye contact. You're furious with me."

"With myself," Mac said. He shut his eyes and tried to relax. "I realized something last night while I was sitting here, and it just . . . ruined my mood I guess. Sorry."

"Do you want to talk about?"

"No."

Sam stood up. "All right. I'm doing cereal for breakfast. You can shower and eat whatever you want. I'm leaving in twenty. You can come with me or not."

"That sounds about right," Mac muttered.

Sam kicked him in the shin with her bare foot. "This is why you need sleep! You're such a grump when you're tired."

"I'm not tired."

"Mac, I'm sorry I put you through this."

He looked up at her in confusion. "What do you mean?"

"I know this isn't easy for you. You got out. Got away from me, and you were safe. This whole time-travel nonsense. You deserve so much better. I know you've got to be stressed out. I know . . ." She sighed, and he thought he saw the shimmer of a tear in her eye. "I'm sorry, all right. You shouldn't be here, but I need you here. It's selfish, and I know it, but I need you. You're my rock, Mac. But I don't want you losing sleep over me. That's not fair. I feel safe, because you're here, but . . ." She shook her head. "If it's too much, say so. Please. I understand if you need to go back to Chicago."

"I wouldn't sleep any better there."

"Where would you sleep better?"

"Your bed."

"Fine," Sam said. "I'll take the couch." Her lips quirked up in a smile. "That's what you meant, right?"

Mac smiled. "Of course."

"Because you wouldn't have been suggesting anything else without at least buying me flowers first."

"I thought I'd bought you flowers before."

"Nope. Still waiting on those."

"Were you expecting them?"

"I figured they'd fit into our relationship eventually."

"Any particular type I should be looking for?"

"Pretty?" San suggested. "I like sunflowers and hibiscus and anything big and bright."

"Yeah?"

She nodded. "Are you going to get breakfast now?"

"Yeah." He stood up. "I don't want to go back to Chicago."

"Good. I don't want you to go back either. You'll have to, eventually, but I have some leave coming up, and I'll be due to transfer in another year. This district's too small for me to grow my career. Maybe I could visit you and do some house hunting while I'm out there."

"Or we could house hunt together."

She raised an eyebrow. "Pretty sure you need to make that kind of proposal with a ring."

"Yeah?"

"Yeah."

"Any kind of ring?"

"I'm partial to opals, and I think sapphires are bad luck."

"I'll keep that in mind."

"You do that," Sam said. "I'm going to go get dressed."

Mac leaned so he could watch her walk down the hall. "Need any help?"

"No, I just needed to see you smile."

Watching her move was more than enough reason to do just that.

CHAPTER 17

We made a horrible mistake dismissing evolution. In the quest to control time, we forgot that time changes all things. People change, and we will never find a way to control who they become.

~ private conversation with Agent 5 (retired)

Saturday March 29, 2070
Florida District 8
Commonwealth of North America
Iteration 2

Steam coiled out of the swamp into the primal darkness of night. Gant paced the perimeter of the building, not certain if he was more concerned about the creatures with glowing eyes swimming in the swamps or the man inside, whose temper was fraying by the hour.

"Will you stop pacing!" Donovan shouted, punching the aluminum siding of the shack for emphasis. "You're not helping."

Gant considered the gun in his hand. Lucky for Donovan, he wasn't worth the few remaining bullets. Besides, after all they'd been through, he felt Donovan deserved something a bit more personal. "The notes say the machine won't work tonight." He'd read them and understood them well enough. If the dates were all correct, there wasn't a chance to cross back to his reality until tomorrow night. "We have time."

"This isn't kindergarten math," Donovan said through clenched teeth. "I'm not waiting to the last minute to do everything."

Grumbling profanities in Spanish and English under his breath, Gant continued pacing. He knew what was wrong. Clone or not, leaving Detective Rose alive was an insult. It tore him apart knowing she was out there breathing—any of her. She'd shrugged off his threats. Treated him as inconsequential.

Ignored me.

"Go get a drink before I kill you," Donovan said. "I can't stand your pacing anymore! Go get laid. Whatever. There's a liquor store about ten miles down the main road."

Gant looked at him, thumb stroking the trigger guard of his gun.

Not.

Worth.

The.

Bullets.

He pivoted on his heel and stalked over to where they'd found two beat-up four-wheelers. One was charged enough to get him to town, where they'd left the college kid's car.

"Be back by noon!" Donovan called after him.

Flipping the other man a rude gesture, Gant called back, "Yes, Mother." He gunned the engine and raced across the dirt road. Whiskey sounded good. Maybe a little ninety-proof moonshine. What he wanted was . . . something flammable. Something that would light up the night sky like the fires of hell.

Sam kicked her blanket off and rolled onto her side. The cool breeze from the air-conditioning sent shivers down her back. She tugged the blanket up, then pushed it off again.

Hoss whined quietly in protest. She was interrupting his sleep.

Rolling onto her back, Sam dropped her arm over the edge of the bed and stroked Hoss's fur. Something had pulled her from sleep, but it wasn't the heat of the night. Adrenaline raced through her veins, pushing her heart rate up, making her hyperaware of everything around her. Downstairs, the neighbor had left their TV on again, and she could hear the hollow sounds of a synthetic laugh track. Tree branches rattled against the siding of the apartment. In the distance, she could hear the faint rumble of a truck charging down the highway.

This wasn't like waking up from a nightmare with a faint sense of dread and cold sweat making her skin clammy. This was liking waking up *to* a nightmare. Opening her eyes to see monsters.

Sam swung her legs out of bed. She slid her foot over Hoss's flank until it found the soft carpet, stood, and dressed in the darkness. Something had pulled her from a deep sleep to perfect awareness. Quietly opening the door, she tiptoed to the living room.

Mac lay sprawled across the couch, one arm over his forehead, the other dangling off the side of the couch. She really should have offered him the bed. Their green couch just wasn't built for a tall person. Funny how she'd come to think of in terms of Us and We and Ours.

Car tires squealed in the parking lot outside. All thoughts of relationships pushed aside, Sam ran to the window. A dark car took the turn too fast, slowed for a fraction of a second, and something like a giant cigarette butt flew out the car window. There was a crashing sprinkle of glass, and Hoss yelped in the bedroom.

"Hoss!" She ran down the hall and opened the door to see a bottle with a lit rag explode. The heat of the explosion knocked her backward. "Hoss!" She choked, coughing on smoke.

Strong hands grabbed her under the armpits and hauled her backward. Sam tried to break free.

Hoss limped out of the room. She clapped her hands.

"Out," Mac ordered, opening the door. "Right now."

"There's a fire extinguisher"—she coughed as smoke started filling the room—"under the sink."

Fire alarms were going off. Mac was dialing someone, probably the fire department.

She looped a leash over Hoss's head and dragged him outside. Hurrying barefoot down the wooden stairs, she banged on her neighbor's door, praying the elderly woman would hear something over the sound of her TV.

Slowly, it was dawning on her that someone had thrown a Molotov cocktail on her bed. Delayed shock froze her limbs. If she'd been in bed . . . She dropped her hand down to pet Hoss.

A car rolled up beside her. Sam looked over, expecting to see a neighbor.

The man who stepped out of the car with a twisted grin was no friend of hers. "Hello, Detective Rose."

"Gant." Sam stepped back, hand tightening on Hoss's leash.

He lifted a gun. "Good-bye, Detective."

Sam lunged forward, but Hoss was faster. Five shots, and Hoss fell backward. Sam lurched sideways as Mac tackled her. All she could do was watch Gant's car peel away into the night as tears ran down her face.

"I am fine." Mac tried once again to wrestle the IV needle away from his arm.

The nurse, a middle aged woman with dark skin, bright cherry-red hair, and a Spanish accent snarled at him. "You are going to hold still, or I will sedate you."

"Mac!"

He looked up to see Sam standing in the doorway, wearing an oversized sweatshirt and a pair of navy-blue scrub pants.

"Let her put the IV in," Sam ordered.

He narrowed his eyes at her betrayal but sat back in the hospital bed. "I'm not in pain."

"You have a bruised rib, a concussion, damage to your lungs, and that's only the partial list." Sam's eyes were tight with fear.

He winced as the needle cut his skin. "Sam, sweetie, I'm fine. Come here." He held out his free hand. "It's not that bad."

"You jumped off the balcony, you idiot," she said through clenched teeth.

The nurse grumbled something in Spanish that was certainly a commentary on his brains, or lack thereof, but he ignored her. "Sam? Are you all right?"

"Hoss is dead. You're in a hospital bed. And you ask if I'm okay?"

Right. He took a deep breath and was rewarded with a stabbing pain. "Sam . . . I'll say anything you want. How do I make it better?"

She turned to the window and pulled aside the thick green curtains. There was nothing to see but a streetlamp in the parking lot. "This isn't on you, Mac. You have plane tickets for Chicago. In forty-eight hours, you will be released from the hospital and fly home."

"And?"

The room filled with an arctic chill as she turned.

"There is no 'and.' I arrest Gant. You go to Chicago. We all file our paperwork and move on."

"You think I'm going to leave after this?" The machine next to him let out a shrill scream as his blood pressure skyrocketed. "Not just no, Sam. *Hell* no. I'm not leaving you. Nothing you say is going to change that."

There were marble statues with more emotion on their faces than hers as she crossed to him. She was shutting him out. Closing down all the nonessential systems so she could survive. He'd seen soldiers do it in war zones and at home. He'd done it more times than he cared to consider, but Sam had pulled him out. Forced him to feel something other than burning self-hatred.

"Don't even try to pull rank," he warned with a snarl. He wasn't going to let her slip into the same mire he'd only barely escaped. "I'll pay off my government contract and retire down here if that's what it takes. I'm not abandoning you."

She pressed a bittersweet kiss to his cheek. Her lips were as cold as the grave. "What if I ask?" she whispered.

Ice filled his veins. His free hand curled around her wrist. "Why?"

"You're hurting me." Her eyes were so cold. So dark and distant it was like looking into the face of a corpse.

He dropped his hand, but he wasn't sure that it was his touch causing the pain.

"Please leave. If you love me at all, you won't want

to see me hurt, so leave. Let me have my life back. What little is left, I want to live free."

There wasn't a medicine in the hospital that would fix his breaking heart. No way to return the stolen air to his lungs. No measure for the pain as she walked away.

"**W**here have you been?" Donovan demanded, as Gant got off the four-wheeler.

He glowered. "Getting more bullets. And a drink." And revenge. The first light of day was breaking across the swamp, and already the humidity was something near a hundred percent. It felt good.

Donovan rolled his eyes. "You're pathetic. Get in here."

"What's got your panties in a twist?"

"Look here." Donovan held up a rod with a viscous purple liquid. "Know what this is?"

"Poison?"

"A stabilizing catalytic liquid," Donovan said with the careful enunciation of someone who'd read the word but didn't quite know it meant. "Keeps us from going boom."

"Does it get us back to reality?" Nothing else mattered.

Donovan nodded. "We turn this on at three this afternoon, and we should wind up back in our timeline a few days before your prison break."

"How do we go farther back?" A few days wasn't

enough. The airports would still have him on the no-fly list. Detective Rose would still have his fortune sitting in an evidence locker.

"We'd have to wait six more weeks to go back farther, and it would still only buy us a few more days." Donovan hurled the notebook they'd stolen from the wrecked car at Gant. "Read it over."

Donovan finished putting the machine together as Gant read over the notes. Most of it was over his head, not that he'd ever admit that. He had the sneaking suspicion that Donovan was, possibly, smarter than he. At least with the book work and math. School hadn't been a bastion of safety and learning as much as a building full of marks waiting to be taken for their money. Gant had spent more time breaking into cars in the parking lot than in class. Up to this point, it hadn't affected his upward momentum.

Book smarts weren't necessary for a con unless you played a professor. It was better posing as an accountant. Numbers never lied, but they could dance if you had the knack.

"Donovan?"

"Eh?"

"What's an einselected node?" Gant asked as he leaned against a support beam of the warehouse. The metal was refreshingly cool, nicely shaded from the blazing sun outside.

Donovan washed machine grease off his hands from a water donkey they'd found tucked in one corner. "I think it's like a pillar-of-the-world type of thing. You know in a house where you have walls you can knock out and walls that have to stay because the house collapses without 'em?"

"Sure," Gant lied as he flipped a page of notes with the Zoetimax watermark.

"Haven't you ever demolished a building?"

Gant looked up from the stolen pages with disgust. "Why would I want to damage a building? I use finesse."

"Killing people is finesse?"

"Sometimes it's the only way to get the lock open," Gant said calmly. Some part of him recognized that murder was not an option for the average person. He was equally aware that keeping murder as an option broadened his choice of options considerably. Really, it was the difference between believing that only the people with keys should open doors and the belief that anyone who could pick the lock should open doors to take what they wanted. It was baffling that more people didn't view life that way. For which Gant was grateful to his fellow man. Competition—competent competition—wasn't good for him.

Donovan sighed.

"Tired of me already?" Gant asked.

"A week with you is more than I planned for," Donovan said. There was no malice in his tone.

Gant's fingers slipped to the reassuring shape of the gun tucked into his pants. Killing Donovan was tempting but not yet practical. If the other man was anything like him, then Donovan was holding a crucial detail back so that Gant wouldn't be able to use the machine alone. It's what he would have done. Once again, he felt like his control over the situation was slipping.

He rubbed sweating palms along the rough denim of his pants. Detective Rose was dead. His eye twitched. There'd been a dog, a dark shadow of a monster lunging for him. But surely, *surely*, the bullets had gone through. He'd seen her fall . . .

Gant nodded to himself. Yes, Rose was dead. For good this time. They were out of hell. In the swamps, but away from the English-speaking abomination of a country that had infested Florida. The gas station had strange beer, no sugar skulls, no chili-covered mangoes. Part of his mind ticked over and started calculating how much he could charge the locals to escape. No reason to be greedy. A few grand a head, and he'd still make money hand over fist.

But that meant staying longer.

Not worth it then.

He flipped another page over. Someone had scrawled dates on the back with sparkling purple ink. The loops of the s's gave it away. Detective Rose had written herself some notes. Purple. He snorted in derision but read the notes carefully. "Donovan?"

"What?" the other man demanded angrily.

"What's an Emir?"

Donovan stomped across the warehouse. "A what? An emir?"

"Yeah." Gant held the note up. "Rose said to watch out for an emir. Avoid at all cost."

"It's a . . . whatchamacallit . . . prince sort of title. Exalted one. Commander. It's an Arab title, I think." Donovan shrugged and passed the paper back. "Who knows, maybe if you travel on the wrong day, this is the Federated States of Arabia or something."

Gant tried to remember anything about the Arab nations as Donovan walked away. They weren't Mexican trade partners, and the Middle East wasn't a place he ever intended to visit. Too much sand. He couldn't even remember if they had decent dried mangoes.

Something whined behind him.

Looking over his shoulder, Gant scanned the visible parts of the swamp. The low, keening sound didn't sound entirely organic. "Donovan!"

"I hear it." The other man pulled his gun. "Four bullets left."

"I've got five."

"Did you get any more when you went out?"

Gant nodded. "They don't have standard sizes, but these will work in a pinch." Donovan grimaced. A too-small bullet in their guns was risky, but the measurements here were all off by a millimeter or two. They risked a misfire or the guns exploding. Between that risk and the possibility of landing in jail here, though, the gun was a better bet.

"Take the north side," Donovan said, as he walked out the south entrance. In the daylight, he wasn't silhouetted against a backlit warehouse, but it was a dumb move anyway.

Gant took more care as he went to check the swamp

side of the hideout. He peered around the corner and waited, watching for any changes. The birds were still singing peacefully. Somewhere, a cricket was humming. The keening whine seemed to come from all directions at once. He would say it was an echo, but there was nothing for the sound to echo off. Swamps weren't known for their rocky canyons for a reason.

Biting back a curse, Gant moved carefully through the tall grass. Tiny insects rose in black swarms. Prickly sticker seedpods clung to his pant leg as his boots squelched in the mud. The water was still. No ripples caused by an underwater intruder or an incoming airboat. He looked around to see Donovan peering down the road using a sniper scope Gant hadn't known the other man had. A nice tidbit to file away for later use.

You've been keeping secrets from me, friend.

Donovan shook his head and circled his hand.

With a nod, Gant followed the order to walk the perimeter, looking for anything out of place. A bent blade of grass, a suspicious glint of metal, anything to tell him what was making the sound. He looked up at the gray clouds rolling in from the coast. Just how far out could one hear a drone approaching? He watched the tree line for movement, peering at the dark green canopy as if he could pierce it by will alone.

The warehouse walls rumbled. "Oh, hells, no." *Underground? How could anyone possibly tunnel through this wet earth?* He ran in the direction he'd seen Donovan go as the ground shook. The walls of the warehouse buckled outward. "Donovan!"

As the ground bucked, rippling under his feet, he stumbled and rolled. Clutching his gun with white knuckles, Gant scrambled to his feet.

"Gant!" Donovan skidded around the corner.

"What did you do?"

Donovan shook his head and lifted a finger to his lips in a command for silence.

There were voices inside the damaged warehouse. "Team One, check the perimeter. Team Two, identify the machine. Commander, where is this place?" The voice was definitely a man with an accent that Gant pegged as British, but it wasn't quite British. University English, perhaps, learned as a second language at an expensive school.

"Unknown, sir. The location is not listed as any known contact site."

Gant's hand tensed around the handle of his gun. He knew *that* voice.

Donovan tilted his head to the side in question.

With a nod, Gant confirmed what they'd heard. Detective Rose just wouldn't die. He shook his head. Five bullets left, and every single one had her name etched on it.

Heavy boots stomped on the cement floor of the warehouse. Sounded like Team One was moving out.

"Do we run for the tree line?" Donovan asked breathlessly. "We can't survive a shoot-out with them."

"What's the standard *federales* team have? Six men? Five?"

"For a sting, it's twelve," Donovan said with an angry frown. "Too many for us to take out quickly."

Gant felt himself cheering up. Long odds against overwhelming force was his forte. "But they're moving together, with no eyes outside. They go out, we go in."

"And going in gets us, what, exactly?"

"The four-wheelers, you idiot. Shoot Rose. Grab machines. Leave in a roar. They'll follow the tracks. We can drop the four-wheelers by the main road and take a boat back while they're still hunting." It would work because it had to work. Their window of opportunity was too narrow for anything else.

Clearly, Donovan agreed—with the sentiment, if not with the plan. With a nod, he led the way, which suited Gant to the bone. The bigger should always go first. Donovan was his shield. That way, at least, the smart one in the partnership got out alive. They moved away from the sound of Team One's beating the grass to circle the building. Inside, six people stood hovering around the machine and a bright blue portal. Four were dressed in gray scrubs and held various bits of tech. The other two stood to the side supervising: an older man with a trim goatee and Detective Rose, still alive but thinner than Gant remembered her being hours before.

"I'm beginning to see why you hate this woman," Donovan muttered.

The old man looked up. "Mr. Donovan, is that you?"

Donovan's brow furrowed.

"Captain Joachim Donovan? Dishonorable discharge was it, or did you walk away in another fit of morals?" The man laughed at a joke no one else saw.

Rose turned, a sneer etched into her elegant face. "We can see you, Donovan. Stop being an idiot and get over here."

Rage poured through Gant like lava in an erupting volcano. "You traitor!" He struck Donovan across the head with the butt of his gun. "You filthy, lying, whoreson!" Another beat against Donovan's thick skull. Gant brought his knee up, catching the larger man in his kidneys.

Donovan lashed back, slamming a heavy fist into Gant's ribs. "Shut up. They don't know me."

"On the contrary, Captain, I've studied your life quite extensively," the man with the goatee said over the sound of their brawl.

Gant got ahold of Donovan's neck and squeezed. "Who is he?"

Donovan's face turned red as he choked out the words, "Don't. Know." He pushed Gant away with brute force and brought his gun up, aimed at the strangers. "Who are you? Why are you here?"

"To kill you," Rose said. "Iteration three is already crumbling, fracturing in your absence. Faster than we anticipated, but your presence here is subverting predominance."

Strong arms gripped Gant from behind. He snarled, bent his back to crack his head backward into a nose, and hit the solid plastic of body armor. He roared in fury, squirmed, and felt his shoulder pop out of place.

The old man watched him with the scholarly interest of an entomologist spotting a new species of flea. "Bring them inside. The heat outside is quite oppressive."

"An excellent reminder of why such iterations should not be preserved," Rose said. She was ignoring him again. Acting as if she hadn't fumed at his court case, demanding his death. Acting as if he hadn't tried to kill her hours before. Acting as if she were another clone of the Rose he'd killed. How many Roses existed?

"So very calm, Detective Rose," Gant said through gritted teeth and pain. "I see you washed the smoke off."

She raised a perfectly sculpted eyebrow. "Smoke?"

"I set your apartment on fire!" Fleck of spittle fell from his mouth as he screamed. Gant didn't care. Let her see the anger. Let her see the fire burning in him.

"You're mistaken, sir. I live in residential building 3–42, and there has never been a fire in that building."

The old man patted his shoulder. "Perhaps he saw another iteration of you. A detective, you say? How typical of the Roses of the world, don't you think? Always enforcing laws." He chuckled, as if this were a joke.

Donovan was pushed beside him, held by two soldiers wearing full black body armor.

"A detective shows a lack of initiative," Rose said. "This is an iteration with a strong military. If the shadow of me living here had ambition, she would have sought glory there."

The old man nodded. "A weakness. Make a note of it. It will make her easy to destroy in the long run."

Rose wrinkled her nose, giving the impression that such concerns were beneath her. "This iteration is flawed. The entire historical structure is baseless. They'll topple without our help. Fade into the oblivion of nightmares."

"You—" The soldier holding Gant jerked him backward so he bit his tongue instead of shouting at Rose again. With a snarl, he spat the bloody salvia at her feet. "I'm not done with you."

"You never started with me," she said. It was a cold dismissal. Too cold.

For the first time since the fire, Gant felt a tremor of fear unsettling his soul. This . . . wasn't what he'd imagined. Detective Rose wasn't supposed to ignore him. It went against everything he knew. Dread touched him, the knowing that came before the fall of the axe. His death was coming, and it was wrong in every way.

"Captain Donovan," Rose said, ignoring Gant. "You and I must talk."

"I got nothing to say to you, lady." Donovan sneered at her.

She smiled, and Gant realized she was a monster. The pretty outfits and pageant-queen smiles were the disguise of a monster, and now he saw the teeth. "Oh, no, Captain. We have much to say to each other. I spoke to your crew in Iteration 3 yesterday. They were very, what is the word, hmmm . . . broken?" Her dark eyes flashed with devilish delight. "Yes, broken is the term. Arms. Legs. Fingers. Jaws eventually. The youngest one held out longer than anticipated, but I know there is more than one way to skin a man."

"Cat," Donovan corrected. "The term is more than one way to skin a cat."

She raised an eyebrow. "Is that so? I'll make a note of the wording. However, I was skinning a man. He only screamed after that, but it was enough. I had what I wanted from him. Clever of you to hide here in another iteration."

"I don't know what you're talking about," Donovan said.

"You don't need to," Rose said.

The man with the goatee clapped. "Oh, bravo, Commander. So much menace."

Rose's glare promised pain to the man, but he missed the glance. "You don't approve, Dr. Emir?"

"Torture produces erratic results."

"The promise of torture produces good results," she countered.

"But in this case, it isn't required. Question the captain and let's be done with this. Our window is small."

The soldier holding Gant shook him. "Sir? What do you want done with this one?"

"Captain Donovan's little pet?" Emir looked at him with eyes filled with a glittering madness. He'd seen the look in the eyes of prisoners in isolation. The ones on death row who would go cackling to their executions looked like that. "Put him in the corner in case the captain needs persuasion. That is your weakness, isn't it, Donovan? You never left a man behind." Emir chuckled, and even the birds went quiet.

"Don't you dismiss me!" Gant shrieked, straining away from his captors. "I'm worth ten of him! Ten! Do you even know who I am?"

Emir looked at him. "You are nothing. Donovan is an einselected node."

Gant gasped in shock. "A pillar?"

"You've heard of them?" Emir's voice couldn't have been more surprised if a fish rode a unicycle past him. "The beasts are learning, Commander. What do you make of that?"

"They're still only shadows of things," Rose said. "When we're done, this one won't even be a memory."

Sam's phone rang with a piercing wail she'd programmed in for Ivy Clemens. She grabbed it, aware of the hazard lights turning on in her side mirrors. "This is Rose. Give me good news." She steered the car to the side of the road and left the wipers on.

"We found a body," Ivy said breathlessly. "He's not going to make it."

"Gant?" *Please, God, let it be Gant. Let me lock this bastard away forever. Let me put my nightmare behind bars.*

Thunder grumbled across the sky. "No," Ivy said. "He's been muttering in Spanish, but he's said Gant's name a few times."

"How much longer does he have?"

Ivy took a deep breath. "Ma'am, the ambulance is here, and they don't even think he's worth the ride back. The only reason I found him is that I saw lights in the scrub. It's a restricted area because it's box tortoise breeding ground, so I followed. I found this guy before I got too far in."

"They wanted him to be found." She tried to wrap that around Gant's sick obsession with her and couldn't. "Was there anything on him? Marks, other than the beating?"

"Nothing," Ivy said. "But whoever worked him over knew what they were doing. All the cuts are neatly spaced out."

"Either a serial killer or an interrogation." She swore under her breath, then switched to French blasphemies because they sounded better. "Did you write down everything he said?"

"Better than that, I had my recorder on. Want me to send you a transcript?" Ivy sucked in a breath. "Oh. He's gone, ma'am. Dead. The EMTs are pulling the blanket over his head." There was a heavy silence. "Why don't I feel anything?"

Sam knew that one. "Because you're still on the job. When you get home after this is all over, you'll cry. You'll wonder if you could have done something more. You'll wonder if this was fate, or destiny, or divine intervention. You'll be able to see his face every time you close your eyes. But we're still at work, Ivy. We still need to find Gant. I need that transcript."

Ivy drew in a deep breath and exhaled. "Yes, ma'am. I'll transmit it right away."

"To my phone," Sam ordered. "And send me your GPS coordinates. Call Edwin to meet us."

"Yes, ma'am." Ivy hung up, and twenty seconds later, Sam's phone buzzed with an incoming file.

She programmed the coordinates into her car's GPS first. As it calculated a route, she played the audio file. Broken phrases streamed past in bastard Spanish.

Timemyst Machine. . .
Federated States of Mexico. . .
Escape with Gant. . .
Rose followed. . .
Emir is coming. . .
Emir is here. . .
Emir knows he was a soldier. . .
Einselected.

The words changed to pleas for help as she sped through the rain.

Gant stood in front of the warehouse in the rain. His heart raced as his vision blurred. He swayed on his feet, not certain anymore if he was dying or not.

A car drove cautiously down the muddy road. It stopped, headlights framing him. No bright red sports car. No windows rolling down so the occupant could look at him chained like a dog. But still he knew who was there.

He took his gun out and took the safety off. There was one bullet left. For him or for her, he hadn't decided yet. "Come out, Detective Rose!"

The dome light turned on, and he saw her, black hair pulled back, tan skin wan from fatigue and stress, pale lips unpainted. She was a ghost of herself.

Gant chuckled. "Come out, Detective. Come out and arrest me."

She cocked her head to the side, her shoulder shrugged as if she were sighing, then the door of the little gray car opened. The car beeped in protest as she excited with the engine still turned on. "Mr. Gant?"

Gant held up his gun. "Present."

"I've come to help you, Mr. Gant. My name is Agent Rose from the Commonwealth Bureau of Investigation." Metal flashed in the light from the car; he aimed but realized the shape was wrong for a gun. "This is my badge, Mr. Gant. Do you see it?" She waited, then repeated everything in Spanish.

"I know English, Detective."

She shook her head. "I'm not a detective," she said in English. "I'm not with the police. I'm with the bureau, and I want to help you. Can I walk over to you? Can we talk?"

"Talk all you want." Gant laughed. "Talk 'til you die. You can't make me go back to prison."

She took two steps toward him. "Which prison were you in, Mr. Gant?" Her voice was perfectly calm, unruffled, unstressed.

His eye twitched. "Repisa de la Roca Prisión. You put me away for fraud. Tried to get me to hang for murder. Didn't happen, though."

"Repisa de la Roca Prisión? Rockledge doesn't have a prison, Mr. Gant. They have a rehab center. The Hammond Center has always been a rehab, from day one, although I admit it does look a bit like a prison. I checked, but they have no record of you ever being there."

His breath escaped in a hiss. "I've haven't gone there yet! I will! In 2072, you sent me there. You chased me like a terrier chasing a rat! You hunted me down, and in 2074, I escaped. I killed them all. Killed Wilhite in the parking lot. Killed the guard in the laundry, too."

"There is no Wilhite," Rose said as she came close to him. "These people you remember killing do not exist. They never did. Not here."

"No." Gant shook his head. "No. I know they exist. I saw 'em. I broke their necks with my bare hands. I felt their pulses stop." He remembered it like it was yesterday, or like it was a dream. When he slept, the memories were strongest. He dreamt and relived his life breath by breath.

She stopped in front of him, rain streaming down her unadorned face, dark green T-shirt plastered to her skin.

"You wore jeans?"

"Kitten heels and a pencil skirt seemed out of place." She shrugged. "Where's your friend, Mr. Gant?"

Gant pointed the gun at swamp. "In there. Dead

probably. They took him away still screaming, but now it's quiet." Too quiet. His throat tightened with an unwelcome sensation of fear. "We found the machine."

"Emir's time machine?"

His eye twitched at the name. "Didn't know about him until today. The rich use it as a toy. Hop back in time. Go forward, too, I suppose."

"I don't think it goes forward."

"Has to. I'm making it. I'm going to make it take me home." He realized he was trembling. "I've got to go home."

Rose lifted the gun from his hand. She flipped the safety on. "You are home. This is reality now. I'm sorry for your loss."

"NO!" His shout echoed across the empty lot, and thunder rumbled in response. "No. This isn't where I belong. Send me back!" He grabbed fistfuls of her shirt. "Send me back! No one knows me here. No one respects me here."

She touched his cheek with a cold hand. *A ghost. She really was a ghost.* "I'm sorry, Mr. Gant. I can't let you use the machine."

"I know how to use it. I'll share with you." He fumbled in his pant pocket for the notebook he'd grabbed from the dust. Donovan's blood was splattered across the cover "Here. Emir dropped this. He knew all about the machine. Said everything was over now. Anything you want, you can have. I'll go my way. You go yours." Same deal that had gotten him into this mess could get him out.

She took the notebook from him and slowly turned the first few pages. "Just to be clear, we're talking about a shorter man? Not much taller than me? Santa beard with a nice tan and looked like he'd been living off diet shakes?"

"Yes."

"That's Dr. Abdul Emir." She closed the notebook. "He's a narcissistic sociopath with the morals of, well, hmmm . . ." She tilted her head to the side and looked up at the growling clouds. "I'd say with the morals of a parasitic leech, but that's very unfair to leeches. He's not a nice man."

"He tortured Donovan."

"Yes, that's something I can see him doing."

Pain pierced Gant's head. It felt like someone was twisting a knife behind his eyes. He clutched at his forehead. "Please. Please make it stop." His knees sagged, and he sank to the ground.

Rose sat down with him.

"I'm being ripped apart. I'm being . . . hurt!"

She pulled his head close so it rested on her shoulder. "I'm sorry. If I understand the notes from Henry and Emir, you're being cut off. And I'm going to make it worse."

The pain brought tears to his eyes. "Make it stop. Send me home."

"There is no home but this. Donovan was a node. If Emir killed him, there is no reality for you to return to."

He shook, great rolling tremors ripping into his muscles. "I killed people."

"No," she said, patting his arm. "Well, you killed the Jane Doe in the purple shirt. She was an iteration of me, but that's not the sort of thing I can write in my report." Rose shifted in the mud, settling in as if they were about to have a picnic. "She had a nice funeral. We named her Juanita in the end. Oh, and there was Bradet. We didn't hit it off, but he was a citizen in my district, and I feel responsible for him. Did you cut him?"

Gant shook his head. "Donovan."

"Well, then, you probably won't go to trial ever. It would be a waste of the judge's time, and the Commonwealth frowns on that sort of thing. Big show trials are a waste of taxpayer money." She sighed and patted his head again.

"What's happening to me?"

"The worst possible thing I can imagine. You're going to the hospital. They'll give you an IV, patch you up, and in the morning, someone will come to talk to you. The state provides excellent therapy care. You'll probably tell them everything. You'll talk about the machine, and Donovan, and the strange man who came through the blue portal to kill you."

"I'll tell them his name," Gant said.

"Yes, and they'll look it up. Dr. Emir was executed outside his laboratory in Alabama last summer. Murdered by a rogue CBI agent who wanted to go back in time to change the nationhood vote." Rose put a companionable arm around his shoulder as he shivered. "You see, no matter what you tell them, no one will believe you. You and I will be the only ones who know the whole truth. Others will suspect. My partner will make a very educated guess, but he'll also keep his mouth shut. When I tell everyone you're mad, they will believe me."

Lightning illuminated the dark purple clouds. "Marrins. He was the agent. He didn't understand you can't change your past. You can go back and witness the past, but it won't change what you remember, what you lived. You can't change your past, only your future. You can only step forward. Even if it means your future tomorrow starts two years ago. You will keep moving forward."

"I went back in time." Gant sat up as an idea took hold, a life raft of sanity in the sea of madness. "You don't know me because I haven't murdered anyone yet. You're saying my past is your future. I remember killing those people, but they aren't dead yet. I still have to kill them." He looked her in the eye. "I will."

She raised one eyebrow in mocking question. Then she smiled pityingly. "No, Mr. Gant. You will go to the hospital. You will tell your story, then you will be taken to a care facility for people like you. People who have lost touch with reality."

"It's the truth! You know it is! You know I traveled through time!" Fear choked him, strangled his words. "I'm sane."

"I know it's the truth. I believe you . . . but no one else will. No one will ever, ever believe your story." She leaned closer. "Why did you come here, Mr. Gant? What were you trying to gain?"

He took a deep breath. "I came to escape my past. I was going to run away before my crimes were ever committed and live in freedom forever. It would be the perfect crime."

"Congratulations, Mr. Gant, you succeeded. You got away with murder."

CHAPTER 18

> *C–130 rolling down the strip. Airborne Ranger going to take a little trip. Mission unspoken. Destination unknown. Don't even know if we're ever coming home.*
>
> ~ **Airborne Ranger running cadence I2–2025**

Tuesday April 1, 2070
Florida District 8
Commonwealth of North America
Iteration 2

Sam slept on the leather couch of the regional director's office, ignoring the mud that dried on her pant legs. She woke foggy headed to a still and gray morning. The sounds of everyday office life filtered through the walls like ghosts. Everything felt ever so slightly off, like she was skating on ice that she knew would crack at any moment, but she kept drifting farther from shore.

It was a weightless feeling brought on by closing the case, she told herself. But even that felt like a lie.

Thou Shalt Not Kill. How many times had she repeated the phrase as part of the Ten Commandments? How many times had the nuns repeated the little song, "Shed not life in wanton ways?"

All these needless deaths.

She tried to imagine what Henry had felt when he stepped through the time portal into the muggy predawn hours of July 4, 2069. Had the dew clung to his shoes as he stepped on the grass outside N-V Nova Labs? Had he seen the other Emir? Had he seen Marrins lift the gun to execute Henry's mentor? Or had he been too far away, hidden in the tree line? The missing bullet they'd assumed lost last summer had certainly been meant for Troom.

But had Marrins known?

Was Marrins surprised when Henry pulled up to the lab the night she was kidnapped?

She sat at an empty desk, chin resting on her folded hands, and stared out the window at the palm trees. That morning in 2069 she'd rushed to the lab, angry at Emir for waking her up. Angry at herself for letting herself be pushed around by everyone else's agenda.

The morning Henry died, she'd felt confident, certain she could handle it all. She closed her eyes against the threat of tears. Now she felt deflated. Empty. Adrift. Lost in a world of possibilities where each one was worse than the last.

It was all so meaningless.

"Agent Rose?"

She looked up at a young woman she'd never met peering in from the doorway.

"Yes?"

"The director is ready to meet with you. Would you like a coffee?"

"No, thank you." Sam stood up, brushing the remains of the previous night's debacle off her pants as best she could. "Where is he?"

Director Loren was waiting in a secondary conference room; nine screens filled one wall, images of men in military fatigues moving soundlessly. "Good morning, Agent Rose. How was my couch?"

"I wouldn't recommend it if you aren't tired, but last night it was perfect. What's this?" She gestured to the screens. Emir's machine was with the men in uniform. "Are they dismantling it?"

"Testing it," Director Loren said. "We shipped it up to Fort Benning while you were catching forty winks. The first test was thirty minutes ago. It went well."

"Went well?" The words tasted like ash in her mouth. "What did you do?" The ice was beginning to crack under her.

Director Loren frowned at her in confusion. "We tested it. Took all those notes you found and gave it to one of the science teams. This thing's great."

"No. No, you can't," Sam stuttered. "It's dangerous."

"I know. I read the report about the safety circles and crushed bones and everything. We're being very careful. No one is going to get injured." His frown deepened. "Rose, are you feeling all right? You've gone all pale."

"The machine needs to be destroyed."

"That's an argument, certainly." Director Loren nodded and picked up his coffee mug from the conference table. "But before we destroy it, we're studying it. Making sure there are no uses for it."

"It's killed people."

"So have guns. We still have those," he said, giving her a significant look as he sipped his drink.

She knew that look. It was the one superiors gave to lower-ranking agents to tell them to shut up and get in line. "We know how guns work, sir. This isn't a new kind of projectile weapon. It's the new atom bomb. The new radium and mercury. It's going to kill us if we try to use it."

"Don't take this the wrong way, Rose. I like cautious agents. I like the people who think of the worst-case scenarios and are prepared for them. I like that in you. But in this case, I think you need to remember there are reasons we have radium, and mercury, and the atom bomb. We aren't Marie Curie leaving the thing out to slowly poison us. It's controlled."

"How can you possibly control something you don't understand?"

"We'll understand it soon enough." He sighed. "You think you can hold it together long enough to debrief the rest of the senior agents? There's a lot of gossip on social media about this. Your car wreck stirred up a tempest in a teapot like I've never seen. You should have seen how many demands I've had for your resignation."

"My resignation? For what . . . not dying?" Sam was indignant, but Director Loren was clearly done with the interruptions. She withered under his glare. "I'm sorry, sir."

"Trust me—I'm not going to ask you to resign. It's not your fault, Rose. There's always that one agent who catches media attention like a lightning rod. You just happen to be it."

"I don't try to get their attention."

"You know the bureau, though. Attention means promotion. It's hard for other agents to see your record as anything but self-aggrandizing stunts."

"I'm sorry iterations of me keep getting killed. I'll try to keep that under control. Maybe I can send a group memo to myselves." She crossed her arms and scowled at him.

"Agent . . ."

He gave her a long look, somewhere between stern and sympathetic. Finally, he said, "You sure you don't want something to eat before we go into the debrief? There are some donuts in the main office."

Her stomach cramped at the suggestion. "I'll be fine."

"Okay, right in there then." Director Loren led her into the main conference room, where the rest of the region's senior agents were waiting.

The room held a row of tables set in a U-shape

with computers, locking desk drawers, and plush red seats that looked comfortable but undoubtedly would feel like torture devices after the first hour. Ten other agents were already there, including Agent Petrilli, and the illustrious Senior Agent Alisha Mada, her inky-black hair twisted out and salted with white. She'd had a decorated thirty-year career, first in the USA FBI then the CBI, and the only reason she'd taken a district was because her nephew had been killed by gang violence and she wanted it cleaned up before her retirement.

It had been cleaned up, and her retirement was imminent.

Not soon enough to avoid her being here for this, though.

Sam met Mada's eyes and tried to smile. Mada's career was the one she'd always modeled, or hoped she was modeling. On days like today, she had serious doubts about her ability to live up to those standards.

Mada wasn't smiling.

Next to Agent Mada was a younger man nervously tapping a stylus on the desktop. He saw Sam's look and folded his hands in his lap.

Director Loren looked around the room. "Are we all here?"

"Yes, sir," the junior agent said. Sam was surprised his voice didn't squeak.

"Who're you?" Director Loren asked.

"Junior Agent Gerrard Wade, sir. Agent Eckleton sent me because he's in the hospital."

"Right. Foot surgery." Director Loren sighed. "What's your clearance level, Wade?"

"Um . . ."

Director Loren jerked his head toward the door. "Get out. Tell Agent Eckleton I'll visit him in the hospital later today."

"Um, yes, sir." Wade gathered his things and hurried out the door.

"Everyone else here has top secret clearance, correct?"

There was a murmur of affirmatives from around the room.

"Good. Let's get started. Has anyone not had a chance to read the statement I sent out this morning." If anyone hadn't, they weren't stupid enough to say so. "Good." Director Loren sat down at the right corner of the U. "Agent Rose will catch us up on what she knows about the events of last night."

Sam looked to the regional director in confusion. "Where do you want me to start, sir?"

"Start with the events of the past few days," Director Loren said.

Sam nodded and tried to gather her harried thoughts. Biting her lip wondering if *In the Beginning was the Word*' was a good response. Director Loren didn't look like he'd enjoy that bit of Catholic school humor.

So . . . the truth it is.

"Last year, a man named Dr. Emir invented a machine that he wanted to use to send messages back in time. It was meant to be an early alert system for natural disasters or terrorist attacks. It failed stupendously in that regard.

"What it did do was create a connection with time-lines similar to our own. Parallel universes in a way. Emir called them iterations. The woman killed earlier this week was Detective Samantha Rose. Me from a different iteration of time. She crossed into our time-line, looking for Gant. She stole my car at least once. She impersonated me, most likely followed me, and, in the end, she died. Gant is a killer with no parallel in our iteration. I don't know what psychosis drove him to pursue me after the other woman was dead, but he did. He firebombed my apartment, shot my dog, and put my partner in the hospital."

"Iteration? Timelines?" Agent Mada's stern frown was skeptical.

Director Loren made a circular motion with his hand, encouraging Sam to open up.

"Explain what an iteration is," Director Loren said. "I doubt anyone understood that part before their morning coffee."

"Time and reality are not as set in stone as we'd like," Sam said. "Emir proved the theory of the Many-Worlds Hypothesis correct. Every choice fractures re-ality into different iterations of time. There are periods of expansion followed by collapses. Eventually, all it-erations come back to one reality, and the others are discarded. Emir termed the event a Decoherence, the collapse of an iteration. When two iterations run paral-lel, it's called a Convergence, and it is possible to cross into other timelines during a convergence. During other periods, it's theoretically possible for a person to travel backward—possibly forward—in their own iteration."

"Why weren't we informed about this earlier?" Agent Mada demanded coolly. "The risk of having untracked criminals from other timelines is a significant security risk. Everyone in the bureau should be aware of what's happening."

Sam glanced at Director Loren and sighed. "We thought the machine was destroyed last year and that we wouldn't experience any more interference from other timelines."

"A foolish assumption," Mada said. "Especially if you didn't have proof the machine was destroyed."

"We had proof," Sam said. She'd smashed the damn thing herself. And she was willing to pick up a sledgehammer and do it again. Then she'd burn Henry's notes. "But it was rebuilt by a student of Dr. Emir's. Actually, he built two. A working prototype and another smaller machine that he tested in his lab and which killed him."

"Give them the full story," Director Loren ordered.

Sam closed her eyes. "Emir's student, Dr. Henry Troom, activated the smaller machine at his lab, crossed back in time to the day of his mentor's death, was shot by then–Senior Agent Marrins of the CBI, fell back into our time dead of a bullet to the head. The smaller machine was unstable and caused an explosion." She could practically see their thought processes. The machine was a shiny new toy of destruction. Like Mac, they were all thinking about that one thing in their past they could change. Contemplating what crimes they could stop before they ever happened.

She was losing them to the madness of the machine. To that siren song everyone heard but her. "I need to be clear: These are not toys," Sam said. "The machine has killed at least two people through improper use and been instrumental in the deaths of several others. Leaving our timeline open creates a security breach we are not prepared to deal with."

"We can guard the machine, though, can't we?" Petrilli asked. "Put guards around it and prevent anyone from walking in."

Sam shook her head. "The machine doesn't deliver you to the machine on the other end. At least, that's not been our experience. There is a way to make that happen, but we don't know how. We don't know nearly enough to contemplate keeping the machine active. Most people who cross between timelines wind up in a random location. Unless we have a way to calculate it, this machine creates an open border we can't defend. Look at Gant. He crossed over from another iteration and was hunting us before we knew he existed."

"Not much different than most stalkers," Petrilli said with a shrug. "Usually, we only find them after they've been following the victim for months. We can handle that sort of situation."

She stared at him and wondered if Petrilli realized how stupid he sounded. Probably not. He hadn't spent the last week reading physics notes until his eyes burned. He just . . . couldn't know. Couldn't understand.

"Petrilli is right," Mada said. "If we get ahead of this, we could use it to our advantage."

Petrilli nodded at her encouragingly. "There's a lot to be said for being able to control time."

"Yes, *if* we could control time," Sam said. "We can't. No one alive knows how the machine works. This is the new atom bomb, and we are poking it with a stick waiting to see if confetti comes out. Guess what? We're not going to get confetti and candy." Saints and angels. Why couldn't she be having this argument with someone rational, like MacKenzie? These people were too . . . too . . . too *her*, she realized. This was exactly what Agent Rose would look like after ten years of service in the bureau. Able to rationalize anything in the name of the greater good, with full faith in the infallibility of the bureau.

Mada raised her hand. "You said we have the research Emir used?"

"Yes." Oh, she did not like where this was going.

"Then we have a way of learning how to control the machine."

Sam opened her mouth to protest, but Mada held her hand up to stop her. "But I also recommend caution. Agent Rose is right, we shouldn't be poking anything with a stick. Yet we also shouldn't dismiss it too easily. There are many things in history we could change."

"That would be a mistake," Sam said, cutting off Director Loren. She'd rather her director fire her than let this go on. "Changing the past will drive you insane.

We have Gant in custody, he's insane. I don't think he started that way, but when he came here, everything that had made his history was erased. Anyone we asked to use the machine would be at risk."

"So we ask for volunteers," Mada said. "Ask them to fix our greatest mistakes, and in exchange, let them fix one of their own."

It was like they weren't even listening. "How would you determine our nation's greatest mistakes?" Sam demanded, hands moving to her hips. "Marrins tried that. He wanted to go back and stop the nationhood vote. Gant wanted to leave the country before he committed his crimes. If you ask any two people what part of history ought to be stopped, you'll get three different answers. Are you willing to risk another civil war to justify using the machine?"

"We won't ask the people. This isn't a referendum. We have a government for a reason." Mada's dark eyes were frosty with contempt.

"So we'll put the power to eradicate parts of our culture into the hands of the wealthy and elite? You'll destroy parts of our heritage with no idea what impact it will have on the future, or our present?" Sam shook her head. "No. This is too dangerous."

Director Loren held up a hand. "Thank you, Agent Rose. Please have a seat. We have a great deal to discuss here."

"Sir—" There was nothing to discuss.

"Your opinion has been noted, Agent Rose," Director Loren said as he stood up. "I appreciate your passion for the topic. But, as your supervisor, I will caution you to examine your own feelings on the matter."

Sam sank reluctantly into the chair opposite the director as she realized his decision was already made. Director Loren might not have even been the one making the decision. While she'd slept, he could have passed it up the chain of command, so the choice to use the machine ended up with a politician. Ended up with someone like her mother, someone who wouldn't think twice before rearranging the universe to suit their whims.

"Dr. Troom was close to you," Director Loran said.

"Not particularly, sir."

"You rescued him last year during the assault on the laboratory where he worked?"

"Yes, sir." Her shoulder tightened in anticipation of what was coming.

"From personal experience, I know how much it hurts to lose an asset you've risked your life for."

She swallowed the angry refutation she wanted to use. "I regret the loss of Henry's life, but I assure you that's not why I object to using the machine, sir."

"Your dog was killed by this. Your partner injured. You are too closely tied, and too emotionally invested, to think clearly about the possibilities," Director Loren said with a patient smile.

Sam resisted the urge to cross her arms. Looking combative wouldn't help her stance. "With all due respect, sir, that's a weak argument. I've been dealing with this for over a year. I'm the only person with any direct experience in this field. That makes *me* the expert. I'm not being emotional when I tell you that using the machine will cost more lives than you or I are willing to spend. You're about to make the Battle of the Somme look like a picnic. *Sir*."

Director Loren stared at her, face a mask of emotionless rigidity. "I'll take that under advisement. Agents, we will follow Agent Mada's direction to proceed with caution. That being said, let us discuss the possible ways this new device could help our nation."

"Putting a positive spin on it won't make it better," Sam muttered. Director Loren sent her another harsh glare, and she snapped her mouth shut. Her teeth ground together as the other agents talked about the things that could be changed. Old cases worth revisiting. Being able to place a person at the scene of the crime to witness it without interfering, stopping tragic deaths in advance. They hadn't heard a word she'd said.

An hour later, her stomach was in knots, and nothing had changed.

Director Loren dismissed them. "Agent Rose, stay a moment please."

She stopped at the door, not willing to turn. "Sir."

"I know this is hard for you. You've been on the front lines, and it's left an impression. Have you considered taking a few days off?"

"I'll take it under advisement, sir." Just like he'd taken her suggestions under advisement.

"You're going to go down in history, Agent. A hundred years from now, they'll be reading about you in history class."

"A hundred years from now, there won't be anyone left to attend class."

The hospital was oddly quiet for an afternoon. Sam walked down the halls, heels clicking on the floor with a comforting familiarity. The smell of antiseptic and the slow beeps of the machines guarding the patients helped soothe her. She slipped into Mac's room and checked the nurse's notes on the computer screen by his bed. Poor security there. Someone should have logged out before leaving the room. Still, she was grateful for the oversight. Mac's vitals were good. He'd recover in time.

She sat down in a hard plastic chair next to his bed. "Mac?" The whisper didn't wake him. She gently reached for his hand. He was cold. So still. Corpselike . . . almost dead when she needed him most. She squeezed his hand and bit back the tears. There was so much she needed to tell him, to ask him, to take from him, she realized with a sickened sensation. She always took from Mac. Stole his time, and his couch, and his attention . . . She had endangered his career more than once.

She put her head on the bed beside his hand, waiting for him to wake up. She wanted one more thing from him: a chance to say good-bye.

A nurse bustled in, regarded her in speculative silence, and retreated after checking the monitors.

She was still waiting for Mac to wake up when Agent Petrilli knocked on the door.

"Hi." He smiled like a movie star waiting for the camera flash.

Sam forced a smile of her own. "Hi."

"Your phone was off, and Director Loren asked if I could check on you on my way back home."

Sam sat up. *What had they done?*

"I figured you'd be here." Petrilli smiled. "I always wondered who I was competing with for your attention. You two are quite something, aren't you?"

"No, just friends," she said for what felt like the hundredth time. She pulled her hand away from Mac's. Petrilli couldn't know what Mac meant to her. No one could. Not if Mac was ever going to have a normal life. "He saved my life once. I figured the least I could do was visit the hospital and check up on him."

"Is he going to be okay?"

"He'll be fine. He has a minor concussion, a couple of scrapes and bruises. Nothing serious." Hoss had taken bullets for her. Mac had taken the bruises. She ought to be dead twice over, but here she sat unscathed, while everyone around her suffered. "Did you need anything?"

"No. I just wanted you to know they ran the first op with the machine up at Fort Benning."

Her heartbeat slowed, stuttering, threatening to

stop as cold fear gripped her. "Oh?" She kept her voice light and calm.

"They went back a week in time and saved a baby who was going to be killed in a car collision. I thought you might need to hear that."

"Really?" Even to her ears, her voice sounded strained.

"We're going to do good with this, Rose. I know you're worried it could all go sideways, but it isn't. I promise. I'm on your side. I agree we need to be careful. But we saved a kid's life today, what's better than that?"

"Nothing," Sam lied. "I'm sure the family is relieved." She waited a moment. "How did they react?"

He glanced down the hall and shrugged. "They were good."

"You're lying."

Petrilli winced. "There was some shock. The family was grieving, and then it hadn't happened, it was an adjustment. We sent a therapist to work it out with them. In the future, we'll probably try to hit these things within a few hours. Giving people too long to adjust to changes only gives them more psychological dissonance to worry about."

"What do you think is going to happen if we erase tragedy from life?"

He shrugged. "Who knows? Maybe we'll create Utopia. Maybe it'll just lower the number people using antidepressants. It's a sea star thing; you can't save them all maybe, but you can save the one you throw back in the water. You know?"

"Do you think everyone is going to have a fabulous life because you stop every death, every car accident, every suicide? *Are* you going to stop death? We can't even keep people from being unemployed when the world population is so low that no single country could scrape together a halfway-decent army, and you think you can create Utopia by stopping car accidents? Life without tragedy isn't life, Petrilli. If we didn't ever experience a loss, we'd never understand how good it feels to have someone survive. You can't appreciate sunshine if you've never seen night."

"That is a very pessimistic view, Rose. If people need tragedy in life, they can read Shakespeare. Pull out some old Russian literature, maybe. No one needs real heartbreak in their life."

"Who would we be without tragedy? I wouldn't be me. Are you going to erase all the moments that defined my life?"

"Maybe this will mean your life won't need to be defined by horrible things!" Petrilli threw his arms up in exasperation. "You know? How much happier would you be if your life was influenced by a series of happy memories instead of whatever trauma you're hauling around. Drop your baggage, Rose."

She lifted her chin. "There is no such thing as a perfect life. Even if to everyone else your life was flawless, you would hate the days that weren't euphorically beautiful. You'd be an addict always looking for the next bit of happiness. You'd destroy yourself in a quest for something that doesn't exist."

"I give up," Petrilli said. He turned away, then turned back, ready to jump into the fray once more. "We saved a *baby*." Petrilli raised his eyebrows. "Don't you think that means something? Can't you see the value of a single life?"

"I can. I'm glad the baby is alive, but I want to make sure the baby grows up in a world where its choices determine its future. No one sitting in a lab with a tinker-toy time machine has the right to decide how history is shaped. That's not our job. We aren't God."

"I was always taught God helps those who help themselves. We were given a wonderful new way to help people. I think God would want us to use it."

"That's probably what people said about the atom bomb."

"And the bomb brought an end to the world wars. It isn't a black-and-white thing."

"Exactly! Don't you see: You can't just decide this machine will only do good because you want it to. There are people who will use it for their own ends. Nothing ever exists in a vacuum. And maybe it won't be immediate, but given enough time—and we are talking about a time machine here—someone is going to turn that machine on and hurt others." Sam pushed past him and walked furiously down the hall.

"Where are you going, Rose?" Petrilli asked as he chased after her.

"Home." *No.* There wasn't an apartment left to go home to. "Never mind, I'm going to the office."

"Are you upset with me?" He honestly sounded wounded.

Sam came to a screeching halt in the hospital hallway. "Petrilli, I know this might be hard for you to wrap your mind around, but my life doesn't actually revolve around you. In the past seventy-two hours, I've lost my residence, my dog, and my best friend has been hospitalized. I have paperwork piling up in my office and a junior agent who needs to be debriefed and given some leave time before he breaks from the stress."

"I'm just checking. You're were a hot second away from trashing your career this morning, arguing with Loren. I don't want our friendship caught in the cross fire."

"We're fine," she lied.

"Good." He fell into step with her. "Wanna do lunch next week? I found this awesome Mexican grill near the border of our districts. Hole-in-the-wall, but the queso deserves a letter of commendation."

Sam glanced sideways at him. "Really?" He couldn't be serious.

"Oh, yeah. If you like spicy food, you will love this place!"

He was incredible. Nothing bruised Feo Petrilli's ego. Something would have to get through to his little pin-sized brain for that to happen.

"You game?"

"Sure. Let me check my calendar, and I'll let you know when I'm free." She'd probably be free second

Thursday after never, but she'd say just about anything to get him to shut up at this point.

"It's a date then." If he'd had a hat on, he would have tipped it. She almost laughed at the image.

Almost.

Sam stabbed the elevator CALL button and realized that was a tactical error. Being trapped with Petrilli even a minute more might result in a homicide, and she didn't want more paperwork. The elevator dinged as the doors opened. She waited for Petrilli to step in, and said, "You know what, I think I'll take the stairs." She waved good-bye, then leaned back, looking up at the ceiling, trying to picture heaven beyond the faded white tiles dimpled with black paint.

Director Loren wasn't going to listen to her. Petrilli had already dismissed every warning. The chances for divine intervention were low . . . Maybe this was what Julius Cesar had felt like before he crossed the Rubicon, like he was the only one in the world who could do things right.

Noah before the flood might have been a better analogy, she admitted as she walked back to Mac's room. She hesitated in the doorway, watching him sleep for a moment. He hadn't looked this peaceful since after he'd rescued her from Marrins and Emir the previous summer, and even then, things hadn't been good.

Mac would never admit it, but being with her would kill him. She closed the distance between them and pressed a gentle kiss against his forehead, leaving a faint trace of her lipstick. "Good-bye."

"Do you want a drink of water?" Agent Edwin asked. He was sitting at his desk, fiddling nervously with a pen.

Ivy looked at him. "Hmm?"

"Water, there's, um, a watercooler in the county records office downstairs. I can got get you a drink if you want."

"Sure." She smiled and tried to not fidget. Agent Rose hadn't given her any clue as to why she wanted to meet. All the paperwork had been turned in. Senior Agent Petrilli had met with her last night, debriefed her, and sworn her to secrecy. The department had given her the third degree this morning, then—after a phone call the chief wouldn't talk about—she'd been told to take the rest of the day off. She'd been on her way to home—and her bed—when Agent Rose called.

The door opened, and Ivy jumped to her feet.

Agent Rose walked in, looking thinner and harder than Ivy could have ever imagined. She'd heard of women described as whiplike and always imagined them as leanly muscled people with sharp tongues and killer looks. Now she knew that whiplike meant ready to crack. "Good afternoon, Agent Rose. I was surprised you called."

"Thank you for coming. I'm glad you were able to come here today." There was no emotion on Rose's face or in her voice.

"Busy schedule?" Ivy asked, trying to hide her worry.

"Something like that."

"I hear Boca's great this time of year. You could make a weekend of it. Catch up on your sleep." She smiled nervously.

Agent Rose's answering smile was brittle. "I'll take that under advisement for a later date. My weekend is already booked."

"Right. I bet you and Agent MacKenzie have things to do." *Probably naked things.* If she had a man like MacKenzie looking at her the way Agent MacKenzie looked at Rose, she'd be spending her weekends indulging every erotic fantasy she'd ever had.

Rose's face was statuesque in its emptiness. "Yes, but not together. He's headed home to Chicago tomorrow."

Ivy looked at the floor and wondered if it could swallow her whole. "Oh." *What a waste of a weekend.*

"Let me grab something," Agent Rose said. She unlocked her office, cautiously opened the door, then stepped in, returning a moment later with a small folder of dead-wood papers. "This is for you, Officer Clemens, with the thanks and gratitude of a grateful nation."

Ivy took the proffered paper and read it. "A commendation?"

"For exemplary service and quick thinking under pressure." Agent Rose held out the rest of the folder. "This is a recommendation to the bureau training program with testimonies from myself, Agent Edwin, Agent MacKenzie, and District Supervisor Loren. We all feel your service went above and beyond the call of duty and that your talent is being wasted in the police department here. It's your choice, of course, but I think you'd be an amazing bureau agent."

Ivy's vision blurred as tears filled her eyes. "Agent Rose, I don't . . . I don't know what to say! You think I could be like you? I'm not . . . I'm nothing as good as you."

"You said you admired me for being the only clone in the bureau? But then you learned I wasn't. I was a fraud. The clone movement wanted to make me a figurehead because they needed a champion. But I'm not and never could be. You, though—you could be that champion. *Should* be that champion. A clone police officer graduating from the academy? You'd be everything you wanted me to be. I don't want to pressure you, or tell you that people need you to do this, but they need someone. They need a hero."

Ivy wiped the tears away with the cuff of her uniform. "Agent Rose, you have no idea what this means to me."

"I have an idea." She opened her arms. "Are you a hugger?"

Rose had just spoken of heroes, and Ivy wrapped her arms around hers. "Thank you!" She squeezed Agent Rose tight. "Oh, gosh, I will not let you down. You'll see. I'm going to make you proud. You won't regret this. I promise."

"I know I won't." Rose squeezed her back and let go. "There's one more thing." She reached up and unclasped a chain from around her neck. "This is my

Saint Samantha medallion, my namesake and the patron saint of spirituality. You may never need a god in your life, but you'll need faith. The days ahead are going to be dark. Everything you do will be scrutinized. Everything you say will be questioned. On the days you can't believe in yourself, know that I believe in you. No matter what happens. No matter what the future holds, I believe in you."

There was a rush of air from the hall as Agent Edwin came back in. "Oh! Did you tell her, ma'am?"

Agent Rose smiled, and this time she looked less defeated. "I did. Officer Clemens hasn't made a decision yet, but I did present her with her award and the letters of recommendation."

Edwin held out a cup of water to her. "I wrote one, too. Said I'd be honored to have you in my district if I was ever a senior agent."

"By the time she graduates the academy, you will be a senior agent," Rose said. "You could request her for your district. That is if you're going, Officer Clemens."

Ivy took the water and lifted it in a toast as she beamed with joy. "To the academy!"

Mac shook his arm, trying to regain some feeling now that the IV needle was gone. The phone rang and went to voice mail. He dialed again.

"This is Agent Rose."

"Sam! It's me," he said as if she didn't make a habit of checking her caller ID when the phone rang. Or that she wouldn't guess that from his voice. "The nurse said you came to see me but left with some man."

"Agent Petrilli hunted me down." There was a small sneer to her tone that suggested she hadn't welcomed the other agent's intrusion.

"Are you okay?"

"I'm fine." Her voice was distant, closed off. "How are you doing?"

"I have a clean bill of health, and I'm starving. Want to meet somewhere for dinner?"

"I can't. I'm sorry. The paperwork is Sisyphean." The words were all in the right order, but the tone was wrong. Dismissive. Cold. Distant.

He was losing her again. "Sam?" He tried to stay calm. "What's wrong?"

"Nothing." There was a moment of silence and a little defeated sigh. "It's not you. I'm tired. I have bureau paperwork and stuff for the apartment complex, and I'm so tired."

He relaxed a little. "Why not go find a hotel for the night and tackle it in the morning. It's already past six."

"I just want to get it out of the way. Get it done and cut my losses, you know."

"Yeah, I know, I just want to make sure you'll take care of yourself."

"I'll be fine. Agent Edwin has manfully volunteered to stay here and fill out everything he knows the details for. We'll be done in an hour or two."

He thought he heard a smile in there. "Okay, well, maybe we could get together tomorrow?"

"You aren't at the hotel yet?" Sam asked.

He hadn't left the hospital yet. Checking on Sam had seemed more important. "No, why?"

"The bureau bought you a return ticket to Chicago for tomorrow. Your flight leaves at eight in the morning."

"Oh." So this is what heartbreak felt like. "I thought . . . never mind. I thought wrong."

Sam sighed. "Don't be like that. I'm going to take some leave soon. I can come visit. We can call each other."

He heard the words, and in them, he heard the lie.

"Sam . . . I love you." He sat down in the hospital hallway, leaned against the wall. "I love you."

"I know . . . but I can't love you. You're wonderful." He heard her move things on her desk and settle in to her chair. "The bureau approved use of Emir's machine. They've already started testing it. I'm living with a death sentence. No matter what I do in the next year or two, I'm going to die sooner rather than later. I can't do that to you."

"We could be happy while it lasted." A day, a year or two—he could accept there might be a time limit on their being together, but he couldn't stomach the idea of never having time with her again.

"No." Sam's voice broke through his thoughts. "Mac, we couldn't. You'd always be trying to figure out a way to stop it. I'd always be trying to find a way to protect you. I don't want to see you broken again. I can't die knowing how much it would hurt you if you loved me."

He closed his eyes. "If you were trying to make this easier, this isn't the right speech. Tell me you love someone else. Tell me you're moving to Aruba with Agent Edwin."

She laughed, a bitter, heartbroken sound of a woman who had lost too much laughing at the world asking her for another drop of blood. "You'd know I was lying. You always know when I'm lying."

"Sam . . . please. Don't do this to us. We're so happy together."

"Good-bye, Mac. Have a safe flight." She turned off her phone.

He dialed again, but it went straight to voice mail. Two more tries, two more messages asking her to call back.

"Sir?" A nurse stopped in front of him. "Are you all right?"

He held up the phone. "My girlfriend just broke up with me."

"Is she in the hospital?"

"No, ma'am."

"Then sitting here isn't going to do you any good," the nurse said.

He looked up at a middle-aged woman whose no-nonsense face was filled with empathy.

"If you want her back, you have to go get her. That's how these things work. Always have. If you want something, you have to go out and get it." The nurse held up a hand to help him up.

He took it and stood up. "You're right, thanks. She'll probably be at work for a little while longer."

"Take some flowers," the nurse suggested. "Makes you look like less of a stalker."

"Ah . . . right."

Sam signed the last piece of paper and shut down her computer. She picked up her purse, then her phone. After a moment's consideration, she tossed the phone in her trash bin. She walked out of her office and closed the door behind her.

"Ready to go home, ma'am?" Edwin asked. He turned beet red with embarrassment. "I mean, to the hotel."

"Yes. Are Agent MacKenzie's travel arrangements all set?"

"I was just finalizing them now, ma'am."

"Good. I already told him he's leaving in the morning."

Edwin grimaced. "Are you sure he wants to take off tomorrow, ma'am? Traveling right after getting out of the hospital is a bad, um, not advised," he said, hastily editing his vocabulary.

"He said he was eager to get home. There are cases piling up in Chicago that need his attention." Mac might be able to catch her lying, but Edwin didn't know her well enough.

"Are you sure?"

"You can call him," Sam said.

"I tried. The number you gave me for his private cell phone seems to be turned off."

"Really?" Sam frowned with genuine concern. "How strange. I'm sure it's the right number." And the sun was covered in ice, and cats were vegetarians. "He must want some privacy." She laid her papers on his stack. "Can you sign and file these for me when you get a chance?"

"Sure, ma'am. Anything urgent in there."

"No," Sam said. "It's just my final paperwork for the Troom case. No rush. The bureau already is fully aware of my thoughts on the matter."

"I'll get it done when I'm finished with everything else then," he said.

"Great. Don't work too late. This has been a hard week for all of us."

Edwin blushed. "I'll be fine, ma'am. One of the girls from the WIC office brought me up some of their fish fry. She said we're reinvited to the building Christmas party! I think she likes me."

"Well, that's good news!" Sam said with forced enthusiasm. "I'll start planning my ugly sweater!"

"Mine has reindeer," Edwin said.

"I look forward to seeing it. I'll be at the hotel downtown. If you need anything, just call." Sam walked out of the office for the last time. She wanted to cry. No, that was a lie, too. She'd been wanting to cry for months. Ever since she'd buried her father, she'd been carrying a weight she couldn't escape. Every day, her knees bent a little more. Every sunrise hailed another day of battle. One without Hoss.

And one without her anchor . . .

Her throat tightened with grief.

The bureau had signed her death sentence. Anywhere they took this project would be the path of her destruction. And Mac's

She crossed the parking lot to where her new car sat, a used, gray Alexian Virgo. Mac was just the kind of person they'd get to volunteer to go through the machine. If they told him he could go back and save his friends from the ambush, he wouldn't even stop to think about it. No one would. It seemed she was the only one who didn't want to change the past.

All she wanted to do was change the future.

Mac pushed open the door to Sam's office and looked in. Her flustered junior agent stared at him with a shocked look on his face.

"C-can I help you, sir?"

"I'm looking for Agent Rose; do you know where she is?" Maybe he should have stopped for the flowers.

"Uh-uh." The younger man shook his head.

"Do you know when she'll be back?"

Edwin frowned in confusion. "What?"

"Agent Rose?" Mac stepped forward not quite sure how to proceed. "Do you know if she's returning tonight?"

"She resigned!" Agent Edwin blurted out. "She left!"

Mac closed on the desk and gently took the paperwork that the junior agent was clutching tightly. Sam's signature was at the bottom of a resignation form. Reason for leaving was listed as personal.

For a moment, his heart leapt with joy. Personal reasons. She was going to come to Chicago with him! But . . . no. That would be a transfer. There was no reason to resign if she wanted to come with him. "What did Agent Rose do this morning?"

"She went to the district meeting. I mean, I think . . ." Mac gave him a steady, questioning look. "I wasn't supposed to know about it," Edwin admitted. "Definitely wasn't supposed to be there."

"I don't care—I'm not going to get you in trouble. What did you hear?"

He shrugged. "Maybe Agent Rose arguing with the regional director. Something about her dog, and warnings, and a machine they took to Fort Benning. Maybe. I was outside waiting to ask her a question."

"Not listening." Mac nodded. "The director told her to toe the line, didn't he? I bet that went over well."

"Like telling a hurricane the city is a no-fly zone, sir."

Mac set the paperwork down, tapping it as he stared into space. She couldn't go back to her apartment. She hadn't stayed around to take him home from the hospital.

In retrospect, he should have seen that as a huge, glaring red flag.

Sam was trying to get him out of the picture. Which meant there was really only one place she would go.

"Sit on this," he ordered Agent Edwin. "Give me forty-eight hours to see if I can talk some sense into her."

Agent Edwin slowly nodded. "How are you going to reach her?"

"I'll start with a phone call."

"I tried; she left her phone and badge in her office." Edwin grimaced. "In the trash can."

Smart girl. She wasn't leaving anything for someone to track. The Alexia Virgo she drove was old enough that it didn't have a speed restrictor in it. It was tenuous, but he didn't think she was just going off the grid, like Connor and Nealie. Which meant she was doing it for a reason—that someone's being able to follow her would be either dangerous, illegal . . . or both.

And if he had to guess, he would say she was on the road to Fort Benning.

Mac smiled. "I know where she went."

He drove back to the hotel first, parking the rental in the back of the lot. It had been years since he had done anything remotely black ops or covert, but the training was still there. The bureau couldn't be fooled for long, but he didn't need more than a head start. Once he was gone, there were only a few possible endings, death and imprisonment being the most likely options. With luck, and possibly divine intervention, he might be able to swing success.

Adrenaline burned through his veins. Time slowed to a crawl. It had been a long time since he'd been in the zone, but he was back now. In control and sure of himself like he hadn't been since Afghanistan.

With careful attention, he tore through his luggage, discarding anything memorable. Nothing traceable was coming. Nothing that would garner attention. The government phone stayed, credit cards, all of it. There was no way the rental car could come, but it did mean he needed transportation that could move fast.

He looked out the window at the library down the street. Dereliction of duty. Fraud. Forgery. Possibly grand theft auto . . . it helped if he acted like this was hostile territory. He wouldn't think twice if he were behind enemy lines and in a military uniform. Here, the lines were blurred. This was supposed to be home, but the people gunning at him were the ones in uniform.

Mac called down to the front desk—the room was reserved for another six days. By accident or design, Sam had it covered. Still in his suit, he walked down to the library and called the rental company. Thirty minutes later a young man named Kori picked him up.

"Thank you," Mac said as he climbed into the car. "My transmission broke, I called the tow truck, but that doesn't get me home to Columbia tonight. If I'm not at that meeting tomorrow, my boss will kill me."

Kori laughed. "Yeah, my dad's like that. I miss curfew, and I'm grounded for a week!"

Ah, to be seventeen again.

Kori dropped him off at the main desk and Mac spent another hour filing paperwork under the name of Cole Clary. Mr. Clary was a scruffy individual about Mac's height who had been engrossed in a computer game when Mac walked past him at the library. Apparently, the computer game was pay-as-you-go, and the hapless Mr. Clary had forgotten to put his wallet away.

Mac had turned it in to the main desk like a good citizen after he lifted the driver's license and cash.

"What kind of car, Mr. Clary?" the clerk asked as he signed the last page of waivers.

"Anything that runs," Mac said. "Nothing flashy. I just need to get there on time."

"I have the perfect car."

A beat-up, brown Moka Black with twenty thousand miles on the tires. Mac checked the engine—there was a driver's black box that would keep him from speeding, but he could work with that. "Looks great."

"Just drop her off in the Columbia office when you get there, and you'll get your fifty dollar safety deposit back when you plug her into the charge station."

"Perfect." Mac took the keys and pulled out of the lot. The first stop was the beach with the mud parking lot. He turned donuts in the empty lot until there was a good layer of mud on the car, then smeared the license plates and covered the rental sticker. He stripped off his suit and stuffed the bureau uniform in the trash. The chances of his ever needing that again were dwindling with every passing second. T-shirt and jeans were what this op called for. And sunglasses.

Time to chase Sam.

He drove the speed limit for an hour, then pulled into a good-sized town and stopped at an auto-parts store for two basic travel essentials: an auditor and a radar detector. Popping the hood, he fixed the auditor in place. It would read the allowed speed limit and tell the restrictor box that the car was within seven miles of that limit at all times. Then he hooked the radar detector in and set it to search for large radio signals, radars, and police bands. Traveling just shy of two hundred miles an hour wasn't good for the tires, but it ate the miles between the Space Coast and the Home of the Infantry in record time.

CHAPTER 19

*Ten thousand deaths, my beloved. Let me fall before
you. Let my death be the one that wins you life anew.*

**~ excerpt from the poem "A Living
Death" by Jorge Sabio 12–2068**

*Wednesday April 2, 2070
Fort Benning, Georgia
Commonwealth of North America
Iteration 2*

Sam parked her car behind a charging station down
the street from the main research facility and left the
windows cracked and the keys lying on the driver's
seat. There should have been a storm brewing in the
distance. Big thunderclouds boiling in the atmosphere
promising a torrent of rain and shattering thunder.
The wind should have picked up, gusting around her
or howling down the street like the song of a damned
soul. Birdsong and a gentle afternoon zephyr seemed
wholly inappropriate.

It was a metaphor for her life, really. Every grand plan with which she set out fizzled into obscurity. Not failure, she didn't fail. But all her efforts were swept away in the great rolling tide of time, lost, forgotten, erased like footprints on the sand.

She parked her car in the back and made her way to the station bathroom to freshen up. The woman in the mirror was a stranger. Sleepless nights had left bruises on her cheeks. Stress had thinned her, sharpened her features, and left her wan. Aside from the faint heartbeat fluttering her neck, she was already a corpse.

"Why are you doing this, Samantha?"

The woman in the mirror stared back with unforgiving eyes.

"What do you think this will get you? Another year? Another decade? Everyone dies in the end."

Ten thousand deaths, wasn't that what Mac had said? There were ten thousand deaths needed to make a life. The machine would take ten million. Everyone here would die if Emir and Loren had their way.

"I swore an oath," she told the woman in the mirror. "I promised to sacrifice everything if that's what it took to defend the nation. Everyone else is blind. I'm the only one who sees the danger, so I'm the only one who can prevent the destruction."

Saying it aloud almost made it possible to believe all that.

Or maybe she really was delusional. Maybe Loren and Petrilli were right.

She had to wonder how many other Sams had repeated that in other iterations? She wondered if they'd reached this point, too. If the detective who chased Gant had hesitated, then run into the vortex, telling herself she had to stop Gant before anyone else did. Maybe Juanita's last thoughts were of how she was dying to protect her people.

Or maybe they were all as selfish as she. Wanting to keep themselves away from the nightmares of crossed timelines and greedy men.

There really was no way of knowing.

Fort Benning. Talk about ghosts. He'd done basic training there, and Ranger school, and airborne school. Most his life between nineteen and twenty-five revolved around the ancient army post. Somewhere in his wallet, he still had the ID they'd issued him before his last deployment.

By the time he'd sobered up and started thinking straight, the brown card was little more than a souvenir, a memento of a shattered lifetime. He'd kept it out of misplaced sentimentalism. The lockdown was an annexed portion on the southwest side of Fort Benning that UNATBI had taken over in 2066. Part of the old training grounds outside Jamestown off Blueridge Road.

He recharged the car at a rest stop just inside Georgia before turning north on 520 as the sun set. Sam was bureau-trained. She would wait until it was late, and the guards were tired, before she tried anything. He tried to take some comfort from that.

Knowing that Sam was an absolute rookie charging in to steal a device that had already been involved with six deaths and more than one murder attempt made him drive faster. At Cusseta, he pulled over at a pawnshop. They sold him a small gun and ammo with no questions. Insanity all around. He wouldn't have handed a weapon to a man who looked like him.

Maybe they just wanted to get me out of their store.

He didn't blame them.

A quarter to eleven, he abandoned the rental in the woods outside the lockdown. He wiped it down for prints, left the keys in the driver's seat, and Cole Clary's driver's license on the dashboard. Hopefully, the guy had a decent alibi.

Now, where would his errant senior agent be? He scanned the tree line around the lockdown as he secured his new gun. There was a darker pocket of shadow under a thick layer of broad-leafed vines. Something glinted in the yellow light from the building. Amateur—she hadn't taken her jewelry off.

He smiled as he melted into the brush in the way only a Ranger could.

Lying on her stomach, Sam crawled forward, timing the cameras on the outside of the lockdown. A hand covered her mouth, and she was pulled forcibly backward, landing on something warm. Her nose told her who it was even before Mac hissed "Be quiet!" in her ear. She was wrapped in his arms, sitting on his lap in a tent of vines

"What are you doing here?" she whispered, turning so she could look at him.

"That's my line."

She tried to wiggle free, but Mac just tightened his grip, pulling her closer. Her heart rate picked up. "I don't have a choice, Mac."

"You'll break it, they'll rebuild it. You aren't going to accomplish anything. Let's go back to Florida. Agent Edwin is sitting on your resignation. We can think of something else."

"I already have. I'm not breaking the machine." She froze as a guard's flashlight swept the foliage. Someone standing behind them and looking at the light might have seen their profile, but the guard standing by the building could only see vines. He moved on.

Sam lowered her voice. "I'm not breaking the machine," she said again. "I'm removing it from the timeline. Emir said that all timelines eventually collapsed back into one, didn't he?"

"Phased back into balance," Mac corrected. "I remember."

"So I remove the machine from the timeline, and it will eventually be removed from *all* the timelines."

He shifted position, his five o'clock shadow grazing her face. "How?"

"Take the time machine *through* the time warp."

Mac held her in silence. It seemed he was holding her tighter. She could smell his soap and hear the high-pitched buzz of mosquitoes.

"I have to go, Mac. This is the only option I have.

There's nothing for me here. I've lost everything. I have nothing."

He kissed her cheek. "You have me."

"But I don't. Not like this. Not with my head already in the guillotine." She bit her lip, trying not to cry. "You should leave." She couldn't keep pushing him away. She wasn't that strong.

"I can't lose you."

"Thank you."

She could feel Mac swallow hard. He gestured toward the lockdown. "You have a plan for this?"

"The director's keycard, running shoes, and a couple of prayers." She'd managed to get a tour of the outer labs, but even her sunny smile and a bureau badge hadn't been enough to get her near the machine. Thankfully, the lab director was the careless sort who left her badge sitting on her desk when she went to the break room for lunch.

"I would have preferred a fragment grenade."

In the distance, someone shouted.

"Ah, they found the car," Mac said.

She glared at him, a look he probably missed in the dark.

"Call it a distraction," he said. With a light push, she was crouching. "Time to run."

They waited for the guards and cameras to move, then sprinted for the side door. Sam slid the director's card in, and the lock turned green.

"This is way too easy," Mac breathed.

"Tell me that in five minutes. This is after hours."

"So, what, six minutes before the lockdown turns this into a pretty mausoleum?"

"Three." Bureau security didn't believe in second chances. Once lockdown was initiated, vents would flood the halls with a knockout gas that would leave them incapacitated.

She ran headlong down the tiled hallways, following the map in her head. Two lefts, a right, the third right . . . and there it was. *Bastard*. The machine that would ultimately kill her. Emir's theory meant she could take the time machine out of play, but it also meant Jane Doe would still get buried in 2069. She would be buried in a pauper's grave after months of hideous torture finally killed her.

Mac's hand rested on her back. "Sam?"

"I hate this machine."

"Two minutes and counting."

She unlocked the door. The buttons were easy. She'd watched the remote video presentation with the taste of bile in her mouth, but that didn't mean she didn't need to know how to work the thing. Ironically, Petrilli had sent her the video because he hoped it would win her over to the bureau's way of thinking.

"When are we going?" Mac asked.

"If it's still the same setting from the lab, we'll move back in time a year. April of '69. We might jump a few miles." Thirty seconds for it to power up. "My math might be a bit off, though."

"Let's just hope it doesn't drop us in a live-fire range out on the post."

"Let's hope our bones aren't twisted like a wrung-out towel."

Mac grimaced.

Forty seconds more for the machine to rattle to life. A claxon sounded in the building. Red lights flashed.

"We begin losing oxygen in five . . . four . . . three . . . two . . ."

Sam hit the button. "One."

A blue-green mist swirled as she held the button down. Time slowed. "I love you."

"I love you, too."

She clutched the machine to her chest and leaned in for a kiss. Mac wrapped his arms around her, and they fell into the portal together.

CHAPTER 20

We are never so lost as when we believe we know everything.

~ excerpt from *Among the Wildflowers*
by Andria Toskoshi

Date Unknown
Location Unknown
Iteration Unknown

Sunlight burned Sam's eyes. She had been expecting night and the cover of darkness. Heart racing, she rolled away from the portal, still clutching the machine. It seemed her grip was loosening. She looked down and saw the metal dissolving, steaming into the air like dry ice on a hot road.

Mac scrambled to his feet beside her. "That's not supposed to happen, is it?"

"This plan didn't come with a training manual."

They watched it vanish until there was nothing left but a glass tube with a metal fitting on each end filled with a viscous purple liquid that moved like mercury. Sam looked up at Mac. "Thoughts?"

"Don't break the tube."

"Good thinking." She tucked it into her pocket and looked around. "This . . . could be Alabama."

"This could be anywhere."

Sam shrugged. "Let's find a road. Some sign of human civilization would be nice."

"Just so we know we didn't accidentally wander into a dystopian wasteland populated only by rabid dogs?"

"You're not allowed to watch sci-fi movies anymore."

"Considering I think we're currently *living* a sci-fi movie, I feel it's good preparation for time traveling."

"We're not time traveling. That was a onetime deal. Now it's over. No more machine."

"We still have the pieces."

"We're going to lose the pieces as soon as I find a convenient abyss." She took a deep breath. "Do you smell something . . . weird? Like, museumish?"

"Museumish?" Mac inhaled and shook his head. "I smell grass, wildflowers, maybe jasmine or magnolia. Not to mention asphalt, tar, and diesel."

"Diesel?" Sam raised an eyebrow. "Who runs anything on fossil fuels?"

"We're not arresting anyone," Mac warned.

"It's illegal to use fossil fuels! The pollution fines alone . . ." Sam trailed off as she noticed a face in the distance. Or at least the outline of a human body. "Mac, is there a little green man over there?"

He spun around, squinted, and raised an eyebrow. "That is a soldier in a combat uniform."

"We did not go back to the Civil War!" Sister Mary Francis would be horrified to hear how bad her math skills had failed. They couldn't have possibly traveled back further than 2069. That's when Emir made the machine . . . "Mac." She turned to him in a panic. "When are we?"

"That's the uniform we had from 2057 until America became part of the Commonwealth." Mac shrugged. "We didn't leave Fort Benning."

"We didn't land in 2069, either," she growled.

"Hands where we can see them!" a man shouted from behind Sam.

"Mac?" She raised her eyebrows and willed him to find an exit plan. He'd been a Ranger. He was supposed to have a plan for disasters like this.

"Put your hands out and let me talk."

"We're relying on your people skills for survival?" *We're going to die.*

Mac flashed her a grin. "Exciting, right?"

"A laugh a minute." She closed her eyes and prayed to St. Jude. If there was ever a hopeless cause, this was it. "Don't kick him in the nuts," Sam muttered.

"Would I do that?"

"You're not good at making friends."

"I have you." Mac winked and turned to the soldiers stalking up to them with unfamiliar rifles in their hands.

Mac could probably name the rifles. Heck, he could

probably fieldstrip or undress or whatever it was soldiers did with guns with their eyes closed in under thirty seconds. Right now, she hoped that he could get out of this without their winding up in jail, or worse.

"Hi," Mac said. "We are a little lost."

"No kidding," the soldier said. His uniform had the name BENTLY embroidered on the right side of his chest. "This is a training ground."

"I know, we were just trying to take a short cut. My car died, and my girlfriend's got to catch a flight home from Atlanta. I thought we could cut across here and catch the main road, but I think I took a wrong turn." Mac patted his pocket. "Here, I've got my ID."

Sam closed her eyes. They didn't know what year it was, and he wanted to use his ID. This was going to be so much fun.

"Right here." Mac held out his wallet.

The soldier took it. "Lieutenant MacKenzie? This ID expires next month you know."

"Yeah."

"You fail landnav, LT?"

"I . . ." Mac winced. "I might have been paying more attention to my girlfriend than my step count."

Bently eyed Sam. His look traveled up, down, and back up to rest on her chest before making eye contact again. "I guess that makes sense."

Sam swallowed an angry reproach as Mac put an arm around her. If they survived this, she was going to give him a long lecture on believable lies. It was a stretch to think anyone, even MacKenzie, was so distracted by her nonexistent beauty that he wasn't paying attention to their surroundings. Actually, it made even less sense with Mac, since he took hyperawareness to a whole new level.

"Can you point us in the direction of the main post?" Mac asked.

Bently sighed. "You've got a good ten-mile hike, and this is a restricted area. We're out here on exercises. If the MPs had found you"—he grimaced—"boy howdy would you be in trouble. Look. One Ranger to another, my car is just behind those trees. You know the roads here?"

"Better than I know the fields," Mac said.

"Can you drop my car off at the PX?"

"Sure thing," Mac said with a smile.

Bently took a set of keys out of his pocket. "It's the black truck with the sniper sticker on the back. Leave it at the PX with a full tank of gas."

"Hooah." Mac saluted. "Come on, Sam. We can get a taxi from the PX."

"Thanks." Sam waved good-bye to the soldiers and hurried to follow Mac. "What is a PX and where are we taking the taxi? There's no way I can fly anywhere. All I have is my passport, and it was issued in 2066."

"The PX is the post exchange. It's the general store on base, where you can buy everything from clothes to gardening supplies. It's across from the commissary."

"A food court?"

"A grocery store. And it's October, 2064. My lieutenant's ID expires in November."

Sam frowned as she followed him through the grass. "I thought you were a captain."

He nodded. "Officially promoted just before I left for Afghanistan. I never pinned the rank on." Mac clicked a button on the keys, and a black truck flashed its lights and unlocked. "Here's our ride to our taxi, which will take us to the bus station."

"I can't believe you're stealing a soldier's car!"

"I'm not stealing it!" Mac said as he climbed into the driver's seat. "He's letting us borrow it. Soldiers did this all the time before we joined the Commonwealth. If your car was low on gas or you needed a ride, you borrowed a buddy's car. No big deal. Fill the gas tank and leave it somewhere easy to find. Sergeant Bently will hitch a ride with a friend and pick up the car. No one thinks twice about this sort of stuff."

Sam strapped herself in. "What is that smell?"

Mac sniffed. "Stale french fries, gun cleaner, boot polish, and wet dog. Why?"

She peeked at the back bench of the truck. "This is filthy."

"It's a soldier's truck! What do you expect?" Mac turned the key, and the engine roared like a jet.

Sam covered her ears. "Is it broken?"

"It's an old gasoline truck. Haven't you ever been in one?"

"We had electric cars in Canada."

Mac laughed. "Oh, you are in for a ride."

She looked nervously at the field behind them. "Where's the taxi going to take us?"

"The bus station, for a start. Fifty dollars can get you a ticket to anywhere. If we're in our iteration, we can head to my place up in D.C. I just got home from Afghanistan, and between the pain meds and the alcohol, I wouldn't know if a stranger walked into my place at all. Plus, there's a sweet combat bonus waiting to be cashed in that expires in January. I'll never know it is missing."

"Your plan is to rely on your past self's inebriation for safety and rob yourself blind?"

He shrugged. "Pretty sure it's not illegal."

"Why not go all the way to my place in Canada?" Sam said sarcastically.

"Because the border is closed, and you're currently not old enough to vote." He winked at her.

Sam frowned. "What if this isn't our iteration?"

"Let's deal with one thing at a time. First, we need a phone."

"First, we need a plan!" She crossed her arms and tried not to breathe deeply. "I can't believe you used to live like this."

"You know you love me." His voice warmed her to the core.

Sam smiled in spite of yourself. "You're my Captain United. Always there to save the day."

He leaned over and kissed her cheek. "Always and only yours, baby."

She shook her head. "Nope. Don't call me baby. You've got to find something else."

"Love?"

"I could work with that."

CHAPTER 21

*And we danced to the music of the spheres. Our fates
entwined. Our fears forgotten. Our hearts luminous.*

**~ from the *Song of the Radiant Lover*
poet unknown I4–2061**

*Monday October 27, 2064
District of Columbia
United States of America
Iteration 2 (probably)*

The taxi rolled up in front of a brick building with part
of the roof missing and several windows missing on
the second floor.

"This is the right address?" Sam asked, looking at
Mac in bewilderment. Six hundred dollars, nineteen
hours, thirty-seven minutes, and three buses had
hauled them northward to dump them in front of a
dump.

"Home sweet home."

She looked at the domicile in despair. "You should

not be allowed to pick housing. Why . . . just . . . WHY? I thought the place in Alabama was bad." The apartments had been so bad, the owner tried to set them on fire. How had Mac found something worse?

"That'll be sixty dollars, seventeen cents," the cabby said.

Mac handed him a green bill and opened the door for Sam. "Come on."

"Mac, there's no roof. This can't be the right place."

"It blew off in a storm during the summer. The landlord swears it'll get fixed soon." He hesitated. "This is a good sign."

"Is it?" Sam demanded, as the cab pulled away leaving them stranded in the slum. "Saints and angels, protect me." She closed her eyes. "We're going to die of tetanus poisoning."

"It's not that bad."

"Yes it is!"

He walked up to a door and kicked the faded welcome mat to the side. "No key."

"Great. So we can't even break in." Sam tried counting to ten, but that didn't work. "Let's call the cab back, go find a hotel, and figure out what we're doing from there."

"We can't get our names in the system," Mac said. "We need to avoid cameras and public places. We need to lie low. Right now, I'm considered a risk to public safety."

"You?" She stared at him in bafflement. When she met him she'd have doubted Mac's ability to win a fight against a cockroach. He was a danger to himself, not anyone else.

He raised an eyebrow. "A soldier fresh from the war zone with training and no support network? Didn't you watch horror movies when you were a teen? I'm the bogeyman of this era."

A car rolled up behind them, and Mac stepped in front of her.

"Captain MacKenzie?" a man's voice shouted from the car.

"See?" he said. "Even the house is being watched." Mac turned around and stiffened.

"Captain?" the man in the car repeated.

"Yes?" Mac sounded like he wanted to say no. He hadn't sounded that hesitant even when they'd first met. Sam leaned to the side, trying to peer around him.

"I'm Sergeant Gillam, sir. I'm here to drive you to the service."

Sam tapped Mac's shoulder. "What service?" Mac froze under her hand.

"We have an hour before we need to leave, sir," the sergeant said.

Mac's hand found hers and squeezed hard.

"What service is he talking about?"

"The funeral," Mac whispered. She could hear the pain. "It's the funeral I missed."

Sam hugged him quickly and squeezed his hand back, than she stepped around him. "Sergeant, we still need to get dressed. I just flew in, and my luggage went missing. Would it be a problem if we met you there?"

The sergeant looked from her to MacKenzie. "You sure, ma'am? I can wait."

She gave her sunniest smile and prayed it would work. "I really don't want to inconvenience you. And"—she looked at her abused running shoes and pretended to blush before looking back up—"we haven't seen each other in a long time." She drew out the word long. He was staring at her, and Sam wondered how obtuse a soldier could be. Time to draw him a nice verbal map. "I'd really like to reconnect with my boyfriend. *Alone*. Without an audience."

Understanding widened the sergeant's eyes. "Of course, ma'am. I'll see you two at the service."

"We'll see you there!" Sam waved cheerfully and turned back to Mac. "I need a dress."

"We?" Mac looked at her. "We're going?"

"Yes, and we have a whole hour to break into the apartment, find me a dress, and get there."

He shook his head. "We don't need to go."

The pain in his eyes nearly broke her. She'd do anything to take it away. "We don't, but you do. You need a chance to say good-bye. Please?" She could tell it was the please that got him.

"Fine."

The door swung open. A filthy man wobbled on his feet. "Who're you?"

"You," MacKenzie said as the man toppled forward, unconscious. "I smell foul."

"Mac!" Sam shook her head. There were so many things wrong with this.

"Get his feet," Mac said. "We'll put him in the bedroom."

Grabbing the younger MacKenzie's feet, she waited for Mac to grab his shoulders, and they carried him into the house. He was heavier than she expected, not yet lost to the prescription pills but certainly well on his way. She guided them through the filthy apartment, which smelled of rancid meat and stale sorrows. "Why did you live here?"

"Because I thought I deserved it." Mac tossed his younger self on the bed.

"Don't break him!"

"It's too late for that." He crossed his arms. "We have nothing to wear to a funeral."

Sam walked to the closet and opened it. As she'd suspected, his dress uniform was hanging there in a dry-cleaning bag. "Some things never change." She saw his frown and smiled. "You had one in the closet in Alabama. If you were dragging it around then, there's no reason you wouldn't have it now."

"And what are you wearing?"

"The first black dress I find at the nearest shopping mall. Hurry up. We have less than an hour." She surveyed the disaster. "Where do you keep your trash bags?"

"Under the sink," Mac said, as he reached for the uniform. "Why?"

She smiled. "I'm going to do a little spring cleaning while you get changed."

"I don't even know if this will fit."

She gave him her tough-senior-bureau-agent look. "It will fit. We will go. It's time for a proper good-bye." She walked over to a tall dresser and shifted through the debris to find something that had caught her eye. A set of golden captain's bars waiting to be put on the dress uniform. Sam held them out. "Do you want me to pin them on?"

Bone-white headstones marked the final resting places of the dead. Row upon row, a sea of fallen soldiers resting beneath the parched earth. It was raining now. Dark, sullen clouds had rolled in before dawn and sat over the city like a dark blanket. Mac hesitated. Already, they could see the funeral party. Twenty freshly dug graves with the grieving families in front of them.

Sam's hand touched the small of his back. "Are you okay?"

He took a step forward and a deep breath, then kept walking as Taps played. His old dress uniform felt uncomfortable, the starch and the pins and everything about it was wrong. This was why he hadn't come the first time. Even now, six years removed from the original stabbing despair of loss, the pain was staggering. A week ago, all these men had been alive. Now he was the only one still breathing.

They approached the back of the crowd, and Mac started looking for familiar faces.

Alina Matthews, the single mother of the lieutenant about to make captain who led the fateful charge, sat in the front row in a black dress, hat, and veil. Beside her was the wife of Top Sergeant Abel, a woman who was herself a veteran of more funerals than Mac cared to count. Her two sons wore crisp navy uniforms. None of them had tears. Not here. Not yet. She'd told him once that army wives learned not to cry at funerals.

There were others crying, though.

Flags were taken off the coffins, folded, and handed to the families. One of the POWs must have been very young, his widow was holding an infant as a confused and crying toddler sat beside her.

He would have given anything to trade places with the man in the coffin. Done anything to bring the men back to their families. He closed his eyes and let the funeral end around him as tears ran down his cheeks, and his fingernails dug into his skin.

The scent of an overly floral perfume made him open his eyes. An elderly woman with an American-flag pin on the lapel of her black dress suit stood in front of him. "Captain MacKenzie?"

"Yes." It was a shaky whisper, and he was aware of Sam's moving closer, getting ready to intervene if need be.

"I'm Mrs. Hastings, one of the Arlington Ladies. I thought it would be appropriate to present you with a condolence card, too." She held out a white envelope with beautiful calligraphy handwriting on the outside. "Thank you for your service to our great nation. You are an example to us all."

He couldn't move his arm.

Sam took the envelope with a small smile. "Thank you for your condolences. This has been a very difficult time, for both of us."

Mrs. Hastings frowned politely at Sam. "I'm so sorry. I didn't catch your name."

"Samantha Rose."

"Of course. Thank you for supporting our soldier. Being an army wife isn't the easiest job in the world. But, Lord, do they need us. You take good care of our captain here." She patted Mac's arm gently and walked away to fuss over someone else.

Sam tucked the envelope into her purse. "You okay?"

"Are you going to ask anything else?"

"I don't know what to say. The only funeral I've ever been to is my father's, and at that point we were so estranged, it was like being at the funeral of a stranger." She leaned against him for a second and moved away. "What do you need?"

He shook his head. "To go back four more months and stop all this. It was an insane plan to start with. Jerry-rigged to hell. We couldn't get negotiations to go through. Everything was stalled out. I wasn't even supposed to be in the unit—I was on leave—but they needed a medic." He shrugged.

It had been raining that day, too. A summer deluge was washing the streets out, and he'd remembered grinning as his truck dipped through potholes. The plan had been to stop in to see his old buddies at Benning. Maybe go out for dinner or hit the town. Drive up to Atlanta for a day. Then he was flying home to

Idaho to finish out his R&R before reporting to the medical unit at Fort Carson. He'd walked into a planning session. Colonel Kawsay was trying to talk some sense into his troops. The mission was too dangerous, and they'd never get permission. Flying in without backup was risky. The army was being held together by duct tape and tradition as it was; one more good push, and they'd all be gone.

Then Mac opened his big, fat mouth. Said he'd go along. A medic to back up the six-man team. He had the training. He was a good battlefield surgeon with an amazing record. Kawsay had finally allowed it. A few favors were called in, a commercial jet took them to a friendly port in the Middle East. A navy helicopter had taken them to a no-fly zone to drop them under the radar. They'd hiked in, infiltrated the base, got their guys out, and almost been home.

Almost been safe.

"You're shaking," Sam said as she took his hand.

"We were almost home."

"I know." She gave his arm a tug. "Let's sit down for a minute."

He let her lead the way to the abandoned seats, still warm from the mourners who were leaving. "Sam . . ." He stood up. "I don't belong here. I'm on the wrong side." There should have been a grave for him.

She followed his gaze, understood the despair in his voice. "No, you aren't." Wrapping her arms around his she pulled in close. "You weren't meant to die with them."

He closed his eyes. It would have been so much easier to take the bullet there in Afghanistan. A moment of pain in exchange for a lifetime of anguish.

"Eric?" a quavering but familiar voice from his nightmares asked. *Bring my baby home.*

He turned, tears running down his face. "Mrs. Matthews, I am so sorry for the loss of your son."

She launched herself at him, wrapping skinny arms around his chest and squeezing him tight. "I didn't see you here. I thought you were angry with me." She sobbed. "I'm so sorry." She leaned back and reached up to pat his face. "All my babies." She hugged him again. "I thank God every night you came back. I prayed for you all. I prayed for Daniel. Lit candles for him every day while you were gone. I was so selfish, praying only for my son."

Mac shook his head. "No. That's the right thing to do." His family had prayed for him, he knew it. He hated knowing that only their prayers were answered. Hated God and himself for failing to bring his fellow soldiers home.

"I still pray for them. Every night I tell God to keep them. And I pray for you." She patted his cheek again. "To survive all that? If this is what God chooses to train you with? What must God have in store for you?"

"I don't know." He looked to Sam, elegant in a simple black dress, black hair framing her face, and wondered if she was the reason. Prayer wasn't something he'd wanted. Answers . . . he kept asking why he was alive, and there she was, smiling at him, caring for him, silently standing beside him at his worst. He reached for her.

Sam took his hand and stepped closer.

"Mrs. Matthews, this is Sam, she's um . . ."

"His girlfriend," Sam said.

Something like that. No—something much more than that. She was his lifeline. His heart and soul. The reason he woke up in the morning. "Sam, this is Dan Matthews's mom." He stumbled over his friend's name, not sure if he'd ever mentioned Dan or the rest of the soldiers to her.

"It's an honor to meet you," Sam said. "Mac has told me so much about your son. He was an amazing young man. I'm so sorry for your loss." Of course she had the right words. Sam always did.

Alina Matthews reached out and patted Sam's face. "Thank you."

Mac shook as she walked away. Thunder rumbled in the distance. Everyone was leaving. All but the dead. He leaned his head back, letting the rain wash away the tears. Sam wrapped her arms around him. He hugged her tight, needing the warmth. And then he rested his head on hers and cried.

Sam slid down the wall until her rump hit the faux hardwood of the floor. The only sound aside from the lashing rain were the snores and occasional whimpers of Li'l Eric MacKenzie sleeping in his bedroom.

Mac sat down beside her. "How you doing?"

"I could be worse." He offered her a can of a soda—a brand she didn't recognize. She opened it and tasted it gingerly. It was better than the tap water, but not by much. *Was everything so sickeningly sweet back then?*

"I realized today I've never been to a funeral that wasn't related to a murder investigation. I don't know what to do when I'm not looking for a killer. It's a little surreal."

"You did fine," Mac said. He chugged his pop, then crushed the can. "You did . . . amazing."

She blushed slightly. She'd been hearing things like that from him for so long, but she had never really let herself listen. Now, though . . . it filled her with warmth. Warmth she wanted to share. "How are you holding up?"

He did an odd, one-sided shoulder-to-ear shrug. "I'm empty. I know they say that funerals are for the living, one last chance to say good-bye, but I never really believed it. Most funerals I've been to have been celebrations. You don't grieve someone who dies peacefully in their sleep at ninety surrounded by friends and family. You break out the old journals, read about their school-yard crushes, and tell stories. This felt like good-bye. Good-bye to my friends, good-bye to my life, good-bye army, good-bye everything. This is where it all fell apart." He gestured vaguely at the molding walls. "I thought I'd die here."

"Here in D.C.? Why?"

"That's what all the alcohol was for. I thought it was a poison, I guess. The news always had stories about someone drinking too much and getting alcohol poisoning, so I bought all the liquor I could afford.

"I was trying to drown the pain. Not the injuries. There was something inside, stabbing me and smothering me. I felt trapped in my own body." He looked at her. "Does that make sense?"

"It doesn't have to, Mac. Don't you get it: You *didn't* kill yourself. All on your own—for whatever reason—you lived in order to meet me in Alabama. And look how far you came from *that* person. Do you feel better now?"

"Most days."

"We're getting you back to therapy once we figure out where we're staying." She took a deep breath as the enormity of the situation hit her. "We are going to find somewhere else to stay, aren't we? Somewhere not here?"

Mac nodded. "That's the plan."

"Oh, you have a plan?" She drank some more of the carbonated sugar water and hoped it kicked her brain in gear.

He grimaced. "Part of a plan?"

"You fill me with such hope."

He scrambled to his feet, went into the bedroom, and brought back a large black duffel, shutting the door on the sleeping Eric as he passed. "On my way up to find you at Fort Benning, I stopped at a little pawnshop to see if I could find an unregistered gun."

Sam covered her ears. "I'm not hearing this."

Mac pulled her hands away from her face laughing. "Who broke into a government building and stole an

ID card? That was you. Don't give me a hard time. I paid for the gun."

Mac unzipped the duffel to reveal faded green rectangles of United States currency. "My reup bonus. I took it out in cash because I thought it was better than a bank at the time."

Sam held up a stack of twenty-dollar bills. "Your country had really ugly money."

"Thanks, remind me to compliment Canada sometime. What was on them? An old woman and a crazy bird?"

She made a face and stuck out her tongue.

"Right now, this currency is good, but the exchange rate after the nationhood vote was ridiculous. Five thousand USD got you thirteen cents of Commonwealth cash. The United States dollar was dead, and everyone got a check to help them start over."

"How far away is that?"

"The vote is on November 11, but the polls will close early when it's obvious the overwhelming majority of the citizens want to join the Commonwealth." Mac took the cash back. "The spring after we joined the Commonwealth, the online DIY sites were full of ways to use cash to decorate. People used them for wallpaper and covered lamps in them."

Sam's eyes went wide with horror. "That's beyond tacky. Why didn't I hear about it?"

"Eh, it was only in style for a minute or two, and it's not like Canada had the same problems with the transition that we did."

"Okay, so we have capital. It's a good way to make a fresh start. The question is: Where Do We Go?"

Mac pulled a piece of glossy printed paper from his back pocket. He unfolded it and passed it to Sam.

She read it aloud, " 'Come visit beautiful Australia and find your new dream home'?"

"Australia lost nearly eighty percent of its population in the plague."

"Only because they were trafficking sex slaves from all over Asia," Sam said. "They shut down the ports in time, but they didn't shut down the human traffickers."

He pointed a finger at her. "Ancient history."

"Nineteen years ago isn't ancient history."

"Listen, right now, Australia is taking skilled immigrants and offering them a move-in bonus, a job-signing bonus, and housing. There are houses sitting empty, and we can have one."

She narrowed her eyes. "What's the catch?"

"The offer is going to expire in four days, when several major politicians come out in favor of the nationhood vote."

"And?"

"And I can't fly right now. The airports are using fingerprint scanners, and I'm on the no-fly list because of my combat status. The soonest I can leave the country is when we hit the transition period between the vote and the Commonwealth government's actually taking over. All the airports will lose security, but the airlines will do big business for a few weeks while people try to escape. Europe is the most popular destination, but there will be flights to Australia."

"If nothing changes."

"If nothing changes," Mac agreed.

"That's a really big IF."

He shrugged. "It's a way out. And you don't have to wait: With a few bribes, we can get you on a plane by tomorrow night. You go to Australia, and you'll have a house and job before the end of the month. You'll be safe."

CHAPTER 22

> A strong man trusts to the strength of his arm. A wise
> man trusts to the wisdom of his learning. A great man
> trusts only that he is not yet perfect. Greatness can only
> come from a place of patient humility.
>
> ~ excerpt from *A Greater Fall of
> Man* by Indel Nazti I1—2070

*Tuesday October 28, 2064
District of Columbia
United States of America
Iteration 2*

Sam's shoe stuck to a tar-like substance embedded in the low pile carpet. "What . . ."

"Don't ask," Mac said as he steered her forward. "This isn't our world."

"Marble tiles are fashionable flooring because they're easy to clean."

"And easy to break things on. Like heads."

As if to remind her, the floor sank slightly as she

stepped, like sinking into wet grass with her heels. "Is the floor padded?"

"All the government offices were given padded main floors after the suicide crisis in the thirties." Mac led the way to a winding line filled with people wearing faded clothes and weary looks. He smiled at her. "That's a joke, by the way."

"Then make it funny." She stuck her tongue out at him, then inched closer. "Do they go out of their way to make it depressing?"

Mac looked around and shrugged. "Dunno. I had a sergeant once who said that most places like this were designed at the epicenters of evil. It was some feng shui thing. If you mapped out government offices, they were always in the worst possible place for progress and enlightenment."

A Canadian Marine walked past, a bleach stain on his hem making her eye twitch. "The last days of the old republic."

"Shh!"

The people closest to Sam and Mac turned, eyes full of questions and fear.

"The vote isn't until next week," Mac said to her. She didn't realize how bad it was . . . how bad it was going to get. He remembered. He'd been old enough to vote. She'd still been behind the ivy-laced walls of the all-girls Catholic school she'd lived at most her life. Even then, she'd lived in United Territories, safely hidden away from the horrors that rocked the United States.

For twenty minutes, they waited in mute terror as the past slipped by. Everything was ever so slightly out of phase. The faces, the clothes, even the colors seemed wrong, dulled by the national despair that finally drove the States to combine with the Territories and form the Commonwealth.

"Next!" A woman with naturally blond hair rang the bell at her station and smiled as Sam approached with her passport. "How can I help you today?"

"Well, ah . . ." Mac laughed and rubbed the back of his head before hitting her with an aww-shucks-country-boy smile. "My girlfriend's about to leave for this college trip, and we had to get her a new passport and um . . ." He took Sam's passport. "You can see the problem."

The woman frowned. "Everything looks right for a Canadian passport."

"The date," Sam said. "There's a typo." There wasn't. She'd gotten the passport when her Spanish one expired in 2066, but that was going to be real tough to explain to a customs agent.

"Oh my gosh!" The woman laughed. She tried scratching the date with her thumbnail. "How weird is that? I've never heard of a typo! Hey, Charlie!" she called to a coworker. "Chuck, come look at this!"

An older man with a handlebar mustache ambled over, shuffling a well-worn groove in the threadbare carpet. His glasses slid to the end of his nose as he peered at the passport. "Says 2066? Are you a time traveler, ma'am?"

Sam froze as her worst fears came true. There was no sane way to explain this. They were going to lock her in an insane asylum. She'd be executed as a clone . . .

Mac laughed. He nudged her, and she managed a weak smile.

"There's no such thing as time travel," Mac said with an encouraging smile.

"Exactly," Sam said, trying to fake cheerfulness as she fought to remember how to breathe.

"It'll take us a few hours to get the new one made," the woman said. "I can print it here, but we have a backlog right now."

"Can you have it before you close today?" Mac asked. His hand reached across the counter, and a stack of bills dropped down out of sight. "She's got a flight to catch tomorrow night."

The woman's eyes barely dipped to count the money before she turned a sunny smile back to them. "Sure thing! Come back by four, and they'll let you in to wait. I'll make sure this gets done by then." She waved Sam's passport and walked away.

Mac took her hand. "Come on."

"She has my passport," Sam muttered, grabbing Mac's arm in a white-knuckled grip.

"That's fine."

"No, it most certainly isn't. I've got no ID on me!"

"So what? You'll have one in a few hours. If anyone asks, just tell them the truth."

"That I'm from the future?"

"That you're getting a new passport made at the consulate."

"Oh." She looked up at him and almost fell into his glorious eyes. She caressed his face. "You'll come after me, won't you?"

"When have I not?" Mac caught her hand and pressed a kiss into her palm. "There's nowhere you can go that I won't follow."

CHAPTER 23

No one can do my job and carry regrets. The temptation to misuse our control of time would be too great. Still, we are human. We long for the same things everyone wants: recognition, friendship, comfort, love.

~ private conversation with Agent 5 of
the Ministry of Defense I1—2073

Saturday November 1, 2064
Sydney
Australia
Iteration 2

As a girl, Sam's least favorite book from the library had been *Lost at the Park*. In it, little Ellie Sweet took a dare to enter an abandoned amusement park at midnight. There was a plot somewhere in faded pages, something about foiling a bank robbery, but what stuck with Sam was the terror of the abandoned park. Empty benches. Row upon row of derelict cars. Buildings with paint peeling off smiling faces. The book had given her nightmares for weeks afterward, and she'd suppressed it all until the trip to the carnival when she turned six. Seeing the clown castle had sent her running back to Sister Mary Peter and refusing to leave the elderly nun's side for the rest of the day for fear of being left there overnight.

Sydney reminded her of the abandoned park.

There were no clown castles or bank robbers, but the buildings were empty. Several had been torn down in the wake of the Yellow Plague, and many that survived did so with only a few floors lit at night. As the sun set, she looked out her hotel window at a stygian vista. This was the darkness that first drove mankind to find safety in fire. This was the blackness that swallowed the soul and left bleached bones in the desert.

She shivered with primal fear before securing the curtains tightly. Australia had been one of the nations hardest hit by the plagues. Seventy percent of the population was infected in the first wave. Over 50 percent of them died in 2045. A second wave in 2047, when the borders opened and another 20 percent were killed. Birth rates were down. A population that had soared past the expected 32 million was reduced very quickly to less than 9 million. Inadequate medical care over the intervening nineteen years had slowly chipped away at the population base.

The incentives offered to come and rebuild the country were tempting for many who wanted to escape the financial collapse of the northern hemisphere. Australia was at least self-sustaining, isolated, safe from the chaos of the United States nationhood vote and the collapse of the American dollar.

Sam flipped through the folder she'd been given upon arrival. There was a choice of lovely homes, all certified plague-free, and jobs to accompany them. She'd live tax-free for the first five years and be paid an incentive for marrying and having a baby—to the tune of a hundred thousand dollars per child. The woman who'd greeted Sam had talked about the joy of having families for over an hour. No amount of polite refusal could convince the Aussie woman that children just weren't in the cards. Claiming to have a fatal disease would get her booted back to the Americas, where Commonwealth surveillance would tag her as a clone within a few weeks of taking over the United States. It wouldn't matter if she told the truth, the early Commonwealth had been brutally clonephobic. Stating she was infertile was equally problematic. So she'd fallen back on the "waiting for true love" response.

That had gotten her a list of eligible Aussie bachelors in each town.

Sleep eluded her, so she packed her bags and checked out before dawn. She drove northward on the paid highway, her newly assigned, solar-powered car zipping along the empty road at an excess of 250 kilometers an hour.

A few hours before noon, she stopped to stretch and find food in Goondiwindi. The air was baking as she pulled the car to a stop at a strip mall with a small carnival going on. A group of students was holding a car wash to fund-raise for some vague event. One of the boutiques had rolled most their wares outside, children ran around mirrors with bright pink frames as their parents tried on sunglasses and held up shirts with the critical eyes of professional window-shoppers.

Sam dug through her purse for the Aussie money she'd gotten just for arriving and sought out the scent of hot dogs and caramelized onions that flowed on the breeze like the perfume of the gods. "One, please," she told the vendor as she sorted through her change.

He gave her an odd look.

She held up her pointer finger, and he nodded. Probably the accent, but it was hard to tell. She could hear at least three different languages being spoken in the plaza. English was considered the main language, but the welcoming immigration policy meant people from everywhere were rushing to rebuild Australia. And she was beginning to realize her Eurocentric education wasn't going to get her very far.

"Come pet a puppy! Dogs make the best pets! Come find the love of your life!" a woman shouted from somewhere in the crowd.

Sam swapped cash for lunch and went in search of puppies. She found them in the shade of the buildings romping in temporary playpens. Tiny teacup poodles, a terrier mix that looked ready to do flips on command, and . . . her heart lurched . . . a tiny tan mastiff with a black mask just like Hoss's. Suddenly, she wasn't so hungry.

"Would you like to pet one?" the woman sitting

under broad white straw hat asked as she moved a braid of silver hair out of the way to reveal a name tag that proclaimed her to be Jill. "They're all adoptable." She held a poodle up for Sam's inspection. "Microchipped, vaccinated, spayed or neutered, and they come with two weeks' worth of food and a leash!"

"Can I . . . could I pet the mastiff?" Sam asked.

"Sure thing!" Jill said. "This cute little guy is Bosco, and he won't stay small forever."

Bosco was already a forty-pound bundle of wiggling, wagging, licking love. He squirmed on Sam's lap, turned two circles, and collapsed in typical mastiff exhaustion.

"They get huge," Jill said. "He's a—"

"—Boerboel," Sam said. "I know. I had one." Her heart tightened. Sorrow squeezed her chest, and she pulled Bosco closer, sobbing into his fur. "I miss him. I miss him so much!"

Jill patted her tentatively on the shoulder. "Would you like a hanky?"

She nodded, forcing herself to release her death grip on the puppy. "I'm sorry, I just . . . I can't believe he's gone."

"I understand," Jill said. "I was the same way when my Tofu passed away. Silly thing, she was a Yorkie, and I adored her. It was the cancer that got her in the end. I cried for weeks! What was your puppy's name?"

"Hoss."

"Sounds like a real gentleman."

Sam nodded reluctantly as she stroked Bosco's back. "He was a wonderful dog."

"What happened to him?"

"There was . . ." *a serial killer who wanted me dead* " . . . an accident. It was over very quickly, but it felt like losing a limb. Every time I turn around, Hoss is missing. I have a dog-shaped hole in my life."

Jill nodded.

Bosco looked up, noticed the uneaten hot dog in Sam's hand, and obviously decided the delicious gift was for him. The hot dog was gone in two bites, and Sam was smiling. "Can he come home with me?"

"Sure!" Jill said. "Do you live here?"

Sam shook her head. "I'm moving north of here, near Airlie Beach? A city called Cannonvale. There's a house waiting for me."

"Oh . . ." The other woman frowned. "Bit brave of you to go back to a tourist destination. Half the town was burned, you know, to get rid of all the germs."

With a weak smile, Sam nodded. "There are worse things than ghost towns."

"I can't think of any."

Sam hugged Bosco to her chest. He licked her chin, leaving onion-scented drool behind. "I'm sure there's worse." Like being cast adrift from your own time and place. Or being tortured and hideously mutilated before being dumped back in time and buried in a pauper's grave. Or being erased from history entirely. That was worse. Her gaze was drawn to the car on the other side of the crowd. No one here knew about the stability core she'd smuggled through time. They were all blissfully naive.

Bosco licked her again and gave a tiny mastiff growl of content.

"I'll have a big, drooling, lazy mastiff to protect me!" Sam said with a cheery smile. "What could possibly go wrong?"

Jill sighed sadly.

"Don't answer that," Sam said. "Let's just sign the adoption paperwork."

Forty minutes and three hot dogs later—two more for Bosco, who was a growing boy, and one for Sam—and she and the lazy puppy were back on the road. And, for the first time since arriving in 2064, Sam thought she could see a light at the end of the tunnel.

CHAPTER 24

*I look at the sea and see the incarnation of eternity.
Time, the elusive goddess wed to death, is present in
every wave.*

~ excerpt from *The Heart of Fear* by Liedjie Slaan

*Saturday November 23, 2064
Cannonvale, Queensland
Australia
Iteration 2*

A pale moon hung low over the Coral Sea like a luminous opal. Mac parked his truck in the driveway of
the only house with lights on without checking the address. According to Sam's e-mails, no one else lived in
a three-block radius. The sweet aroma of woodsmoke
and charcoal pulled him forward. He walked up the
terraced stone steps to the house and knocked on the
door.

A ferocious bark made Mac step back.

"Down, Bosco! Sit!" The door opened to the thumping of a heavy tail on tiled floors. "Hi, Mac. I'm glad you made it!" Sam reached out with one hand and hugged him, pulling away far too quickly. "How was the flight?"

"The one up from Sydney wasn't bad. The one down here from New York was . . . long." He watched the puppy smear his pant leg with drool. "He has a tail."

"Yup, they didn't dock it when he was born. Watch it, it's lethal. Especially when he's happy." She smiled fondly down at the puppy, looking happier than she had when she'd left him.

Mac reached down and rubbed Bosco's ear. "Did I smell the charcoal grill going when I pulled up?"

"You did. I was just about to put on some lamb steaks, and I have a salad I'm tossing in the kitchen." Her smile was the warmth of sunshine after a long winter.

He reached for her, needing to know there was something for him. Needing to know she was really with him again. "Tell me you missed me."

"Every day." Sam walked into his embrace, resting her head on his chest as she wrapped her arms around him. "I kept waiting for you to call and say you weren't coming." The fear in her voice broke his heart.

He kissed the top of her head, gentle and reassuring. "Why would I do that?"

"You could have gone anywhere. Vanished. Gone home to Idaho or joined one of the mercenary companies the news keeps going on about. You had choices."

"You know I didn't want any of those. Not if there was a chance to be with you." He squeezed her tight, then let her go.

Sam stepped away with a sigh. "It's been strange here without you, honestly. There are days I can wake up and almost pretend it was all a silly dream. Without any proof to hold except my own memory, I catch myself thinking the memory is faulty. Having you here with me makes it real again."

"I'm sorry." The words weren't enough. They had the ability to travel back in time, and some days he wished he'd stopped to tell his younger self not to tell Sam about Jane Doe's true identity. It was tempting to think that other choices would have led to an easier life, but there was always a shadow of doubt. A dark faith that any other action would have led to death. He couldn't put it in words, but he knew it in the same way he knew the sun would rise in the morning. There was only one way to get through this, and that was together.

"Don't be sorry," Sam said. "Ignoring the problem won't make it go away. Come on, let's have dinner. We can plan for the future tomorrow."

Dinner was a quiet affair. Sam filled him in on the few locals, her on-paper-only job as an on-call manager at the boathouse in the harbor, and Bosco's training. She talked, he listened, and they danced around the difficult topics.

Sam cleared the table in silence, then said, "I forgot the cider."

"What?" Mac ran a nervous hand over his jeans pockets.

"Sparkling cider. I bought it for your 'Welcome to Australia' dinner."

"We can have it for dessert," he said.

She nodded. "And drink it on the porch. We have a beautiful view of the ocean."

"I'll pour," Mac said, jumping at the opening. He filled two champagne glasses with the bubbling golden cider and joined Sam on the wooden deck that looked over the edge of a hill to the sea. "Beautiful." He handed Sam her glass.

"It is a gorgeous view."

"I wasn't talking about the view." He set his glass on the wooden railing and wrapped his arms around her. She leaned back into his chest, right where she belonged.

"I'm glad you're here."

"Me too." He'd lived for this night since the day she'd boarded the plane. Dreamed of her. Wanted her so much, it became a physical pain.

"You realize this is just the calm before the storm, right? It's all going to get crazy from here. We have time to plan, but reality is collapsing, and Emir isn't going to let his vision go without a fight."

He held her tighter, breathing in the scent of the vanilla-and-cinnamon soap she'd used in the kitchen. Feeling their heartbeats falling into sync. "We'll be fine."

"You think so." She sounded amused.

"I know so."

Sam's chuckle vibrated against him. "I have a million questions about the future."

"Really? I only have one." He reached into his pocket and pulled a ring. Black opal ovals were defined on two silver infinity signs on either side of an Asscher-cut diamond.

"Sam, will you marry me?"

THE END

CHAPTER 25

Nothing changes faster than the future.

~ excerpt from *A Brief Summary of Time*
by Dr. Henry Troom I4—2065

Day 187/365
Year 5 of Progress
Central Command
Third Continent
Prime Reality

Commander Rose moved around the quiet command room. The lights were at 30 percent, mimicking night and discouraging anyone from lingering after their shift was over. She was alone with the soft hum of data collection interrupted only by the occasional chirp of a computer spitting out data.

This was the very center of the universe. Her fingers brushed across the synthapaper scrolls that showed the constant sine wave of time. With training, she'd learned to read each dip of the iterations. Here, the birth of an einselected node. There, the tragic outcome of an event that crushed a million iterations and left only four struggling forward.

The future had a unique brilliance. During the times of expansion, all of time looked like a rainbow fracturing into infinite color. Now the lines of possibility were thickening, collapsing. Decoherence was drowning the rainbow in brutal black.

Quietly, the machine drew the newest line. Tomorrow shifted into view.

Her Prime iteration—the master control of the iterations, heartbeat of the universe—appeared as a thin black line at the base of the sine wave. The scroll rolled out, and the black line surged up like a wave, following the possibilities of the lesser iterations. Hour by hour, ink drop by ink drop, the future appeared. She held her breath as the wave crested and crashed down, back to where it belonged at the baseline.

But this time, the Prime iteration didn't crash far enough.

Heartbeat stuttering with an unpleasant rush of fear, she watched another iteration take its place. Another line touched the baseline and took dominance as Prime iteration. Someone was stealing her future.

Rose went to the communications board and dialed a number she thought she'd never need to use.

After a moment, the screen shimmered as the stern visage of a world leader appeared.

"Dr. Emir, my apologies for calling at this late hour, there's been a mishap here at the command center."

He raised a bushy white eyebrow. "A mishap? A flood perhaps? Did you run out of synthapaper? You're a commander. You are supposed to be able to handle these things on your own."

Rose bristled at his tone. "There is a problem with the machine, sir." She only barely managed to keep her tone respectful because she knew how easily commanders could be replaced. There was no place for dissenters in the world now.

"Impossible." Emir sneered. "The machine is infallible."

"If that is the case, sir, than we have lost our place as the dominant iteration."

"Impossible!"

"Then the machine is broken. Sir."

Emir's scowl burned through the screen. "Prepare a hit team. I'll be there in two hours."

ACKNOWLEDGMENTS

It takes a village to raise a child and it takes no less to create a book. I want to thank everyone who was in this from the beginning. Amy, Derek, Dave, Jason, Christina . . . just to name a few. You got me through the early drafts. Special thanks to my battle buddy Samantha for loaning me her name for a character (love you!), my agent Marlene for believing in me even when I didn't, and my editor David for all he does.

ABOUT THE AUTHOR

LIANA BROOKS is a full-time mom and a part-time author who would rather slay dragons than budget the checkbook any day. Alas, Adventuring Hero is not a recognized course of study in American universities. She graduated from college with a bachelor's degree in marine biology, a husband, and no job prospects in her field. To fill the free time, she started writing. Now her books are read all over the world (she says she's big in Canada) and she's free to explore the universe one page at a time. You can find Liana on the Web at www.lianabrooks.com, on Twitter as @LianaBrooks, or on Facebook under the same name.

Discover great authors, exclusive offers, and more at hc.com